U0106918

Oscar Wilde 著

榮如德 譯

THE PICTURE OF DORIAN GRAY

道林·格雷的畫像

商務印書館

本書譯文由上海譯文出版社有限公司授權使用

責任編輯	陳朝暉
裝幀設計	郭梓琪
排　版	周　榮
責任校對	趙會明
印　務	龍寶祺

道林·格雷的畫像 *The Picture of Dorian Gray*

作　者	Oscar Wilde
譯　者	榮如德
出　版	商務印書館（香港）有限公司
	香港筲箕灣耀興道 3 號東滙廣場 8 樓
	http://www.commercialpress.com.hk
發　行	香港聯合書刊物流有限公司
	香港新界荃灣德士古道 220－248 號荃灣工業中心 16 樓
印　刷	永經堂印刷有限公司
	香港新界荃灣德士古道 188－202 號立泰工業中心第 1 座 3 樓
版　次	2024 年 7 月第 1 版第 1 次印刷
	© 2024 商務印書館（香港）有限公司
	ISBN 978 962 07 0440 6
	Printed in China

Publisher's Note　出版説明

　　《道林·格雷的畫像》以主角道林·格雷的個人成長和道德墮落為主線展開。道林·格雷是一位年輕貴族,他通過一幅畫像將自己的青春和美貌永遠定格——畫像代替他老去,而他容顏永駐。這看似完美的交易背後,卻隱藏着難以言喻的代價。隨着歲月的流逝,道林·格雷內心的黑暗與墮落逐漸浮現,畫像則成為了他內心真實世界的鏡像。

　　這是王爾德出版的唯一一部長篇小說,也是十九世紀唯美主義的經典巨著,探討了外表和內心之間的對立,個人選擇對道德發展的影響,蘊含許多深刻的哲理命題。讀者可思考感官放縱與道德價值之間的衝突取捨,探索在物慾橫流的世代中保持善良敦厚之法門。

　　初、中級英語程度讀者使用本書時,先閱讀英文原文,如遇到理解障礙,則參考中譯作為輔助。在英文原文後附加註解,標註古英語、非現代詞彙拼寫形式及語法;在譯文後附加註釋,以幫助讀者理解原文背景。讀者如有餘力,可在閱讀原文部分段落後,查閱相應中譯,揣摩同樣詞句在雙語中的不同表達。

商務印書館 (香港) 有限公司

編輯出版部

Contents　目錄

The Picture of Dorian Gray　1

The Preface　3

道林・格雷的畫像　293

Preface to the Chinese Translation　中文譯本序　295

自序　306

The Picture of
Dorian Gray

The Preface

The artist is the creator of beautiful things.

To reveal art and conceal the artist is art's aim.

The critic is he who can translate into another manner or a new material his impression of beautiful things.

The highest as the lowest form of criticism is a mode of autobiography.

Those who find ugly meanings in beautiful things are corrupt without being charming. This is a fault.

Those who find beautiful meanings in beautiful things are the cultivated. For these there is hope.

They are the elect to whom beautiful things mean only Beauty.

There is no such thing as a moral or an immoral book. Books are well written, or badly written. That is all.

The nineteenth century dislike of Realism is the rage of Caliban seeing his own face in a glass.

The nineteenth century dislike of Romanticism is the rage of Caliban not seeing his own face in a glass.

The moral life of man forms part of the subject-matter[1] of the artist, but the morality of art consists in the perfect use of an imperfect medium.

No artist desires to prove anything. Even things that are true can be proved.

No artist has ethical sympathies. An ethical sympathy in an artist is an unpardonable mannerism of style.

No artist is ever morbid. The artist can express everything.

Thought and language are to the artist instruments of an art.

Vice and virtue are to the artist materials for an art.

From the point of view of form, the type of all the arts is the art of the musician. From the point of view of feeling, the actor's craft is the type.

All art is at once surface and symbol.

Those who go beneath the surface do so at their peril.

Those who read the symbol do so at their peril.

It is the spectator, and not life, that art really mirrors.

Diversity of opinion about a work of art shows that the work is new, complex, and vital.

When critics disagree the artist is in accord with himself.

We can forgive a man for making a useful thing as long as he does not admire it. The only excuse for making a useless thing is that one admires it intensely.

All art is quite useless.

OSCAR WILDE

Chapter 1

The studio was filled with the rich odour of roses, and when the light summer wind stirred amidst the trees of the garden there came through the open door the heavy scent of the lilac, or the more delicate perfume of the pink-flowering thorn.

From the corner of the divan of Persian saddlebags on which he was lying, smoking, as was his custom, innumerable cigarettes, Lord Henry Wotton could just catch the gleam of the honey-sweet and honey-coloured blossoms of a laburnum, whose tremulous branches seemed hardly able to bear the burden of a beauty so flame-like as theirs; and now and then the fantastic shadows of birds in flight flitted across the long tussore-silk curtains that were stretched in front of the huge window, producing a kind of momentary Japanese effect, and making him think of those pallid jade-faced painters of Tokio[2] who, through the medium of an art that is necessarily immobile, seek to convey the sense of swiftness and motion. The sullen murmur of the bees shouldering their way through the long unmown grass, or circling with monotonous insistence round the dusty gilt horns of the straggling woodbine, seemed to make the stillness more oppressive. The dim roar of London was like the bourdon note of a distant organ.

In the centre of the room, clamped to an upright easel, stood the full-length portrait of a young man of extraordinary personal beauty, and in front of it, some little distance away, was sitting the artist himself, Basil Hallward, whose sudden disappearance some years ago caused, at the time, such public excitement, and gave rise to so many strange conjectures.

As the painter looked at the gracious and comely form he had so skilfully mirrored in his art, a smile of pleasure passed across his face, and seemed about to linger there. But he suddenly started up, and, closing his eyes, placed his fingers upon the lids, as though he sought to imprison within his brain some curious dream from which he feared he might awake.

'It is your best work, Basil, the best thing you have ever done,' said Lord Henry, languidly. 'You must certainly send it next year to the Grosvenor. The Academy is too large and too vulgar. Whenever I have gone there, there have been either so many people that I have not been able to see the pictures, which was dreadful, or so many pictures that I have not been able to see the people, which was worse. The Grosvenor is really the only place.'

'I don't think I shall send it anywhere,' he answered, tossing his head back in that odd way that used to make his friends laugh at him at Oxford. 'No: I won't send it anywhere.'

Lord Henry elevated his eyebrows, and looked at him in amazement through the thin blue wreaths of smoke that curled up in such fanciful whorls from his heavy opium-tainted cigarette. 'Not send it anywhere? My dear fellow, why? Have you any reason? What odd chaps you painters are! You do anything in the world to gain a reputation. As soon as you have one, you seem to want to throw it away. It is silly of you, for there is only one thing in the world worse than being talked about, and that is not being talked about. A portrait like this would set you far above all the young men in England, and make the old men quite jealous, if old men are ever capable of any emotion.'

'I know you will laugh at me,' he replied, 'but I really can't exhibit it. I have put too much of myself into it.'

Lord Henry stretched himself out on the divan and laughed.

'Yes, I knew you would; but it is quite true, all the same.'

'Too much of yourself in it! Upon my word, Basil, I didn't know you were so vain; and I really can't see any resemblance between you, with your rugged strong face and your coal-black hair, and this young Adonis, who looks as if he was made out of ivory and rose-leaves. Why, my dear Basil, he is a Narcissus, and you—well, of course you have an intellectual expression, and all that. But beauty, real beauty, ends where an intellectual expression begins. Intellect is in itself a mode of exaggeration, and destroys the harmony of any face. The moment one sits down to think, one becomes all nose, or all forehead, or something horrid. Look at the successful men in any of the learned professions. How perfectly hideous they are! Except, of course, in the Church. But then in the Church they don't think. A bishop keeps on saying at the age of eighty what he was told to say when he was a boy of eighteen, and as a natural consequence he always looks absolutely delightful. Your mysterious young friend, whose name you have never told me, but whose picture really fascinates me, never thinks. I feel quite sure of that. He is some brainless, beautiful creature, who should be always here in winter when we have no flowers to look at, and always here in summer when we want something to chill our intelligence. Don't flatter yourself, Basil: you are not in the least like him.'

'You don't understand me, Harry,' answered the artist. 'Of course I am not like him. I know that perfectly well. Indeed, I should be sorry to look like him. You shrug your shoulders? I am telling you the truth. There is a fatality about all physical and intellectual distinction, the sort of fatality that seems to dog through history the faltering steps of kings. It is better not to be different from one's fellows. The ugly and the stupid have the best of it in this world. They can sit at their ease and gape at the play. If they know nothing of victory, they are at least spared the knowledge of defeat. They live as we all should live, undisturbed, indifferent, and without disquiet. They neither bring ruin upon others, nor ever receive it from alien hands. Your rank and wealth, Harry; my brains, such as they are—my art, whatever it may be worth; Dorian Gray's good looks—we shall all suffer for what the gods have given us, suffer terribly.'

'Dorian Gray? Is that his name?' asked Lord Henry, walking across the studio towards Basil Hallward.

'Yes, that is his name. I didn't intend to tell it to you.'

'But why not?'

'Oh, I can't explain. When I like people immensely I never tell their names to any one[3]. It is like surrendering a part of them. I have grown to love secrecy. It seems to be the one thing that can make modern life mysterious or marvellous to us. The commonest thing is delightful if one only hides it. When I leave town now I never tell my people where I am going. If I did, I would lose all my pleasure. It is a silly habit, I dare say, but somehow it seems to bring a great deal of romance into one's life. I suppose you think me awfully foolish about it?'

'Not at all,' answered Lord Henry, 'not at all, my dear Basil. You seem to forget that I am married, and the one charm of marriage is that it makes a life of deception absolutely necessary for both parties. I never know where my wife is, and my wife never knows what I am doing. When we meet—we do meet occasionally, when we dine out together, or go down to the Duke's—we tell each other the most absurd stories with the most serious faces. My wife is very good at it—much better, in fact, than I am. She never gets confused over her dates, and I always do. But when she does find me out, she makes no row at all. I sometimes wish she would; but she merely laughs at me.'

'I hate the way you talk about your married life, Harry,' said

Basil Hallward, strolling towards the door that led into the garden. 'I believe that you are really a very good husband, but that you are thoroughly ashamed of your own virtues. You are an extraordinary fellow. You never say a moral thing, and you never do a wrong thing. Your cynicism is simply a pose.'

'Being natural is simply a pose, and the most irritating pose I know,' cried Lord Henry, laughing; and the two young men went out into the garden together, and ensconced themselves on a long bamboo seat that stood in the shade of a tall laurel bush. The sunlight slipped over the polished leaves. In the grass, white daisies were tremulous.

After a pause, Lord Henry pulled out his watch. 'I am afraid I must be going, Basil,' he murmured, 'and before I go, I insist on your answering a question I put to you some time ago.'

'What is that?' said the painter, keeping his eyes fixed on the ground.

'You know quite well.'

'I do not, Harry.'

'Well, I will tell you what it is. I want you to explain to me why you won't exhibit Dorian Gray's picture. I want the real reason.'

'I told you the real reason.'

'No, you did not. You said it was because there was too much of yourself in it. Now, that is childish.'

'Harry,' said Basil Hallward, looking him straight in the face, 'every portrait that is painted with feeling is a portrait of the artist, not of the sitter. The sitter is merely the accident, the occasion. It is not he who is revealed by the painter; it is rather the painter who, on the coloured canvas, reveals himself. The reason I will not exhibit this picture is that I am afraid that I have shown in it the secret of my own soul.'

Lord Henry laughed. 'And what is that?' he asked.

'I will tell you,' said Hallward; but an expression of perplexity came over his face.

'I am all expectation, Basil,' continued his companion, glancing at him.

'Oh, there is really very little to tell, Harry,' answered the painter; 'and I am afraid you will hardly understand it. Perhaps you will hardly believe it.'

Lord Henry smiled, and, leaning down, plucked a pink-petalled daisy from the grass and examined it. 'I am quite sure I shall understand it,' he replied, gazing intently at the little golden white-feathered disk, 'and as for believing things, I can believe anything, provided that it is quite incredible.'

The wind shook some blossoms from the trees, and the heavy lilac-blooms, with their clustering stars, moved to and fro in the languid air. A grasshopper began to chirrup by the wall, and like a blue thread a long thin dragon-fly[4] floated past on its brown gauze wings. Lord Henry felt as if he could hear Basil Hallward's heart beating, and wondered what was coming.

'The story is simply this,' said the painter after some time. 'Two months ago I went to a crush at Lady Brandon's. You know we poor artists have to show ourselves in society from time to time, just to remind the public that we are not savages. With an evening coat and a white tie, as you told me once, anybody, even a stock-broker[5], can gain a reputation for being civilized. Well, after I had been in the room about ten minutes, talking to huge overdressed dowagers and tedious Academicians, I suddenly became conscious that some one[6] was looking at me. I turned half-way[7] round, and saw Dorian Gray for the first time. When our eyes met, I felt that I was growing pale. A curious sensation of terror came over me. I knew that I had come face to face with some one whose mere personality was so fascinating that, if I allowed it to do so, it would absorb my whole nature, my whole soul, my very art itself. I did not want any external influence in my life. You know yourself, Harry, how independent I am by nature. I have always been my own master; had at least always been so, till I met Dorian Gray. Then—but I don't know how to explain it to you. Something seemed to tell me that I was on the verge of a terrible crisis in my life. I had a strange feeling that Fate had in store for me exquisite joys and exquisite sorrows. I grew afraid, and turned to quit the room. It was not conscience that made me do so: it was a sort of cowardice. I take no credit to myself for trying to escape.'

'Conscience and cowardice are really the same things, Basil. Conscience is the trade-name[8] of the firm. That is all.'

'I don't believe that, Harry, and I don't believe you do either. However, whatever was my motive—and it may have been pride, for I used to be very proud—I certainly struggled to the door. There, of course, I stumbled against Lady Brandon. "You are not going to run away so soon, Mr Hallward?" she screamed out. You know her curiously shrill voice?'

'Yes; she is a peacock in everything but beauty,' said Lord Henry, pulling the daisy to bits with his long, nervous fingers.

'I could not get rid of her. She brought me up to Royalties, and people with Stars and Garters, and elderly ladies with gigantic tiaras and parrot noses. She spoke of me as her dearest friend. I had only met her once before, but she took it into her head to lionize me. I believe some picture of mine had made a great success at the time, at least had been chattered about in the penny newspapers, which is the nineteenth-century standard of immortality. Suddenly I found myself face to face with the young man whose personality had so strangely stirred me. We were quite close, almost touching. Our eyes met again. It was reckless of me, but I asked Lady Brandon to introduce me to him. Perhaps it was not so reckless, after all. It was simply inevitable. We would have spoken to each other without any introduction. I am sure of that. Dorian told me so afterwards. He, too, felt that we were destined to know each other.'

'And how did Lady Brandon describe this wonderful young man?' asked his companion. 'I know she goes in for giving a rapid *précis* of all her guests. I remember her bringing me up to a truculent and red-faced old gentleman covered all over with orders and ribbons, and hissing into my ear, in a tragic whisper which must have been perfectly audible to everybody in the room, the most astounding details. I simply fled. I like to find out people for myself. But Lady Brandon treats her guests exactly as an auctioneer treats his goods. She either explains them entirely away, or tells one everything about them except what one wants to know.'

'Poor Lady Brandon! You are hard on her, Harry!' said Hallward, listlessly.

'My dear fellow, she tried to found a *salon*, and only succeeded in opening a restaurant. How could I admire her? But tell me, what did she say about Mr Dorian Gray?'

'Oh, something like, "Charming boy—poor dear mother and I absolutely inseparable. Quite forget what he does—afraid he—doesn't do anything—oh, yes, plays the piano—or is it the violin, dear Mr Gray?" Neither of us could help laughing, and we became friends at once.'

'Laughter is not at all a bad beginning for a friendship, and it is far the best ending for one,' said the young lord, plucking another daisy.

Hallward shook his head. 'You don't understand what friendship is, Harry,' he murmured—'or what enmity is, for that matter. You like every one[9]; that is to say, you are indifferent to every one.'

'How horribly unjust of you!' cried Lord Henry, tilting his hat back and looking up at the little clouds that, like ravelled skeins of glossy white silk, were drifting across the hollowed turquoise of the summer sky. 'Yes; horribly unjust of you. I make a great difference between people. I choose my friends for their good looks, my acquaintances for their good characters, and my enemies for their good intellects. A man cannot be too careful in the choice of his enemies. I have not got one who is a fool. They are all men of some intellectual power, and consequently they all appreciate me. Is that very vain of me? I think it is rather vain.'

'I should think it was, Harry. But according to your category I must be merely an acquaintance.'

'My dear old Basil, you are much more than an acquaintance.'

'And much less than a friend. A sort of brother, I suppose?'

'Oh, brothers! I don't care for brothers. My elder brother won't die, and my younger brothers seem never to do anything else.'

'Harry!' exclaimed Hallward, frowning.

'My dear fellow, I am not quite serious. But I can't help detesting my relations. I suppose it comes from the fact that none of us can stand other people having the same faults as ourselves. I quite sympathize with the rage of the English democracy against what they call the vices of the upper orders. The masses feel that drunkenness, stupidity, and immorality should be their own special property, and that if any one of us makes an ass of himself he is poaching on their preserves. When poor Southwark got into the Divorce Court, their indignation was quite magnificent. And yet I don't suppose that ten per cent. of the proletariat live correctly.'

'I don't agree with a single word that you have said, and, what is more, Harry, I feel sure you don't either.'

Lord Henry stroked his pointed brown beard, and tapped the toe of his patent-leather boot with a tasselled ebony cane. 'How English you are Basil! That is the second time you have made that observation. If one puts forward an idea to a true Englishman— always a rash thing to do—he never dreams of considering whether the idea is right or wrong. The only thing he considers of any importance is whether one believes it oneself. Now, the value of an idea has nothing whatsoever to do with the sincerity of the man who expresses it. Indeed, the probabilities are that the more insincere the man is, the more purely intellectual will the idea be, as in that case it will not be coloured by either his wants, his desires, or his prejudices. However, I don't propose to discuss politics, sociology, or metaphysics with you. I like persons better than principles, and I like persons with no principles better than anything else in the world. Tell me more about Mr Dorian Gray. How often do you see him?'

'Every day. I couldn't be happy if I didn't see him every day. He is absolutely necessary to me.'

'How extraordinary! I thought you would never care for anything but your art.'

'He is all my art to me now,' said the painter, gravely. 'I sometimes think, Harry, that there are only two eras of any importance in the world's history. The first is the appearance of a new medium for art, and the second is the appearance of a new personality for art also. What the invention of oil-painting was to the Venetians, the face of Antinoüs[10] was to late Greek sculpture, and the face of Dorian Gray will some day be to me. It is not merely that I paint from him, draw from him, sketch from him. Of course, I have done all that. But he is much more to me than a model or a sitter. I won't tell you that I am dissatisfied with what I have done of him, or that his beauty is such that Art cannot express it. There is nothing that Art cannot express, and I know that the work I have done, since I met Dorian Gray, is good work, is the best work of my life. But in some curious way—I wonder will you understand me?—his personality has suggested to me an entirely new manner in art, an entirely new mode of style. I see things differently, I think of them differently. I can now recreate life in a way that was hidden from me before. "A dream of form in days of thought" —who is it who says that? I forget; but it is what Dorian Gray has been to me. The merely visible presence of this lad—for he seems to me little more than a lad, though he is really over twenty—his merely visible presence—ah! I wonder can you realise all that that means? Unconsciously he defines for me the lines of a fresh school, a school that is to have in it all the passion of the romantic spirit, all the perfection of the spirit that is Greek. The harmony of soul and body—how much that is! We in our madness have separated the two, and have invented a realism that is vulgar, an ideality that is void. Harry! if[11] you only knew what Dorian Gray is to me! You remember that landscape of mine, for which Agnew offered me such a huge price, but which I would not part with? It is one of the best things I have ever done. And why is it so? Because while I was painting it, Dorian Gray sat beside me. Some subtle influence passed from him to me, and for the first time in my life I saw in the plain woodland the wonder I had always looked for, and always missed.'

'Basil, this is extraordinary! I must see Dorian Gray.'

Hallward got up from the seat, and walked up and down the garden. After some time he came back. 'Harry,' he said, 'Dorian Gray is to me simply a motive in art. You might see nothing in him. I see everything in him. He is never more present in my work than when no image of him is there. He is a suggestion, as I have said, of a new manner. I find him in the curves of certain lines, in the loveliness and subtleties of certain colours. That is all.'

'Then why won't you exhibit his portrait?' asked Lord Henry.

'Because, without intending it, I have put into it some expression of all this curious artistic idolatry, of which, of course, I have never cared to speak to him. He knows nothing about it. He shall never know anything about it. But the world might guess it; and I will not bare my soul to their shallow, prying eyes. My heart shall never be put under their microscope. There is too much of myself in the thing, Harry—too much of myself!'

'Poets are not so scrupulous as you are. They know how useful passion is for publication. Nowadays a broken heart will run to many editions.'

'I hate them for it,' cried Hallward. 'An artist should create beautiful things, but should put nothing of his own life into them. We live in an age when men treat art as if it were meant to be a form of autobiography. We have lost the abstract sense of beauty. Some day I will show the world what it is; and for that reason the world shall never see my portrait of Dorian Gray.'

'I think you are wrong, Basil, but I won't argue with you. It is only the intellectually lost who ever argue. Tell me, is Dorian Gray very fond of you?'

The painter considered for a few moments. 'He likes me,' he answered, after a pause; 'I know he likes me. Of course I flatter him dreadfully. I find a strange pleasure in saying things to him that I know I shall be sorry for having said. As a rule, he is charming to me, and we sit in the studio and talk of a thousand things. Now and then, however, he is horribly thoughtless, and seems to take a real delight in giving me pain. Then I feel, Harry, that I have given away my whole soul to some one who treats it as if it were a flower to put in his coat, a bit of decoration to charm his vanity, an ornament for a summer's day.'

'Days in summer, Basil, are apt to linger,' murmured Lord Henry. 'Perhaps you will tire sooner than he will. It is a sad thing to think of, but there is no doubt that Genius lasts longer than Beauty. That accounts for the fact that we all take such pains to over-educate ourselves. In the wild struggle for existence, we want to have something that endures, and so we fill our minds with rubbish and facts, in the silly hope of keeping our place. The thoroughly well-informed man—that is the modern ideal. And the mind of the thoroughly well-informed man is a dreadful thing. It is like a bric-à-brac[12] shop, all monsters and dust, with everything priced above its proper value. I think you will tire first, all the same. Some day you will look at your friend, and he will seem to you to be a little out of drawing, or you won't like his tone of colour, or something. You will bitterly reproach him in your own heart, and seriously think that he has behaved very badly to you. The next time he calls, you will be perfectly cold and indifferent. It will be a great pity, for it will alter you. What you have told me is quite a romance, a romance of art one might call it, and the worst of having a romance of any kind is that it leaves one so unromantic.'

'Harry, don't talk like that. As long as I live, the personality of Dorian Gray will dominate me. You can't feel what I feel. You change too often.'

'Ah, my dear Basil, that is exactly why I can feel it. Those who are faithful know only the trivial side of love: it is the faithless who know love's tragedies.' And Lord Henry struck a light on a dainty silver case, and began to smoke a cigarette with a self-conscious and satisfied air, as if he had summed up the world in a phrase. There was a rustle of chirruping sparrows in the green lacquer leaves of the ivy, and the blue cloud-shadows chased themselves across the grass like swallows. How pleasant it was in the garden! And how delightful other people's emotions were!—much more delightful than their ideas, it seemed to him. One's own soul, and the passions of one's friends—those were the fascinating things in life. He pictured to himself with silent amusement the tedious luncheon that he had missed by staying so long with Basil Hallward. Had he gone to his aunt's, he would have been sure to have met Lord Goodbody there, and the whole conversation would have been about the feeding of the poor, and the necessity for model lodging-houses[13]. Each class would have preached the importance of those virtues, for whose exercise there was no necessity in their own lives. The rich would have spoken on the value of thrift, and the idle grown eloquent over the dignity of labour. It was charming to have escaped all that! As he thought of his aunt, an idea seemed to strike him. He turned to Hallward and said, 'My dear fellow, I have just remembered.'

'Remembered what, Harry?'

'Where I heard the name of Dorian Gray.'

'Where was it?' asked Hallward, with a slight frown.

'Don't look so angry, Basil. It was at my aunt, Lady Agatha's. She told me she had discovered a wonderful young man, who was going to help her in the East End, and that his name was Dorian Gray. I am bound to state that she never told me he was good-looking. Women have no appreciation of good looks; at least, good women have not. She said that he was very earnest, and had a beautiful nature. I at once pictured to myself a creature with spectacles and lank hair, horribly freckled, and tramping about on huge feet. I wish I had known it was your friend.'

'I am very glad you didn't, Harry.'

'Why?'

'I don't want you to meet him.'

'You don't want me to meet him?'

'No.'

'Mr Dorian Gray is in the studio, sir,' said the butler, coming into the garden.

'You must introduce me now,' cried Lord Henry, laughing.

The painter turned to his servant, who stood blinking in the sunlight. 'Ask Mr Gray to wait, Parker: I shall be in in a few moments.' The man bowed, and went up the walk.

Then he looked at Lord Henry. 'Dorian Gray is my dearest friend,' he said. 'He has a simple and a beautiful nature. Your aunt was quite right in what she said of him. Don't spoil him. Don't try to influence him. Your influence would be bad. The world is wide, and has many marvellous people in it. Don't take away from me the one person who gives to my art whatever charm it possesses: my life as an artist depends on him. Mind, Harry, I trust you.' He spoke very slowly, and the words seemed wrung out of him almost against his will.

'What nonsense you talk!' said Lord Henry, smiling, and, taking Hallward by the arm, he almost led him into the house.

Chapter 2

As they entered they saw Dorian Gray. He was seated at the piano, with his back to them, turning over the pages of a volume of Schumann's 'Forest Scenes'. 'You must lend me these, Basil,' he cried. 'I want to learn them. They are perfectly charming.'

'That entirely depends on how you sit to-day[14], Dorian.'

'Oh, I am tired of sitting, and I don't want a life-sized portrait of myself,' answered the lad, swinging round on the music-stool, in a wilful, petulant manner. When he caught sight of Lord Henry, a faint blush coloured his cheeks for a moment, and he started up. 'I beg your pardon, Basil, but I didn't know you had any one with you.'

'This is Lord Henry Wotton, Dorian, an old Oxford friend of mine. I have just been telling him what a capital sitter you were, and now you have spoiled everything.'

'You have not spoiled my pleasure in meeting you, Mr Gray,' said Lord Henry, stepping forward and extending his hand. 'My aunt has often spoken to me about you. You are one of her favourites, and, I am afraid, one of her victims also.'

'I am in Lady Agatha's black books at present,' answered Dorian, with a funny look of penitence. 'I promised to go to a club in Whitechapel with her last Tuesday, and I really forgot all about it. We were to have played a duet together—three duets, I believe. I don't know what she will say to me. I am far too frightened to call.'

'Oh, I will make your peace with my aunt. She is quite devoted to you. And I don't think it really matters about your not being there. The audience probably thought it was a duet. When Aunt Agatha sits down to the piano she makes quite enough noise for two people.'

'That is very horrid to her, and not very nice to me,' answered Dorian, laughing.

Lord Henry looked at him. Yes, he was certainly wonderfully handsome, with his finely-curved scarlet lips, his frank blue eyes, his crisp gold hair. There was something in his face that made one trust him at once. All the candour of youth was there, as well as all youth's passionate purity. One felt that he had kept himself unspotted from the world. No wonder Basil Hallward worshipped him.

'You are too charming to go in for philanthropy, Mr Gray—far too charming.' And Lord Henry flung himself down on the divan, and opened his cigarette-case[15].

The painter had been busy mixing his colours and getting his brushes ready. He was looking worried, and when he heard Lord Henry's last remark he glanced at him, hesitated for a moment, and then said, 'Harry, I want to finish this picture to-day. Would you think it awfully rude of me if I asked you to go away?'

Lord Henry smiled and looked at Dorian Gray. 'Am I to go, Mr Gray?' he asked.

'Oh, please don't, Lord Henry. I see that Basil is in one of his sulky moods; and I can't bear him when he sulks. Besides, I want you to tell me why I should not go in for philanthropy.'

'I don't know that I shall tell you that, Mr Gray. It is so tedious a subject that one would have to talk seriously about it. But I certainly shall not run away, now that you have asked me to stop. You don't really mind, Basil, do you? You have often told me that you liked your sitters to have some one to chat to.'

Hallward bit his lip. 'If Dorian wishes it, of course you must stay. Dorian's whims are laws to everybody, except himself.'

Lord Henry took up his hat and gloves. 'You are very pressing, Basil, but I am afraid I must go. I have promised to meet a man at the Orleans. Good-bye, Mr Gray. Come and see me some afternoon in Curzon Street. I am nearly always at home at five o'clock. Write to me when you are coming. I should be sorry to miss you.'

'Basil,' cried Dorian Gray, 'if Lord Henry Wotton goes I shall go too. You never open your lips while you are painting, and it is horribly dull standing on a platform and trying to look pleasant. Ask him to stay. I insist upon it.'

'Stay, Harry, to oblige Dorian, and to oblige me,' said Hallward, gazing intently at his picture. 'It is quite true, I never talk when I am working, and never listen either, and it must be dreadfully tedious for my unfortunate sitters. I beg you to stay.'

'But what about my man at the Orleans?'

The painter laughed. 'I don't think there will be any difficulty about that. Sit down again, Harry. And now, Dorian, get up on the platform, and don't move about too much, or pay any attention to what Lord Henry says. He has a very bad influence over all his friends, with the single exception of myself.'

Dorian Gray stepped up on the dais, with the air of a young Greek martyr, and made a little *moue* of discontent to Lord Henry, to whom he had rather taken a fancy. He was so unlike Basil. They made a delightful contrast. And he had such a beautiful voice. After a few moments he said to him, 'Have you really a very bad influence, Lord Henry? As bad as Basil says?'

'There is no such thing as a good influence, Mr Gray. All influence is immoral—immoral from the scientific point of view.'

'Why?'

'Because to influence a person is to give him one's own soul. He does not think his natural thoughts, or burn with his natural passions. His virtues are not real to him. His sins, if there are such things as sins, are borrowed. He becomes an echo of some one else's music, an actor of a part that has not been written for him. The aim of life is self-development. To realise one's nature perfectly—that is what each of us is here for. People are afraid of themselves, nowadays. They have forgotten the highest of all duties, the duty that one owes to one's self. Of course they are charitable. They feed the hungry, and clothe the beggar. But their own souls starve, and are naked. Courage has gone out of our race. Perhaps we never really had it. The terror of society, which is the basis of morals, the terror of God, which is the secret of religion— these are the two things that govern us. And yet—'

'Just turn your head a little more to the right, Dorian, like a good boy,' said the painter, deep in his work, and conscious only that a look had come into the lad's face that he had never seen there before.

'And yet,' continued Lord Henry, in his low, musical voice, and with that graceful wave of the hand that was always so characteristic of him, and that he had even in his Eton days, 'I believe that if one man were to live out his life fully and completely, were to give form to every feeling, expression to every thought, reality to every dream—I believe that the world would gain such a fresh impulse of joy that we would forget all the maladies of mediaevalism, and return to the Hellenic ideal—to something finer, richer than the Hellenic ideal, it may be. But the bravest man amongst us is afraid of himself. The mutilation of the savage has its tragic survival in the self-denial that mars our lives. We are punished for our refusals. Every impulse that we strive to strangle broods in the mind, and poisons us. The body sins once, and has done with its sin, for action is a mode of purification. Nothing remains then but the recollection of a pleasure, or the luxury of a regret. The only way to get rid of a temptation is to yield to it. Resist it, and your soul grows sick with longing for the things it has forbidden to itself, with desire for what its monstrous laws have made monstrous and unlawful. It has been said that the great events of the world take place in the brain. It is in the brain, and the brain only, that the great sins of the world take place also. You, Mr Gray, you yourself, with your rose-red youth and your rose-white boyhood, you have had passions that have made you afraid, thoughts that have filled you with terror, day-dreams[16] and sleeping dreams whose mere memory might stain your cheek with shame—'

'Stop!' faltered Dorian Gray, 'stop! you[17] bewilder me. I don't know what to say. There is some answer to you, but I cannot find it. Don't speak. Let me think. Or, rather, let me try not to think.'

For nearly ten minutes he stood there, motionless, with parted lips, and eyes strangely bright. He was dimly conscious that entirely fresh influences were at work within him. Yet they seemed to him to have come really from himself. The few words that Basil's friend had said to him—words spoken by chance, no doubt, and with wilful paradox in them—had touched some secret chord that had never been touched before, but that he felt was now vibrating and throbbing to curious pulses.

Music had stirred him like that. Music had troubled him many times. But music was not articulate. It was not a new world, but rather another chaos, that it created in us. Words! Mere words! How terrible they were! How clear, and vivid, and cruel! One could not escape from them. And yet what a subtle magic there was in them! They seemed to be able to give a plastic form to formless things, and to have a music of their own as sweet as that of viol or of lute. Mere words! Was there anything so real as words?

Yes; there had been things in his boyhood that he had not understood. He understood them now. Life suddenly became fiery-coloured to him. It seemed to him that he had been walking in fire. Why had he not known it?

With his subtle smile, Lord Henry watched him. He knew the precise psychological moment when to say nothing. He felt intensely interested. He was amazed at the sudden impression that his words had produced, and, remembering a book that he had read when he was sixteen, a book which had revealed to him much that he had not known before, he wondered whether Dorian Gray was passing through a similar experience. He had merely shot an arrow into the air. Had it hit the mark? How fascinating the lad was!

Hallward painted away with that marvellous bold touch of his, that had the true refinement and perfect delicacy that in art, at any rate, comes only from strength. He was unconscious of the silence.

'Basil, I am tired of standing,' cried Dorian Gray, suddenly. 'I must go out and sit in the garden. The air is stifling here.'

'My dear fellow, I am so sorry. When I am painting, I can't think of anything else. But you never sat better. You were perfectly still. And I have caught the effect I wanted—the half-parted lips, and the bright look in the eyes. I don't know what Harry has been saying to you, but he has certainly made you have the most wonderful expression. I suppose he has been paying you compliments. You mustn't believe a word that he says.'

'He has certainly not been paying me compliments. Perhaps that is the reason that I don't believe anything he has told me.'

'You know you believe it all,' said Lord Henry, looking at him with his dreamy, languorous eyes. 'I will go out to the garden with you. It is horribly hot in the studio. Basil, let us have something iced to drink, something with strawberries in it.'

'Certainly, Harry. Just touch the bell, and when Parker comes I will tell him what you want. I have got to work up this background, so I will join you later on. Don't keep Dorian too long. I have never been in better form for painting than I am to-day. This is going to be my masterpiece. It is my masterpiece as it stands.'

Lord Henry went out to the garden, and found Dorian Gray burying his face in the great cool lilac-blossoms[18], feverishly drinking in their perfume as if it had been wine. He came close to him, and put his hand upon his shoulder. 'You are quite right to do that,' he murmured. 'Nothing can cure the soul but the senses, just as nothing can cure the senses but the soul.'

The lad started and drew back. He was bare-headed, and the leaves had tossed his rebellious curls and tangled all their gilded threads. There was a look of fear in his eyes, such as people have when they are suddenly awakened. His finely-chiselled nostrils quivered, and some hidden nerve shook the scarlet of his lips and left them trembling.

'Yes,' continued Lord Henry, 'that is one of the great secrets of life—to cure the soul by means of the senses, and the senses by means of the soul. You are a wonderful creation. You know more than you think you know, just as you know less than you want to know.'

Dorian Gray frowned and turned his head away. He could not help liking the tall, graceful young man who was standing by him. His romantic, olive-coloured face and worn expression interested him. There was something in his low, languid voice that was absolutely fascinating. His cool, white, flower-like hands, even, had a curious charm. They moved, as he spoke, like music, and seemed to have a language of their own. But he felt afraid of him, and ashamed of being afraid. Why had it been left for a stranger to reveal him to himself? He had known Basil Hallward for months, but the friendship between them had never altered him.

Suddenly there had come some one across his life who seemed to have disclosed to him life's mystery. And, yet, what was there to be afraid of? He was not a schoolboy or a girl. It was absurd to be frightened.

'Let us go and sit in the shade,' said Lord Henry. 'Parker has brought out the drinks, and if you stay any longer in this glare you will be quite spoiled, and Basil will never paint you again. You really must not allow yourself to become sunburnt. It would be unbecoming.'

'What can it matter?' cried Dorian Gray, laughing, as he sat down on the seat at the end of the garden.

'It should matter everything to you, Mr Gray.'

'Why?'

'Because you have the most marvellous youth, and youth is the one thing worth having.'

'I don't feel that, Lord Henry.'

'No, you don't feel it now. Some day, when you are old and wrinkled and ugly, when thought has seared your forehead with its lines, and passion branded your lips with its hideous fires, you will feel it, you will feel it terribly. Now, wherever you go, you charm the world. Will it always be so? ...You have a wonderfully beautiful face, Mr Gray. Don't frown. You have. And Beauty is a form of Genius—is higher, indeed, than Genius, as it needs no explanation. It is one of the great facts of the world, like sunlight, or spring-time, or the reflection in dark waters of that silver shell we call the moon. It cannot be questioned. It has its divine right of sovereignty. It makes princes of those who have it. You smile? Ah! when[19] you have lost it you won't smile....People say sometimes that Beauty is only superficial. That may be so. But at least it is not so superficial as Thought is. To me, Beauty is the wonder of wonders. It is only shallow people who do not judge by appearances. The true mystery of the world is the visible, not the invisible....Yes, Mr Gray, the gods have been good to you. But what the gods give they quickly take away. You have only a few years in which to live really, perfectly, and fully. When your youth goes, your beauty will go with it, and then you will suddenly discover that there are no triumphs left for you, or have to content yourself with those mean triumphs that the memory of your past will make more bitter than defeats. Every month as it wanes brings you nearer to something dreadful. Time is jealous of you, and wars against your lilies and your roses. You will become sallow, and hollow-cheeked, and dull-eyed. You will suffer horribly....Ah! realise[20] your youth while you have it. Don't squander the gold of your days, listening to the tedious, trying to improve the hopeless failure, or giving away your life to the ignorant, the common, and the vulgar. These are the sickly aims, the false ideals, of our age. Live! Live the wonderful life that is in you! Let nothing be lost upon you. Be always searching for new sensations. Be afraid of nothing....A new Hedonism—that is what our century wants. You might be its visible symbol. With your personality there is nothing you could not do. The world belongs to you for a season....The moment I met you I saw that you were quite unconscious of what you really are, of what you really might be. There was so much in you that charmed me that I felt I must tell you something about yourself. I thought how tragic it would be if you were wasted. For there is such a little time that your youth will last—such a little time. The common hill-flowers wither, but they blossom again. The laburnum will be as yellow next June as it is now. In a month there will be purple stars on the clematis, and year after year the green night of its leaves will hold its purple stars. But we never get back our youth. The pulse of joy that beats in us at twenty, becomes sluggish. Our limbs fail, our senses rot. We degenerate into hideous puppets, haunted by the memory of the passions of which we were too much afraid, and the exquisite temptations that we had not the courage to yield to. Youth! Youth! There is absolutely nothing in the world but youth!'

Dorian Gray listened, open-eyed and wondering. The spray of lilac fell from his hand upon the gravel. A furry bee came and buzzed round it for a moment. Then it began to scramble all over the oval stellated globe of the tiny blossoms. He watched it with that strange interest in trivial things that we try to develop when things of high import make us afraid, or when we are stirred by some new emotion for which we cannot find expression, or when some thought that terrifies us lays sudden siege to the brain and calls on us to yield. After a time the bee flew away. He saw it creeping into the stained trumpet of a Tyrian convolvulus. The flower seemed to quiver, and then swayed gently to and fro.

Suddenly the painter appeared at the door of the studio, and made staccato signs for them to come in. They turned to each other, and smiled.

'I am waiting,' he cried. 'Do come in. The light is quite perfect, and you can bring your drinks.'

They rose up, and sauntered down the walk together. Two green-and-white butterflies fluttered past them, and in the pear-tree at the corner of the garden a thrush began to sing.

'You are glad you have met me, Mr Gray,' said Lord Henry, looking at him.

'Yes, I am glad now. I wonder shall I always be glad?'

'Always! That is a dreadful word. It makes me shudder when I hear it. Women are so fond of using it. They spoil every romance by trying to make it last for ever. It is a meaningless word, too. The only difference between a caprice and a life-long[21] passion is that the caprice lasts a little longer.'

As they entered the studio, Dorian Gray put his hand upon Lord Henry's arm. 'In that case, let our friendship be a caprice,' he murmured, flushing at his own boldness, then stepped up on the platform and resumed his pose.

Lord Henry flung himself into a large wicker arm-chair[22], and watched him. The sweep and dash of the brush on the canvas made the only sound that broke the stillness, except when, now and then, Hallward stepped back to look at his work from a distance. In the slanting beams that streamed through the open doorway the dust danced and was golden. The heavy scent of the roses seemed to brood over everything.

After about a quarter of an hour Hallward stopped painting, looked for a long time at Dorian Gray, and then for a long time at the picture, biting the end of one of his huge brushes, and frowning. 'It is quite finished,' he cried at last, and stooping down he wrote his name in long vermilion letters on the left-hand corner of the canvas.

Lord Henry came over and examined the picture. It was certainly a wonderful work of art, and a wonderful likeness as well.

'My dear fellow, I congratulate you most warmly,' he said. 'It is the finest portrait of modern times. Mr Gray, come over and look at yourself.'

The lad started, as if awakened from some dream. 'Is it really finished?' he murmured, stepping down from the platform.

'Quite finished,' said the painter. 'And you have sat splendidly to-day. I am awfully obliged to you.'

'That is entirely due to me,' broke in Lord Henry. 'Isn't it, Mr Gray?'

Dorian made no answer, but passed listlessly in front of his picture and turned towards it. When he saw it he drew back, and his cheeks flushed for a moment with pleasure. A look of joy came into his eyes, as if he had recognized himself for the first time. He stood there motionless and in wonder, dimly conscious that Hallward was speaking to him, but not catching the meaning of his words. The sense of his own beauty came on him like a revelation. He had never felt it before. Basil Hallward's compliments had seemed to him to be merely the charming exaggeration of friendship. He had listened to them, laughed at them, forgotten them. They had not influenced his nature. Then had come Lord

Henry Wotton with his strange panegyric on youth, his terrible warning of its brevity. That had stirred him at the time, and now, as he stood gazing at the shadow of his own loveliness, the full reality of the description flashed across him. Yes, there would be a day when his face would be wrinkled and wizen, his eyes dim and colourless, the grace of his figure broken and deformed. The scarlet would pass away from his lips, and the gold steal from his hair. The life that was to make his soul would mar his body. He would become dreadful, hideous, and uncouth.

As he thought of it, a sharp pang of pain struck through him like a knife, and made each delicate fibre of his nature quiver. His eyes deepened into amethyst, and across them came a mist of tears. He felt as if a hand of ice had been laid upon his heart.

'Don't you like it?' cried Hallward at last, stung a little by the lad's silence, not understanding what it meant.

'Of course he likes it,' said Lord Henry. 'Who wouldn't like it? It is one of the greatest things in modern art. I will give you anything you like to ask for it. I must have it.'

'It is not my property, Harry.'

'Whose property is it?'

'Dorian's, of course,' answered the painter.

'He is a very lucky fellow.'

'How sad it is!' murmured Dorian Gray, with his eyes still fixed upon his own portrait. 'How sad it is! I shall grow old, and horrible, and dreadful. It will never be older than this particular day of June....If it were only the other way! If it were I who was to be always young, and the picture that was to grow old! For that—for that—I would give everything! Yes, there is nothing in the whole world I would not give! I would give my soul for that!'

'You would hardly care for such an arrangement, Basil,' cried Lord Henry, laughing. 'It would be rather hard lines on your work.'

'I should object very strongly, Harry,' said Hallward.

Dorian Gray turned and looked at him. 'I believe you would, Basil. You like your art better than your friends. I am no more to you than a green bronze figure. Hardly as much, I dare say.'

The painter stared in amazement. It was so unlike Dorian to speak like that. What had happened? He seemed quite angry. His face was flushed and his cheeks burning.

'Yes,' he continued, 'I am less to you than your ivory Hermes[23] or your silver Faun[24]. You will like them always. How long will you like me? Till I have my first wrinkle, I suppose. I know, now, that when one loses one's good looks, whatever they may be, one loses everything. Your picture has taught me that. Lord Henry Wotton is perfectly right. Youth is the only thing worth having. When I find that I am growing old, I shall kill myself.'

Hallward turned pale, and caught his hand. 'Dorian! Dorian!' he cried, 'don't talk like that. I have never had such a friend as you, and I shall never have such another. You are not jealous of material things, are you?—you who are finer than any of them!'

'I am jealous of everything whose beauty does not die. I am jealous of the portrait you have painted of me. Why should it keep what I must lose? Every moment that passes takes something from me, and gives something to it. Oh, if it were only the other way! If the picture could change, and I could be always what I am now! Why did you paint it? It will mock me some day—mock me horribly!' The hot tears welled into his eyes; he tore his hand away, and, flinging himself on the divan, he buried his face in the cushions, as though he was praying.

'This is your doing, Harry,' said the painter, bitterly.

Lord Henry shrugged his shoulders. 'It is the real Dorian Gray—that is all.'

'It is not.'

'If it is not, what have I to do with it?'

'You should have gone away when I asked you,' he muttered.

'I stayed when you asked me,' was Lord Henry's answer.

'Harry, I can't quarrel with my two best friends at once, but between you both you have made me hate the finest piece of work I have ever done, and I will destroy it. What is it but canvas and colour? I will not let it come across our three lives and mar them.'

Dorian Gray lifted his golden head from the pillow, and with pallid face and tear-stained eyes looked at him, as he walked over to the deal painting-table[25] that was set beneath the high curtained window. What was he doing there? His fingers were straying about among the litter of tin tubes and dry brushes, seeking for something. Yes, it was for the long palette-knife[26], with its thin blade of lithe steel. He had found it at last. He was going to rip up the canvas.

With a stifled sob the lad leaped from the couch, and, rushing over to Hallward, tore the knife out of his hand, and flung it to the end of the studio. 'Don't, Basil, don't!' he cried. 'It would be murder!'

'I am glad you appreciate my work at last, Dorian,' said the painter, coldly, when he had recovered from his surprise. 'I never thought you would.'

'Appreciate it? I am in love with it, Basil. It is part of myself. I feel that.'

'Well, as soon as you are dry, you shall be varnished, and

framed, and sent home. Then you can do what you like with yourself.' And he walked across the room and rang the bell for tea. 'You will have tea, of course, Dorian? And so will you, Harry? Or do you object to such simple pleasures?'

'I adore simple pleasures,' said Lord Henry. 'They are the last refuge of the complex. But I don't like scenes, except on the stage. What absurd fellows you are, both of you! I wonder who it was defined man as a rational animal. It was the most premature definition ever given. Man is many things, but he is not rational. I am glad he is not, after all: though I wish you chaps would not squabble over the picture. You had much better let me have it, Basil. This silly boy doesn't really want it, and I really do.'

'If you let any one have it but me, Basil, I shall never forgive you!' cried Dorian Gray; 'and I don't allow people to call me a silly boy.'

'You know the picture is yours, Dorian. I gave it to you before it existed.'

'And you know you have been a little silly, Mr Gray, and that you don't really object to being reminded that you are extremely young.'

'I should have objected very strongly this morning, Lord Henry.'

'Ah! this[27] morning! You have lived since then.'

There came a knock at the door, and the butler entered with a laden tea-tray[28] and set it down upon a small Japanese table. There was a rattle of cups and saucers and the hissing of a fluted Georgian urn. Two globe-shaped china dishes were brought in by a page. Dorian Gray went over and poured out the tea. The two men sauntered languidly to the table, and examined what was under the covers.

'Let us go to the theatre to-night[29],' said Lord Henry. 'There is sure to be something on, somewhere. I have promised to dine at White's, but it is only with an old friend, so I can send him a wire to say that I am ill, or that I am prevented from coming in consequence of a subsequent engagement. I think that would be a rather nice excuse: it would have all the surprise of candour.'

'It is such a bore putting on one's dress-clothes[30],' muttered Hallward. 'And, when one has them on, they are so horrid.'

'Yes,' answered Lord Henry, dreamily, 'the costume of the nineteenth century is detestable. It is so sombre, so depressing. Sin is the only real colour-element[31] left in modern life.'

'You really must not say things like that before Dorian, Harry.'

'Before which Dorian? The one who is pouring out tea for us, or the one in the picture?'

'Before either.'

'I should like to come to the theatre with you, Lord Henry,' said the lad.

'Then you shall come; and you will come too, Basil, won't you?'

'I can't, really. I would sooner not. I have a lot of work to do.'

'Well, then, you and I will go alone, Mr Gray.'

'I should like that awfully.'

The painter bit his lip and walked over, cup in hand, to the picture. 'I shall stay with the real Dorian,' he said, sadly.

'Is it the real Dorian?' cried the original of the portrait, strolling across to him. 'Am I really like that?'

'Yes; you are just like that.'

'How wonderful, Basil!'

'At least you are like it in appearance. But it will never alter,' sighed Hallward. 'That is something.'

'What a fuss people make about fidelity!' exclaimed Lord Henry. 'Why, even in love it is purely a question for physiology. It has nothing to do with our own will. Young men want to be faithful, and are not; old men want to be faithless, and cannot: that is all one can say.'

'Don't go to the theatre to-night, Dorian,' said Hallward. 'Stop and dine with me.'

'I can't, Basil.'

'Why?'

'Because I have promised Lord Henry Wotton to go with him.'

'He won't like you the better for keeping your promises. He always breaks his own. I beg you not to go.'

Dorian Gray laughed and shook his head.

'I entreat you.'

The lad hesitated, and looked over at Lord Henry, who was watching them from the tea-table[32] with an amused smile.

'I must go, Basil,' he answered.

'Very well,' said Hallward; and he went over and laid down his cup on the tray. 'It is rather late, and, as you have to dress, you had better lose no time. Good-bye, Harry. Good-bye, Dorian. Come and see me soon. Come to-morrow[33].'

'Certainly.'

'You won't forget?'

'No, of course not,' cried Dorian.

'And...Harry!'

'Yes, Basil?'

'Remember what I asked you, when we were in the garden this morning.'

'I have forgotten it.'

'I trust you.'

'I wish I could trust myself,' said Lord Henry, laughing. 'Come, Mr Gray, my hansom is outside, and I can drop you at your own place. Good-bye, Basil. It has been a most interesting afternoon.'

As the door closed behind them, the painter flung himself down on a sofa, and a look of pain came into his face.

Chapter 3

At half-past twelve next day Lord Henry Wotton strolled from Curzon Street over to the Albany to call on his uncle, Lord Fermor, a genial if somewhat rough-mannered old bachelor, whom the outside world called selfish because it derived no particular benefit from him, but who was considered generous by Society as he fed the people who amused him. His father had been our ambassador at Madrid when Isabella was young, and Prim unthought of, but had retired from the Diplomatic Service in a capricious moment of annoyance on not being offered the Embassy at Paris, a post to which he considered that he was fully entitled by reason of his birth, his indolence, the good English of his dispatches, and his inordinate passion for pleasure. The son, who had been his father's secretary, had resigned along with his chief, somewhat foolishly as was thought at the time, and on succeeding some months later to the title, had set himself to the serious study of the great aristocratic art of doing absolutely nothing. He had two large town houses, but preferred to live in chambers as it was less trouble, and took most of his meals at his club. He paid some attention to the management of his collieries in the Midland counties, excusing himself for this taint of industry on the ground that the one advantage of having coal was that it enabled a gentleman to afford the decency of burning wood on his own hearth. In politics he was a Tory, except when the Tories were in office, during which period he roundly abused them for being a pack of Radicals. He was a hero to his valet, who bullied him, and a terror to most of his relations, whom he bullied in turn. Only England could have produced him, and he always said that the country was going to the dogs. His principles were out of date, but there was a good deal to be said for his prejudices.

When Lord Henry entered the room, he found his uncle sitting in a rough shooting coat, smoking a cheroot and grumbling over *The Times*. 'Well, Harry,' said the old gentleman, 'what brings you out so early? I thought you dandies never got up till two, and were not visible till five.'

'Pure family affection, I assure you, Uncle George. I want to get something out of you.'

'Money, I suppose,' said Lord Fermor, making a wry face. 'Well, sit down and tell me all about it. Young people, nowadays, imagine that money is everything.'

'Yes,' murmured Lord Henry, settling his buttonhole in his coat; 'and when they grow older they know it. But I don't want money. It is only people who pay their bills who want that, Uncle George, and I never pay mine. Credit is the capital of a younger son, and one lives charmingly upon it. Besides, I always deal with Dartmoor's tradesmen, and consequently they never bother me. What I want is information: not useful information, of course; useless information.'

'Well, I can tell you anything that is in an English Blue-book[34], Harry, although those fellows nowadays write a lot of nonsense. When I was in the Diplomatic, things were much better. But I hear they let them in now by examination. What can you expect? Examinations, sir, are pure humbug from beginning to end. If a man is a gentleman, he knows quite enough, and if he is not a gentleman, whatever he knows is bad for him.'

'Mr Dorian Gray does not belong to Blue-books, Uncle George,' said Lord Henry, languidly.

'Mr Dorian Gray? Who is he?' asked Lord Fermor, knitting his bushy white eyebrows.

'That is what I have come to learn, Uncle George. Or rather, I know who he is. He is the last Lord Kelso's grandson. His mother was a Devereux, Lady Margaret Devereux. I want you to tell me about his mother. What was she like? Whom did she marry? You have known nearly everybody in your time, so you might have known her. I am very much interested in Mr Gray at present. I have only just met him.'

'Kelso's grandson!' echoed the old gentleman—'Kelso's grandson!...Of course....I knew his mother intimately. I believe I was at her christening. She was an extraordinarily beautiful girl,

Margaret Devereux, and made all the men frantic by running away with a penniless young fellow, a mere nobody, sir, a subaltern in a foot regiment, or something of that kind. Certainly. I remember the whole thing as if it happened yesterday. The poor chap was killed in a duel at Spa a few months after the marriage. There was an ugly story about it. They said Kelso got some rascally adventurer, some Belgian brute, to insult his son-in-law in public, paid him, sir, to do it, paid him, and that the fellow spitted his man as if he had been a pigeon. The thing was hushed up, but, egad, Kelso ate his chop alone at the club for some time afterwards. He brought his daughter back with him, I was told, and she never spoke to him again. Oh, yes; it was a bad business. The girl died too, died within a year. So she left a son, did she? I had forgotten that. What sort of boy is he? If he is like his mother he must be a good-looking chap.'

'He is very good-looking,' assented Lord Henry.

'I hope he will fall into proper hands,' continued the old man. 'He should have a pot of money waiting for him if Kelso did the right thing by him. His mother had money too. All the Selby property came to her, through her grandfather. Her grandfather hated Kelso, thought him a mean dog. He was, too. Came to Madrid once when I was there. Egad, I was ashamed of him. The Queen used to ask me about the English noble who was always quarrelling with the cabmen about their fares. They made quite a story of it. I didn't dare show my face at Court for a month. I hope he treated his grandson better than he did the jarvies.'

'I don't know,' answered Lord Henry. 'I fancy that the boy will be well off. He is not of age yet. He has Selby, I know. He told me so. And...his mother was very beautiful?'

'Margaret Devereux was one of the loveliest creatures I ever saw, Harry. What on earth induced her to behave as she did, I never could understand. She could have married anybody she chose. Carlington was mad after her. She was romantic, though. All the women of that family were. The men were a poor lot, but, egad! the[35] women were wonderful. Carlington went on his knees to her. Told me so himself. She laughed at him, and there wasn't a girl in London at the time who wasn't after him. And by the way, Harry, talking about silly marriages, what is this humbug your father tells me about Dartmoor wanting to marry an American? Ain't English girls good enough for him?'

'It is rather fashionable to marry Americans just now, Uncle George.'

'I'll back English women against the world, Harry,' said Lord Fermor, striking the table with his fist.

'The betting is on the Americans.'

'They don't last, I am told,' muttered his uncle.

'A long engagement exhausts them, but they are capital at a steeplechase. They take things flying. I don't think Dartmoor has a chance.'

'Who are her people?' grumbled the old gentleman. 'Has she got any?'

Lord Henry shook his head. 'American girls are as clever at concealing their parents, as English women are at concealing their past,' he said, rising to go.

'They are pork-packers, I suppose?'

'I hope so, Uncle George, for Dartmoor's sake. I am told that pork-packing is the most lucrative profession in America, after politics.'

'Is she pretty?'

'She behaves as if she was beautiful. Most American women do. It is the secret of their charm.'

'Why can't these American women stay in their own country? They are always telling us that it is the Paradise for women.'

'It is. That is the reason why, like Eve, they are so excessively anxious to get out of it,' said Lord Henry. 'Good-bye, Uncle George. I shall be late for lunch, if I stop any longer. Thanks for giving me the information I wanted. I always like to know everything about my new friends, and nothing about my old ones.'

'Where are you lunching, Harry?'

'At Aunt Agatha's. I have asked myself and Mr Gray. He is her latest *protégé*.'

'Humph! tell[36] your Aunt Agatha, Harry, not to bother me any more with her charity appeals. I am sick of them. Why, the good woman thinks that I have nothing to do but to write cheques for her silly fads.'

'All right, Uncle George, I'll tell her, but it won't have any effect. Philanthropic people lose all sense of humanity. It is their distinguishing characteristic.'

The old gentleman growled approvingly, and rang the bell for his servant. Lord Henry passed up the low arcade into Burlington Street, and turned his steps in the direction of Berkeley Square.

So that was the story of Dorian Gray's parentage. Crudely as it had been told to him, it had yet stirred him by its suggestion of a strange, almost modern romance. A beautiful woman risking everything for a mad passion. A few wild weeks of happiness cut short by a hideous, treacherous crime. Months of voiceless agony, and then a child born in pain. The mother snatched away by death, the boy left to solitude and the tyranny of an old and loveless man. Yes; it was an interesting background. It posed the lad, made him more perfect as it were. Behind every exquisite thing that existed, there was something tragic. Worlds had to be in travail, that the meanest flower might blow....And how charming he had been at dinner the night before, as with startled eyes and lips parted in frightened pleasure he had sat opposite to him at the club, the red candle shades staining to a richer rose the wakening wonder of his face. Talking to him was like playing upon an exquisite violin. He answered to every touch and thrill of the bow....There was something terribly enthralling in the exercise of influence. No other activity was like it. To project one's soul into some gracious form, and let it tarry there for a moment; to hear one's own intellectual views echoed back to one with all the added music of passion and youth; to convey one's temperament into another as though it were a subtle fluid or a strange perfume: there was a real joy in that—perhaps the most satisfying joy left to us in an age so limited and vulgar as our own, an age grossly carnal in its pleasures, and grossly common in its aims....He was a marvellous type, too, this lad, whom by so curious a chance he had met in Basil's studio, or could be fashioned into a marvellous type, at any rate. Grace was his, and the white purity of boyhood, and beauty such as old Greek marbles kept for us. There was nothing that one could not do with him. He could be made a Titan or a toy. What a pity it was that such beauty was destined to fade!...And Basil? From a psychological point of view, how interesting he was! The new manner in art, the fresh mode of looking at life, suggested so strangely by the merely visible presence of one who was unconscious of it all; the silent spirit that dwelt in dim woodland, and walked unseen in open field, suddenly showing herself, Dryad-like and not afraid, because in his soul who sought for her there had been wakened that wonderful vision to which alone are wonderful things revealed; the mere shapes and patterns of things becoming, as it were, refined, and gaining a kind of symbolical value, as though they were themselves patterns of some other and more perfect form whose shadow they made real: how strange it all was! He remembered something like it in history. Was it not Plato, that artist in thought, who had first analysed it? Was it not Buonarotti who had carved it in the coloured marbles of a sonnet-sequence[37]? But in our own century it was strange....Yes; he would try to be to Dorian Gray what, without knowing it, the lad was to the painter who had fashioned the wonderful portrait. He would seek to dominate him—had already, indeed, half done so. He would make that wonderful spirit his own. There was something fascinating in this son of Love and Death.

Suddenly he stopped and glanced up at the houses. He found that he had passed his aunt's some distance, and, smiling to himself, turned back. When he entered the somewhat sombre hall, the butler told him that they had gone in to lunch. He gave one of the footmen his hat and stick, and passed into the dining-room[38].

'Late as usual, Harry,' cried his aunt, shaking her head at him.

He invented a facile excuse, and having taken the vacant seat next to her, looked round to see who was there. Dorian bowed to him shyly from the end of the table, a flush of pleasure stealing into his cheek. Opposite was the Duchess of Harley, a lady of admirable good-nature[39] and good temper, much liked by every one who knew her, and of those ample architectural proportions that in women who are not Duchesses are described by contemporary historians as stoutness. Next to her sat, on her right, Sir Thomas Burdon, a Radical member of Parliament, who followed his leader in public life, and in private life followed the best cooks, dining with the Tories, and thinking with the Liberals, in accordance with a wise and well-known rule. The post on her left was occupied by Mr Erskine of Treadley, an old gentleman of considerable charm and culture, who had fallen, however, into bad habits of silence, having, as he explained once to Lady Agatha, said everything that he had to say before he was thirty. His own neighbour was Mrs Vandeleur, one of his aunt's oldest friends, a perfect saint amongst women, but so dreadfully dowdy that she reminded one of a badly bound hymn-book[40]. Fortunately for him she had on the other side Lord Faudel, a most intelligent middle-aged mediocrity, as bald as a Ministerial statement in the House of Commons, with whom she was conversing in that intensely earnest manner which is the one unpardonable error, as he remarked once himself, that all really good people fall into, and from which none of them ever quite escape.

'We are talking about poor Dartmoor, Lord Henry,' cried the Duchess, nodding pleasantly to him across the table. 'Do you think he will really marry this fascinating young person?'

'I believe she has made up her mind to propose to him, Duchess.'

'How dreadful!' exclaimed Lady Agatha. 'Really, some one should interfere.'

'I am told, on excellent authority, that her father keeps an American dry-goods store,' said Sir Thomas Burdon, looking supercilious.

'My uncle has already suggested pork-packing, Sir Thomas.'

'Dry-goods! What are American dry-goods?' asked the Duchess, raising her large hands in wonder, and accentuating the verb.

'American novels,' answered Lord Henry, helping himself to some quail.

The Duchess looked puzzled.

'Don't mind him, my dear,' whispered Lady Agatha. 'He never means anything that he says.'

'When America was discovered,' said the Radical member, and he began to give some wearisome facts. Like all people who try to exhaust a subject, he exhausted his listeners. The Duchess sighed, and exercised her privilege of interruption. 'I wish to goodness it never had been discovered at all!' she exclaimed. 'Really, our girls have no chance nowadays. It is most unfair.'

'Perhaps, after all, America never has been discovered,' said Mr Erskine; 'I myself would say that it had merely been detected.'

'Oh! but[41] I have seen specimens of the inhabitants,' answered the Duchess, vaguely. 'I must confess that most of them are extremely pretty. And they dress well, too. They get all their dresses in Paris. I wish I could afford to do the same.'

'They say that when good Americans die they go to Paris,' chuckled Sir Thomas, who had a large wardrobe of Humour's cast-off clothes.

'Really! And where do bad Americans go to when they die?' inquired the Duchess.

'They go to America,' murmured Lord Henry.

Sir Thomas frowned. 'I am afraid that your nephew is prejudiced against that great country,' he said to Lady Agatha. 'I have travelled all over it, in cars provided by the directors, who, in such matters, are extremely civil. I assure you that it is an education to visit it.'

'But must we really see Chicago in order to be educated?' asked Mr Erskine, plaintively. 'I don't feel up to the journey.'

Sir Thomas waved his hand. 'Mr Erskine of Treadley has the world on his shelves. We practical men like to see things, not to read about them. The Americans are an extremely interesting people. They are absolutely reasonable. I think that is their distinguishing characteristic. Yes, Mr Erskine, an absolutely reasonable people. I assure you there is no nonsense about the Americans.'

'How dreadful!' cried Lord Henry. 'I can stand brute force, but brute reason is quite unbearable. There is something unfair about its use. It is hitting below the intellect.'

'I do not understand you,' said Sir Thomas, growing rather red.

'I do, Lord Henry,' murmured Mr Erskine, with a smile.

'Paradoxes are all very well in their way...' rejoined the Baronet.

'Was that a paradox?' asked Mr Erskine. 'I did not think so. Perhaps it was. Well, the way of paradoxes is the way of truth. To test Reality we must see it on the tight-rope[42]. When the Verities become acrobats we can judge them.'

'Dear me!' said Lady Agatha, 'how you men argue! I am sure I never can make out what you are talking about. Oh! Harry, I am quite vexed with you. Why do you try to persuade our nice Mr Dorian Gray to give up the East End? I assure you he would be quite invaluable. They would love his playing.'

'I want him to play to me,' cried Lord Henry, smiling, and he looked down the table and caught a bright answering glance.

'But they are so unhappy in Whitechapel,' continued Lady Agatha.

'I can sympathize with everything, except suffering,' said Lord Henry, shrugging his shoulders. 'I cannot sympathize with that. It is too ugly, too horrible, too distressing. There is something terribly morbid in the modern sympathy with pain. One should sympathize with the colour, the beauty, the joy of life. The less said about life's sores the better.'

'Still, the East End is a very important problem,' remarked Sir Thomas, with a grave shake of the head.

'Quite so,' answered the young lord. 'It is the problem of slavery, and we try to solve it by amusing the slaves.'

The politician looked at him keenly. 'What change do you propose, then?' he asked.

Lord Henry laughed. 'I don't desire to change anything in England except the weather,' he answered. 'I am quite content with philosophic contemplation. But, as the nineteenth century has gone bankrupt through an over-expenditure of sympathy, I would suggest that we should appeal to Science to put us straight. The advantage of the emotions is that they lead us astray, and the advantage of science is that it is not emotional.'

'But we have such grave responsibilities,' ventured Mrs Vandeleur, timidly.

'Terribly grave,' echoed Lady Agatha.

Lord Henry looked over at Mr Erskine. 'Humanity takes itself too seriously. It is the world's original sin. If the caveman had known how to laugh, History would have been different.'

'You are really very comforting,' warbled the Duchess. 'I have always felt rather guilty when I came to see your dear aunt, for I take no interest at all in the East End. For the future I shall be able to look her in the face without a blush.'

'A blush is very becoming, Duchess,' remarked Lord Henry.

'Only when one is young,' she answered. 'When an old woman like myself blushes, it is a very bad sign. Ah! Lord Henry, I wished you would tell me how to become young again.'

He thought for a moment. 'Can you remember any great error that you committed in your early days, Duchess?' he asked, looking at her across the table.

'A great many, I fear,' she cried.

'Then commit them over again,' he said, gravely. 'To get back one's youth, one has merely to repeat one's follies.'

'A delightful theory!' she exclaimed. 'I must put it into practice.'

'A dangerous theory!' came from Sir Thomas's tight lips. Lady Agatha shook her head, but could not help being amused. Mr Erskine listened.

'Yes,' he continued, 'that is one of the great secrets of life. Nowadays most people die of a sort of creeping common sense, and discover when it is too late that the only things one never regrets are one's mistakes.'

A laugh ran round the table.

He played with the idea, and grew wilful; tossed it into the air and transformed it; let it escape and recaptured it; made it iridescent with fancy, and winged it with paradox. The praise of folly, as he went on, soared into a philosophy, and Philosophy herself became young, and catching the mad music of Pleasure, wearing, one might fancy, her wine-stained robe and wreath of ivy, danced like a Bacchante[43] over the hills of life, and mocked the slow Silenus[44] for being sober. Facts fled before her like frightened forest things. Her white feet trod the huge press at which wise Omar sits, till the seething grape-juice[45] rose round her bare limbs in waves of purple bubbles, or crawled in red foam over the vat's black, dripping, sloping sides. It was an extraordinary improvisation. He felt that the eyes of Dorian Gray were fixed on him, and the consciousness that amongst his audience there was one whose temperament he wished to fascinate, seemed to give his wit keenness, and to lend colour to his imagination. He was brilliant, fantastic, irresponsible. He charmed his listeners out of themselves, and they followed his pipe laughing. Dorian Gray never took his gaze off him, but sat like one under a spell, smiles chasing each other over his lips, and wonder growing grave in his darkening eyes.

At last, liveried in the costume of the age, Reality entered the room in the shape of a servant to tell the Duchess that her carriage was waiting. She wrung her hands in mock despair. 'How annoying!' she cried. 'I must go. I have to call for my husband at the club, to take him to some absurd meeting at Willis's Rooms, where he is going to be in the chair. If I am late he is sure to be furious, and I couldn't have a scene in this bonnet. It is far too fragile. A harsh word would ruin it. No, I must go, dear Agatha. Good-bye, Lord Henry, you are quite delightful, and dreadfully demoralizing. I am sure I don't know what to say about your views. You must come and dine with us some night. Tuesday? Are you disengaged Tuesday?'

'For you I would throw over anybody, Duchess,' said Lord Henry, with a bow.

'Ah! that[46] is very nice, and very wrong of you,' she cried; 'so mind you come;' and she swept out of the room, followed by Lady Agatha and the other ladies.

When Lord Henry had sat down again, Mr Erskine moved

round, and taking a chair close to him, placed his hand upon his arm.

'You talk books away,' he said; 'why don't you write one?'

'I am too fond of reading books to care to write them, Mr Erskine. I should like to write a novel certainly, a novel that would be as lovely as a Persian carpet and as unreal. But there is no literary public in England for anything except newspapers, primers, and encyclopaedias. Of all people in the world the English have the least sense of the beauty of literature.'

'I fear you are right,' answered Mr Erskine. 'I myself used to have literary ambitions, but I gave them up long ago. And now, my dear young friend, if you will allow me to call you so, may I ask if you really meant all that you said to us at lunch?'

'I quite forget what I said,' smiled Lord Henry. 'Was it all very bad?'

'Very bad indeed. In fact I consider you extremely dangerous, and if anything happens to our good Duchess we shall all look on you as being primarily responsible. But I should like to talk to you about life. The generation into which I was born was tedious. Some day, when you are tired of London, come down to Treadley, and expound to me your philosophy of pleasure over some admirable Burgundy I am fortunate enough to possess.'

'I shall be charmed. A visit to Treadley would be a great privilege. It has a perfect host, and a perfect library.'

'You will complete it,' answered the old gentleman, with a courteous bow. 'And now I must bid good-bye to your excellent aunt. I am due at the Athenaeum. It is the hour when we sleep there.'

'All of you, Mr Erskine?'

'Forty of us, in forty arm-chairs. We are practising for an English Academy of Letters.'

Lord Henry laughed, and rose. 'I am going to the Park,' he cried.

As he was passing out of the door Dorian Gray touched him on the arm. 'Let me come with you,' he murmured.

'But I thought you had promised Basil Hallward to go and see him,' answered Lord Henry.

'I would sooner come with you; yes, I feel I must come with you. Do let me. And you will promise to talk to me all the time? No one talks so wonderfully as you do.'

'Ah! I have talked quite enough for to-day,' said Lord Henry, smiling. 'All I want now is to look at life. You may come and look at it with me, if you care to.'

Chapter 4

One afternoon, a month later, Dorian Gray was reclining in a luxurious arm-chair, in the little library of Lord Henry's house in Mayfair. It was, in its way, a very charming room, with its high panelled wainscoting of olive-stained oak, its cream-coloured frieze and ceiling of raised plasterwork, and its brickdust felt carpet strewn with silk long-fringed Persian rugs. On a tiny satinwood table stood a statuette by Clodion, and beside it lay a copy of 'Les Cent Nouvelles', bound for Margaret of Valois by Clovis Eve, and powdered with the gilt daisies that Queen had selected for her device. Some large blue china jars and parrot-tulips[47] were ranged on the mantelshelf, and through the small leaded panes of the window streamed the apricot-coloured light of a summer day in London.

Lord Henry had not yet come in. He was always late on principle, his principle being that punctuality is the thief of time. So the lad was looking rather sulky, as with listless fingers he turned over the pages of an elaborately-illustrated edition of 'Manon Lescaut' that he had found in one of the bookcases. The formal monotonous ticking of the Louis Quatorze clock annoyed him. Once or twice he thought of going away.

At last he heard a step outside, and the door opened. 'How late you are, Harry!' he murmured.

'I am afraid it is not Harry, Mr Gray,' answered a shrill voice.

He glanced quickly round, and rose to his feet. 'I beg your pardon. I thought—'

'You thought it was my husband. It is only his wife. You must let me introduce myself. I know you quite well by your photographs. I think my husband has got seventeen of them.'

'Not seventeen, Lady Henry?'

'Well, eighteen, then. And I saw you with him the other night at the Opera.' She laughed nervously as she spoke, and watched him with her vague forget-me-not eyes. She was a curious woman, whose dresses always looked as if they had been designed in a rage and put on in a tempest. She was usually in love with somebody, and, as her passion was never returned, she had kept all her illusions. She tried to look picturesque, but only succeeded in being untidy. Her name was Victoria, and she had a perfect mania for going to church.

'That was at "Lohengrin", Lady Henry, I think?'

'Yes; it was at dear "Lohengrin". I like Wagner's music better than anybody's. It is so loud that one can talk the whole time without other people hearing what one says. That is a great advantage: don't you think so, Mr Gray?'

The same nervous staccato laugh broke from her thin lips, and her fingers began to play with a long tortoise-shell paper-knife[48].

Dorian smiled, and shook his head: 'I am afraid I don't think so, Lady Henry. I never talk during music—at least, during good music. If one hears bad music, it is one's duty to drown it in conversation.'

'Ah! that is one of Harry's views, isn't it, Mr Gray? I always hear Harry's views from his friends. It is the only way I get to know of them. But you must not think I don't like good music. I adore it, but I am afraid of it. It makes me too romantic. I have simply worshipped pianists—two at a time, sometimes, Harry tells me. I don't know what it is about them. Perhaps it is that they are foreigners. They all are, ain't they? Even those that are born in England become foreigners after a time, don't they? It is so clever of them, and such a compliment to art. Makes it quite cosmopolitan, doesn't it? You have never been to any of my parties, have you, Mr Gray? You must come. I can't afford orchids, but I spare no expense in foreigners. They make one's rooms look so picturesque. But here is Harry!—Harry, I came in to look for you, to ask you something—I forget what it was—and I found Mr Gray here. We have had such a pleasant chat about music. We have quite the same ideas. No; I think our ideas are quite different. But he has been most pleasant. I am so glad I've seen him.'

'I am charmed, my love, quite charmed,' said Lord Henry, elevating his dark crescent-shaped eyebrows and looking at them both with an amused smile. 'So sorry I am late, Dorian. I went to look after a piece of old brocade in Wardour Street and had to bargain for hours for it. Nowadays people know the price of everything, and the value of nothing.'

'I am afraid I must be going,' exclaimed Lady Henry, breaking an awkward silence with her silly sudden laugh. 'I have promised to drive with the Duchess. Good-bye, Mr Gray. Good-bye, Harry. You are dining out, I suppose? So am I. Perhaps I shall see you at Lady Thornbury's.'

'I dare say, my dear,' said Lord Henry, shutting the door behind her, as, looking like a bird of paradise that had been out all night in the rain, she flitted out of the room, leaving a faint odour of frangipanni. Then he lit a cigarette, and flung himself down on the sofa.

'Never marry a woman with straw-coloured hair, Dorian,' he said, after a few puffs.

'Why, Harry?'

'Because they are so sentimental.'

'But I like sentimental people.'

'Never marry at all, Dorian. Men marry because they are tired; women, because they are curious: both are disappointed.'

'I don't think I am likely to marry, Harry. I am too much in love. That is one of your aphorisms. I am putting it into practice, as I do everything that you say.'

'Who are you in love with?' asked Lord Henry, after a pause.

'With an actress,' said Dorian Gray, blushing.

Lord Henry shrugged his shoulders. 'That is a rather commonplace *début*[49].'

'You would not say so if you saw her, Harry.'

'Who is she?'

'Her name is Sibyl Vane.'

'Never heard of her.'

'No one has. People will some day, however. She is a genius.'

'My dear boy, no woman is a genius. Women are a decorative sex. They never have anything to say, but they say it charmingly. Women represent the triumph of matter over mind, just as men represent the triumph of mind over morals.'

'Harry, how can you?'

'My dear Dorian, it is quite true. I am analysing women at present, so I ought to know. The subject is not so abstruse as I thought it was. I find that, ultimately, there are only two kinds of women, the plain and the coloured. The plain women are very useful. If you want to gain a reputation for respectability, you have merely to take them down to supper. The other women are very charming. They commit one mistake, however. They paint in order to try and look young. Our grandmothers painted in order to try and talk brilliantly. *Rouge* and *esprit* used to go together. That is all over now. As long as a woman can look ten years younger than her own daughter, she is perfectly satisfied. As for conversation, there are only five women in London worth talking to, and two of these can't be admitted into decent society. However, tell me about your genius. How long have you known her?'

'Ah! Harry, your views terrify me.'

'Never mind that. How long have you known her?'

'About three weeks.'

'And where did you come across her?'

'I will tell you, Harry; but you mustn't be unsympathetic about it. After all, it never would have happened if I had not met you. You filled me with a wild desire to know everything about life. For days after I met you, something seemed to throb in my veins. As I lounged in the Park or strolled down Piccadilly, I used to look at every one who passed me, and wonder, with a mad curiosity, what sort of lives they led. Some of them fascinated me. Others filled me with terror. There was an exquisite poison in the air. I had a passion for sensations....Well, one evening about seven o'clock, I determined to go out in search of some adventure. I felt that this grey, monstrous London of ours, with its myriads of people, its sordid sinners, and its splendid sins, as you once phrased it, must have something in store for me. I fancied a thousand things. The mere danger gave me a sense of delight. I remembered what you had said to me on that wonderful evening when we first dined together, about the search for beauty being the real secret of life. I don't know what I expected, but I went out and wandered eastward, soon losing my way in a labyrinth of grimy streets and black, grassless squares. About half-past eight I passed by an absurd little theatre, with great flaring gas-jets[50] and gaudy play-bills[51]. A hideous Jew, in the most amazing waistcoat I ever beheld in my life, was standing at the entrance, smoking a vile cigar. He had greasy ringlets, and an enormous diamond blazed in the centre of a soiled shirt. 'Have a box, my Lord?' he said, when he saw me, and he took off his hat with an air of gorgeous servility. There was something about him, Harry, that amused me. He was such a monster. You will laugh at me, I know, but I really went in and paid a whole guinea for the stage-box. To the present day I can't make out why I did so; and yet if I hadn't—my dear Harry, if I hadn't, I should have missed the greatest romance of my life. I see you are laughing. It is horrid of you!'

'I am not laughing, Dorian; at least I am not laughing at you. But you should not say the greatest romance of your life. You should say the first romance of your life. You will always be loved, and you will always be in love with love. A *grande passion* is the privilege of people who have nothing to do. That is the one use of the idle classes of a country. Don't be afraid. There are exquisite things in store for you. This is merely the beginning.'

'Do you think my nature so shallow?' cried Dorian Gray, angrily.

'No; I think your nature so deep.'

'How do you mean?'

'My dear boy, the people who love only once in their lives are really the shallow people. What they call their loyalty, and their fidelity, I call either the lethargy of custom or their lack of imagination. Faithfulness is to the emotional life what consistency is to the life of the intellect—simply a confession of failure. Faithfulness! I must analyse it some day. The passion for property is in it. There are many things that we would throw away if we were not afraid that others might pick them up. But I don't want to interrupt you. Go on with your story.'

'Well, I found myself seated in a horrid little private box, with a vulgar drop-scene[52] staring me in the face. I looked out from behind the curtain, and surveyed the house. It was a tawdry affair, all Cupids and cornucopias, like a third-rate wedding-cake. The gallery and pit were fairly full, but the two rows of dingy stalls were quite empty, and there was hardly a person in what I suppose they called the dress-circle[53]. Women went about with oranges and ginger-beer[54], and there was a terrible consumption of nuts going on.'

'It must have been just like the palmy days of the British Drama.'

'Just like, I should fancy, and very depressing. I began to wonder what on earth I should do, when I caught sight of the play-bill. What do you think the play was, Harry?'

'I should think "The Idiot Boy, or Dumb but Innocent". Our fathers used to like that sort of piece, I believe. The longer I live, Dorian, the more keenly I feel that whatever was good enough for our fathers is not good enough for us. In art, as in politics, *les grandpères ont toujours tort.*[55]'

'This play was good enough for us, Harry. It was "Romeo and Juliet". I must admit that I was rather annoyed at the idea of seeing Shakespeare done in such a wretched hole of a place. Still, I felt interested, in a sort of way. At any rate, I determined to wait for the first act. There was a dreadful orchestra, presided over by a young Hebrew who sat at a cracked piano, that nearly drove me away, but at last the drop-scene was drawn up, and the play began. Romeo was a stout elderly gentleman, with corked eyebrows, a husky tragedy voice, and a figure like a beer-barrel[56]. Mercutio was almost as bad. He was played by the low-comedian[57], who had introduced gags of his own and was on most friendly terms with the pit. They were both as grotesque as the scenery, and that looked as if it had come out of a country-booth. But Juliet! Harry, imagine a girl, hardly seventeen years of age, with a little flower-like face, a small Greek head with plaited coils of dark-brown hair, eyes that were violet wells of passion, lips that were like the petals of a rose. She was the loveliest thing I had ever seen in my life. You said to me once that pathos left you unmoved, but that beauty, mere beauty, could fill your eyes with tears. I tell you, Harry, I could hardly see this girl for the mist of tears that came across me.

And her voice—I never heard such a voice. It was very low at first, with deep mellow notes, that seemed to fall singly upon one's ear. Then it became a little louder, and sounded like a flute or a distant hautbois[58]. In the garden-scene[59] it had all the tremulous ecstasy that one hears just before dawn when nightingales are singing. There were moments, later on, when it had the wild passion of violins. You know how a voice can stir one. Your voice and the voice of Sibyl Vane are two things that I shall never forget. When I close my eyes, I hear them, and each of them says something different. I don't know which to follow. Why should I not love her? Harry, I do love her. She is everything to me in life. Night after night I go to see her play. One evening she is Rosalind[60], and the next evening she is Imogen[61]. I have seen her die in the gloom of an Italian tomb, sucking the poison from her lover's lips. I have watched her wandering through the forest of Arden, disguised as a pretty boy in hose and doublet and dainty cap. She has been mad, and has come into the presence of a guilty king, and given him rue to wear, and bitter herbs to taste of. She has been innocent, and the black hands of jealousy have crushed her reed-like throat. I have seen her in every age and in every costume. Ordinary women never appeal to one's imagination. They are limited to their century. No glamour ever transfigures them. One knows their minds as easily as one knows their bonnets. One can always find them. There is no mystery in any of them. They ride in the Park in the morning, and chatter at tea-parties[62] in the afternoon. They have their stereotyped smile, and their fashionable manner. They are quite obvious. But an actress! How different an actress is! Harry! why[63] didn't you tell me that the only thing worth loving is an actress?'

'Because I have loved so many of them, Dorian.'

'Oh, yes, horrid people with dyed hair and painted faces.'

'Don't run down dyed hair and painted faces. There is an extraordinary charm in them, sometimes,' said Lord Henry.

'I wish now I had not told you about Sibyl Vane.'

'You could not have helped telling me, Dorian. All through your life you will tell me everything you do.'

'Yes, Harry, I believe that is true. I cannot help telling you things. You have a curious influence over me. If I ever did a crime, I would come and confess it to you. You would understand me.'

'People like you—the wilful sunbeams of life—don't commit crimes, Dorian. But I am much obliged for the compliment, all the same. And now tell me—reach me the matches, like a good boy: thanks—what are your actual relations with Sibyl Vane?'

Dorian Gray leaped to his feet, with flushed cheeks and burning eyes. 'Harry! Sibyl Vane is sacred!'

'It is only the sacred things that are worth touching, Dorian,' said Lord Henry, with a strange touch of pathos in his voice. 'But why should you be annoyed? I suppose she will belong to you some day. When one is in love, one always begins by deceiving one's self, and one always ends by deceiving others. That is what the world calls a romance. You know her, at any rate, I suppose?'

'Of course I know her. On the first night I was at the theatre, the horrid old Jew came round to the box after the performance was over, and offered to take me behind the scenes and introduce me to her. I was furious with him, and told him that Juliet had been dead for hundreds of years, and that her body was lying in a marble tomb in Verona. I think, from his blank look of amazement, that he was under the impression that I had taken too much champagne, or something.'

'I am not surprised.'

'Then he asked me if I wrote for any of the newspapers. I told him I never even read them. He seemed terribly disappointed at that, and confided to me that all the dramatic critics were in a conspiracy against him, and that they were every one of them to be bought.'

'I should not wonder if he was quite right there. But, on the other hand, judging from their appearance, most of them cannot be at all expensive.'

'Well, he seemed to think they were beyond his means,' laughed Dorian. 'By this time, however, the lights were being put out in the theatre, and I had to go. He wanted me to try some cigars that he strongly recommended. I declined. The next night, of course, I arrived at the place again. When he saw me he made me a low bow, and assured me that I was a munificent patron of art. He was a most offensive brute, though he had an extraordinary passion for Shakespeare. He told me once, with an air of pride, that his five bankruptcies were entirely due to "The Bard", as he insisted on calling him. He seemed to think it a distinction.'

'It was a distinction, my dear Dorian—a great distinction. Most people become bankrupt through having invested too heavily in the prose of life. To have ruined one's self over poetry is an honour. But when did you first speak to Miss Sibyl Vane?'

'The third night. She had been playing Rosalind. I could not help going round. I had thrown her some flowers, and she had looked at me; at least I fancied that she had. The old Jew was persistent. He seemed determined to take me behind, so I consented. It was curious my not wanting to know her, wasn't it?'

'No; I don't think so.'

'My dear Harry, why?'

'I will tell you some other time. Now I want to know about the girl.'

'Sibyl? Oh, she was so shy, and so gentle. There is something of a child about her. Her eyes opened wide in exquisite wonder when I told her what I thought of her performance, and she seemed quite unconscious of her power. I think we were both rather nervous. The old Jew stood grinning at the doorway of the dusty greenroom, making elaborate speeches about us both, while we stood looking at each other like children. He would insist on calling me 'My Lord', so I had to assure Sibyl that I was not anything of the kind. She said quite simply to me, "You look more like a prince. I must call you Prince Charming." '

'Upon my word, Dorian, Miss Sibyl knows how to pay compliments.'

'You don't understand her, Harry. She regarded me merely as a person in a play. She knows nothing of life. She lives with her mother, a faded tired woman who played Lady Capulet in a sort of magenta dressing-wrapper on the first night, and looks as if she had seen better days.'

'I know that look. It depresses me,' murmured Lord Henry, examining his rings.

'The Jew wanted to tell me her history, but I said it did not interest me.'

'You were quite right. There is always something infinitely mean about other people's tragedies.'

'Sibyl is the only thing I care about. What is it to me where she came from? From her little head to her little feet, she is absolutely and entirely divine. Every night of my life I go to see her act, and every night she is more marvellous.'

'That is the reason, I suppose, that you never dine with me now. I thought you must have some curious romance on hand. You have; but it is not quite what I expected.'

'My dear Harry, we either lunch or sup together every day, and I have been to the Opera with you several times,' said Dorian, opening his blue eyes in wonder.

'You always come dreadfully late.'

'Well, I can't help going to see Sibyl play,' he cried, 'even if it is only for a single act. I get hungry for her presence; and when I think of the wonderful soul that is hidden away in that little ivory body, I am filled with awe.'

'You can dine with me to-night, Dorian, can't you?'

He shook his head. 'To-night she is Imogen,' he answered, 'and to-morrow night she will be Juliet.'

'When is she Sibyl Vane?'

'Never.'

'I congratulate you.'

'How horrid you are! She is all the great heroines of the world in one. She is more than an individual. You laugh, but I tell you she has genius. I love her, and I must make her love me. You, who know all the secrets of life, tell me how to charm Sibyl Vane to love me! I want to make Romeo jealous. I want the dead lovers of the world to hear our laughter, and grow sad. I want a breath of our passion to stir their dust into consciousness, to wake their ashes into pain. My God, Harry, how I worship her!' He was walking up and down the room as he spoke. Hectic spots of red burned on his cheeks. He was terribly excited.

Lord Henry watched him with a subtle sense of pleasure. How different he was now from the shy, frightened boy he had met in Basil Hallward's studio! His nature had developed like a flower, had borne blossoms of scarlet flame. Out of its secret hiding-place[64] had crept his Soul, and Desire had come to meet it on the way.

'And what do you propose to do?' said Lord Henry, at last.

'I want you and Basil to come with me some night and see her act. I have not the slightest fear of the result. You are certain to acknowledge her genius. Then we must get her out of the Jew's hands. She is bound to him for three years—at least for two years and eight months—from the present time. I shall have to pay him something, of course. When all that is settled, I shall take a West End theatre and bring her out properly. She will make the world as mad as she has made me.'

'That would be impossible, my dear boy!'

'Yes, she will. She has not merely art, consummate art-instinct[65], in her, but she has personality also; and you have often told me that it is personalities, not principles, that move the age.'

'Well, what night shall we go?'

'Let me see. To-day is Tuesday. Let us fix to-morrow. She plays Juliet to-morrow.'

'All right. The Bristol at eight o'clock; and I will get Basil.'

'Not eight, Harry, please. Half-past six. We must be there before the curtain rises. You must see her in the first act, where she meets Romeo.'

'Half-past six! What an hour! It will be like having a meat-tea[66], or reading an English novel. It must be seven. No gentleman dines before seven. Shall you see Basil between this and then? Or shall I write to him?'

'Dear Basil! I have not laid eyes on him for a week. It is rather horrid of me, as he has sent me my portrait in the most wonderful frame, specially designed by himself, and, though I am a little jealous of the picture for being a whole month younger than I am, I must admit that I delight in it. Perhaps you had better write to him. I don't want to see him alone. He says things that annoy me. He gives me good advice.'

Lord Henry smiled. 'People are very fond of giving away what they need most themselves. It is what I call the depth of generosity.'

'Oh, Basil is the best of fellows, but he seems to me to be

just a bit of a Philistine. Since I have known you, Harry, I have discovered that.'

'Basil, my dear boy, puts everything that is charming in him into his work. The consequence is that he has nothing left for life but his prejudices, his principles, and his common sense. The only artists I have ever known, who are personally delightful, are bad artists. Good artists exist simply in what they make, and consequently are perfectly uninteresting in what they are. A great poet, a really great poet, is the most unpoetical of all creatures. But inferior poets are absolutely fascinating. The worse their rhymes are, the more picturesque they look. The mere fact of having published a book of second-rate sonnets makes a man quite irresistible. He lives the poetry that he cannot write. The others write the poetry that they dare not realise.'

'I wonder is that really so, Harry?' said Dorian Gray, putting some perfume on his handkerchief out of a large gold-topped bottle that stood on the table. 'It must be, if you say it. And now I am off. Imogen is waiting for me. Don't forget about to-morrow. Good-bye.'

As he left the room, Lord Henry's heavy eyelids drooped, and he began to think. Certainly few people had ever interested him so much as Dorian Gray, and yet the lad's mad adoration of some one else caused him not the slightest pang of annoyance or jealousy. He was pleased by it. It made him a more interesting study. He had been always enthralled by the methods of natural science, but the ordinary subject-matter of that science had seemed to him trivial and of no import. And so he had begun by vivisecting himself, as he had ended by vivisecting others. Human life—that appeared to him the one thing worth investigating. Compared to it there was nothing else of any value. It was true that as one watched life in its curious crucible of pain and pleasure, one could not wear over one's face a mask of glass, nor keep the sulphurous fumes from troubling the brain and making the imagination turbid with monstrous fancies and misshapen dreams. There were poisons so subtle that to know their properties one had to sicken of them. There were maladies so strange that one had to pass through them if one sought to understand their nature. And, yet, what a great reward one received! How wonderful the whole world became to one! To note the curious hard logic of passion, and the emotional coloured life of the intellect—to observe where they met, and where they separated, at what point they were in unison, and at what point they were at discord—there was a delight in that! What matter what the cost was? One could never pay too high a price for any sensation.

He was conscious—and the thought brought a gleam of pleasure into his brown agate eyes—that it was through certain words of his, musical words said with musical utterance, that Dorian Gray's soul had turned to this white girl and bowed in worship before her. To a large extent the lad was his own creation. He had made him premature. That was something. Ordinary people waited till life disclosed to them its secrets, but to the few, to the elect, the mysteries of life were revealed before the veil was drawn away. Sometimes this was the effect of art, and chiefly of the art of literature, which dealt immediately with the passions and the intellect. But now and then a complex personality took the place and assumed the office of art, was indeed, in its way, a real work of art, Life having its elaborate masterpieces, just as poetry has, or sculpture, or painting.

Yes, the lad was premature. He was gathering his harvest while it was yet spring. The pulse and passion of youth were in him, but he was becoming self-conscious. It was delightful to watch him. With his beautiful face, and his beautiful soul, he was a thing to wonder at. It was no matter how it all ended, or was destined to end. He was like one of those gracious figures in a pageant or a play, whose joys seem to be remote from one, but whose sorrows stir one's sense of beauty, and whose wounds are like red roses.

Soul and body, body and soul—how mysterious they were! There was animalism in the soul, and the body had its moments of spirituality. The senses could refine, and the intellect could degrade. Who could say where the fleshly impulse ceased, or the psychical impulse began? How shallow were the arbitrary definitions of ordinary psychologists! And yet how difficult to decide between the claims of the various schools! Was the soul a shadow seated in the house of sin? Or was the body really in the soul, as Giordano Bruno thought? The separation of spirit from matter was a mystery, and the union of spirit with matter was a mystery also.

He began to wonder whether we could ever make psychology so absolute a science that each little spring of life would be revealed to us. As it was, we always misunderstood ourselves, and rarely understood others. Experience was of no ethical value. It was merely the name men gave to their mistakes. Moralists had, as a rule, regarded it as a mode of warning, had claimed for it a certain ethical efficacy in the formation of character, had praised it as something that taught us what to follow and showed us what to avoid. But there was no motive power in experience. It was as little of an active cause as conscience itself. All that it really demonstrated was that our future would be the same as our past, and that the sin we had done once, and with loathing, we would do many times, and with joy.

It was clear to him that the experimental method was the only method by which one could arrive at any scientific analysis of the passions; and certainly Dorian Gray was a subject made to his hand, and seemed to promise rich and fruitful results. His sudden mad love for Sibyl Vane was a psychological phenomenon of no small interest. There was no doubt that curiosity had much to do with it, curiosity and the desire for new experiences; yet it was not a simple but rather a very complex passion. What there was in it of the purely sensuous instinct of boyhood had been transformed by the workings of the imagination, changed into something that seemed to the lad himself to be remote from sense, and was for that very reason all the more dangerous. It was the passions about whose origin we deceived ourselves that tyrannized most strongly over us. Our weakest motives were those of whose nature we were conscious. It often happened that when we thought we were experimenting on others we were really experimenting on ourselves.

While Lord Henry sat dreaming on these things, a knock came to the door, and his valet entered, and reminded him it was time to dress for dinner. He got up and looked out into the street. The sunset had smitten into scarlet gold the upper windows of the houses opposite. The panes glowed like plates of heated metal. The sky above was like a faded rose. He thought of his friend's young fiery-coloured life, and wondered how it was all going to end.

When he arrived home, about half-past twelve o'clock, he saw a telegram lying on the hall table. He opened it, and found it was from Dorian Gray. It was to tell him that he was engaged to be married to Sibyl Vane.

Chapter 5

'Mother, mother, I am so happy!' whispered the girl, burying her face in the lap of the faded, tired-looking woman who, with back turned to the shrill intrusive light, was sitting in the one arm-chair that their dingy sitting-room[67] contained. 'I am so happy!' she repeated, 'and you must be happy too!'

Mrs Vane winced, and put her thin bismuth-whitened hands on her daughter's head. 'Happy!' she echoed, 'I am only happy, Sibyl, when I see you act. You must not think of anything but your acting. Mr Isaacs has been very good to us, and we owe him money.'

The girl looked up and pouted. 'Money, mother?' she cried, 'what does money matter? Love is more than money.'

'Mr Isaacs has advanced us fifty pounds to pay off our debts, and to get a proper outfit for James. You must not forget that, Sibyl. Fifty pounds is a very large sum. Mr Isaacs has been most considerate.'

'He is not a gentleman, mother, and I hate the way he talks to me,' said the girl, rising to her feet, and going over to the window.

'I don't know how we could manage without him,' answered the elder woman, querulously.

Sibyl Vane tossed her head and laughed. 'We don't want him any more, mother. Prince Charming rules life for us now.' Then she paused. A rose shook in her blood, and shadowed her cheeks. Quick breath parted the petals of her lips. They trembled. Some southern wind of passion swept over her, and stirred the dainty folds of her dress. 'I love him,' she said, simply.

'Foolish child! foolish[68] child!' was the parrot-phrase[69] flung in answer. The waving of crooked, false-jewelled fingers gave grotesqueness to the words.

The girl laughed again. The joy of a caged bird was in her voice. Her eyes caught the melody, and echoed it in radiance: then closed for a moment, as though to hide their secret. When they opened, the mist of a dream had passed across them.

Thin-lipped wisdom spoke at her from the worn chair, hinted

at prudence, quoted from that book of cowardice whose author apes the name of common sense. She did not listen. She was free in her prison of passion. Her prince, Prince Charming, was with her. She had called on Memory to remake him. She had sent her soul to search for him, and it had brought him back. His kiss burned again upon her mouth. Her eyelids were warm with his breath.

Then Wisdom altered its method and spoke of espial and discovery. This young man might be rich. If so, marriage should be thought of. Against the shell of her ear broke the waves of worldly cunning. The arrows of craft shot by her. She saw the thin lips moving, and smiled.

Suddenly she felt the need to speak. The wordy silence troubled her. 'Mother, mother,' she cried, 'why does he love me so much? I know why I love him. I love him because he is like what Love himself should be. But what does he see in me? I am not worthy of him. And yet—why, I cannot tell—though I feel so much beneath him, I don't feel humble. I feel proud, terribly proud. Mother, did you love my father as I love Prince Charming?'

The elder woman grew pale beneath the coarse powder that daubed her cheeks, and her dry lips twitched with a spasm of pain. Sybil rushed to her, flung her arms round her neck, and kissed her. 'Forgive me, mother. I know it pains you to talk about our father. But it only pains you because you loved him so much. Don't look so sad. I am as happy to-day as you were twenty years ago. Ah! let[70] me be happy for ever!'

'My child, you are far too young to think of falling in love. Besides, what do you know of this young man? You don't even know his name. The whole thing is most inconvenient, and really, when James is going away to Australia, and I have so much to think of, I must say that you should have shown more consideration. However, as I said before, if he is rich...'

'Ah! mother[71], mother, let me be happy!'

Mrs Vane glanced at her, and with one of those false theatrical gestures that so often become a mode of second nature to a stage-player[72], clasped her in her arms. At this moment the door opened, and a young lad with rough brown hair came into the room. He was thick-set[73] of figure, and his hands and feet were large, and somewhat clumsy in movement. He was not so finely bred as his sister. One would hardly have guessed the close relationship that existed between them. Mrs Vane fixed her eyes on him, and intensified her smile. She mentally elevated her son to the dignity of an audience. She felt sure that the *tableau* was interesting.

'You might keep some of your kisses for me, Sibyl, I think,' said the lad, with a good-natured grumble.

'Ah! but you don't like being kissed, Jim,' she cried. 'You are a dreadful old bear.' And she ran across the room and hugged him.

James Vane looked into his sister's face with tenderness. 'I want you to come out with me for a walk, Sibyl. I don't suppose I shall ever see this horrid London again. I am sure I don't want to.'

'My son, don't say such dreadful things,' murmured Mrs Vane, taking up a tawdry theatrical dress, with a sigh, and beginning to patch it. She felt a little disappointed that he had not joined the group. It would have increased the theatrical picturesqueness of the situation.

'Why not, mother? I mean it.'

'You pain me, my son. I trust you will return from Australia in a position of affluence. I believe there is no society of any kind in the Colonies, nothing that I would call society; so when you have made your fortune you must come back and assert yourself in London.'

'Society!' muttered the lad. 'I don't want to know anything about that. I should like to make some money to take you and Sibyl off the stage. I hate it.'

'Oh, Jim!' said Sibyl, laughing, 'how unkind of you! But are you really going for a walk with me? That will be nice! I was afraid you were going to say good-bye to some of your friends—to Tom Hardy, who gave you that hideous pipe, or Ned Langton, who makes fun of you for smoking it. It is very sweet of you to let me have your last afternoon. Where shall we go? Let us go to the Park.'

'I am too shabby,' he answered, frowning. 'Only swell people go to the Park.'

'Nonsense, Jim,' she whispered, stroking the sleeve of his coat.

He hesitated for a moment. 'Very well,' he said at last, 'but don't be too long dressing.' She danced out of the door. One could hear her singing as she ran upstairs. Her little feet pattered overhead.

He walked up and down the room two or three times. Then he turned to the still figure in the chair. 'Mother, are my things ready?' he asked.

'Quite ready, James,' she answered, keeping her eyes on her work. For some months past she had felt ill at ease when she was alone with this rough, stern son of hers. Her shallow secret nature was troubled when their eyes met. She used to wonder if he suspected anything. The silence, for he made no other observation, became intolerable to her. She began to complain. Women defend themselves by attacking, just as they attack by sudden and strange surrenders. 'I hope you will be contented, James, with your seafaring life,' she said. 'You must remember that it is your own choice. You might have entered a solicitor's office. Solicitors are a very respectable class, and in the country often dine with the best families.'

'I hate offices, and I hate clerks,' he replied. 'But you are quite right. I have chosen my own life. All I say is, watch over Sibyl. Don't let her come to any harm. Mother, you must watch over her.'

'James, you really talk very strangely. Of course I watch over Sibyl.'

'I hear a gentleman comes every night to the theatre, and goes behind to talk to her. Is that right? What about that?'

'You are speaking about things you don't understand, James. In the profession we are accustomed to receive a great deal of most gratifying attention. I myself used to receive many bouquets at one time. That was when acting was really understood. As for Sibyl, I do not know at present whether her attachment is serious or not. But there is no doubt that the young man in question is a perfect gentleman. He is always most polite to me. Besides, he has the appearance of being rich, and the flowers he sends are lovely.'

'You don't know his name, though,' said the lad, harshly.

'No,' answered his mother, with a placid expression in her face. 'He has not yet revealed his real name. I think it is quite romantic of him. He is probably a member of the aristocracy.'

James Vane bit his lip. 'Watch over Sibyl, mother,' he cried, 'watch over her.'

'My son, you distress me very much. Sibyl is always under my special care. Of course, if this gentleman is wealthy, there is no reason why she should not contract an alliance with him. I trust he is one of the aristocracy. He has all the appearance of it, I must say.'

It might be a most brilliant marriage for Sibyl. They would make a charming couple. His good looks are really quite remarkable; everybody notices them.'

The lad muttered something to himself, and drummed on the window-pane[74] with his coarse fingers. He had just turned round to say something, when the door opened, and Sibyl ran in.

'How serious you both are!' she cried. 'What is the matter?'

'Nothing,' he answered. 'I suppose one must be serious sometimes. Good-bye, mother; I will have my dinner at five o'clock. Everything is packed, except my shirts, so you need not trouble.'

'Good-bye, my son,' she answered, with a bow of strained stateliness.

She was extremely annoyed at the tone he had adopted with her, and there was something in his look that had made her feel afraid.

'Kiss me, mother,' said the girl. Her flower-like lips touched the withered cheek, and warmed its frost.

'My child! my[75] child!' cried Mrs Vane, looking up to the ceiling in search of an imaginary gallery.

'Come, Sibyl,' said her brother, impatiently. He hated his mother's affectations.

They went out into the flickering wind-blown sunlight, and strolled down the dreary Euston Road. The passers-by glanced in wonder at the sullen, heavy youth, who, in coarse, ill-fitting clothes, was in the company of such a graceful, refined-looking girl. He was like a common gardener walking with a rose.

Jim frowned from time to time when he caught the inquisitive glance of some stranger. He had that dislike of being stared at which comes on geniuses late in life, and never leaves the commonplace. Sibyl, however, was quite unconscious of the effect she was producing. Her love was trembling in laughter on her lips. She was thinking of Prince Charming, and, that she might think of him all the more, she did not talk of him, but prattled on about the ship in which Jim was going to sail, about the gold he was certain to find, about the wonderful heiress whose life he was to save from the wicked, red-shirted bushrangers. For he was not to remain a sailor, or a super-cargo[76], or whatever he was going to be. Oh, no! A sailor's existence was dreadful. Fancy being cooped up in a horrid ship, with the hoarse, hump-backed waves trying to get in, and a black wind blowing the masts down, and tearing the sails into long screaming ribands! He was to leave the vessel at Melbourne, bid a polite good-bye to the captain, and go off at once to the gold-fields[77]. Before a week was over he was to come across a large nugget of pure gold, the largest nugget that had ever been discovered, and bring it down to the coast in a waggon guarded by six mounted policemen. The bushrangers were to attack them three times, and be defeated with immense slaughter. Or, no. He was not to go to the gold-fields at all. They were horrid places, where men got intoxicated, and shot each other in bar-rooms[78], and used bad language. He was to be a nice sheep-farmer[79], and one evening, as he was riding home, he was to see the beautiful heiress being carried off by a robber on a black horse, and give chase, and rescue her. Of course she would fall in love with him, and he with her, and they would get married, and come home, and live in an immense house in London. Yes, there were delightful things in store for him. But he must be very good, and not lose his temper, or spend his money foolishly. She was only a year older than he was, but she knew so much more of life. He must be sure, also, to write to her by every mail, and to say his prayers each night before he went to sleep. God was very good, and would watch over him. She would pray for him too, and in a few years he would come back quite rich and happy.

The lad listened sulkily to her, and made no answer. He was heart-sick[80] at leaving home.

Yet it was not this alone that made him gloomy and morose. Inexperienced though he was, he had still a strong sense of the danger of Sibyl's position. This young dandy who was making love to her could mean her no good. He was a gentleman, and he hated him for that, hated him through some curious race-instinct[81] for which he could not account, and which for that reason was all the more dominant within him. He was conscious also of the shallowness and vanity of his mother's nature, and in that saw infinite peril for Sibyl and Sibyl's happiness. Children begin by loving their parents; as they grow older they judge them; sometimes they forgive them.

His mother! He had something on his mind to ask of her, something that he had brooded on for many months of silence. A chance phrase that he had heard at the theatre, a whispered sneer that had reached his ears one night as he waited at the stage-door[82], had set loose a train of horrible thoughts. He remembered it as if it had been the lash of a hunting-crop[83] across his face. His brows knit together into a wedge-like furrow, and with a twitch of pain he bit his under-lip[84].

'You are not listening to a word I am saying, Jim,' cried Sibyl, 'and I am making the most delightful plans for your future. Do say something.'

'What do you want me to say?'

'Oh! that you will be a good boy, and not forget us,' she answered, smiling at him.

He shrugged his shoulders. 'You are more likely to forget me, than I am to forget you, Sibyl.'

She flushed. 'What do you mean, Jim?' she asked.

'You have a new friend, I hear. Who is he? Why have you not told me about him? He means you no good.'

'Stop, Jim!' she exclaimed. 'You must not say anything against him. I love him.'

'Why, you don't even know his name,' answered the lad. 'Who is he? I have a right to know.'

'He is called Prince Charming. Don't you like the name. Oh! you silly boy! you should never forget it. If you only saw him, you would think him the most wonderful person in the world. Some day you will meet him: when you come back from Australia. You will like him so much. Everybody likes him, and I...love him. I wish you could come to the theatre to-night. He is going to be there, and I am to play Juliet. Oh! how[85] I shall play it! Fancy, Jim, to be in love and play Juliet! To have him sitting there! To play for his delight! I am afraid I may frighten the company, frighten or enthral them. To be in love is to surpass one's self. Poor dreadful Mr Isaacs will be shouting "genius" to his loafers at the bar. He has preached me as a dogma; to-night he will announce me as a revelation. I feel it. And it is all his, his only, Prince Charming, my wonderful lover, my god of graces. But I am poor beside him. Poor? What does that matter? When poverty creeps in at the door, love flies in through the window. Our proverbs want rewriting. They were made in winter, and it is summer now; spring-time[86] for me, I think, a very dance of blossoms in blue skies.'

'He is a gentleman,' said the lad, sullenly.

'A prince!' she cried, musically. 'What more do you want?'

'He wants to enslave you.'

'I shudder at the thought of being free.'

'I want you to beware of him.'

'To see him is to worship him, to know him is to trust him.'

'Sibyl, you are mad about him.'

She laughed, and took his arm. 'You dear old Jim, you talk as if you were a hundred. Some day you will be in love yourself. Then you will know what it is. Don't look so sulky. Surely you should be glad to think that, though you are going away, you leave me happier than I have ever been before. Life has been hard for us both, terribly hard and difficult. But it will be different now. You are going to a new world, and I have found one. Here are two chairs; let us sit down and see the smart people go by.'

They took their seats amidst a crowd of watchers. The tulip-beds[87] across the road flamed like throbbing rings of fire. A white dust, tremulous cloud of orris-root[88] it seemed, hung in the panting air. The brightly-coloured parasols danced and dipped like monstrous butterflies.

She made her brother talk of himself, his hopes, his prospects. He spoke slowly and with effort. They passed words to each other as players at a game pass counters. Sibyl felt oppressed. She could not communicate her joy. A faint smile curving that sullen mouth was all the echo she could win. After some time she became silent. Suddenly she caught a glimpse of golden hair and laughing lips, and in an open carriage with two ladies Dorian Gray drove past.

She started to her feet. 'There he is!' she cried.

'Who?' said Jim Vane.

'Prince Charming,' she answered, looking after the victoria.

He jumped up, and seized her roughly by the arm. 'Show him to me. Which is he? Point him out. I must see him!' he exclaimed; but at that moment the Duke of Berwick's four-in-hand came between, and when it had left the space clear, the carriage had swept out of the Park.

'He is gone,' murmured Sibyl, sadly. 'I wish you had seen him.'

'I wish I had, for as sure as there is a God in heaven, if he ever does you any wrong, I shall kill him.'

She looked at him in horror. He repeated his words. They cut the air like a dagger. The people round began to gape. A lady standing close to her tittered.

'Come away, Jim; come away,' she whispered. He followed her doggedly, as she passed through the crowd. He felt glad at what he had said.

When they reached the Achilles Statue she turned round. There was pity in her eyes that became laughter on her lips. She shook her head at him. 'You are foolish, Jim, utterly foolish; a bad-tempered boy, that is all. How can you say such horrible things?

You don't know what you are talking about. You are simply jealous and unkind. Ah! I wish you would fall in love. Love makes people good, and what you said was wicked.'

'I am sixteen,' he answered, 'and I know what I am about. Mother is no help to you. She doesn't understand how to look after you. I wish now that I was not going to Australia at all. I have a great mind to chuck the whole thing up. I would, if my articles hadn't been signed.'

'Oh, don't be so serious, Jim. You are like one of the heroes of those silly melodramas mother used to be so fond of acting in. I am not going to quarrel with you. I have seen him, and oh! to[89] see him is perfect happiness. We won't quarrel. I know you would never harm any one I love, would you?'

'Not as long as you love him, I suppose,' was the sullen answer.

'I shall love him for ever!' she cried.

'And he?'

'For ever, too!'

'He had better.'

She shrank from him. Then she laughed and put her hand on his arm. He was merely a boy.

At the Marble Arch they hailed an omnibus, which left them close to their shabby home in the Euston Road. It was after five o'clock, and Sibyl had to lie down for a couple of hours before acting. Jim insisted that she should do so. He said that he would sooner part with her when their mother was not present. She would be sure to make a scene, and he detested scenes of every kind.

In Sybil's own room they parted. There was jealousy in the lad's heart, and a fierce, murderous hatred of the stranger who, as it seemed to him, had come between them. Yet, when her arms were flung round his neck, and her fingers strayed through his hair, he softened, and kissed her with real affection. There were tears in his eyes as he went downstairs.

His mother was waiting for him below. She grumbled at his unpunctuality, as he entered. He made no answer, but sat down to his meagre meal. The flies buzzed round the table, and crawled over the stained cloth. Through the rumble of omnibuses, and the clatter of street-cabs, he could hear the droning voice devouring each minute that was left to him.

After some time, he thrust away his plate, and put his head in his hands. He felt that he had a right to know. It should have been told to him before, if it was as he suspected. Leaden with fear, his mother watched him. Words dropped mechanically from her lips. A tattered lace handkerchief twitched in her fingers. When the clock struck six, he got up, and went to the door. Then he turned back, and looked at her. Their eyes met. In hers he saw a wild appeal for mercy. It enraged him.

'Mother, I have something to ask you,' he said. Her eyes wandered vaguely about the room. She made no answer. 'Tell me the truth. I have a right to know. Were you married to my father?'

She heaved a deep sigh. It was a sigh of relief. The terrible moment, the moment that night and day, for weeks and months, she had dreaded, had come at last, and yet she felt no terror. Indeed in some measure it was a disappointment to her. The vulgar directness of the question called for a direct answer. The situation had not been gradually led up to. It was crude. It reminded her of a bad rehearsal.

'No,' she answered, wondering at the harsh simplicity of life.

'My father was a scoundrel then!' cried the lad, clenching his fists.

She shook her head. 'I knew he was not free. We loved each other very much. If he had lived, he would have made provision for us. Don't speak against him, my son. He was your father, and a gentleman. Indeed, he was highly connected.'

An oath broke from his lips. 'I don't care for myself,' he exclaimed, 'but don't let Sibyl....It is a gentleman, isn't it, who is in love with her, or says he is? Highly connected, too, I suppose.'

For a moment a hideous sense of humiliation came over the woman. Her head drooped. She wiped her eyes with shaking hands. 'Sibyl has a mother,' she murmured; 'I had none.'

The lad was touched. He went towards her, and stooping down he kissed her. 'I am sorry if I have pained you by asking about my father,' he said, 'but I could not help it. I must go now. Good-bye. Don't forget that you will have only one child now to look after, and believe me that if this man wrongs my sister, I will find out who he is, track him down, and kill him like a dog. I swear it.'

The exaggerated folly of the threat, the passionate gesture that accompanied it, the mad melodramatic words, made life seem more vivid to her. She was familiar with the atmosphere. She breathed more freely, and for the first time for many months she really admired her son. She would have liked to have continued the scene on the same emotional scale, but he cut her short. Trunks had to be carried down, and mufflers looked for. The lodging-house drudge bustled in and out. There was the bargaining with the cabman. The moment was lost in vulgar details. It was with a renewed feeling of disappointment that she waved the tattered lace handkerchief from the window, as her son drove away. She was conscious that a great opportunity had been wasted. She consoled herself by telling Sibyl how desolate she felt her life would be, now that she had only one child to look after. She remembered the phrase. It had pleased her. Of the threat she said nothing. It was vividly and dramatically expressed. She felt that they would all laugh at it some day.

Chapter 6

'I suppose you have heard the news, Basil?' said Lord Henry that evening, as Hallward was shown into a little private room at the Bristol where dinner had been laid for three.

'No, Harry,' answered the artist, giving his hat and coat to the bowing waiter. 'What is it? Nothing about politics, I hope? They don't interest me. There is hardly a single person in the House of Commons worth painting; though many of them would be the better for a little whitewashing.'

'Dorian Gray is engaged to be married,' said Lord Henry, watching him as he spoke.

Hallward started and then frowned. 'Dorian engaged to be married!' he cried. 'Impossible!'

'It is perfectly true.'

'To whom?'

'To some little actress or other.'

'I can't believe it. Dorian is far too sensible.'

'Dorian is far too wise not to do foolish things now and then, my dear Basil.'

'Marriage is hardly a thing that one can do now and then, Harry.'

'Except in America,' rejoined Lord Henry, languidly. 'But I didn't say he was married. I said he was engaged to be married. There is a great difference. I have a distinct remembrance of being married, but I have no recollection at all of being engaged. I am inclined to think that I never was engaged.'

'But think of Dorian's birth, and position, and wealth. It would be absurd for him to marry so much beneath him.'

'If you want to make him marry this girl tell him that, Basil. He is sure to do it, then. Whenever a man does a thoroughly stupid thing, it is always from the noblest motives.'

'I hope the girl is good, Harry. I don't want to see Dorian tied to some vile creature, who might degrade his nature and ruin his intellect.'

'Oh, she is better than good—she is beautiful,' murmured Lord Henry, sipping a glass of vermouth and orange-bitters[90]. 'Dorian says she is beautiful; and he is not often wrong about things of that kind. Your portrait of him has quickened his appreciation of the personal appearance of other people. It has had that excellent effect, amongst others. We are to see her to-night, if that boy doesn't forget his appointment.'

'Are you serious?'

'Quite serious, Basil. I should be miserable if I thought I should ever be more serious than I am at the present moment.'

'But do you approve of it, Harry?' asked the painter, walking up and down the room, and biting his lip. 'You can't approve of it, possibly. It is some silly infatuation.'

'I never approve, or disapprove, of anything now. It is an absurd attitude to take towards life. We are not sent into the world to air our moral prejudices. I never take any notice of what common people say, and I never interfere with what charming people do. If a personality fascinates me, whatever mode of expression that personality selects is absolutely delightful to me. Dorian Gray falls in love with a beautiful girl who acts Juliet, and proposes to marry her. Why not? If he wedded Messalina[91] he would be none the less interesting. You know I am not a champion of marriage. The real drawback to marriage is that it makes one unselfish. And unselfish people are colourless. They lack individuality. Still, there are certain temperaments that marriage makes more complex. They retain their egotism, and add to it many other egos. They are forced to have more than one life. They become more highly organized, and to be highly organized is, I should fancy, the object of man's existence. Besides, every experience is of value, and, whatever one may say against marriage, it is certainly an experience. I hope that Dorian Gray will make this girl his wife, passionately adore her for six months, and then suddenly become fascinated by some one else. He would be a wonderful study.'

'You don't mean a single word of all that, Harry; you know you don't. If Dorian Gray's life were spoiled, no one would be sorrier than yourself. You are much better than you pretend to be.'

Lord Henry laughed. 'The reason we all like to think so well of others is that we are all afraid for ourselves. The basis of optimism is sheer terror. We think that we are generous because we credit our neighbour with the possession of those virtues that are likely to be a benefit to us. We praise the banker that we may overdraw our account, and find good qualities in the highwayman in the hope that he may spare our pockets. I mean everything that I have said. I have the greatest contempt for optimism. As for a spoiled life, no life is spoiled but one whose growth is arrested. If you want to mar a nature, you have merely to reform it. As for marriage, of course that would be silly, but there are other and more interesting bonds between men and women. I will certainly encourage them. They have the charm of being fashionable. But here is Dorian himself. He will tell you more than I can.'

'My dear Harry, my dear Basil, you must both congratulate me!' said the lad, throwing off his evening cape with its satin-lined wings and shaking each of his friends by the hand in turn. 'I have never been so happy. Of course it is sudden: all really delightful things are. And yet it seems to me to be the one thing I have been looking for all my life.' He was flushed with excitement and pleasure, and looked extraordinarily handsome.

'I hope you will always be very happy, Dorian,' said Hallward, 'but I don't quite forgive you for not having let me know of your engagement. You let Harry know.'

'And I don't forgive you for being late for dinner,' broke in Lord Henry, putting his hand on the lad's shoulder, and smiling as he spoke. 'Come, let us sit down and try what the new *chef* here is like, and then you will tell us how it all came about.'

'There is really not much to tell,' cried Dorian, as they took their seats at the small round table. 'What happened was simply this. After I left you yesterday evening, Harry, I dressed, had some dinner at that little Italian restaurant in Rupert Street, you introduced me to, and went down at eight o'clock to the theatre. Sibyl was playing Rosalind. Of course the scenery was dreadful, and the Orlando absurd. But Sibyl! You should have seen her! When she came on in her boy's clothes she was perfectly wonderful. She wore a moss-coloured velvet jerkin with cinnamon sleeves, slim brown cross-gartered hose, a dainty little green cap with a hawk's feather caught in a jewel, and a hooded cloak lined with dull red. She had never seemed to me more exquisite. She had all the delicate grace of that Tanagra figurine that you have in your studio, Basil. Her hair clustered round her face like dark leaves round a pale rose. As for her acting—well, you shall see her to-night. She is simply a born artist. I sat in the dingy box absolutely enthralled. I forgot that I was in London and in the nineteenth century. I was away with my love in a forest that no man had ever seen. After the performance was over I went behind, and spoke to her. As we were sitting together, suddenly there came into her eyes a look that I had never seen there before. My lips moved towards hers. We kissed each other. I can't describe to you what I felt at that moment. It seemed to me that all my life had been narrowed to one perfect point of rose-coloured joy. She trembled all over, and shook like a white narcissus. Then she flung herself on her knees and kissed my hands. I feel that I should not tell you all this, but I can't help it. Of course our engagement is a dead secret. She has not even told her own mother. I don't know what my guardians will say. Lord Radley is sure to be furious. I don't care. I shall be of age in less than a year, and then I can do what I like. I have been right, Basil, haven't I, to take my love out of poetry, and to find my wife in Shakespeare's plays? Lips that Shakespeare taught to speak have whispered their secret in my ear. I have had the arms of Rosalind around me, and kissed Juliet on the mouth.'

'Yes, Dorian, I suppose you were right,' said Hallward, slowly.

'Have you seen her to-day?' asked Lord Henry.

Dorian Gray shook his head. 'I left her in the forest of Arden, I shall find her in an orchard in Verona.'

Lord Henry sipped his champagne in a meditative manner. 'At what particular point did you mention the word marriage, Dorian? And what did she say in answer? Perhaps you forgot all about it.'

'My dear Harry, I did not treat it as a business transaction, and I did not make any formal proposal. I told her that I loved her, and she said she was not worthy to be my wife. Not worthy! Why, the whole world is nothing to me compared with her.'

'Women are wonderfully practical,' murmured Lord Henry,— 'much more practical than we are. In situations of that kind we often forget to say anything about marriage, and they always remind us.'

Hallward laid his hand upon his arm. 'Don't Harry. You have annoyed Dorian. He is not like other men. He would never bring misery upon any one. His nature is too fine for that.'

Lord Henry looked across the table. 'Dorian is never annoyed with me,' he answered. 'I asked the question for the best reason possible, for the only reason, indeed, that excuses one for asking any question—simple curiosity. I have a theory that it is always the women who propose to us, and not we who propose to the women. Except, of course, in middle-class life. But then the middle classes are not modern.'

Dorian Gray laughed, and tossed his head. 'You are quite incorrigible, Harry; but I don't mind. It is impossible to be angry with you. When you see Sibyl Vane you will feel that the man who could wrong her would be a beast, a beast without a heart. I cannot understand how any one can wish to shame the thing he loves. I love Sibyl Vane. I want to place her on a pedestal of gold, and to see the world worship the woman who is mine. What is marriage? An irrevocable vow. You mock at it for that. Ah! don't[92] mock. It is an irrevocable vow that I want to take. Her trust makes me faithful, her belief makes me good. When I am with her, I regret all that you have taught me. I become different from what you have known me to be. I am changed, and the mere touch of Sibyl Vane's hand makes me forget you and all your wrong, fascinating, poisonous, delightful theories.'

'And those are...?' asked Lord Henry, helping himself to some salad.

'Oh, your theories about life, your theories about love, your theories about pleasure. All your theories, in fact, Harry.'

'Pleasure is the only thing worth having a theory about,' he answered, in his slow, melodious voice. 'But I am afraid I cannot claim my theory as my own. It belongs to Nature, not to me. Pleasure is Nature's test, her sign of approval. When we are happy we are always good, but when we are good we are not always happy.'

'Ah! but what do you mean by good?' cried Basil Hallward.

'Yes,' echoed Dorian, leaning back in his chair, and looking at Lord Henry over the heavy clusters of purple-lipped irises that stood in the centre of the table, 'what do you mean by good, Harry?'

'To be good is to be in harmony with one's self,' he replied, touching the thin stem of his glass with his pale, fine-pointed fingers. 'Discord is to be forced to be in harmony with others. One's own life—that is the important thing. As for the lives of one's neighbours, if one wishes to be a prig or a Puritan, one can flaunt one's moral views about them, but they are not one's concern. Besides, Individualism has really the higher aim. Modern morality consists in accepting the standard of one's age. I consider that for any man of culture to accept the standard of his age is a form of the grossest immorality.'

'But, surely, if one lives merely for one's self, Harry, one pays a terrible price for doing so?' suggested the painter.

'Yes, we are overcharged for everything nowadays. I should fancy that the real tragedy of the poor is that they can afford nothing but self-denial. Beautiful sins, like beautiful things, are the privilege of the rich.'

'One has to pay in other ways but money.'

'What sort of ways, Basil?'

'Oh! I should fancy in remorse, in suffering, in...well, in the consciousness of degradation.'

Lord Henry shrugged his shoulders. 'My dear fellow, mediaeval art is charming, but mediaeval emotions are out of date. One can use them in fiction, of course. But then the only things that one can use in fiction are the things that one has ceased to use in fact. Believe me, no civilized man ever regrets a pleasure, and no uncivilized man ever knows what a pleasure is.'

'I know what pleasure is,' cried Dorian Gray. 'It is to adore some one.'

'That is certainly better than being adored,' he answered, toying with some fruits. 'Being adored is a nuisance. Women treat us just as Humanity treats its gods. They worship us, and are always bothering us to do something for them.'

'I should have said that whatever they ask for they had first given to us,' murmured the lad, gravely. 'They create Love in our natures. They have a right to demand it back.'

'That is quite true, Dorian,' cried Hallward.

'Nothing is ever quite true,' said Lord Henry.

'This is,' interrupted Dorian. 'You must admit, Harry, that women give to men the very gold of their lives.'

'Possibly,' he sighed, 'but they invariably want it back in such very small change. That is the worry. Women, as some witty Frenchman once put it, inspire us with the desire to do masterpieces, and always prevent us from carrying them out.'

'Harry, you are dreadful! I don't know why I like you so much.'

'You will always like me, Dorian,' he replied. 'Will you have some coffee, you fellows?—Waiter, bring coffee, and *fine-champagne*[93], and some cigarettes. No: don't mind the cigarettes; I have some. Basil, I can't allow you to smoke cigars. You must have a cigarette. A cigarette is the perfect type of a perfect pleasure. It is exquisite, and it leaves one unsatisfied. What more can one want? Yes, Dorian, you will always be fond of me. I represent to you all the sins you have never had the courage to commit.'

'What nonsense you talk, Harry!' cried the lad, taking a light from a fire-breathing silver dragon that the waiter had placed on the table. 'Let us go down to the theatre. When Sibyl comes on the stage you will have a new ideal of life. She will represent something to you that you have never known.'

'I have known everything,' said Lord Henry, with a tired look in his eyes, 'but I am always ready for a new emotion. I am afraid, however, that, for me at any rate, there is no such thing. Still, your wonderful girl may thrill me. I love acting. It is so much more real than life. Let us go. Dorian, you will come with me. I am so sorry, Basil, but there is only room for two in the brougham. You must follow us in a hansom.'

They got up and put on their coats, sipping their coffee standing. The painter was silent and preoccupied. There was a gloom over him. He could not bear this marriage, and yet it seemed to him to be better than many other things that might have happened. After a few minutes, they all passed downstairs. He drove off by himself, as had been arranged, and watched the flashing lights of the little brougham in front of him. A strange sense of loss came over him. He felt that Dorian Gray would never again be to him all that he had been in the past. Life had come between them....His eyes darkened, and the crowded, flaring streets became blurred to his eyes. When the cab drew up at the theatre, it seemed to him that he had grown years older.

Chapter 7

For some reason or other, the house was crowded that night, and the fat Jew manager who met them at the door was beaming from ear to ear with an oily, tremulous smile. He escorted them to their box with a sort of pompous humility, waving his fat jewelled hands, and talking at the top of his voice. Dorian Gray loathed him more than ever. He felt as if he had come to look for Miranda[94] and had been met by Caliban[95]. Lord Henry, upon the other hand, rather liked him. At least he declared he did, and insisted on shaking him by the hand, and assuring him that he was proud to meet a man who had discovered a real genius and gone bankrupt over a poet. Hallward amused himself with watching the faces in the pit. The heat was terribly oppressive, and the huge sunlight flamed like a monstrous dahlia with petals of yellow fire. The youths in the gallery had taken off their coats and waistcoats and hung them over the side. They talked to each other across the theatre, and shared their oranges with the tawdry girls who sat beside them. Some women were laughing in the pit. Their voices were horribly shrill and discordant. The sound of the popping of corks came from the bar.

'What a place to find one's divinity in!' said Lord Henry.

'Yes!' answered Dorian Gray. 'It was here I found her, and she is divine beyond all living things. When she acts you will forget everything. These common, rough people, with their coarse faces and brutal gestures, become quite different when she is on the stage. They sit silently and watch her. They weep and laugh as she wills them to do. She makes them as responsive as a violin. She spiritualizes them, and one feels that they are of the same flesh and blood as one's self.'

'The same flesh and blood as one's self! Oh, I hope not!' exclaimed Lord Henry, who was scanning the occupants of the gallery through his opera-glass[96].

'Don't pay any attention to him, Dorian,' said the painter. 'I understand what you mean, and I believe in this girl. Any one you love must be marvellous, and any girl who has the effect you describe must be fine and noble. To spiritualize one's age— that is something worth doing. If this girl can give a soul to those who have lived without one, if she can create the sense of beauty in people whose lives have been sordid and ugly, if she can strip them of their selfishness and lend them tears for sorrows that are not their own, she is worthy of all your adoration, worthy of the adoration of the world. This marriage is quite right. I did not think so at first, but I admit it now. The gods made Sibyl Vane for you. Without her you would have been incomplete.'

'Thanks, Basil,' answered Dorian Gray, pressing his hand. 'I knew that you would understand me. Harry is so cynical, he terrifies me. But here is the orchestra. It is quite dreadful, but it only lasts for about five minutes. Then the curtain rises, and you will see the girl to whom I am going to give all my life, to whom I have given everything that is good in me.'

A quarter of an hour afterwards, amidst an extraordinary turmoil of applause, Sibyl Vane stepped on to the stage. Yes, she was certainly lovely to look at—one of the loveliest creatures, Lord Henry thought, that he had ever seen. There was something of the fawn in her shy grace and startled eyes. A faint blush, like the shadow of a rose in a mirror of silver, came to her cheeks as she glanced at the crowded, enthusiastic house. She stepped back a few paces, and her lips seemed to tremble. Basil Hallward leaped to his feet and began to applaud. Motionless, and as one in a dream, sat Dorian Gray, gazing at her. Lord Henry peered through his glasses, murmuring, 'Charming! charming[97]!'

The scene was the hall of Capulet's house, and Romeo in his pilgrim's dress had entered with Mercutio and his other friends. The band, such as it was, struck up a few bars of music, and the dance began. Through the crowd of ungainly, shabbily-dressed actors, Sibyl Vane moved like a creature from a finer world. Her body swayed, while she danced, as a plant sways in the water. The curves of her throat were the curves of a white lily. Her hands seemed to be made of cool ivory.

Yet she was curiously listless. She showed no sign of joy when her eyes rested on Romeo. The few words she had to speak—

> *Good pilgrim, you do wrong your hand too much,*
> *Which mannerly devotion shows in this;*
> *For saints have hands that pilgrims' hands do touch,*
> *And palm to palm is holy palmers' kiss—*

with the brief dialogue that follows, were spoken in a thoroughly artificial manner. The voice was exquisite, but from the point of view of tone it was absolutely false. It was wrong in colour. It took away all the life from the verse. It made the passion unreal.

Dorian Gray grew pale as he watched her. He was puzzled and anxious. Neither of his friends dared to say anything to him. She seemed to them to be absolutely incompetent. They were horribly disappointed.

Yet they felt that the true test of any Juliet is the balcony scene of the second act. They waited for that. If she failed there, there was nothing in her.

She looked charming as she came out in the moonlight. That could not be denied. But the staginess of her acting was unbearable, and grew worse as she went on. Her gestures became absurdly artificial. She over-emphasized everything that she had to say. The beautiful passage—

Thou[98] *knowest the mask of night is on my face,*
Else would a maiden blush bepaint my cheek
For that which thou hast[99] *heard me speak to-night—*

was declaimed with the painful precision of a school-girl[100] who has been taught to recite by some second-rate professor of elocution. When she leaned over the balcony and came to those wonderful lines—

Although I joy in thee[101]*,*
I have no joy of this contract to-night:
It is too rash, too unadvised, too sudden;
Too like the lightning, which doth[102] *cease to be*
Ere[103] *one can say, 'It lightens.' Sweet, good-night!*
This bud of love by summer's ripening breath
May prove a beauteous flower when next we meet—

she spoke the words as though they conveyed no meaning to her. It was not nervousness. Indeed, so far from being nervous, she was absolutely self-contained. It was simply bad art. She was a complete failure.

Even the common, uneducated audience of the pit and gallery lost their interest in the play. They got restless, and began to talk loudly and to whistle. The Jew manager, who was standing at the back of the dress-circle, stamped and swore with rage. The only person unmoved was the girl herself.

When the second act was over there came a storm of hisses, and Lord Henry got up from his chair and put on his coat. 'She is quite beautiful, Dorian,' he said, 'but she can't act. Let us go.'

'I am going to see the play through,' answered the lad, in a hard, bitter voice. 'I am awfully sorry that I have made you waste an evening, Harry. I apologize to you both.'

'My dear Dorian, I should think Miss Vane was ill,' interrupted Hallward. 'We will come some other night.'

'I wish she were ill,' he rejoined. 'But she seems to me to be simply callous and cold. She has entirely altered. Last night she was a great artist. This evening she is merely a commonplace, mediocre actress.'

'Don't talk like that about any one you love, Dorian. Love is a more wonderful thing than Art.'

'They are both simply forms of imitation,' remarked Lord Henry. 'But do let us go. Dorian, you must not stay here any longer. It is not good for one's morals to see bad acting. Besides, I don't suppose you will want your wife to act. So what does it matter if she plays Juliet like a wooden doll? She is very lovely, and if she knows as little about life as she does about acting, she will be a delightful experience. There are only two kinds of people who are really fascinating—people who know absolutely everything, and people who know absolutely nothing. Good heavens, my dear boy, don't look so tragic! The secret of remaining young is never to have an emotion that is unbecoming. Come to the club with Basil and myself. We will smoke cigarettes and drink to the beauty of Sibyl Vane. She is beautiful. What more can you want?'

'Go away, Harry,' cried the lad. 'I want to be alone. Basil, you must go. Ah! can't[104] you see that my heart is breaking?' The hot tears came to his eyes. His lips trembled, and, rushing to the back of the box, he leaned up against the wall, hiding his face in his hands.

'Let us go, Basil,' said Lord Henry, with a strange tenderness in his voice; and the two young men passed out together.

A few moments afterwards the footlights flared up, and the curtain rose on the third act. Dorian Gray went back to his seat. He looked pale, and proud, and indifferent. The play dragged on, and seemed interminable. Half of the audience went out, tramping in heavy boots, and laughing. The whole thing was a *fiasco*. The last act was played to almost empty benches. The curtain went down on a titter, and some groans.

As soon as it was over, Dorian Gray rushed behind the scenes into the greenroom. The girl was standing there alone, with a look of triumph on her face. Her eyes were lit with an exquisite fire. There was a radiance about her. Her parted lips were smiling over some secret of their own.

When he entered, she looked at him, and an expression of infinite joy came over her. 'How badly I acted to-night, Dorian!' she cried.

'Horribly!' he answered, gazing at her in amazement—'horribly! It was dreadful. Are you ill? You have no idea what it was. You have no idea what I suffered.'

The girl smiled. 'Dorian,' she answered, lingering over his name with long-drawn music in her voice, as though it were sweeter than honey to the red petals of her mouth—'Dorian, you should have understood. But you understand now, don't you?'

'Understand what?' he asked, angrily.

'Why I was so bad to-night. Why I shall always be bad. Why I shall never act well again.'

He shrugged his shoulders. 'You are ill, I suppose. When you are ill you shouldn't act. You make yourself ridiculous. My friends were bored. I was bored.'

She seemed not to listen to him. She was transfigured with joy. An ecstasy of happiness dominated her.

'Dorian, Dorian,' she cried, 'before I knew you, acting was the one reality of my life. It was only in the theatre that I lived. I thought that it was all true. I was Rosalind one night, and Portia[105] the other. The joy of Beatrice[106] was my joy, and the sorrows of Cordelia[107] were mine also. I believed in everything. The common people who acted with me seemed to me to be godlike. The painted scenes were my world. I knew nothing but shadows, and I thought them real. You came—oh, my beautiful love!— and you freed my soul from prison. You taught me what reality really is. To-night, for the first time in my life, I saw through the hollowness, the sham, the silliness of the empty pageant in which I had always played. To-night, for the first time, I became conscious that the Romeo was hideous, and old, and painted, that the moonlight in the orchard was false, that the scenery was vulgar, and that the words I had to speak were unreal, were not my words, were not what I wanted to say. You had brought me something higher, something of which all art is but a reflection. You had made me understand what love really is. My love! my love! Prince Charming! Prince of life! I have grown sick of shadows. You are more to me than all art can ever be. What have I to do with the puppets of a play? When I came on to-night, I could not understand how it was that everything had gone from me. I thought that I was going to be wonderful. I found that I could do nothing. Suddenly it dawned on my soul what it all meant. The knowledge was exquisite to me. I heard them hissing, and I smiled. What could they know of love such as ours? Take me away, Dorian—take me away with you, where we can be quite alone. I hate the stage. I might mimic a passion that I do not feel, but I cannot mimic one that burns me like fire. Oh, Dorian, Dorian, you understand now what it signifies? Even if I could do it, it would be profanation for me to play at being in love. You have made me see that.'

He flung himself down on the sofa, and turned away his face. 'You have killed my love,' he muttered.

She looked at him in wonder, and laughed. He made no answer. She came across to him, and with her little fingers stroked his hair. She knelt down and pressed his hands to her lips. He drew them away, and a shudder ran through him.

Then he leaped up and went to the door. 'Yes,' he cried, 'you have killed my love. You used to stir my imagination. Now you don't even stir my curiosity. You simply produce no effect. I loved you because you were marvellous, because you had genius and intellect, because you realised the dreams of great poets and gave shape and substance to the shadows of art. You have thrown it all away. You are shallow and stupid. My God! how mad I was to love you! What a fool I have been! You are nothing to me now. I will never see you again. I will never think of you. I will never mention your name. You don't know what you were to me, once. Why, once...Oh, I can't bear to think of it! I wish I had never laid eyes upon you! You have spoiled the romance of my life. How little you can know of love, if you say it mars your art! Without your art you are nothing. I would have made you famous, splendid, magnificent. The world would have worshipped you, and you would have borne my name. What are you now? A third-rate actress with a pretty face.'

The girl grew white, and trembled. She clenched her hands

together, and her voice seemed to catch in her throat. 'You are not serious, Dorian?' she murmured. 'You are acting.'

'Acting! I leave that to you. You do it so well,' he answered, bitterly.

She rose from her knees, and, with a piteous expression of pain in her face, came across the room to him. She put her hand upon his arm, and looked into his eyes. He thrust her back. 'Don't touch me!' he cried.

A low moan broke from her, and she flung herself at his feet, and lay there like a trampled flower. 'Dorian, Dorian, don't leave me!' she whispered. 'I am so sorry I didn't act well. I was thinking of you all the time. But I will try—indeed, I will try. It came so suddenly across me, my love for you. I think I should never have known it if you had not kissed me—if we had not kissed each other. Kiss me again, my love. Don't go away from me. I couldn't bear it. Oh! don't go away from me. My brother...No; never mind. He didn't mean it. He was in jest....But you, oh! can't you forgive me for to-night? I will work so hard, and try to improve. Don't be cruel to me because I love you better than anything in the world. After all, it is only once that I have not pleased you. But you are quite right, Dorian. I should have shown myself more of an artist. It was foolish of me; and yet I couldn't help it. Oh, don't leave me, don't leave me.' A fit of passionate sobbing choked her. She crouched on the floor like a wounded thing, and Dorian Gray, with his beautiful eyes, looked down at her, and his chiselled lips curled in exquisite disdain. There is always something ridiculous about the emotions of people whom one has ceased to love. Sibyl Vane seemed to him to be absurdly melodramatic. Her tears and sobs annoyed him.

'I am going,' he said at last, in his calm, clear voice. 'I don't wish to be unkind, but I can't see you again. You have disappointed me.'

She wept silently, and made no answer, but crept nearer. Her little hands stretched blindly out, and appeared to be seeking for him. He turned on his heel, and left the room. In a few moments he was out of the theatre.

Where he went to he hardly knew. He remembered wandering through dimly-lit streets, past gaunt black-shadowed archways and evil-looking houses. Women with hoarse voices and harsh laughter had called after him. Drunkards had reeled by cursing, and chattering to themselves like monstrous apes. He had seen grotesque children huddled upon doorsteps, and heard shrieks and oaths from gloomy courts.

As the dawn was just breaking he found himself close to Covent Garden. The darkness lifted, and, flushed with faint fires, the sky hollowed itself into a perfect pearl. Huge carts filled with nodding lilies rumbled slowly down the polished empty street. The air was heavy with the perfume of the flowers, and their beauty seemed to bring him an anodyne for his pain. He followed into the market, and watched the men unloading their waggons. A white-smocked carter offered him some cherries. He thanked him, wondered why he refused to accept any money for them, and began to eat them listlessly. They had been plucked at midnight, and the coldness of the moon had entered into them. A long line of boys carrying crates of striped tulips, and of yellow and red roses, defiled in front of him, threading their way through the huge jade-green piles of vegetables. Under the portico, with its grey sun-bleached pillars, loitered a troop of draggled bareheaded girls, waiting for the auction to be over. Others crowded round the swinging doors of the coffee-house[108] in the Piazza. The heavy cart-horses[109] slipped and stamped upon the rough stones, shaking their bells and trappings. Some of the drivers were lying asleep on a pile of sacks. Iris-necked, and pink-footed, the pigeons ran about picking up seeds.

After a little while, he hailed a hansom, and drove home. For a few moments he loitered upon the doorstep, looking round at the silent Square with its blank close-shuttered windows, and its staring blinds. The sky was pure opal now, and the roofs of the houses glistened like silver against it. From some chimney opposite a thin wreath of smoke was rising. It curled, a violet riband, through the nacre-coloured air.

In the huge gilt Venetian lantern, spoil of some Doge's barge, that hung from the ceiling of the great oak-panelled hall of entrance, lights were still burning from three flickering jets: thin blue petals of flame they seemed, rimmed with white fire. He turned them out, and, having thrown his hat and cape on the table, passed through the library towards the door of his bedroom, a large octagonal chamber on the ground floor that, in his new-born feeling for luxury, he had just had decorated for himself, and hung with some curious Renaissance tapestries that had been discovered stored in a disused attic at Selby Royal. As he was turning the handle of the door, his eye fell upon the portrait Basil Hallward had painted of him. He started back as if in surprise. Then he went on into his own room, looking somewhat puzzled. After he had taken the buttonhole out of his coat, he seemed to hesitate. Finally he came back, went over to the picture, and examined it. In the dim arrested light that struggled through the cream-coloured silk blinds, the face appeared to him to be a little changed. The expression looked different. One would have said that there was a touch of cruelty in the mouth. It was certainly strange.

He turned round, and, walking to the window, drew up the blind. The bright dawn flooded the room, and swept the fantastic shadows into dusky corners, where they lay shuddering. But the strange expression that he had noticed in the face of the portrait seemed to linger there, to be more intensified even. The quivering, ardent sunlight showed him the lines of cruelty round the mouth as clearly as if he had been looking into a mirror after he had done some dreadful thing.

He winced, and, taking up from the table an oval glass framed in ivory Cupids, one of Lord Henry's many presents to him, glanced hurriedly into its polished depths. No line like that warped his red lips. What did it mean?

He rubbed his eyes, and came close to the picture, and examined it again. There were no signs of any change when he looked into the actual painting, and yet there was no doubt that the whole expression had altered. It was not a mere fancy of his own. The thing was horribly apparent.

He threw himself into a chair, and began to think. Suddenly there flashed across his mind what he had said in Basil Hallward's studio the day the picture had been finished. Yes, he remembered it perfectly. He had uttered a mad wish that he himself might remain young, and the portrait grow old; that his own beauty might be untarnished, and the face on the canvas bear the burden of his passions and his sins; that the painted image might be seared with the lines of suffering and thought, and that he might keep all the delicate bloom and loveliness of his then just conscious boyhood. Surely his wish had not been fulfilled? Such things were impossible. It seemed monstrous even to think of them. And, yet, there was the picture before him, with the touch of cruelty in the mouth.

Cruelty! Had he been cruel? It was the girl's fault, not his. He had dreamed of her as a great artist, had given his love to her because he had thought her great. Then she had disappointed him. She had been shallow and unworthy. And, yet, a feeling of infinite regret came over him, as he thought of her lying at his feet sobbing like a little child. He remembered with what callousness he had watched her. Why had he been made like that? Why had such a soul been given to him? But he had suffered also. During the three terrible hours that the play had lasted, he had lived centuries of pain, aeon upon aeon of torture. His life was well worth hers. She had marred him for a moment, if he had wounded her for an age. Besides, women were better suited to bear sorrow than men. They lived on their emotions. They only thought of their emotions. When they took lovers, it was merely to have some one with whom they could have scenes. Lord Henry had told him that, and Lord Henry knew what women were. Why should he trouble about Sibyl Vane? She was nothing to him now.

But the picture? What was he to say of that? It held the secret of his life, and told his story. It had taught him to love his own beauty. Would it teach him to loathe his own soul? Would he ever look at it again?

No; it was merely an illusion wrought on the troubled senses. The horrible night that he had passed had left phantoms behind it. Suddenly there had fallen upon his brain that tiny scarlet speck that makes men mad. The picture had not changed. It was folly to think so.

Yet it was watching him, with its beautiful marred face and its cruel smile. Its bright hair gleamed in the early sunlight. Its blue eyes met his own. A sense of infinite pity, not for himself, but for the painted image of himself, came over him. It had altered already, and would alter more. Its gold would wither into grey. Its red and white roses would die. For every sin that he committed, a stain would fleck and wreck its fairness. But he would not sin. The picture, changed or unchanged, would be to him the visible emblem of conscience. He would resist temptation. He would not see Lord Henry any more—would not, at any rate, listen to those subtle poisonous theories that in Basil Hallward's garden had first stirred within him the passion for impossible things. He would go back to Sibyl Vane, make her amends, marry her, try to love her again. Yes, it was his duty to do so. She must have suffered more than he had. The fascination that she had exercised over him would return. They would be happy together. His life with her would be beautiful and pure.

He got up from his chair, and drew a large screen right in front of the portrait, shuddering as he glanced at it. 'How horrible!' he murmured to himself, and he walked across to the window and opened it. When he stepped out on to the grass, he drew a deep breath. The fresh morning air seemed to drive away all his sombre passions. He thought only of Sibyl. A faint echo of his love came back to him. He repeated her name over and over again. The birds that were singing in the dew-drenched garden seemed to be telling the flowers about her.

Chapter 8

It was long past noon when he awoke. His valet had crept several times on tiptoe into the room to see if he was stirring, and had wondered what made his young master sleep so late. Finally his bell sounded, and Victor came in softly with a cup of tea, and a pile of letters, on a small tray of old Sèvres china, and drew back the olive-satin curtains, with their shimmering blue lining, that hung in front of the three tall windows.

'Monsieur has well slept this morning,' he said, smiling.

'What o'clock is it, Victor?' asked Dorian Gray, drowsily.

'One hour and a quarter, Monsieur.'

How late it was! He sat up, and, having sipped some tea, turned over his letters. One of them was from Lord Henry, and had been brought by hand that morning. He hesitated for a moment, and then put it aside. The others he opened listlessly. They contained the usual collection of cards, invitations to dinner, tickets for private views, programmes of charity concerts, and the like, that are showered on fashionable young men every morning during the season. There was a rather heavy bill, for a chased silver Louis-Quinze toilet-set[110], that he had not yet had the courage to send on to his guardians, who were extremely old-fashioned people and did not realise that we live in an age when unnecessary things are our only necessities; and there were several very courteously worded communications from Jermyn Street money-lenders[111] offering to advance any sum of money at a moment's notice and at the most reasonable rates of interest.

After about ten minutes he got up, and, throwing on an elaborate dressing-gown[112] of silk-embroidered cashmere wool, passed into the onyx-paved bathroom. The cool water refreshed him after his long sleep. He seemed to have forgotten all that he had gone through. A dim sense of having taken part in some strange tragedy came to him once or twice, but there was the unreality of a dream about it.

As soon as he was dressed, he went into the library and sat down to a light French breakfast, that had been laid out for him on a small round table close to the open window. It was an exquisite day. The warm air seemed laden with spices. A bee flew in, and buzzed round the blue-dragon bowl that, filled with sulphur-yellow roses, stood before him. He felt perfectly happy.

Suddenly his eye fell on the screen that he had placed in front of the portrait, and he started.

'Too cold for Monsieur?' asked his valet, putting an omelette on the table. 'I shut the window?'

Dorian shook his head. 'I am not cold,' he murmured.

Was it all true? Had the portrait really changed? Or had it been simply his own imagination that had made him see a look of evil where there had been a look of joy? Surely a painted canvas could not alter? The thing was absurd. It would serve as a tale to tell Basil some day. It would make him smile.

And, yet, how vivid was his recollection of the whole thing! First in the dim twilight, and then in the bright dawn, he had seen the touch of cruelty round the warped lips. He almost dreaded his valet leaving the room. He knew that when he was alone he would have to examine the portrait. He was afraid of certainty. When the coffee and cigarettes had been brought and the man turned to go, he felt a wild desire to tell him to remain. As the door was closing behind him he called him back. The man stood waiting for his orders. Dorian looked at him for a moment. 'I am not at home to any one, Victor,' he said, with a sigh. The man bowed and retired.

Then he rose from the table, lit a cigarette, and flung himself down on a luxuriously-cushioned couch that stood facing the screen. The screen was an old one, of gilt Spanish leather, stamped and wrought with a rather florid Louis-Quatorze pattern. He scanned it curiously, wondering if ever before it had concealed the secret of a man's life.

Should he move it aside, after all? Why not let it stay there? What was the use of knowing? If the thing was true, it was terrible. If it was not true, why trouble about it? But what if, by some fate or deadlier chance, eyes other than his spied behind, and saw the horrible change? What should he do if Basil Hallward came and asked to look at his own picture? Basil would be sure to do that. No; the thing had to be examined, and at once. Anything would be better than this dreadful state of doubt.

He got up, and locked both doors. At least he would be alone when he looked upon the mask of his shame. Then he drew the screen aside, and saw himself face to face. It was perfectly true. The portrait had altered.

As he often remembered afterwards, and always with no small wonder, he found himself at first gazing at the portrait with a feeling of almost scientific interest. That such a change should have taken place was incredible to him. And yet it was a fact. Was there some subtle affinity between the chemical atoms, that shaped themselves into form and colour on the canvas, and the soul that was within him? Could it be that what that soul thought, they realised?—that what it dreamed, they made true? Or was there some other, more terrible reason? He shuddered, and felt afraid, and, going back to the couch, lay there, gazing at the picture in sickened horror.

One thing, however, he felt that it had done for him. It had made him conscious how unjust, how cruel, he had been to Sibyl Vane. It was not too late to make reparation for that. She could still be his wife. His unreal and selfish love would yield to some higher influence, would be transformed into some nobler passion, and the portrait that Basil Hallward had painted of him would be a guide to him through life, would be to him what holiness is to some, and conscience to others, and the fear of God to us all. There were opiates for remorse, drugs that could lull the moral sense to sleep. But here was a visible symbol of the degradation of sin. Here was an ever-present sign of the ruin men brought upon their souls.

Three o'clock struck, and four, and the half-hour rang its double chime, but Dorian Gray did not stir. He was trying to gather up the scarlet threads of life, and to weave them into a pattern; to find his way through the sanguine labyrinth of passion through which he was wandering. He did not know what to do, or what to think. Finally, he went over to the table and wrote a passionate letter to the girl he had loved, imploring her forgiveness, and accusing himself of madness. He covered page after page with wild words of sorrow, and wilder words of pain. There is a luxury in self-reproach. When we blame ourselves we feel that no one else has a right to blame us. It is the confession, not the priest, that gives us absolution. When Dorian had finished the letter, he felt that he had been forgiven.

Suddenly there came a knock to the door, and he heard Lord Henry's voice outside. 'My dear boy, I must see you. Let me in at once. I can't bear your shutting yourself up like this.'

He made no answer at first, but remained quite still. The knocking still continued, and grew louder. Yes, it was better to let Lord Henry in, and to explain to him the new life he was going to lead, to quarrel with him if it became necessary to quarrel, to part if parting was inevitable. He jumped up, drew the screen hastily across the picture, and unlocked the door.

'I am so sorry for it all, Dorian,' said Lord Henry, as he entered. 'But you must not think too much about it.'

'Do you mean about Sibyl Vane?' asked the lad.

'Yes, of course,' answered Lord Henry, sinking into a chair, and slowly pulling off his yellow gloves. 'It is dreadful, from one point of view, but it was not your fault. Tell me, did you go behind and see her, after the play was over?'

'Yes.'

'I felt sure you had. Did you make a scene with her?'

'I was brutal, Harry—perfectly brutal. But it is all right now. I am not sorry for anything that has happened. It has taught me to know myself better.'

'Ah, Dorian, I am so glad you take it in that way! I was afraid I would find you plunged in remorse, and tearing that nice curly hair of yours.'

'I have got through all that,' said Dorian, shaking his head, and smiling. 'I am perfectly happy now. I know what conscience is, to begin with. It is not what you told me it was. It is the divinest thing in us. Don't sneer at it, Harry, any more—at least not before me. I want to be good. I can't bear the idea of my soul being hideous.'

'A very charming artistic basis for ethics, Dorian! I congratulate you on it. But how are you going to begin?'

'By marrying Sibyl Vane.'

'Marrying Sibyl Vane!' cried Lord Henry, standing up, and looking at him in perplexed amazement. 'But, my dear Dorian—'

'Yes, Harry, I know what you are going to say. Something dreadful about marriage. Don't say it. Don't ever say things of that kind to me again. Two days ago I asked Sibyl to marry me. I am not going to break my word to her. She is to be my wife.'

'Your wife! Dorian!...Didn't you get my letter? I wrote to you this morning, and sent the note down, by my own man.'

'Your letter? Oh, yes, I remember. I have not read it yet, Harry. I was afraid there might be something in it that I wouldn't like. You cut life to pieces with your epigrams.'

'You know nothing then?'

'What do you mean?'

Lord Henry walked across the room, and, sitting down by Dorian Gray, took both his hands in his own, and held them tightly. 'Dorian,' he said, 'my letter—don't be frightened—was to tell you that Sibyl Vane is dead.'

A cry of pain broke from the lad's lips, and he leaped to his feet, tearing his hands away from Lord Henry's grasp. 'Dead! Sibyl dead! It is not true! It is a horrible lie! How dare you say it?'

'It is quite true, Dorian,' said Lord Henry, gravely. 'It is in all the morning papers. I wrote down to you to ask you not to see any one till I came. There will have to be an inquest, of course, and you must not be mixed up in it. Things like that make a man fashionable in Paris. But in London people are so prejudiced. Here, one should never make one's *début* with a scandal. One should reserve that to give an interest to one's old age. I suppose they don't know your name at the theatre? If they don't, it is all right. Did any one see you going round to her room? That is an important point.'

Dorian did not answer for a few moments. He was dazed with horror. Finally he stammered, in a stifled voice, 'Harry, did you say an inquest? What did you mean by that? Did Sibyl —— ? Oh, Harry, I can't bear it! But be quick. Tell me everything at once.'

'I have no doubt it was not an accident, Dorian, though it must be put in that way to the public. It seems that as she was leaving the theatre with her mother, about half-past twelve or so, she said she had forgotten something upstairs. They waited some time for her, but she did not come down again. They ultimately found her lying dead on the floor of her dressing-room[113]. She had swallowed something by mistake, some dreadful thing they use at theatres. I don't know what it was, but it had either prussic acid or white lead in it. I should fancy it was prussic acid, as she seems to have died instantaneously.'

'Harry, Harry, it is terrible!' cried the lad.

'Yes; it is very tragic, of course, but you must not get yourself mixed up in it. I see by *The Standard* that she was seventeen. I should have thought she was almost younger than that. She looked such a child, and seemed to know so little about acting. Dorian, you mustn't let this thing get on your nerves. You must come and dine with me, and afterwards we will look in at the Opera. It is a Patti night, and everybody will be there. You can come to my sister's box. She has got some smart women with her.'

'So I have murdered Sibyl Vane,' said Dorian Gray, half to himself—'murdered her as surely as if I had cut her little throat with a knife. Yet the roses are not less lovely for all that. The birds sing just as happily in my garden. And to-night I am to dine with you, and then go on to the Opera, and sup somewhere, I suppose, afterwards. How extraordinarily dramatic life is! If I had read all this in a book, Harry, I think I would have wept over it. Somehow, now that it has happened actually, and to me, it seems far too wonderful for tears. Here is the first passionate love-letter[114] I have ever written in my life. Strange, that my first passionate love-letter should have been addressed to a dead girl. Can they feel, I wonder, those white silent people we call the dead? Sibyl! Can she feel, or know, or listen? Oh, Harry, how I loved her once! It seems years ago to me now. She was everything to me. Then came that dreadful night—was it really only last night?—when she played so badly, and my heart almost broke. She explained it all to me. It was terribly pathetic. But I was not moved a bit. I thought her shallow. Suddenly something happened that made me afraid. I can't tell you what it was, but it was terrible. I said I would go back to her. I felt I had done wrong. And now she is dead. My God! my God! Harry, what shall I do? You don't know the danger I am in, and there is nothing to keep me straight. She would have done that for me. She had no right to kill herself. It was selfish of her.'

'My dear Dorian,' answered Lord Henry, taking a cigarette from his case, and producing a gold-latten matchbox, 'the only way a woman can ever reform a man is by boring him so completely that he loses all possible interest in life. If you had married this girl you would have been wretched. Of course, you would have treated her kindly. One can always be kind to people about whom one cares nothing. But she would have soon found out that you were absolutely indifferent to her. And when a woman finds that out about her husband, she either becomes dreadfully dowdy, or wears very smart bonnets that some other woman's husband has to pay for. I say nothing about the social mistake, which would have been abject, which, of course, I would not have allowed, but I assure you that in any case the whole thing would have been an absolute failure.'

'I suppose it would,' muttered the lad, walking up and down the room, and looking horribly pale. 'But I thought it was my duty. It is not my fault that this terrible tragedy has prevented my doing what was right. I remember your saying once that there is a fatality about good resolutions—that they are always made too late. Mine certainly were.'

'Good resolutions are useless attempts to interfere with scientific laws. Their origin is pure vanity. Their result is absolutely *nil*. They give us, now and then, some of those luxurious sterile emotions that have a certain charm for the weak. That is all that can be said for them. They are simply cheques that men draw on a bank where they have no account.'

'Harry,' cried Dorian Gray, coming over and sitting down

beside him, 'why is it that I cannot feel this tragedy as much as I want to? I don't think I am heartless. Do you?'

'You have done too many foolish things during the last fortnight to be entitled to give yourself that name, Dorian,' answered Lord Henry, with his sweet, melancholy smile.

The lad frowned. 'I don't like that explanation, Harry,' he rejoined, 'but I am glad you don't think I am heartless. I am nothing of the kind. I know I am not. And yet I must admit that this thing that has happened does not affect me as it should. It seems to me to be simply like a wonderful ending to a wonderful play. It has all the terrible beauty of a Greek tragedy, a tragedy in which I took a great part, but by which I have not been wounded.'

'It is an interesting question,' said Lord Henry, who found an exquisite pleasure in playing on the lad's unconscious egotism— 'an extremely interesting question. I fancy that the true explanation is this. It often happens that the real tragedies of life occur in such an inartistic manner that they hurt us by their crude violence, their absolute incoherence, their absurd want of meaning, their entire lack of style. They affect us just as vulgarity affects us. They give us an impression of sheer brute force, and we revolt against that. Sometimes, however, a tragedy that possesses artistic elements of beauty crosses our lives. If these elements of beauty are real, the whole thing simply appeals to our sense of dramatic effect. Suddenly we find that we are no longer the actors, but the spectators of the play. Or rather we are both. We watch ourselves, and the mere wonder of the spectacle enthralls us. In the present case, what is it that has really happened? Some one has killed herself for love of you. I wish that I had ever had such an experience. It would have made me in love with love for the rest of my life. The people who have adored me—there have not been very many, but there have been some—have always insisted on living on, long after I had ceased to care for them, or they to care for me. They have become stout and tedious, and when I meet them they go in at once for reminiscences. That awful memory of woman! What a fearful thing it is! And what an utter intellectual stagnation it reveals! One should absorb the colour of life, but one should never remember its details. Details are always vulgar.'

'I must sow poppies[115] in my garden,' sighed Dorian.

'There is no necessity,' rejoined his companion. 'Life has always poppies in her hands. Of course, now and then things linger. I once wore nothing but violets all through one season, as a form of artistic mourning for a romance that would not die. Ultimately, however, it did die. I forget what killed it. I think it was her proposing to sacrifice the whole world for me. That is always a dreadful moment. It fills one with the terror of eternity. Well—would you believe it? —a week ago, at Lady Hampshire's, I found myself seated at dinner next the lady in question, and she insisted on going over the whole thing again, and digging up the past, and raking up the future. I had buried my romance in a bed of asphodel[116]. She dragged it out again, and assured me that I had spoiled her life. I am bound to state that she ate an enormous dinner, so I did not feel any anxiety. But what a lack of taste she showed! The one charm of the past is that it is the past. But women never know when the curtain has fallen. They always want a sixth act, and as soon as the interest of the play is entirely over they propose to continue it. If they were allowed their own way, every comedy would have a tragic ending, and every tragedy would culminate in a farce. They are charmingly artificial, but they have no sense of art. You are more fortunate than I am. I assure you, Dorian, that not one of the women I have known would have done for me what Sibyl Vane did for you. Ordinary women always console themselves. Some of them do it by going in for sentimental colours. Never trust a woman who wears mauve, whatever her age may be, or a woman over thirty-five who is fond of pink ribbons. It always means that they have a history. Others find a great consolation in suddenly discovering the good qualities of their husbands. They flaunt their conjugal felicity in one's face, as if it were the most fascinating of sins. Religion consoles some. Its mysteries have all the charm of a flirtation, a woman once told me; and I can quite understand it. Besides, nothing makes one so vain as being told that one is a sinner. Conscience makes egotists of us all. Yes; there is really no end to the consolations that women find in modern life. Indeed, I have not mentioned the most important one.'

'What is that, Harry?' said the lad, listlessly.

'Oh, the obvious consolation. Taking some one else's admirer when one loses one's own. In good society that always whitewashes a woman. But really, Dorian, how different Sibyl Vane must have been from all the women one meets! There is something to me quite beautiful about her death. I am glad I am living in a century when such wonders happen. They make one believe in the reality of the things we all play with, such as romance, passion, and love.'

'I was terribly cruel to her. You forget that.'

'I am afraid that women appreciate cruelty, downright cruelty, more than anything else. They have wonderfully primitive instincts. We have emancipated them, but they remain slaves looking for their masters, all the same. They love being dominated. I am sure you were splendid. I have never seen you really and absolutely angry, but I can fancy how delightful you looked. And, after all, you said something to me the day before yesterday that seemed to me at the time to be merely fanciful, but that I see now was absolutely true, and it holds the key to everything.'

'What was that, Harry?'

'You said to me that Sibyl Vane represented to you all the heroines of romance—that she was Desdemona one night, and Ophelia the other; that if she died as Juliet, she came to life as Imogen.'

'She will never come to life again now,' muttered the lad, burying his face in his hands.

'No, she will never come to life. She has played her last part. But you must think of that lonely death in the tawdry dressing-room simply as a strange lurid fragment from some Jacobean tragedy, as a wonderful scene from Webster, or Ford, or Cyril Tourneur[117]. The girl never really lived, and so she has never really died. To you at least she was always a dream, a phantom that flitted through Shakespeare's plays and left them lovelier for its presence, a reed through which Shakespeare's music sounded richer and more full of joy. The moment she touched actual life, she marred it, and it marred her, and so she passed away. Mourn for Ophelia, if you like. Put ashes on your head because Cordelia was strangled. Cry out against Heaven because the daughter of Brabantio died. But don't waste your tears over Sibyl Vane. She was less real than they are.'

There was a silence. The evening darkened in the room.

Noiselessly, and with silver feet, the shadows crept in from the garden. The colours faded wearily out of things.

. After some time Dorian Gray looked up. 'You have explained me to myself, Harry,' he murmured, with something of a sigh of relief. 'I felt all that you have said, but somehow I was afraid of it, and I could not express it to myself. How well you know me! But we will not talk again of what has happened. It has been a marvellous experience. That is all. I wonder if life has still in store for me anything as marvellous.'

'Life has everything in store for you, Dorian. There is nothing that you, with your extraordinary good looks, will not be able to do.'

'But suppose, Harry, I became haggard, and old, and wrinkled? What then?'

'Ah, then,' said Lord Henry, rising to go—'then, my dear Dorian, you would have to fight for your victories. As it is, they are brought to you. No, you must keep your good looks. We live in an age that reads too much to be wise, and that thinks too much to be beautiful. We cannot spare you. And now you had better dress, and drive down to the club. We are rather late, as it is.'

'I think I shall join you at the Opera, Harry. I feel too tired to eat anything. What is the number of your sister's box?'

'Twenty-seven, I believe. It is on the grand tier. You will see her name on the door. But I am sorry you won't come and dine.'

'I don't feel up to it,' said Dorian, listlessly. 'But I am awfully obliged to you for all that you have said to me. You are certainly my best friend. No one has ever understood me as you have.'

'We are only at the beginning of our friendship, Dorian,' answered Lord Henry, shaking him by the hand. 'Good-bye. I shall see you before nine-thirty, I hope. Remember, Patti is singing.'

As he closed the door behind him, Dorian Gray touched the bell, and in a few minutes Victor appeared with the lamps and drew the blinds down. He waited impatiently for him to go. The man seemed to take an interminable time over everything.

As soon as he had left, he rushed to the screen, and drew it back. No; there was no further change in the picture. It had received the news of Sibyl Vane's death before he had known of it himself. It was conscious of the events of life as they occurred. The vicious cruelty that marred the fine lines of the mouth had, no doubt, appeared at the very moment that the girl had drunk the poison, whatever it was. Or was it indifferent to results? Did it merely take cognizance of what passed within the soul? He wondered, and hoped that some day he would see the change taking place before his very eyes, shuddering as he hoped it.

Poor Sibyl! What a romance it had all been! She had often mimicked death on the stage. Then Death himself had touched her, and taken her with him. How had she played that dreadful last scene? Had she cursed him, as she died? No; she had died for love of him, and love would always be a sacrament to him now. She had atoned for everything, by the sacrifice she had made of her life. He would not think any more of what she had made him go through, on that horrible night at the theatre. When he thought of her, it would be as a wonderful tragic figure sent on to the world's stage to show the supreme reality of Love. A wonderful tragic figure? Tears came to his eyes as he remembered her childlike look and winsome fanciful ways and shy tremulous grace. He brushed them away hastily and looked again at the picture.

He felt that the time had really come for making his choice. Or had his choice already been made? Yes, life had decided that for him—life, and his own infinite curiosity about life. Eternal youth, infinite passion, pleasures subtle and secret, wild joys and wilder sins—he was to have all these things. The portrait was to bear the burden of his shame: that was all.

A feeling of pain crept over him as he thought of the desecration that was in store for the fair face on the canvas. Once, in boyish mockery of Narcissus, he had kissed, or feigned to kiss, those painted lips that now smiled so cruelly at him. Morning after morning, he had sat before the portrait wondering at its beauty, almost enamoured of it, as it seemed to him at times. Was it to alter now with every mood to which he yielded? Was it to become a monstrous and loathsome thing, to be hidden away in a locked room, to be shut out from the sunlight that had so often touched to brighter gold the waving wonder of its hair? The pity of it! the pity of it!

For a moment he thought of praying that the horrible sympathy that existed between him and the picture might cease. It had changed in answer to a prayer; perhaps in answer to a prayer it might remain unchanged. And, yet, who, that knew anything about Life, would surrender the chance of remaining always young, however fantastic that chance might be, or with what fateful consequences it might be fraught? Besides, was it really under his control? Had it indeed been prayer that had produced the substitution? Might there not be some curious scientific reason for it all? If thought could exercise an influence upon a living organism, might not thought exercise an influence upon dead and inorganic things? Nay[118], without thought or conscious desire, might not things external to ourselves vibrate in unison with our moods and passions, atom calling to atom in secret love or strange affinity? But the reason was of no importance. He would never again tempt by a prayer any terrible power. If the picture was to alter, it was to alter. That was all. Why inquire too closely into it?

For there would be a real pleasure in watching it. He would be able to follow his mind into its secret places. This portrait would be to him the most magical of mirrors. As it had revealed to him his own body, so it would reveal to him his own soul. And when winter came upon it, he would still be standing where spring trembles on the verge of summer. When the blood crept from its face, and left behind a pallid mask of chalk with leaden eyes, he would keep the glamour of boyhood. Not one blossom of his loveliness would ever fade. Not one pulse of his life would ever weaken. Like the gods of the Greeks, he would be strong, and fleet, and joyous. What did it matter what happened to the coloured image on the canvas? He would be safe. That was everything.

He drew the screen back into its former place in front of the picture, smiling as he did so, and passed into his bedroom, where his valet was already waiting for him. An hour later he was at the Opera, and Lord Henry was leaning over his chair.

Chapter 9

As he was sitting at breakfast next morning, Basil Hallward was shown into the room.

'I am so glad I have found you, Dorian,' he said, gravely. 'I called last night, and they told me you were at the Opera. Of course I knew that was impossible. But I wish you had left word where you had really gone to. I passed a dreadful evening, half afraid that one tragedy might be followed by another. I think you might have telegraphed for me when you heard of it first. I read of it quite by chance in a late edition of *The Globe*, that I picked up at the club. I came here at once, and was miserable at not finding you. I can't tell you how heart-broken[119] I am about the whole thing. I know what you must suffer. But where were you? Did you go down and see the girl's mother? For a moment I thought of following you there. They gave the address in the paper. Somewhere in the Euston Road, isn't it? But I was afraid of intruding upon a sorrow that I could not lighten. Poor woman! What a state she must be in! And her only child, too! What did she say about it all?'

'My dear Basil, how do I know?' murmured Dorian Gray, sipping some pale-yellow wine from a delicate gold-beaded bubble of Venetian glass, and looking dreadfully bored. 'I was at the Opera. You should have come on there. I met Lady Gwendolen, Harry's sister, for the first time. We were in her box. She is perfectly charming; and Patti sang divinely. Don't talk about horrid subjects. If one doesn't talk about a thing, it has never happened.

It is simply expression, as Harry says, that gives reality to things. I may mention that she was not the woman's only child. There is a son, a charming fellow, I believe. But he is not on the stage. He is a sailor, or something. And now, tell me about yourself and what you are painting.'

'You went to the Opera?' said Hallward, speaking very slowly, and with a strained touch of pain in his voice. 'You went to the Opera while Sibyl Vane was lying dead in some sordid lodging? You can talk to me of other women being charming, and of Patti singing divinely, before the girl you loved has even the quiet of a grave to sleep in? Why, man, there are horrors in store for that little white body of hers!'

'Stop, Basil! I won't hear it!' cried Dorian, leaping to his feet. 'You must not tell me about things. What is done is done. What is past is past.'

'You call yesterday the past?'

'What has the actual lapse of time got to do with it? It is only shallow people who require years to get rid of an emotion. A man who is master of himself can end a sorrow as easily as he can invent a pleasure. I don't want to be at the mercy of my emotions. I want to use them, to enjoy them, and to dominate them.'

'Dorian, this is horrible! Something has changed you completely. You look exactly the same wonderful boy who, day after day, used to come down to my studio to sit for his picture. But you were simple, natural, and affectionate then. You were the most unspoiled creature in the whole world. Now, I don't know what has come over you. You talk as if you had no heart, no pity in you. It is all Harry's influence. I see that.'

The lad flushed up, and, going to the window, looked out for a few moments on the green, flickering, sun-lashed garden. 'I owe a great deal to Harry, Basil,' he said, at last—'more than I owe to you. You only taught me to be vain.'

'Well, I am punished for that, Dorian—or shall be some day.'

'I don't know what you mean, Basil,' he exclaimed, turning round. 'I don't know what you want. What do you want?'

'I want the Dorian Gray I used to paint,' said the artist sadly.

'Basil,' said the lad, going over to him, and putting his hand on his shoulder, 'you have come too late. Yesterday, when I heard that Sibyl Vane had killed herself—'

'Killed herself! Good heavens! is[120] there no doubt about that?' cried Hallward, looking up at him with an expression of horror.

'My dear Basil! Surely you don't think it was a vulgar accident? Of course she killed herself.'

The elder man buried his face in his hands. 'How fearful,' he muttered, and a shudder ran through him.

'No,' said Dorian Gray, 'there is nothing fearful about it. It is one of the great romantic tragedies of the age. As a rule, people who act lead the most commonplace lives. They are good husbands, or faithful wives, or something tedious. You know what I mean—middle-class virtue, and all that kind of thing. How different Sibyl was! She lived her finest tragedy. She was always a heroine. The last night she played—the night you saw her—she acted badly because she had known the reality of love. When she knew its unreality, she died, as Juliet might have died. She passed again into the sphere of art. There is something of the martyr about her. Her death has all the pathetic uselessness of martyrdom, all its wasted beauty. But, as I was saying, you must not think I have not suffered. If you had come in yesterday at a particular moment—

about half-past five, perhaps, or a quarter to six—you would have found me in tears. Even Harry, who was here, who brought me the news, in fact, had no idea what I was going through. I suffered immensely. Then it passed away. I cannot repeat an emotion. No one can, except sentimentalists. And you are awfully unjust, Basil. You come down here to console me. That is charming of you. You find me consoled, and you are furious. How like a sympathetic person! You remind me of a story Harry told me about a certain philanthropist who spent twenty years of his life in trying to get some grievance redressed, or some unjust law altered—I forget exactly what it was. Finally he succeeded, and nothing could exceed his disappointment. He had absolutely nothing to do, almost died of *ennui*, and became a confirmed misanthrope. And besides, my dear old Basil, if you really want to console me, teach me rather to forget what has happened, or to see it from a proper artistic point of view. Was it not Gautier who used to write about *la consolation des arts*[121]? I remember picking up a little vellum-covered book in your studio one day and chancing on that delightful phrase. Well, I am not like that young man you told me of when we were down at Marlow together, the young man who used to say that yellow satin could console one for all the miseries of life. I love beautiful things that one can touch and handle. Old brocades, green bronzes, lacquer-work, carved ivories, exquisite surroundings, luxury, pomp, there is much to be got from all these. But the artistic temperament that they create, or at any rate reveal, is still more to me. To become the spectator of one's own life, as Harry says, is to escape the suffering of life. I know you are surprised at my talking to you like this. You have not realised how I have developed. I was a schoolboy when you knew me. I am a man now. I have new passions, new thoughts, new ideas. I am different, but you must not like me less. I am changed, but you must always be my friend. Of course I am very fond of Harry. But I know that you are better than he is. You are not stronger—you are too much afraid of life—but you are better. And how happy we used to be together! Don't leave me, Basil, and don't quarrel with me. I am what I am. There is nothing more to be said.'

The painter felt strangely moved. The lad was infinitely dear to him, and his personality had been the great turning-point[122] in his art. He could not bear the idea of reproaching him any more. After all, his indifference was probably merely a mood that would pass away. There was so much in him that was good, so much in him that was noble.

'Well, Dorian,' he said, at length, with a sad smile, 'I won't speak to you again about this horrible thing, after to-day. I only trust your name won't be mentioned in connection with it. The inquest is to take place this afternoon. Have they summoned you?'

Dorian shook his head, and a look of annoyance passed over his face at the mention of the word 'inquest'. There was something so crude and vulgar about everything of the kind. 'They don't know my name,' he answered.

'But surely she did?'

'Only my Christian name, and that I am quite sure she never mentioned to any one. She told me once that they were all rather curious to learn who I was, and that she invariably told them my name was Prince Charming. It was pretty of her. You must do me a drawing of Sibyl, Basil. I should like to have something more of her than the memory of a few kisses and some broken pathetic words.'

'I will try and do something, Dorian, if it would please you. But you must come and sit to me yourself again. I can't get on without you.'

'I can never sit to you again, Basil. It is impossible!' he exclaimed, starting back.

The painter stared at him. 'My dear boy, what nonsense!' he cried. 'Do you mean to say you don't like what I did of you? Where is it? Why have you pulled the screen in front of it? Let me look at it. It is the best thing I have ever done. Do take the screen away, Dorian. It is simply disgraceful of your servant hiding my work like that. I felt the room looked different as I came in.'

'My servant has nothing to do with it, Basil. You don't imagine I let him arrange my room for me? He settles my flowers for me sometimes—that is all. No; I did it myself. The light was too strong on the portrait.'

'Too strong! Surely not, my dear fellow? It is an admirable place for it. Let me see it.' And Hallward walked towards the corner of the room.

A cry of terror broke from Dorian Gray's lips, and he rushed between the painter and the screen. 'Basil,' he said, looking very pale, 'you must not look at it. I don't wish you to.'

'Not look at my own work! you are not serious. Why shouldn't I look at it?' exclaimed Hallward, laughing.

'If you try to look at it, Basil, on my word of honour I will never speak to you again as long as I live. I am quite serious. I don't offer any explanation, and you are not to ask for any. But, remember, if you touch this screen, everything is over between us.'

Hallward was thunderstruck. He looked at Dorian Gray in absolute amazement. He had never seen him like this before. The lad was actually pallid with rage. His hands were clenched, and the pupils of his eyes were like discs of blue fire. He was trembling all over.

'Dorian!'

'Don't speak!'

'But what is the matter? Of course I won't look at it if you don't want me to,' he said, rather coldly, turning on his heel, and going over towards the window. 'But, really, it seems rather absurd that I shouldn't see my own work, especially as I am going to exhibit it in Paris in the autumn. I shall probably have to give it another coat of varnish before that, so I must see it some day, and why not to-day?'

'To exhibit it! You want to exhibit it?' exclaimed Dorian Gray, a strange sense of terror creeping over him. Was the world going to be shown his secret? Were people to gape at the mystery of his life? That was impossible. Something—he did not know what—had to be done at once.

'Yes; I don't suppose you will object to that. Georges Petit is going to collect all my best pictures for a special exhibition in the

Rue de Sèze[123], which will open the first week in October. The portrait will only be away a month. I should think you could easily spare it for that time. In fact, you are sure to be out of town. And if you keep it always behind a screen, you can't care much about it.'

Dorian Gray passed his hand over his forehead. There were beads of perspiration there. He felt that he was on the brink of a horrible danger. 'You told me a month ago that you would never exhibit it,' he cried. 'Why have you changed your mind? You people who go in for being consistent have just as many moods as others have. The only difference is that your moods are rather meaningless. You can't have forgotten that you assured me most solemnly that nothing in the world would induce you to send it to any exhibition. You told Harry exactly the same thing.' He stopped suddenly, and a gleam of light came into his eyes. He remembered that Lord Henry had said to him once, half seriously and half in jest, 'If you want to have a strange quarter of an hour, get Basil to tell you why he won't exhibit your picture. He told me why he wouldn't, and it was a revelation to me.' Yes, perhaps Basil, too, had his secret. He would ask him and try.

'Basil,' he said, coming over quite close, and looking him straight in the face, 'we have each of us a secret. Let me know yours, and I shall tell you mine. What was your reason for refusing to exhibit my picture?'

The painter shuddered in spite of himself. 'Dorian, if I told you, you might like me less than you do, and you would certainly laugh at me. I could not bear your doing either of those two things. If you wish me never to look at your picture again, I am content. I have always you to look at. If you wish the best work I have ever done to be hidden from the world, I am satisfied. Your friendship is dearer to me than any fame or reputation.'

'No, Basil, you must tell me,' insisted Dorian Gray. 'I think I have a right to know.' His feeling of terror had passed away, and curiosity had taken its place. He was determined to find out Basil Hallward's mystery.

'Let us sit down, Dorian,' said the painter, looking troubled. 'Let us sit down. And just answer me one question. Have you noticed in the picture something curious?—something that probably at first did not strike you, but that revealed itself to you suddenly?'

'Basil!' cried the lad, clutching the arms of his chair with trembling hands, and gazing at him with wild, startled eyes.

'I see you did. Don't speak. Wait till you hear what I have to say. Dorian, from the moment I met you, your personality had the most extraordinary influence over me. I was dominated, soul, brain, and power by you. You became to me the visible incarnation of that unseen ideal whose memory haunts us artists like an exquisite dream. I worshipped you. I grew jealous of every one to whom you spoke. I wanted to have you all to myself. I was only happy when I was with you. When you were away from me you were still present in my art....Of course I never let you know anything about this. It would have been impossible. You would not have understood it. I hardly understood it myself. I only knew that I had seen perfection face to face, and that the world had become wonderful to my eyes—too wonderful, perhaps, for in such mad worships there is peril, the peril of losing them, no less than the peril of keeping them....Weeks and weeks went on, and I grew more and more absorbed in you. Then came a new development. I had drawn you as Paris in dainty armour, and as Adonis with huntsman's cloak and polished boar-spear[124]. Crowned with heavy lotus-blossoms[125] you had sat on the prow of Adrian's barge, gazing across the green turbid Nile. You had leant over the still pool of some Greek woodland, and seen in the water's silent silver the marvel of your own face. And it had all been what art should be, unconscious, ideal, and remote. One day, a fatal day I sometimes think, I determined to paint a wonderful portrait of you as you actually are, not in the costume of dead ages, but in your own dress and in your own time. Whether it was the Realism of the method, or the mere wonder of your own personality, thus directly presented to me without mist or veil, I cannot tell. But I know that as I worked at it, every flake and film of colour seemed to me to reveal my secret. I grew afraid that others would know of my idolatry. I felt, Dorian, that I had told too much, that I had put too much of myself into it. Then it was that I resolved never to allow the picture to be exhibited. You were a little annoyed; but then you did not realise all that it meant to me. Harry, to whom I talked about it, laughed at me. But I did not mind that. When the picture was finished, and I sat alone with it, I felt that I was right....Well, after a few days the thing left my studio, and as soon as I had got rid of the intolerable fascination of its presence it seemed to me that I had been foolish in imagining that I had seen anything in it, more than that you were extremely good-looking and that I could paint. Even now I cannot help feeling that it is a mistake to think that the passion one feels in creation is ever really shown in the work one creates. Art is always more abstract than we fancy. Form and colour tell us of form and colour—that is all. It often seems to me that art conceals the artist far more completely than it ever reveals him. And so when I got this offer from Paris I determined to make your portrait the principal thing in my exhibition. It never occurred to me that you would refuse. I see now that you were right. The picture cannot be shown. You must not be angry with me, Dorian, for what I have told you. As I said to Harry, once, you are made to be worshipped.'

Dorian Gray drew a long breath. The colour came back to his cheeks, and a smile played about his lips. The peril was over. He was safe for the time. Yet he could not help feeling infinite pity for the painter who had just made this strange confession to him, and wondered if he himself would ever be so dominated by the personality of a friend. Lord Henry had the charm of being very dangerous. But that was all. He was too clever and too cynical to be really fond of. Would there ever be some one who would fill him with a strange idolatry? Was that one of the things that life had in store?

'It is extraordinary to me, Dorian,' said Hallward, 'that you should have seen this in the portrait. Did you really see it?'

'I saw something in it,' he answered, 'something that seemed to me very curious.'

'Well, you don't mind my looking at the thing now?'

Dorian shook his head. 'You must not ask me that, Basil. I could not possibly let you stand in front of that picture.'

'You will some day, surely?'

'Never.'

'Well, perhaps you are right. And now good-bye, Dorian. You have been the one person in my life who has really influenced my art. Whatever I have done that is good, I owe to you. Ah! you don't know what it cost me to tell you all that I have told you.'

'My dear Basil,' said Dorian, 'what have you told me? Simply that you felt that you admired me too much. That is not even a compliment.'

'It was not intended as a compliment. It was a confession. Now that I have made it, something seems to have gone out of me. Perhaps one should never put one's worship into words.'

'It was a very disappointing confession.'

'Why, what did you expect, Dorian? You didn't see anything else in the picture, did you? There was nothing else to see?'

'No; there was nothing else to see. Why do you ask? But you mustn't talk about worship. It is foolish. You and I are friends, Basil, and we must always remain so.'

'You have got Harry,' said the painter, sadly.

'Oh, Harry!' cried the lad, with a ripple of laughter. 'Harry spends his days in saying what is incredible, and his evenings in doing what is improbable. Just the sort of life I would like to lead. But still I don't think I would go to Harry if I were in trouble. I would sooner go to you, Basil.'

'You will sit to me again?'

'Impossible!'

'You spoil my life as an artist by refusing, Dorian. No man came across two ideal things. Few come across one.'

'I can't explain it to you, Basil, but I must never sit to you again. There is something fatal about a portrait. It has a life of its own. I will come and have tea with you. That will be just as pleasant.'

'Pleasanter for you, I am afraid,' murmured Hallward, regretfully. 'And now good-bye. I am sorry you won't let me look at the picture once again. But that can't be helped. I quite understand what you feel about it.'

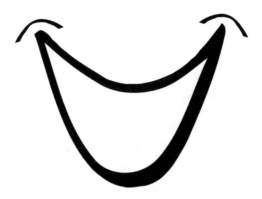

As he left the room, Dorian Gray smiled to himself. Poor Basil! how little he knew of the true reason! And how strange it was that, instead of having been forced to reveal his own secret, he had succeeded, almost by chance, in wresting a secret from his friend! How much that strange confession explained to him! The painter's absurd fits of jealousy, his wild devotion, his extravagant panegyrics, his curious reticences—he understood them all now, and he felt sorry. There seemed to him to be something tragic in a friendship so coloured by romance.

He sighed, and touched the bell. The portrait must be hidden away at all costs. He could not run such a risk of discovery again. It had been mad of him to have allowed the thing to remain, even for an hour, in a room to which any of his friends had access.

Chapter 10

When his servant entered, he looked at him steadfastly, and wondered if he had thought of peering behind the screen. The man was quite impassive, and waited for his orders. Dorian lit a cigarette, and walked over to the glass and glanced into it. He could see the reflection of Victor's face perfectly. It was like a placid mask of servility. There was nothing to be afraid of, there. Yet he thought it best to be on his guard.

Speaking very slowly, he told him to tell the housekeeper that he wanted to see her, and then to go to the frame-maker and ask him to send two of his men round at once. It seemed to him that as the man left the room his eyes wandered in the direction of the screen. Or was that merely his own fancy?

After a few moments, in her black silk dress, with old-fashioned thread mittens on her wrinkled hands, Mrs Leaf bustled into the library. He asked her for the key of the schoolroom.

'The old schoolroom, Mr Dorian?' she exclaimed. 'Why, it is full of dust. I must get it arranged, and put straight before you go into it. It is not fit for you to see, sir. It is not, indeed.'

'I don't want it put straight, Leaf. I only want the key.'

'Well, sir, you'll be covered with cobwebs if you go into it. Why, it hasn't been opened for nearly five years, not since his lordship died.'

He winced at the mention of his grandfather. He had hateful memories of him. 'That does not matter,' he answered. 'I simply want to see the place—that is all. Give me the key.'

'And here is the key, sir,' said the old lady, going over the contents of her bunch with tremulously uncertain hands. 'Here is the key. I'll have it off the bunch in a moment. But you don't think of living up there, sir, and you so comfortable here?'

'No, no,' he cried, petulantly. 'Thank you, Leaf. That will do.'

She lingered for a few moments, and was garrulous over some detail of the household. He sighed, and told her to manage things as she thought best. She left the room, wreathed in smiles.

As the door closed, Dorian put the key in his pocket, and looked round the room. His eye fell on a large purple satin coverlet heavily embroidered with gold, a splendid piece of late seventeenth-century Venetian work that his grandfather had found in a convent near Bologna. Yes, that would serve to wrap the dreadful thing in. It had perhaps served often as a pall for the dead. Now it was to hide something that had a corruption of its own, worse than the corruption of death itself—something that would breed horrors and yet would never die. What the worm was to the corpse, his sins would be to the painted image on the canvas. They would mar its beauty, and eat away its grace. They would defile it, and make it shameful. And yet the thing would still live on. It would be always alive.

He shuddered, and for a moment he regretted that he had not told Basil the true reason why he had wished to hide the picture away. Basil would have helped him to resist Lord Henry's influence, and the still more poisonous influences that came from his own temperament. The love that he bore him—for it was really love—had nothing in it that was not noble and intellectual. It was not that mere physical admiration of beauty that is born of the senses, and that dies when the senses tire. It was such love as Michael Angelo had known, and Montaigne, and Winckelmann, and Shakespeare himself. Yes, Basil could have saved him. But it was too late now. The past could always be annihilated. Regret, denial, or forgetfulness could do that. But the future was inevitable. There were passions in him that would find their terrible outlet, dreams that would make the shadow of their real evil.

He took up from the couch the great purple-and-gold texture that covered it, and, holding it in his hands, passed behind the screen. Was the face on the canvas viler than before? It seemed to him that it was unchanged; and yet his loathing of it was intensified. Gold hair, blue eyes, and rose-red lips—they all were there. It was simply the expression that had altered. That was horrible in its cruelty. Compared to what he saw in it of censure or rebuke, how shallow Basil's reproaches about Sibyl Vane had been!—how shallow, and of what little account! His own soul was looking out at him from the canvas and calling him to judgement. A look of pain came across him, and he flung the rich pall over the picture. As he did so, a knock came to the door. He passed out as his servant entered.

'The persons are here, Monsieur.'

He felt that the man must be got rid of at once. He must not be allowed to know where the picture was being taken to. There was something sly about him, and he had thoughtful, treacherous eyes. Sitting down at the writing-table[126], he scribbled a note to Lord Henry, asking him to send him round something to read, and reminding him that they were to meet at eight-fifteen that evening.

'Wait for an answer,' he said, handing it to him, 'and show the men in here.'

In two or three minutes there was another knock, and Mr Hubbard himself, the celebrated frame-maker of South Audley Street, came in with a somewhat rough-looking young assistant. Mr Hubbard was a florid, red-whiskered little man, whose admiration for art was considerably tempered by the inveterate impecuniosity of most of the artists who dealt with him. As a rule, he never left his shop. He waited for people to come to him. But he always made an exception in favour of Dorian Gray. There was something about Dorian that charmed everybody. It was a pleasure even to see him.

'What can I do for you, Mr Gray?' he said, rubbing his fat freckled hands. 'I thought I would do myself the honour of coming round in person. I have just got a beauty of a frame, sir. Picked it up at a sale. Old Florentine. Came from Fonthill, I believe. Admirably suited for a religious subject, Mr Gray.'

'I am so sorry you have given yourself the trouble of coming round, Mr Hubbard. I shall certainly drop in and look at the frame—though I don't go in much at present for religious art—but to-day I only want a picture carried to the top of the house for me. It is rather heavy, so I thought I would ask you to lend me a couple of your men.'

'No trouble at all, Mr Gray. I am delighted to be of any service to you. Which is the work of art, sir?'

'This,' replied Dorian, moving the screen back. 'Can you move it, covering and all, just as it is? I don't want it to get scratched going upstairs.'

'There will be no difficulty, sir,' said the genial frame-maker, beginning, with the aid of his assistant, to unhook the picture from the long brass chains by which it was suspended. 'And, now, where shall we carry it to, Mr Gray?'

'I will show you the way, Mr Hubbard, if you will kindly follow me. Or perhaps you had better go in front. I am afraid it is right at the top of the house. We will go up by the front staircase, as it is wider.'

He held the door open for them, and they passed out into the hall and began the ascent. The elaborate character of the frame had made the picture extremely bulky, and now and then, in spite of the obsequious protests of Mr Hubbard, who had the true tradesman's spirited dislike of seeing a gentleman doing anything useful, Dorian put his hand to it so as to help them.

'Something of a load to carry, sir,' gasped the little man, when they reached the top landing. And he wiped his shiny forehead.

'I am afraid it is rather heavy,' murmured Dorian, as he unlocked the door that opened into the room that was to keep for him the curious secret of his life and hide his soul from the eyes of men.

He had not entered the place for more than four years—not, indeed, since he had used it first as a play-room[127] when he was a child, and then as a study when he grew somewhat older. It was a large, well-proportioned room, which had been specially built by the last Lord Kelso for the use of the little grandson whom, for his strange likeness to his mother, and also for other reasons, he had always hated and desired to keep at a distance. It appeared to Dorian to have but little changed. There was the huge Italian *cassone*, with its fantastically-painted panels and its tarnished gilt mouldings, in which he had so often hidden himself as a boy. There the satinwood bookcase filled with his dog-eared schoolbooks. On the wall behind it was hanging the same ragged

Flemish tapestry where a faded king and queen were playing chess in a garden, while a company of hawkers rode by, carrying hooded birds on their gauntleted wrists. How well he remembered it all! Every moment of his lonely childhood came back to him as he looked round. He recalled the stainless purity of his boyish life, and it seemed horrible to him that it was here the fatal portrait was to be hidden away. How little he had thought, in those dead days, of all that was in store for him!

But there was no other place in the house so secure from prying eyes as this. He had the key, and no one else could enter it. Beneath its purple pall, the face painted on the canvas could grow bestial, sodden, and unclean. What did it matter? No one could see it. He himself would not see it. Why should he watch the hideous corruption of his soul? He kept his youth—that was enough. And, besides, might not his nature grow finer, after all? There was no reason that the future should be so full of shame. Some love might come across his life, and purify him, and shield him from those sins that seemed to be already stirring in spirit and in flesh—those curious unpictured sins whose very mystery lent them their subtlety and their charm. Perhaps, some day, the cruel look would have passed away from the scarlet sensitive mouth, and he might show to the world Basil Hallward's masterpiece.

No; that was impossible. Hour by hour, and week by week, the thing upon the canvas was growing old. It might escape the hideousness of sin, but the hideousness of age was in store for it. The cheeks would become hollow or flaccid. Yellow crow's-feet would creep round the fading eyes and make them horrible. The hair would lose its brightness, the mouth would gape or droop, would be foolish or gross, as the mouths of old men are.

There would be the wrinkled throat, the cold, blue-veined hands, the twisted body, that he remembered in the grandfather who had been so stern to him in his boyhood. The picture had to be concealed. There was no help for it.

'Bring it in, Mr Hubbard, please,' he said, wearily, turning round. 'I am sorry I kept you so long. I was thinking of something else.'

'Always glad to have a rest, Mr Gray,' answered the frame-maker, who was still gasping for breath. 'Where shall we put it, sir?'

'Oh, anywhere. Here: this will do. I don't want to have it hung up. Just lean it against the wall. Thanks.'

'Might one look at the work of art, sir?'

Dorian started. 'It would not interest you, Mr Hubbard,' he said, keeping his eye on the man. He felt ready to leap upon him and fling him to the ground if he dared to lift the gorgeous hanging that concealed the secret of his life. 'I sha'n't[128] trouble you any more now. I am much obliged for your kindness in coming round.'

'Not at all, not at all, Mr Gray. Ever ready to do anything for you, sir.' And Mr Hubbard tramped downstairs, followed by the assistant, who glanced back at Dorian with a look of shy wonder in his rough, uncomely face. He had never seen any one so marvellous.

When the sound of their footsteps had died away, Dorian locked the door, and put the key in his pocket. He felt safe now. No one would ever look upon the horrible thing. No eye but his would ever see his shame.

On reaching the library, he found that it was just after five o'clock, and that the tea had been already brought up. On a little table of dark perfumed wood thickly incrusted with nacre, a present from Lady Radley, his guardian's wife, a pretty professional invalid, who had spent the preceding winter in Cairo, was lying a note from Lord Henry, and beside it was a book bound in yellow paper, the cover slightly torn and the edges soiled. A copy of the third edition of *The St. James's Gazette* had been placed on the tea-tray. It was evident that Victor had returned. He wondered if he had met the men in the hall as they were leaving the house, and had wormed out of them what they had been doing. He would be sure to miss the picture—had no doubt missed it already, while he had been laying the tea-things. The screen had not been set back, and a blank space was visible on the wall. Perhaps some night he might find him creeping upstairs and trying to force the door of the room. It was a horrible thing to have a spy in one's house. He had heard of rich men who had been blackmailed all their lives by some servant who had read a letter, or overheard a conversation, or picked up a card with an address, or found beneath a pillow a withered flower or a shred of crumpled lace.

He sighed, and, having poured himself out some tea, opened Lord Henry's note. It was simply to say that he sent him round the evening paper, and a book that might interest him, and that he would be at the club at eight-fifteen. He opened *The St. James's* languidly, and looked through it. A red pencil-mark[129] on the fifth page caught his eye. It drew attention to the following paragraph: —

'INQUEST ON AN ACTRESS.—An inquest was held this morning at the Bell Tavern, Hoxton Road, by Mr Danby, the District Coroner, on the body of Sibyl Vane, a young actress recently engaged at the Royal Theatre, Holborn. A verdict of death by misadventure was returned. Considerable sympathy was expressed for the mother of the deceased, who was greatly affected during the giving of her own evidence, and that of Dr Birrell, who had made the post-mortem examination of the deceased.'

He frowned, and, tearing the paper in two, went across the room and flung the pieces away. How ugly it all was! And how horribly real ugliness made things! He felt a little annoyed with Lord Henry for having sent him the report. And it was certainly stupid of him to have marked it with red pencil. Victor might have read it. The man knew more than enough English for that.

Perhaps he had read it, and had begun to suspect something. And, yet, what did it matter? What had Dorian Gray to do with Sibyl Vane's death? There was nothing to fear. Dorian Gray had not killed her.

His eye fell on the yellow book that Lord Henry had sent him. What was it, he wondered. He went towards the little pearl-coloured octagonal stand, that had always looked to him like the work of some strange Egyptian bees that wrought in silver, and taking up the volume, flung himself into an arm-chair, and began to turn over the leaves. After a few minutes he became absorbed. It was the strangest book that he had ever read. It seemed to him that in exquisite raiment, and to the delicate sound of flutes, the sins of the world were passing in dumb show before him. Things that he had dimly dreamed of were suddenly made real to him. Things of which he had never dreamed were gradually revealed.

It was a novel without a plot, and with only one character, being, indeed, simply a psychological study of a certain young Parisian, who spent his life trying to realise in the nineteenth century all the passions and modes of thought that belonged to every century except his own, and to sum up, as it were, in himself the various moods through which the world-spirit[130] had ever passed, loving for their mere artificiality those renunciations that men have unwisely called virtue, as much as those natural rebellions that wise men still call sin. The style in which it was written was that curious jewelled style, vivid and obscure at once, full of *argot* and of archaisms, of technical expressions and of elaborate paraphrases, that characterizes the work of some of the finest artists of the French school of *Symbolistes*[131]. There were in it metaphors as monstrous as orchids, and as subtle in colour. The life of the senses was described in the terms of mystical philosophy. One hardly knew at times whether one was reading the spiritual ecstasies of some mediaeval saint or the morbid confessions of a modern sinner. It was a poisonous book. The heavy odour of incense seemed to cling about its pages and to trouble the brain. The mere cadence of the sentences, the subtle monotony of their music, so full as it was of complex refrains and movements elaborately repeated, produced in the mind of the lad, as he passed from chapter to chapter, a form of reverie, a malady of dreaming, that made him unconscious of the falling day and creeping shadows.

Cloudless, and pierced by one solitary star, a copper-green sky gleamed through the windows. He read on by its wan light till he could read no more. Then, after his valet had reminded him several times of the lateness of the hour, he got up, and going into the next room, placed the book on the little Florentine table that always stood at his bedside, and began to dress for dinner.

It was almost nine o'clock before he reached the club, where he found Lord Henry sitting alone, in the morning-room[132], looking very much bored.

'I am so sorry, Harry,' he cried, 'but really it is entirely your fault. That book you sent me so fascinated me that I forgot how the time was going.'

'Yes: I thought you would like it,' replied his host, rising from his chair.

'I didn't say I liked it, Harry. I said it fascinated me. There is a great difference.'

'Ah, you have discovered that?' murmured Lord Henry. And they passed into the dining-room.

Chapter 11

For years, Dorian Gray could not free himself from the influence of this book. Or perhaps it would be more accurate to say that he never sought to free himself from it. He procured from Paris no less than nine large-paper copies of the first edition, and had them bound in different colours, so that they might suit his various moods and the changing fancies of a nature over which he seemed, at times, to have almost entirely lost control. The hero, the wonderful young Parisian, in whom the romantic and the scientific temperaments were so strangely blended, became to him a kind of prefiguring type of himself. And, indeed, the whole book seemed to him to contain the story of his own life, written before he had lived it.

In one point he was more fortunate than the novel's fantastic hero. He never knew—never, indeed, had any cause to know—that somewhat grotesque dread of mirrors, and polished metal surfaces, and still water, which came upon the young Parisian so early in his life, and was occasioned by the sudden decay of a beauty that had once, apparently, been so remarkable. It was with an almost cruel joy—and perhaps in nearly every joy, as certainly in every pleasure, cruelty has its place—that he used to read the latter part of the book, with its really tragic, if somewhat over-emphasized, account of the sorrow and despair of one who had himself lost what in others, and in the world, he had most dearly valued.

For the wonderful beauty that had so fascinated Basil Hallward, and many others besides him, seemed never to leave him. Even those who had heard the most evil things against him, and from time to time strange rumours about his mode of life crept through London and became the chatter of the clubs, could not believe anything to his dishonour when they saw him. He had always the look of one who had kept himself unspotted from the world. Men who talked grossly became silent when Dorian Gray entered the room. There was something in the purity of his face that rebuked them. His mere presence seemed to recall to them the memory of the innocence that they had tarnished. They wondered how one so charming and graceful as he was could have escaped the stain of an age that was at once sordid and sensual.

Often, on returning home from one of those mysterious and prolonged absences that gave rise to such strange conjecture among those who were his friends, or thought that they were so, he himself would creep upstairs to the locked room, open the door with the key that never left him now, and stand, with a mirror, in front of the portrait that Basil Hallward had painted of him, looking now at the evil and aging face on the canvas, and now at the fair young face that laughed back at him from the polished glass. The very sharpness of the contrast used to quicken his sense of pleasure. He grew more and more enamoured of his own beauty, more and more interested in the corruption of his own soul. He would examine with minute care, and sometimes with a monstrous and terrible delight, the hideous lines that seared the wrinkling forehead or crawled around the heavy sensual mouth, wondering sometimes which were the more horrible, the signs of sin or the signs of age. He would place his white hands beside the coarse bloated hands of the picture, and smile. He mocked the misshapen body and the failing limbs.

There were moments, indeed, at night, when, lying sleepless in his own delicately-scented chamber, or in the sordid room of the little ill-famed tavern near the Docks, which, under an assumed name, and in disguise, it was his habit to frequent, he would think of the ruin he had brought upon his soul, with a pity that was all the more poignant, because it was purely selfish. But moments such as these were rare. That curiosity about life which Lord Henry had first stirred in him, as they sat together in the garden of their friend, seemed to increase with gratification. The more he knew, the more he desired to know. He had mad hungers that grew more ravenous as he fed them.

Yet he was not really reckless, at any rate in his relations to society. Once or twice every month during the winter, and on each Wednesday evening while the season lasted, he would throw open to the world his beautiful house and have the most celebrated musicians of the day to charm his guests with the wonders of their art. His little dinners, in the settling of which Lord Henry always assisted him, were noted as much for the careful selection and placing of those invited, as for the exquisite taste shown in the decoration of the table, with its subtle symphonic arrangements of exotic flowers, and embroidered cloths, and antique plate of gold and silver. Indeed, there were many, especially among the very young men, who saw, or fancied that they saw, in Dorian Gray the true realization of a type of which they had often dreamed in Eton or Oxford days, a type that was to combine something of the real culture of the scholar with all the grace and distinction and perfect manner of a citizen of the world. To them he seemed to be of the company of those whom Dante describes as having sought to 'make themselves perfect by the worship of beauty'. Like Gautier, he was one for whom 'the visible world existed'.

And, certainly, to him Life itself was the first, the greatest, of the arts, and for it all the other arts seemed to be but a preparation. Fashion, by which what is really fantastic becomes for a moment universal, and Dandyism, which, in its own way, is an attempt to assert the absolute modernity of beauty, had, of course, their fascination for him. His mode of dressing, and the particular styles that from time to time he affected, had their marked influence on the young exquisites of the Mayfair balls and Pall Mall club windows, who copied him in everything that he did, and tried to reproduce the accidental charm of his graceful, though to him only half-serious, fopperies.

For, while he was but too ready to accept the position that was almost immediately offered to him on his coming of age, and found, indeed, a subtle pleasure in the thought that he might really become to the London of his own day what to imperial Neronian Rome the author of the 'Satyricon' once had been, yet in his inmost heart he desired to be something more than a mere *arbiter elegantiarum*, to be consulted on the wearing of a jewel, or the knotting of a necktie, or the conduct of a cane. He sought to elaborate some new scheme of life that would have its reasoned philosophy and its ordered principles, and find in the spiritualizing of the senses its highest realization.

The worship of the senses has often, and with much justice, been decried, men feeling a natural instinct of terror about passions and sensations that seem stronger than themselves, and that they are conscious of sharing with the less highly organized forms of existence. But it appeared to Dorian Gray that the true nature of the senses had never been understood, and that they had remained savage and animal merely because the world had sought to starve them into submission or to kill them by pain, instead of aiming at making them elements of a new spirituality, of which a fine instinct for beauty was to be the dominant characteristic. As he looked back upon man moving through History, he was haunted by a feeling of loss. So much had been surrendered! and to such little purpose! There had been mad wilful rejections, monstrous forms of self-torture and self-denial, whose origin was fear, and whose result was a degradation infinitely more terrible than that fancied degradation from which, in their ignorance, they had sought to escape, Nature, in her wonderful irony, driving out the anchorite to feed with the wild animals of the desert and giving to the hermit the beasts of the field as his companions.

Yes: there was to be, as Lord Henry had prophesied, a new Hedonism that was to recreate life, and to save it from that harsh, uncomely puritanism that is having, in our own day, its curious revival. It was to have its service of the intellect, certainly; yet it was never to accept any theory or system that would involve the sacrifice of any mode of passionate experience. Its aim, indeed, was to be experience itself, and not the fruits of experience, sweet or bitter as they might be. Of the asceticism that deadens the senses, as of the vulgar profligacy that dulls them, it was to know nothing. But it was to teach man to concentrate himself upon the moments of a life that is itself but a moment.

There are few of us who have not sometimes wakened before dawn, either after one of those dreamless nights that make us almost enamoured of death, or one of those nights of horror and misshapen joy, when through the chambers of the brain sweep phantoms more terrible than reality itself, and instinct with that vivid life that lurks in all grotesques, and that lends to Gothic art its enduring vitality, this art being, one might fancy, especially the art of those whose minds have been troubled with the malady of reverie. Gradually white fingers creep through the curtains, and they appear to tremble. In black fantastic shapes, dumb shadows crawl into the corners of the room, and crouch there. Outside, there is the stirring of birds among the leaves, or the sound of men going forth to their work, or the sigh and sob of the wind coming down from the hills, and wandering round the silent house, as though it feared to wake the sleepers, and yet must needs call forth sleep from her purple cave. Veil after veil of thin dusky gauze is lifted, and by degrees the forms and colours of things are restored to them, and we watch the dawn remaking the world in its antique pattern. The wan mirrors get back their mimic life. The flameless tapers stand where we had left them, and beside them lies the half-cut book that we had been studying, or the wired flower that we had worn at the ball, or the letter that we had been afraid to read, or that we had read too often. Nothing seems to us changed. Out of the unreal shadows of the night comes back the real life that we had known. We have to resume it where we had left off, and there steals over us a terrible sense of the necessity for the continuance of energy in the same wearisome round of stereotyped habits, or a wild longing, it may be, that our eyelids might open some morning upon a world that had been refashioned anew in the darkness for our pleasure, a world in which things would have fresh shapes and colours, and be changed, or have other secrets, a world in which the past would have little or no place, or survive, at any rate, in no conscious form of obligation or regret, the remembrance even of joy having its bitterness, and the memories of pleasure their pain.

It was the creation of such worlds as these that seemed to Dorian Gray to be the true object, or amongst the true objects, of life; and in his search for sensations that would be at once new and delightful, and possess that element of strangeness that is so essential to romance, he would often adopt certain modes of thought that he knew to be really alien to his nature, abandon himself to their subtle influences, and then, having, as it were, caught their colour and satisfied his intellectual curiosity, leave them with that curious indifference that is not incompatible with a real ardour of temperament, and that indeed, according to certain modern psychologists, is often a condition of it.

It was rumoured of him once that he was about to join the Roman Catholic communion; and certainly the Roman ritual had always a great attraction for him. The daily sacrifice, more awful really than all the sacrifices of the antique world, stirred him as much by its superb rejection of the evidence of the senses as by the primitive simplicity of its elements and the eternal pathos of the human tragedy that it sought to symbolize. He loved to kneel down on the cold marble pavement, and watch the priest, in his stiff flowered dalmatic, slowly and with white hands moving aside the veil of the tabernacle, or raising aloft the jewelled lantern-shaped monstrance with that pallid water that at times, one would fain think, is indeed the '*panis caelestis*', the bread of angels, or, robed in the garments of the Passion of Christ, breaking the Host into the chalice, and smiting his breast for his sins. The fuming censers, that the grave boys, in their lace and scarlet, tossed into the air like great gilt flowers, had their subtle fascination for him. As he passed out, he used to look with wonder at the black confessionals, and long to sit in the dim shadow of one of them and listen to men and women whispering through the worn grating the true story of their lives.

But he never fell into the error of arresting his intellectual development by any formal acceptance of creed or system, or of mistaking, for a house in which to live, an inn that is but suitable for the sojourn of a night, or for a few hours of a night in which there are no stars and the moon is in travail. Mysticism, with its marvellous power of making common things strange to us, and the subtle antinomianism that always seems to accompany it, moved him for a season; and for a season he inclined to the materialistic doctrines of the *Darwinismus* movement in Germany, and found a curious pleasure in tracing the thoughts and passions of men to some pearly cell in the brain, or some white nerve in the body, delighting in the conception of the absolute dependence of the spirit on certain physical conditions, morbid or healthy, normal or diseased. Yet, as has been said of him before, no theory of life seemed to him to be of any importance compared with life itself. He felt keenly conscious of how barren all intellectual speculation is when separated from action and experiment. He knew that the senses, no less than the soul, have their spiritual mysteries to reveal.

And so he would now study perfumes, and the secrets of their manufacture, distilling heavily-scented oils, and burning odorous gums from the East. He saw that there was no mood of the mind that had not its counterpart in the sensuous life, and set himself to discover their true relations, wondering what there was in frankincense that made one mystical, and in ambergris that stirred one's passions, and in violets that woke the memory of dead romances, and in musk that troubled the brain, and in champak that stained the imagination; and seeking often to elaborate a real psychology of perfumes, and to estimate the several influences of sweet-smelling roots, and scented pollen-laden flowers, of aromatic balms, and of dark and fragrant woods, of spikenard that sickens, of hovenia that makes men mad, and of aloes that are said to be able to expel melancholy from the soul.

At another time he devoted himself entirely to music, and in a long latticed room, with a vermilion-and-gold ceiling and walls of olive-green lacquer, he used to give curious concerts in which mad gypsies tore wild music from little zithers, or grave yellow-shawled Tunisians plucked at the strained strings of monstrous lutes, while grinning negroes beat monotonously upon copper drums, and, crouching upon scarlet mats, slim turbaned Indians blew through long pipes of reed or brass, and charmed, or feigned to charm, great hooded snakes and horrible horned adders. The harsh intervals and shrill discords of barbaric music stirred him at times when Schubert's grace, and Chopin's beautiful sorrows, and the mighty harmonies of Beethoven himself, fell unheeded on his ear. He collected together from all parts of the world the strangest instruments that could be found, either in the tombs of dead nations or among the few savage tribes that have survived contact with Western civilizations, and loved to touch and try them. He had the mysterious *juruparis* of the Rio Negro Indians, that women are not allowed to look at, and that even youths may not see till they have been subjected to fasting and scourging, and the earthen jars of the Peruvians that have the shrill cries of birds, and flutes of human bones such as Alfonso de Ovalle heard in Chili, and the sonorous green jaspers that are found near Cuzco and give forth a note of singular sweetness. He had painted gourds filled with pebbles that rattled when they were shaken; the long *clarin* of the Mexicans, into which the performer does not blow, but through which he inhales the air; the harsh *ture* of the Amazon tribes, that is sounded by the sentinels who sit all day long in high trees, and can be heard, it is said, at a distance of three leagues; the *teponaztli*, that has two vibrating tongues of wood, and is beaten with sticks that are smeared with an elastic gum obtained from the milky juice of plants; the *yotl*-bells of the Aztecs, that are hung in clusters like grapes; and a huge cylindrical drum, covered with the skins of great serpents, like the one that Bernal Diaz saw when he went with Cortes into the Mexican temple, and of whose doleful sound he has left us so vivid a description. The fantastic character of these instruments fascinated him, and he felt a curious delight in the thought that Art, like Nature, has her monsters, things of bestial shape and with hideous voices. Yet, after some time, he wearied of them, and would sit in his box at the Opera, either alone or with Lord Henry, listening in rapt pleasure to 'Tannhäuser', and seeing in the prelude to that great work of art a presentation of the tragedy of his own soul.

On one occasion he took up the study of jewels, and appeared at a costume ball as Anne de Joyeuse, Admiral of France, in a dress covered with five hundred and sixty pearls. This taste enthralled him for years, and, indeed, may be said never to have left him. He would often spend a whole day settling and resettling in their cases the various stones that he had collected, such as the olive-green chrysoberyl that turns red by lamplight, the cymophane with its wire-like line of silver, the pistachio-coloured peridot, rose-pink and wine-yellow topazes, carbuncles of fiery scarlet with tremulous four-rayed stars, flame-red cinnamon-stones[133], orange and violet spinels, and amethysts with their alternate layers of ruby and sapphire. He loved the red gold of the sunstone, and the moonstone's pearly whiteness, and the broken rainbow of the milky opal. He procured from Amsterdam three emeralds of extraordinary size and richness of colour, and had a turquoise *de la vieille roche* that was the envy of all the connoisseurs.

He discovered wonderful stories, also, about jewels. In Alphonso's 'Clericalis Disciplina' a serpent was mentioned with eyes of real jacinth, and in the romantic history of Alexander, the Conqueror of Emathia was said to have found in the vale of Jordan snakes 'with collars of real emeralds growing on their backs'. There was a gem in the brain of the dragon, Philostratus told us, and 'by the exhibition of golden letters and a scarlet robe' the monster could be thrown into a magical sleep, and slain. According to the great alchemist, Pierre de Boniface, the diamond rendered a man invisible, and the agate of India made him eloquent. The cornelian appeased anger, and the hyacinth provoked sleep, and the amethyst drove away the fumes of wine. The garnet cast out demons, and the hydropicus deprived the moon of her colour. The selenite waxed and waned with the moon, and the meloceus, that discovers thieves, could be affected only by the blood of kids. Leonardus Camillus had seen a white stone taken from the brain of a newly-killed toad, that was a certain antidote against poison. The bezoar, that was found in the heart of the Arabian deer, was a charm that could cure the plague. In the nests of Arabian birds was the aspilates, that, according to Democritus, kept the wearer from any danger by fire.

The King of Ceilan rode through his city with a large ruby in his hand, as the ceremony of his coronation. The gates of the palace of John the Priest were 'made of sardius, with the horn of the horned snake inwrought, so that no man might bring poison within'. Over the gable were 'two golden apples, in which were two carbuncles', so that the gold might shine by day, and the carbuncles by night. In Lodge's strange romance 'A Margarite of America' it was stated that in the chamber of the queen one could behold 'all the chaste ladies of the world, inchased out of silver, looking through fair mirrours of chrysolites, carbuncles, sapphires, and greene emeraults'. Marco Polo had seen the inhabitants of Zipangu place rose-coloured pearls in the mouths of the dead. A sea-monster[134] had been enamoured of the pearl that the diver brought to King Perozes, and had slain the thief, and mourned for seven moons over its loss. When the Huns lured the king into the great pit, he flung it away—Procopius tells the story—nor was it ever found again, though the Emperor Anastasius offered five hundred-weight of gold pieces for it. The King of Malabar had shown to a certain Venetian a rosary of three hundred and four pearls, one for every god that he worshipped. When the Duke de Valentinois, son of Alexander VI, visited Louis XII of France, his horse was loaded with gold leaves, according to Brantôme, and his cap had double rows of rubies that threw out a great light. Charles of England had ridden in stirrups hung with four hundred and twenty-one diamonds. Richard II had a coat, valued at thirty thousand marks, which was covered with balas rubies. Hall described Henry VIII, on his way to the Tower previous to his coronation, as wearing 'a jacket of raised gold, the placard embroidered with diamonds and other rich stones, and a great bauderike about his neck of large balasses'. The favourites of James I wore earrings of emeralds set in gold filigrane. Edward II gave to Piers Gaveston a suit of red-gold armour studded with jacinths, a collar of gold roses set with turquoise-stones[135], and a skull-cap[136] *parsemé* with pearls. Henry II wore jewelled gloves reaching to the elbow, and had a hawk-glove[137] sewn with twelve rubies and fifty-two great orients. The ducal hat of Charles the Rash, the last Duke of Burgundy of his race, was hung with pear-shaped pearls and studded with sapphires.

How exquisite life had once been! How gorgeous in its pomp and decoration! Even to read of the luxury of the dead was wonderful.

Then he turned his attention to embroideries, and to the tapestries that performed the office of frescoes in the chill rooms of the Northern nations of Europe. As he investigated the subject—and he always had an extraordinary faculty of becoming absolutely absorbed for the moment in whatever he took up— he was almost saddened by the reflection of the ruin that Time brought on beautiful and wonderful things. He, at any rate, had escaped that. Summer followed summer, and the yellow jonquils bloomed and died many times, and nights of horror repeated the story of their shame, but he was unchanged. No winter marred his face or stained his flower-like bloom. How different it was with material things! Where had they passed to? Where was the great crocus-coloured robe, on which the gods fought against the giants, that had been worked by grown girls for the pleasure of Athena? Where, the huge velarium that Nero had stretched across the Colosseum at Rome, that Titan sail of purple on which was represented the starry sky, and Apollo driving a chariot drawn by white gilt-reined steeds? He longed to see the curious table-napkins[138] wrought for the Priest of the Sun, on which were displayed all the dainties and viands that could be wanted for a feast; the mortuary cloth of King Chilperic, with its three hundred golden bees; the fantastic robes that excited the indignation of the Bishop of Pontus, and were figured with 'lions, panthers, bears, dogs, forests, rocks, hunters—all, in fact, that a painter can copy from nature'; and the coat that Charles of Orleans once wore, on the sleeves of which were embroidered the verses of a song beginning 'Madame, je suis tout joyeux'[139], the musical accompaniment of the words being wrought in gold thread, and each note, of square shape in those days, formed with four pearls. He read of the room that was prepared at the palace at Rheims for the use of Queen Joan of Burgundy, and was decorated with 'thirteen hundred and twenty-one parrots, made in broidery, and blazoned with the king's arms, and five hundred and sixty-one butterflies, whose wings were similarly ornamented with the arms of the queen, the whole worked in gold'. Catherine de Médicis had a mourning-bed[140] made for her of black velvet powdered with crescents and suns. Its curtains were of damask, with leafy wreaths and garlands, figured upon a gold and silver ground, and fringed along the edges with broideries of pearls, and it stood in a room hung with rows of the queen's devices in cut black velvet upon cloth of silver. Louis XIV had gold embroidered caryatides fifteen feet high in his apartment. The state bed of Sobieski, King of Poland, was made of Smyrna gold brocade embroidered in turquoises with verses from the Koran. Its supports were of silver gilt, beautifully chased, and profusely set with enamelled and jewelled medallions. It had been taken from the Turkish camp before Vienna, and the standard of Mohammed had stood beneath the tremulous gilt of its canopy.

And so, for a whole year, he sought to accumulate the most exquisite specimens that he could find of textile and embroidered work, getting the dainty Delhi muslins, finely wrought with gold-thread palmates and stitched over with iridescent beetles' wings; the Dacca gauzes, that from their transparency are known in the East as 'woven air', and 'running water', and 'evening dew'; strange figured cloths from Java; elaborate yellow Chinese hangings; books bound in tawny satins or fair blue silks, and wrought with *fleurs de lys*[141], birds, and images; veils of *lacis* worked in Hungary point; Sicilian brocades, and stiff Spanish velvets; Georgian work with its gilt coins, and Japanese *Foukousas* with their green-toned golds and their marvellously-plumaged birds.

He had a special passion, also, for ecclesiastical vestments, as indeed he had for everything connected with the service of the Church. In the long cedar chests that lined the west gallery of his house he had stored away many rare and beautiful specimens of what is really the raiment of the Bride of Christ, who must wear purple and jewels and fine linen that she may hide the pallid macerated body that is worn by the suffering that she seeks for, and wounded by self-inflicted pain. He possessed a gorgeous cope of crimson silk and gold-thread damask, figured with a repeating pattern of golden pomegranates set in six-petalled formal blossoms, beyond which on either side was the pineapple device wrought in seed-pearls[142]. The orphreys were divided into panels representing scenes from the life of the Virgin, and the coronation of the Virgin was figured in coloured silks upon the hood. This was Italian work of the fifteenth century. Another cope was of green velvet, embroidered with heart-shaped groups of acanthus-leaves[143], from which spread long-stemmed white blossoms, the details of which were picked out with silver thread and coloured crystals. The morse bore a seraph's head in gold-thread[144] raised work. The orphreys were woven in a diaper of red and gold silk, and were starred with medallions of many saints and martyrs, among whom was St. Sebastian. He had chasubles, also, of amber-coloured silk, and blue silk and gold brocade, and yellow silk damask and cloth of gold, figured with representations of the Passion and Crucifixion of Christ, and embroidered with lions and peacocks and other emblems; dalmatics of white satin and pink silk damask, decorated with tulips and dolphins and *fleurs de lys*; altar frontals of crimson velvet and blue linen; and many corporals, chalice-veils[145], and sudaria. In the mystic offices to which such things were put, there was something that quickened his imagination.

For these treasures, and everything that he collected in his lovely house, were to be Sto him means of forgetfulness, modes by which he could escape, for a season, from the fear that seemed to him at times to be almost too great to be borne. Upon the walls of the lonely locked room where he had spent so much of his boyhood, he had hung with his own hands the terrible portrait whose changing features showed him the real degradation of his life, and in front of it had draped the purple-and-gold pall as a curtain. For weeks he would not go there, would forget the hideous painted thing, and get back his light heart, his wonderful joyousness, his passionate absorption in mere existence. Then, suddenly, some night he would creep out of the house, go down to dreadful places near Blue Gate Fields, and stay there, day after day, until he was driven away. On his return he would sit in front of the picture, sometimes loathing it and himself, but filled, at other times, with that pride of individualism that is half the fascination of sin, and smiling, with secret pleasure, at the misshapen shadow that had to bear the burden that should have been his own.

After a few years he could not endure to be long out of England, and gave up the villa that he had shared at Trouville with Lord Henry, as well as the little white walled-in house at Algiers where they had more than once spent the winter. He hated to be separated from the picture that was such a part of his life, and was also afraid that during his absence some one might gain access to the room, in spite of the elaborate bars that he had caused to be placed upon the door.

He was quite conscious that this would tell them nothing. It was true that the portrait still preserved, under all the foulness and ugliness of the face, its marked likeness to himself; but what could they learn from that? He would laugh at any one who tried to taunt him. He had not painted it. What was it to him how vile and full of shame it looked? Even if he told them, would they believe it?

Yet he was afraid. Sometimes when he was down at his great house in Nottinghamshire, entertaining the fashionable young men of his own rank who were his chief companions, and astounding the county by the wanton luxury and gorgeous splendour of his mode of life, he would suddenly leave his guests and rush back to town to see that the door had not been tampered with, and that the picture was still there. What if it should be stolen? The mere thought made him cold with horror. Surely the world would know his secret then. Perhaps the world already suspected it.

For, while he fascinated many, there were not a few who distrusted him. He was very nearly blackballed at a West End club of which his birth and social position fully entitled him to become a member, and it was said that on one occasion, when he was brought by a friend into the smoking-room of the Churchill, the Duke of Berwick and another gentleman got up in a marked manner and went out. Curious stories became current about him after he had passed his twenty-fifth year. It was rumoured that he had been seen brawling with foreign sailors in a low den in the distant parts of Whitechapel, and that he consorted with thieves and coiners and knew the mysteries of their trade. His extraordinary absences became notorious, and, when he used to reappear again in society, men would whisper to each other in corners, or pass him with a sneer, or look at him with cold searching eyes, as though they were determined to discover his secret.

Of such insolences and attempted slights he, of course, took no notice, and in the opinion of most people his frank debonnair manner, his charming boyish smile, and the infinite grace of that wonderful youth that seemed never to leave him, were in themselves a sufficient answer to the calumnies, for so they termed them, that were circulated about him. It was remarked, however, that some of those who had been most intimate with him appeared, after a time, to shun him. Women who had wildly adored him, and for his sake had braved all social censure and set convention at defiance, were seen to grow pallid with shame or horror if Dorian Gray entered the room.

Yet these whispered scandals only increased in the eyes of many, his strange and dangerous charm. His great wealth was a certain element of security. Society, civilized society at least, is never very ready to believe anything to the detriment of those who are both rich and fascinating. It feels instinctively that manners are of more importance than morals, and, in its opinion, the highest respectability is of much less value than the possession of a good *chef*. And, after all, it is a very poor consolation to be told that the man who has given one a bad dinner, or poor wine, is irreproachable in his private life. Even the cardinal virtues cannot atone for half-cold *entrées*, as Lord Henry remarked once, in a discussion on the subject; and there is possibly a good deal to be said for his view. For the canons of good society are, or should be, the same as the canons of art. Form is absolutely essential to it. It should have the dignity of a ceremony, as well as its unreality, and should combine the insincere character of a romantic play with the wit and beauty that make such plays delightful to us. Is insincerity such a terrible thing? I think not. It is merely a method by which we can multiply our personalities.

Such, at any rate, was Dorian Gray's opinion. He used to wonder at the shallow psychology of those who conceive the Ego in man as a thing simple, permanent, reliable, and of one essence. To him, man was a being with myriad lives and myriad sensations, a complex multiform creature that bore within itself strange legacies of thought and passion, and whose very flesh was tainted with the monstrous maladies of the dead. He loved to stroll through the gaunt cold picture-gallery of his country house and look at the various portraits of those whose blood flowed in his veins. Here was Philip Herbert, described by Francis Osborne, in his 'Memoires on the Reigns of Queen Elizabeth and King James', as one who was 'caressed by the Court for his handsome face, which kept him not long company'. Was it young Herbert's life that he sometimes led? Had some strange poisonous germ crept from body to body till it had reached his own? Was it some dim sense of that ruined grace that had made him so suddenly, and almost without cause, give utterance, in Basil Hallward's studio, to the mad prayer that had so changed his life? Here, in gold-embroidered red doublet, jewelled surcoat, and gilt-edged ruff and wrist-bands, stood Sir Anthony Sherard, with his silver-and-black armour piled at his feet. What had this man's legacy been? Had the lover of Giovanna of Naples bequeathed him some inheritance of sin and shame? Were his own actions merely the dreams that the dead man had not dared to realise? Here, from the fading canvas, smiled Lady Elizabeth Devereux, in her gauze hood, pearl stomacher, and pink slashed sleeves. A flower was in her right hand, and her left clasped an enamelled collar of white and damask roses. On a table by her side lay a mandolin and an apple. There were large green rosettes upon her little pointed shoes. He knew her life, and the strange stories that were told about her lovers. Had he something of her temperament in him? These oval heavy-lidded eyes seemed to look curiously at him. What of George Willoughby, with his powdered hair and fantastic patches? How evil he looked! The face was saturnine and swarthy, and the sensual lips seemed to be twisted with disdain. Delicate lace ruffles fell over the lean yellow hands that were so overladen with rings. He had been a macaroni of the eighteenth century, and the friend, in his youth, of Lord Ferrars. What of the second Lord Beckenham, the companion of the Prince Regent in his wildest days, and one of the witnesses at the secret marriage with Mrs Fitzherbert? How proud and handsome he was, with his chestnut curls and insolent pose! What passions had he bequeathed? The world had looked upon him as infamous. He had led the orgies at Carlton House. The star of the Garter glittered upon his breast. Beside him hung the portrait of his wife, a pallid, thin-lipped woman in black. Her blood, also, stirred within him. How curious it all seemed! And his mother with her Lady Hamilton face, and her moist wine-dashed lips—he knew what he had got from her. He had got from her his beauty, and his passion for the beauty of others. She laughed at him in her loose Bacchante dress. There were vine leaves in her hair. The purple spilled from the cup she was holding. The carnations of the painting had withered, but the eyes were still wonderful in their depth and brilliancy of colour. They seemed to follow him wherever he went.

Yet one had ancestors in literature, as well as in one's own race, nearer perhaps in type and temperament, many of them, and certainly with an influence of which one was more absolutely conscious. There were times when it appeared to Dorian Gray that the whole of history was merely the record of his own life, not as he had lived it in act and circumstance, but as his imagination had created it for him, as it had been in his brain and in his passions. He felt that he had known them all, those strange terrible figures that had passed across the stage of the world and made sin so marvellous and evil so full of subtlety. It seemed to him that in some mysterious way their lives had been his own.

The hero of the wonderful novel that had so influenced his life had himself known this curious fancy. In the seventh chapter he tells how, crowned with laurel, lest lightning might strike him, he had sat, as Tiberius, in a garden at Capri, reading the shameful books of Elephantis, while dwarfs and peacocks strutted round him and the flute-player[146] mocked the swinger of the censer; and, as Caligula, had caroused with the green-shirted jockeys in their stables, and supped in an ivory manger with a jewel-frontleted horse; and, as Domitian[147], had wandered through a corridor lined with marble mirrors, looking round with haggard eyes for the reflection of the dagger that was to end his days, and sick with that ennui, that terrible *taedium vitae*, that comes on those to whom life denies nothing; and had peered through a clear emerald at the red shambles of the Circus, and then, in a litter of pearl and purple drawn by silver-shod mules, been carried through the Street of Pomegranates to a House of Gold, and heard men cry on Nero Caesar as he passed by; and, as Elagabalus, had painted his face with colours, and plied the distaff among the women, and brought the Moon from Carthage, and given her in mystic marriage to the Sun.

Over and over again Dorian used to read this fantastic chapter, and the two chapters immediately following, in which, as in some curious tapestries or cunningly-wrought enamels, were pictured the awful and beautiful forms of those whom Vice and Blood and Weariness had made monstrous or mad: Filippo, Duke of Milan, who slew his wife, and painted her lips with a scarlet poison that her lover might suck death from the dead thing he fondled; Pietro Barbi, the Venetian, known as Paul the Second, who sought in his vanity to assume the title of Formosus, and whose tiara, valued at two hundred thousand florins, was bought at the price of a terrible sin; Gian Maria Visconti, who used hounds to chase living men, and whose murdered body was covered with roses by a harlot who had loved him; the Borgia on his white horse, with Fratricide riding beside him, and his mantle stained with the blood of Perotto; Pietro Riario, the young Cardinal Archbishop of Florence, child and minion of Sixtus IV, whose beauty was equalled only by his debauchery, and who received Leonora of Aragon in a pavilion of white and crimson silk, filled with nymphs and centaurs, and gilded a boy that he might serve at the feast as Ganymede or Hylas;

Ezzelin, whose melancholy could be cured only by the spectacle of death, and who had a passion for red blood, as other men have for red wine—the son of the Fiend, as was reported, and one who had cheated his father at dice when gambling with him for his own soul; Giambattista Cibo, who in mockery took the name of Innocent, and into whose torpid veins the blood of three lads was infused by a Jewish doctor; Sigismondo Malatesta, the lover of Isotta, and the lord of Rimini, whose effigy was burned at Rome as the enemy of God and man, who strangled Polyssena with a napkin, and gave poison to Ginevra d'Este in a cup of emerald, and in honour of a shameful passion built a pagan church for Christian worship; Charles VI, who had so wildly adored his brother's wife that a leper had warned him of the insanity that was coming on him, and who, when his brain had sickened and grown strange, could only be soothed by Saracen cards painted with the images of Love and Death and Madness; and, in his trimmed jerkin and jewelled cap and acanthus-like curls, Grifonetto Baglioni, who slew Astorre with his bride, and Simonetto with his page, and whose comeliness was such that, as he lay dying in the yellow piazza of Perugia, those who had hated him could not choose but weep, and Atalanta, who had cursed him, blessed him.

There was a horrible fascination in them all. He saw them at night, and they troubled his imagination in the day. The Renaissance knew of strange manners of poisoning—poisoning by a helmet and a lighted torch, by an embroidered glove and a jewelled fan, by a gilded pomander and by an amber chain. Dorian Gray had been poisoned by a book. There were moments when he looked on evil simply as a mode through which he could realise his conception of the beautiful.

Chapter 12

It was on the ninth of November, the eve of his own thirty-eighth birthday, as he often remembered afterwards.

He was walking home about eleven o'clock from Lord Henry's, where he had been dining, and was wrapped in heavy furs, as the night was cold and foggy. At the corner of Grosvenor Square and South Audley Street a man passed him in the mist, walking very fast, and with the collar of his grey ulster turned up. He had a bag in his hand. Dorian recognized him. It was Basil Hallward. A strange sense of fear, for which he could not account, came over him. He made no sign of recognition, and went on quickly, in the direction of his own house.

But Hallward had seen him. Dorian heard him first stopping on the pavement and then hurrying after him. In a few moments his hand was on his arm.

'Dorian! What an extraordinary piece of luck! I have been waiting for you in your library ever since nine o'clock. Finally I took pity on your tired servant, and told him to go to bed, as he let me out. I am off to Paris by the midnight train, and I particularly wanted to see you before I left. I thought it was you, or rather your fur coat, as you passed me. But I wasn't quite sure. Didn't you recognize me?'

'In this fog, my dear Basil? Why, I can't even recognize Grosvenor Square. I believe my house is somewhere about here, but I don't feel at all certain about it. I am sorry you are going away, as I have not seen you for ages. But I suppose you will be back soon?'

'No: I am going to be out of England for six months. I intend to take a studio in Paris, and shut myself up till I have finished a great picture I have in my head. However, it wasn't about myself I wanted to talk. Here we are at your door. Let me come in for a moment. I have something to say to you.'

'I shall be charmed. But won't you miss your train?' said Dorian Gray, languidly, as he passed up the steps and opened the door with his latch-key[148].

The lamp-light[149] struggled out through the fog, and Hallward looked at his watch. 'I have heaps of time,' he answered. 'The train doesn't go till twelve-fifteen, and it is only just eleven. In fact, I was on my way to the club to look for you, when I met you. You see, I sha'n't have any delay about luggage, as I have sent on my heavy things. All I have with me is in this bag, and I can easily get to

Victoria in twenty minutes.'

Dorian looked at him and smiled. 'What a way for a fashionable painter to travel! A Gladstone bag, and an ulster! Come in, or the fog will get into the house. And mind you don't talk about anything serious. Nothing is serious nowadays. At least nothing should be.'

Hallward shook his head, as he entered, and followed Dorian into the library. There was a bright wood fire blazing in the large open hearth. The lamps were lit, and an open Dutch silver spirit-case stood, with some siphons of soda-water[150] and large cut-glass tumblers, on a little marqueterie table.

'You see your servant made me quite at home, Dorian. He gave me everything I wanted, including your best gold-tipped cigarettes. He is a most hospitable creature. I like him much better than the Frenchman you used to have. What has become of the Frenchman, by the bye?'

Dorian shrugged his shoulders. 'I believe he married Lady Radley's maid, and has established her in Paris as an English dressmaker. *Anglomanie* is very fashionable over there now, I hear. It seems silly of the French, doesn't it? But—do you know?—he was not at all a bad servant. I never liked him, but I had nothing to complain about. One often imagines things that are quite absurd. He was really very devoted to me, and seemed quite sorry when he went away. Have another brandy-and-soda? Or would you like hock-and-seltzer? I always take hock-and-seltzer myself. There is sure to be some in the next room.'

'Thanks, I won't have anything more,' said the painter, taking his cap and coat off, and throwing them on the bag that he had placed in the corner. 'And now, my dear fellow, I want to speak to you seriously. Don't frown like that. You make it so much more difficult for me.'

'What is it all about?' cried Dorian, in his petulant way, flinging himself down on the sofa. 'I hope it is not about myself. I am tired of myself to-night. I should like to be somebody else.'

'It is about yourself,' answered Hallward, in his grave, deep voice, 'and I must say it to you. I shall only keep you half an hour.'

Dorian sighed, and lit a cigarette. 'Half an hour!' he murmured.

'It is not much to ask of you, Dorian, and it is entirely for your own sake that I am speaking. I think it right that you should know that the most dreadful things are being said against you in London.'

'I don't wish to know anything about them. I love scandals about other people, but scandals about myself don't interest me. They have not got the charm of novelty.'

'They must interest you, Dorian. Every gentleman is interested in his good name. You don't want people to talk of you as something vile and degraded. Of course you have your position, and your wealth, and all that kind of thing. But position and wealth are not everything. Mind you, I don't believe these rumours at all. At least, I can't believe them when I see you. Sin is a thing that writes itself across a man's face. It cannot be concealed. People talk sometimes of secret vices. There are no such things. If a wretched man has a vice, it shows itself in the lines of his mouth, the droop of his eyelids, the moulding of his hands even. Somebody—I won't mention his name, but you know him—came to me last year to have his portrait done. I had never seen him before, and had never heard anything about him at the time, though I have heard a good deal since. He offered an extravagant price. I refused him. There was something in the shape of his fingers that I hated. I know now that I was quite right in what I fancied about him. His life is dreadful. But you, Dorian, with your pure, bright, innocent face, and your marvellous untroubled youth—I can't believe anything against you. And yet I see you very seldom, and you never come down to the studio now, and when I am away from you, and I hear all these hideous things that people are whispering about you, I don't know what to say. Why is it, Dorian, that a man like the Duke of Berwick leaves the room of a club when you enter it? Why is it that so many gentlemen in London will neither go to your house nor invite you to theirs? You used to be a friend of Lord Staveley. I met him at dinner last week. Your name happened to come up in conversation, in connection with the miniatures you have lent to the exhibition at the Dudley. Staveley curled his lip, and said that you might have the most artistic tastes, but that you were a man whom no pure-minded girl should be allowed to know, and whom no chaste woman should sit in the same room with. I reminded him that I was a friend of yours, and asked him what he meant. He told me. He told me right out before everybody. It was horrible! Why is your friendship so fatal to young men? There was that wretched boy in the Guards who committed suicide. You were his great friend. There was Sir Henry Ashton, who had to leave England, with a tarnished name. You and he were inseparable. What about Adrian Singleton, and his dreadful end? What about Lord Kent's only son, and his career? I met his father yesterday in St. James's Street. He seemed broken with shame and sorrow. What about the young Duke of Perth? What sort of life has he got now? What gentleman would associate with him?'

'Stop, Basil. You are talking about things of which you know nothing,' said Dorian Gray, biting his lip, and with a note of infinite contempt in his voice. 'You ask me why Berwick leaves a room when I enter it. It is because I know everything about his life, not because he knows anything about mine. With such blood as he has in his veins, how could his record be clean? You ask me about Henry Ashton and young Perth. Did I teach the one his vices, and the other his debauchery? If Kent's silly son takes his wife from the streets, what is that to me? If Adrian Singleton writes his friend's name across a bill, am I his keeper? I know how people chatter in England. The middle classes air their moral prejudices over their gross dinner-tables[151], and whisper about what they call the profligacies of their betters in order to try and pretend that they are in smart society, and on intimate terms with the people they slander. In this country it is enough for a man to have distinction and brains for every common tongue to wag against him. And what sort of lives do these people, who pose as being moral, lead themselves? My dear fellow, you forget that we are in the native land of the hypocrite.'

'Dorian,' cried Hallward, 'that is not the question. England is bad enough I know, and English society is all wrong. That is the reason why I want you to be fine. You have not been fine. One has a right to judge of a man by the effect he has over his friends. Yours seem to lose all sense of honour, of goodness, of purity. You have filled them with a madness for pleasure. They have gone down into the depths. You led them there. Yes: you led them there, and yet you can smile, as you are smiling now. And there is worse behind. I know you and Harry are inseparable. Surely for that reason, if for none other, you should not have made his sister's name a by-word[152].'

'Take care, Basil. You go too far.'

'I must speak, and you must listen. You shall listen. When you met Lady Gwendolen, not a breath of scandal had ever touched her. Is there a single decent woman in London now who would drive with her in the Park? Why, even her children are not allowed to live with her. Then there are other stories—stories that you have been seen creeping at dawn out of dreadful houses and slinking in disguise into the foulest dens in London. Are they true? Can they be true? When I first heard them, I laughed. I hear them now, and they make me shudder. What about your country house, and the life that is led there? Dorian, you don't know what is said about you. I won't tell you that I don't want to preach to you. I remember Harry saying once that every man who turned himself into an amateur curate for the moment always began by saying that, and then proceeded to break his word. I do want to preach to you. I want you to lead such a life as will make the world respect you. I want you to have a clean name and a fair record. I want you to get rid of the dreadful people you associate with. Don't shrug your shoulders like that. Don't be so indifferent. You have a wonderful influence. Let it be for good, not for evil. They say that you corrupt every one with whom you become intimate, and that it is quite sufficient for you to enter a house, for shame of some kind to follow after. I don't know whether it is so or not. How should I know? But it is said of you. I am told things that it seems impossible to doubt. Lord Gloucester was one of my greatest friends at Oxford. He showed me a letter that his wife had written to him when she was dying alone in her villa at Mentone. Your name was implicated in the most terrible confession I ever read. I told him that it was absurd—that I knew you thoroughly, and that you were incapable of anything of the kind. Know you? I wonder do I know you? Before I could answer that, I should have to see your soul.'

'To see my soul!' muttered Dorian Gray, starting up from the sofa and turning almost white from fear.

'Yes,' answered Hallward, gravely, and with deep-toned sorrow in his voice—'to see your soul. But only God can do that.'

A bitter laugh of mockery broke from the lips of the younger man. 'You shall see it yourself, to-night!' he cried, seizing a lamp from the table. 'Come: it is your own handiwork. Why shouldn't you look at it? You can tell the world all about it afterwards, if you choose. Nobody would believe you. If they did believe you, they would like me all the better for it. I know the age better than you do, though you will prate about it so tediously. Come, I tell you. You have chattered enough about corruption. Now you shall look on it face to face.'

There was the madness of pride in every word he uttered. He stamped his foot upon the ground in his boyish insolent manner. He felt a terrible joy at the thought that some one else was to share his secret, and that the man who had painted the portrait that was the origin of all his shame was to be burdened for the rest of his life with the hideous memory of what he had done.

'Yes,' he continued, coming closer to him, and looking steadfastly into his stern eyes, 'I shall show you my soul. You shall see the thing that you fancy only God can see.'

Hallward started back. 'This is blasphemy, Dorian!' he cried. 'You must not say things like that. They are horrible, and they don't mean anything.'

'You think so?' He laughed again.

'I know so. As for what I said to you to-night, I said it for your good. You know I have been always a staunch friend to you.'

A twisted flash of pain shot across the painter's face. He paused for a moment, and a wild feeling of pity came over him. After all, what right had he to pry into the life of Dorian Gray? If he had done a tithe of what was rumoured about him, how much he must have suffered! Then he straightened himself up, and walked over to the fireplace, and stood there, looking at the burning logs with their frost-like ashes and their throbbing cores of flame.

'I am waiting, Basil,' said the young man, in a hard, clear voice.

He turned round. 'What I have to say is this,' he cried. 'You must give me some answer to these horrible charges that are made against you. If you tell me that they are absolutely untrue from beginning to end, I shall believe you. Deny them, Dorian, deny them! Can't you see what I am going through? My God! don't tell me that you are bad, and corrupt, and shameful.'

Dorian Gray smiled. There was a curl of contempt in his lips. 'Come upstairs, Basil,' he said, quietly. 'I keep a diary of my life from day to day, and it never leaves the room in which it is written. I shall show it to you if you come with me.'

'I shall come with you, Dorian, if you wish it. I see I have missed my train. That makes no matter. I can go to-morrow. But don't ask me to read anything to-night. All I want is a plain answer to my question.'

'That shall be given to you upstairs. I could not give it here. You will not have to read long.'

Chapter 13

He passed out of the room, and began the ascent, Basil Hallward following close behind. They walked softly, as men do instinctively at night. The lamp cast fantastic shadows on the wall and staircase. A rising wind made some of the windows rattle.

When they reached the top landing, Dorian set the lamp down on the floor, and taking out the key turned it in the lock. 'You insist on knowing, Basil?' he asked, in a low voice.

'Yes.'

'I am delighted,' he answered, smiling. Then he added, somewhat harshly, 'You are the one man in the world who is entitled to know everything about me. You have had more to do with my life than you think:' and, taking up the lamp, he opened the door and went in. A cold current of air passed them, and the light shot up for a moment in a flame of murky orange. He shuddered. 'Shut the door behind you,' he whispered, as he placed the lamp on the table.

Hallward glanced round him with a puzzled expression. The room looked as if it had not been lived in for years. A faded Flemish tapestry, a curtained picture, an old Italian *cassone*, and an almost empty bookcase—that was all that it seemed to contain, besides a chair and a table. As Dorian Gray was lighting a half-burned candle that was standing on the mantelshelf, he saw that the whole place was covered with dust, and that the carpet was in holes. A mouse ran scuffling behind the wainscoting. There was a damp odour of mildew.

'So you think that it is only God who sees the soul, Basil? Draw that curtain back, and you will see mine.'

The voice that spoke was cold and cruel. 'You are mad, Dorian, or playing a part,' muttered Hallward, frowning.

'You won't? Then I must do it myself,' said the young man; and he tore the curtain from its rod, and flung it on the ground.

An exclamation of horror broke from the painter's lips as he saw in the dim light the hideous face on the canvas grinning at him. There was something in its expression that filled him with disgust and loathing. Good heavens! it[153] was Dorian Gray's own face that he was looking at! The horror, whatever it was, had not yet entirely spoiled that marvellous beauty. There was still some gold in the thinning hair and some scarlet on the sensual mouth. The sodden eyes had kept something of the loveliness of their blue, the noble curves had not yet completely passed away from chiselled nostrils and from plastic throat. Yes, it was Dorian himself. But who had done it? He seemed to recognize his own brush-work[154], and the frame was his own design. The idea was monstrous, yet he felt afraid. He seized the lighted candle, and held it to the picture. In the left-hand corner was his own name, traced in long letters of bright vermilion.

It was some foul parody, some infamous, ignoble satire. He had never done that. Still, it was his own picture. He knew it, and he felt as if his blood had changed in a moment from fire to sluggish ice. His own picture! What did it mean? Why had it altered? He turned, and looked at Dorian Gray with the eyes of a sick man. His mouth twitched, and his parched tongue seemed unable to articulate. He passed his hand across his forehead. It was dank with clammy sweat.

The young man was leaning against the mantelshelf, watching him with that strange expression that one sees on the faces of those who are absorbed in a play when some great artist is acting. There was neither real sorrow in it nor real joy. There was simply the passion of the spectator, with perhaps a flicker of triumph in his eyes. He had taken the flower out of his coat, and was smelling it, or pretending to do so.

'What does this mean?' cried Hallward, at last. His own voice sounded shrill and curious in his ears.

'Years ago, when I was a boy,' said Dorian Gray, crushing the flower in his hand, 'you met me, flattered me, and taught me to be vain of my good looks. One day you introduced me to a friend of yours, who explained to me the wonder of youth, and you finished a portrait of me that revealed to me the wonder of beauty. In a mad moment, that, even now, I don't know whether I regret or not, I made a wish, perhaps you would call it a prayer...'

'I remember it! Oh, how well I remember it! No! the thing is impossible. The room is damp. Mildew has got into the canvas. The paints I used had some wretched mineral poison in them. I tell you the thing is impossible.'

'Ah, what is impossible?' murmured the young man, going over to the window, and leaning his forehead against the cold, mist-stained glass.

'You told me you had destroyed it.'

'I was wrong. It has destroyed me.'

'I don't believe it is my picture.'

'Can't you see your ideal in it?' said Dorian, bitterly.

'My ideal, as you call it...'

'As you called it.'

'There was nothing evil in it, nothing shameful. You were to me such an ideal as I shall never meet again. This is the face of a satyr.'

'It is the face of my soul.'

'Christ! what[155] a thing I must have worshipped! It has the eyes of a devil.'

'Each of us has Heaven and Hell in him, Basil,' cried Dorian, with a wild gesture of despair.

Hallward turned again to the portrait, and gazed at it. 'My God! if it is true,' he exclaimed, 'and this is what you have done with your life, why, you must be worse even than those who talk against you fancy you to be!' He held the light up again to the canvas, and examined it. The surface seemed to be quite undisturbed, and as he had left it. It was from within, apparently, that the foulness and horror had come. Through some strange quickening of inner life the leprosies of sin were slowly eating the thing away. The rotting of a corpse in a watery grave was not so fearful.

His hand shook, and the candle fell from its socket on the floor, and lay there sputtering. He placed his foot on it and put it out. Then he flung himself into the rickety chair that was standing by the table and buried his face in his hands.

'Good God, Dorian, what a lesson! What an awful lesson!' There was no answer, but he could hear the young man sobbing at the window. 'Pray, Dorian, pray,' he murmured. 'What is it that one was taught to say in one's boyhood? "Lead us not into temptation. Forgive us our sins. Wash away our iniquities." Let us say that together. The prayer of your pride has been answered. The prayer of your repentance will be answered also. I worshipped you too much. I am punished for it. You worshipped yourself too much. We are both punished.'

Dorian Gray turned slowly around, and looked at him with tear-dimmed eyes. 'It is too late, Basil,' he faltered.

'It is never too late, Dorian. Let us kneel down and try if we cannot remember a prayer. Isn't there a verse somewhere, "Though your sins be as scarlet, yet I will make them as white as snow"?'

'Those words mean nothing to me now.'

'Hush! don't say that. You have done enough evil in your life. My God! don't you see that accursed thing leering at us?'

Dorian Gray glanced at the picture, and suddenly an uncontrollable feeling of hatred for Basil Hallward came over him, as though it had been suggested to him by the image on the canvas, whispered into his ear by those grinning lips. The mad passions of a hunted animal stirred within him, and he loathed the man who was seated at the table, more than in his whole life he had ever loathed anything. He glanced wildly around. Something glimmered on the top of the painted chest that faced him. His eye fell on it. He knew what it was. It was a knife that he had brought up, some days before, to cut a piece of cord, and had forgotten to take away with him. He moved slowly towards it, passing Hallward as he did so. As soon as he got behind him, he seized it, and turned round. Hallward stirred in his chair as if he was going to rise. He rushed at him, and dug the knife into the great vein that is behind the ear, crushing the man's head down on the table, and stabbing again and again.

There was a stifled groan, and the horrible sound of some one choking with blood. Three times the outstretched arms shot up convulsively, waving grotesque stiff-fingered hands in the air. He stabbed him twice more, but the man did not move. Something began to trickle on the floor. He waited for a moment, still pressing the head down. Then he threw the knife on the table, and listened.

He could hear nothing, but the drip, drip on the threadbare carpet. He opened the door and went out on the landing. The house was absolutely quiet. No one was about. For a few seconds he stood bending over the balustrade, and peering down into the black seething well of darkness. Then he took out the key and returned to the room, locking himself in as he did so.

The thing was still seated in the chair, straining over the table with bowed head, and humped back, and long fantastic arms. Had it not been for the red jagged tear in the neck, and the clotted black pool that was slowly widening on the table, one would have said that the man was simply asleep.

How quickly it had all been done! He felt strangely calm, and, walking over to the window, opened it, and stepped out on the balcony. The wind had blown the fog away, and the sky was like a monstrous peacock's tail, starred with myriads of golden eyes. He looked down, and saw the policeman going his rounds and flashing the long beam of his lantern on the doors of the silent houses. The crimson spot of a prowling hansom gleamed at the corner, and then vanished. A woman in a fluttering shawl was creeping slowly by the railings, staggering as she went. Now and then she stopped, and peered back. Once, she began to sing in a hoarse voice. The policeman strolled over and said something to her. She stumbled away, laughing. A bitter blast swept across the Square. The gas-lamps[156] flickered, and became blue, and the leafless trees shook their black iron branches to and fro. He shivered, and went back, closing the window behind him.

Having reached the door, he turned the key, and opened it. He did not even glance at the murdered man. He felt that the secret of the whole thing was not to realise the situation. The friend who had painted the fatal portrait to which all his misery had been due, had gone out of his life. That was enough.

Then he remembered the lamp. It was a rather curious one of Moorish workmanship, made of dull silver inlaid with arabesques of burnished steel, and studded with coarse turquoises. Perhaps it might be missed by his servant, and questions would be asked. He hesitated for a moment, then he turned back and took it from the table. He could not help seeing the dead thing. How still it was! How horribly white the long hands looked! It was like a dreadful wax image.

Having locked the door behind him, he crept quietly downstairs. The woodwork creaked, and seemed to cry out as if in pain. He stopped several times, and waited. No: everything was still. It was merely the sound of his own footsteps.

When he reached the library, he saw the bag and coat in the corner. They must be hidden away somewhere. He unlocked a secret press that was in the wainscoting, a press in which he kept his own curious disguises, and put them into it. He could easily burn them afterwards. Then he pulled out his watch. It was twenty minutes to two.

He sat down, and began to think. Every year—every month, almost—men were strangled in England for what he had done.

There had been a madness of murder in the air. Some red star had come too close to the earth....And yet, what evidence was there against him? Basil Hallward had left the house at eleven. No one had seen him come in again. Most of the servants were at Selby Royal. His valet had gone to bed....Paris! Yes. It was to Paris that Basil had gone, and by the midnight train, as he had intended. With his curious reserved habits, it would be months before any suspicions would be aroused. Months! Everything could be destroyed long before then.

A sudden thought struck him. He put on his fur coat and hat, and went out into the hall. There he paused, hearing the slow heavy tread of the policeman on the pavement outside, and seeing the flash of the bull's-eye reflected in the window. He waited, and held his breath.

After a few moments he drew back the latch, and slipped out, shutting the door very gently behind him. Then he began ringing the bell. In about five minutes his valet appeared, half dressed, and looking very drowsy.

'I am sorry to have had to wake you up, Francis,' he said, stepping in; 'but I had forgotten my latch-key. What time is it?'

'Ten minutes past two, sir,' answered the man, looking at the clock and blinking.

'Ten minutes past two? How horribly late! You must wake me at nine to-morrow. I have some work to do.'

'All right, sir.'

'Did any one call this evening?'

'Mr Hallward, sir. He stayed here till eleven, and then he went away to catch his train.'

'Oh! I am sorry I didn't see him. Did he leave any message?'

'No, sir, except that he would write to you from Paris, if he did not find you at the club.'

'That will do, Francis. Don't forget to call me at nine tomorrow.'

'No, sir.'

The man shambled down the passage in his slippers.

Dorian Gray threw his hat and coat upon the table, and passed into the library. For a quarter of an hour he walked up and down the room biting his lip, and thinking. Then he took down the Blue Book[157] from one of the shelves and began to turn over the leaves. 'Alan Campbell, 152, Hertford Street, Mayfair.' Yes; that was the man he wanted.

Chapter 14

At nine o'clock the next morning his servant came in with a cup of chocolate on a tray, and opened the shutters. Dorian was sleeping quite peacefully, lying on his right side, with one hand underneath his cheek. He looked like a boy who had been tired out with play, or study.

The man had to touch him twice on the shoulder before he woke, and as he opened his eyes a faint smile passed across his lips, as though he had been lost in some delightful dream. Yet he had not dreamed at all. His night had been untroubled by any images of pleasure or of pain. But youth smiles without any reason. It is one of its chiefest charms.

He turned round, and, leaning upon his elbow, began to sip his chocolate. The mellow November sun came streaming into the room. The sky was bright, and there was a genial warmth in the air. It was almost like a morning in May.

Gradually the events of the preceding night crept with silent blood-stained feet into his brain, and reconstructed themselves there with terrible distinctness. He winced at the memory of all that he had suffered, and for a moment the same curious feeling of loathing for Basil Hallward, that had made him kill him as he sat in the chair, came back to him, and he grew cold with passion. The dead man was still sitting there, too, and in the sunlight now. How horrible that was! Such hideous things were for the darkness, not for the day.

He felt that if he brooded on what he had gone through he would sicken or grow mad. There were sins whose fascination was more in the memory than in the doing of them, strange triumphs that gratified the pride more than the passions, and gave to the intellect a quickened sense of joy, greater than any joy they brought, or could ever bring, to the senses. But this was not one of them. It was a thing to be driven out of the mind, to be drugged with poppies, to be strangled lest it might strangle one itself.

When the half-hour struck, he passed his hand across his forehead, and then got up hastily, and dressed himself with even more than his usual care, giving a good deal of attention to the choice of his necktie and scarf-pin[158], and changing his rings more than once. He spent a long time also over breakfast, tasting the various dishes, talking to his valet about some new liveries that he was thinking of getting made for the servants at Selby, and going through his correspondence. At some of the letters he smiled. Three of them bored him. One he read several times over, and then tore up with a slight look of annoyance in his face. 'That awful thing, a woman's memory!' as Lord Henry had once said.

After he had drunk his cup of black coffee, he wiped his lips slowly with a napkin, motioned to his servant to wait, and going over to the table sat down and wrote two letters. One he put in his pocket, the other he handed to the valet.

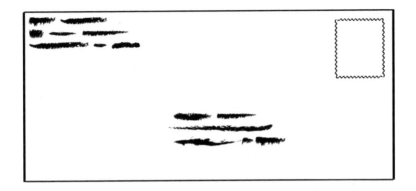

'Take this round to 152, Hertford Street, Francis, and if Mr Campbell is out of town, get his address.'

As soon as he was alone, he lit a cigarette, and began sketching upon a piece of paper, drawing first flowers, and bits of architecture, and then human faces. Suddenly he remarked that every face that he drew seemed to have a fantastic likeness to Basil Hallward. He frowned, and, getting up, went over to the bookcase and took out a volume at hazard. He was determined that he would not think about what had happened until it became absolutely necessary that he should do so.

When he had stretched himself on the sofa, he looked at the title-page[159] of the book. It was Gautier's 'Émaux et Camées', Charpentier's Japanese-paper edition, with the Jacquemart etching. The binding was of citron-green leather, with a design of gilt trellis-work and dotted pomegranates. It had been given to him by Adrian Singleton. As he turned over the pages his eye fell on the poem about the hand of Lacenaire, the cold yellow hand *'du supplice encore mal lavée'*[160], with its downy red hairs and its *'doigts de faune*[161]. He glanced at his own white taper fingers, shuddering slightly in spite of himself, and passed on, till he came to those lovely stanzas upon Venice:—

> *'Sur une gamme chromatique,*
> *Le sein de perles ruisselant,*
> *La Vénus de l'Adriatique*
> *Sort de l'eau son corps rose et blanc.*

> *Les dômes, sur l'azur des ondes*
> *Suivant la phrase au pur contour,*
> *S'enflent comme des gorges rondes*
> *Que soulève un soupir d'amour.*

> *L'esquif aborde et me dépose,*
> *Jetant son amarre au pilier,*
> *Devant une façade rose,*
> *Sur le marbre d'un escalier.'*[162]

How exquisite they were! As one read them, one seemed to be floating down the green waterways of the pink and pearl city, seated in a black gondola with silver prow and trailing curtains. The mere lines looked to him like those straight lines of turquoise-blue that follow one as one pushes out to the Lido. The sudden flashes of colour reminded him of the gleam of the opal-and-iris-throated birds that flutter round the tall honeycombed Campanile, or stalk, with such stately grace, through the dim, dust-stained arcades. Leaning back with half-closed eyes, he kept saying over and over to himself:—

'Devant une façade rose,
Sur le marbre d'un escalier.'

The whole of Venice was in those two lines. He remembered the autumn that he had passed there, and a wonderful love that had stirred him to mad, delightful follies. There was romance in every place. But Venice, like Oxford, had kept the background for romance, and, to the true romantic, background was everything, or almost everything. Basil had been with him part of the time, and had gone wild over Tintoret. Poor Basil! what a horrible way for a man to die!

He sighed, and took up the volume again, and tried to forget. He read of the swallows that fly in and out of the little café at Smyrna where the Hadjis sit counting their amber beads and the turbaned merchants smoke their long tasselled pipes and talk gravely to each other; he read of the Obelisk in the Place de la Concorde that weeps tears of granite in its lonely sunless exile, and longs to be back by the hot lotus-covered Nile, where there are Sphinxes, and rose-red ibises, and white vultures with gilded claws, and crocodiles, with small beryl eyes, that crawl over the green steaming mud; he began to brood over those verses which, drawing music from kiss-stained marble, tell of that curious statue that Gautier compares to a contralto voice, the *'monstre charmant'*[163] that couches in the porphyry-room[164] of the Louvre. But after a time the book fell from his hand. He grew nervous, and a horrible fit of terror came over him. What if Alan Campbell should be out of England? Days would elapse before he could come back. Perhaps he might refuse to come. What could he do then? Every moment was of vital importance.

They had been great friends once, five years before—almost inseparable, indeed. Then the intimacy had come suddenly to an end. When they met in society now, it was only Dorian Gray who smiled: Alan Campbell never did.

He was an extremely clever young man, though he had no real appreciation of the visible arts, and whatever little sense of the beauty of poetry he possessed he had gained entirely from Dorian. His dominant intellectual passion was for science. At Cambridge he had spent a great deal of his time working in the Laboratory, and had taken a good class in the Natural Science Tripos of his year. Indeed, he was still devoted to the study of chemistry, and had a laboratory of his own, in which he used to shut himself up all day long, greatly to the annoyance of his mother, who had set her heart on his standing for Parliament and had a vague idea that a chemist was a person who made up prescriptions. He was an excellent musician, however, as well, and played both the violin and the piano better than most amateurs. In fact, it was music that had first brought him and Dorian Gray together—music and that indefinable attraction that Dorian seemed to be able to exercise whenever he wished, and indeed exercised often without being conscious of it. They had met at Lady Berkshire's the night that Rubinstein played there and after that used to be always seen together at the Opera, and wherever good music was going on. For eighteen months their intimacy lasted. Campbell was always either at Selby Royal or in Grosvenor Square. To him, as to many others, Dorian Gray was the type of everything that is wonderful and fascinating in life. Whether or not a quarrel had taken place between them no one ever knew. But suddenly people remarked that they scarcely spoke when they met, and that Campbell seemed always to go away early from any party at which Dorian Gray was present. He had changed, too—was strangely melancholy at times, appeared almost to dislike hearing music, and would never himself play, giving as his excuse, when he was called upon, that he was so absorbed in science that he had no time left in which to practise. And this was certainly true. Every day he seemed to become more interested in biology, and his name appeared once or twice in some of the scientific reviews, in connection with certain curious experiments.

This was the man Dorian Gray was waiting for. Every second he kept glancing at the clock. As the minutes went by he became horribly agitated. At last he got up, and began to pace up and down the room, looking like a beautiful caged thing. He took long stealthy strides. His hands were curiously cold.

The suspense became unbearable. Time seemed to him to be crawling with feet of lead, while he by monstrous winds was being swept towards the jagged edge of some black cleft of precipice. He knew what was waiting for him there; saw it indeed, and, shuddering, crushed with dank hands his burning lids as though he would have robbed the very brain of sight, and driven the eyeballs back into their cave. It was useless. The brain had its own food on which it battened, and the imagination, made grotesque by terror, twisted and distorted as a living thing by pain, danced like some foul puppet on a stand, and grinned through moving masks. Then, suddenly, Time stopped for him. Yes: that blind, slow-breathing thing crawled no more, and horrible thoughts, Time being dead, raced nimbly on in front, and dragged a hideous future from its grave, and showed it to him. He stared at it. Its very horror made him stone.

At last the door opened, and his servant entered. He turned glazed eyes upon him.

'Mr Campbell, sir,' said the man.

A sigh of relief broke from his parched lips, and the colour came back to his cheeks.

'Ask him to come in at once, Francis.' He felt that he was himself again. His mood of cowardice had passed away.

The man bowed, and retired. In a few moments Alan Campbell walked in, looking very stern and rather pale, his pallor being intensified by his coal-black hair and dark eyebrows.

'Alan! this is kind of you. I thank you for coming.'

'I had intended never to enter your house again, Gray. But you said it was a matter of life and death.' His voice was hard and cold. He spoke with slow deliberation. There was a look of contempt in the steady searching gaze that he turned on Dorian. He kept his hands in the pockets of his Astrakhan coat, and seemed not to have noticed the gesture with which he had been greeted.

'Yes: it is a matter of life and death, Alan, and to more than one person. Sit down.'

Campbell took a chair by the table, and Dorian sat opposite to him. The two men's eyes met. In Dorian's there was infinite pity. He knew that what he was going to do was dreadful.

After a strained moment of silence, he leaned across and said, very quietly, but watching the effects of each word upon the face of him he had sent for, 'Alan, in a locked room at the top of this house, a room to which nobody but myself has access, a dead man is seated at a table. He has been dead ten hours now. Don't stir, and don't look at me like that. Who the man is, why he died, how he died, are matters that do not concern you. What you have to do is this—'

'Stop, Gray. I don't want to know anything further. Whether what you have told me is true or not true, doesn't concern me. I entirely decline to be mixed up in your life. Keep your horrible secrets to yourself. They don't interest me any more.'

'Alan, they will have to interest you. This one will have to interest you. I am awfully sorry for you, Alan. But I can't help myself. You are the one man who is able to save me. I am forced to bring you into the matter. I have no option. Alan, you are scientific. You know about chemistry, and things of that kind. You have made experiments. What you have got to do is to destroy the thing that is upstairs—to destroy it so that not a vestige of it will be left. Nobody saw this person come into the house. Indeed, at the present moment he is supposed to be in Paris. He will not be missed for months. When he is missed, there must be no trace of him found here. You, Alan, you must change him, and everything that belongs to him, into a handful of ashes that I may scatter in the air.'

'You are mad, Dorian.'

'Ah! I was waiting for you to call me Dorian.'

'You are mad, I tell you—mad to imagine that I would raise a finger to help you, mad to make this monstrous confession. I will have nothing to do with this matter, whatever it is. Do you think I am going to peril my reputation for you? What is it to me what devil's work you are up to?'

'It was suicide, Alan.'

'I am glad of that. But who drove him to it? You, I should fancy.'

'Do you still refuse to do this for me?'

'Of course I refuse. I will have absolutely nothing to do with it. I don't care what shame comes on you. You deserve it all. I should not be sorry to see you disgraced, publicly disgraced. How dare you ask me, of all men in the world, to mix myself up in this horror? I should have thought you knew more about people's characters. Your friend Lord Henry Wotton can't have taught you much about psychology, whatever else he has taught you. Nothing will induce me to stir a step to help you. You have come to the wrong man. Go to some of your friends. Don't come to me.'

'Alan, it was murder. I killed him. You don't know what he had made me suffer. Whatever my life is, he had more to do with the making or the marring of it than poor Harry has had. He may not have intended it, the result was the same.'

'Murder! Good God, Dorian, is that what you have come to? I shall not inform upon you. It is not my business. Besides, without my stirring in the matter, you are certain to be arrested. Nobody ever commits a crime without doing something stupid. But I will have nothing to do with it.'

'You must have something to do with it. Wait, wait a moment;

listen to me. Only listen, Alan. All I ask of you is to perform a certain scientific experiment. You go to hospitals and dead-houses[165], and the horrors that you do there don't affect you. If in some hideous dissecting-room[166] or fetid laboratory you found this man lying on a leaden table with red gutters scooped out in it for the blood to flow through, you would simply look upon him as an admirable subject. You would not turn a hair. You would not believe that you were doing anything wrong. On the contrary, you would probably feel that you were benefiting the human race, or increasing the sum of knowledge in the world, or gratifying intellectual curiosity, or something of that kind. What I want you to do is merely what you have often done before. Indeed, to destroy a body must be far less horrible than what you are accustomed to work at. And, remember, it is the only piece of evidence against me. If it is discovered, I am lost; and it is sure to be discovered unless you help me.'

'I have no desire to help you. You forget that. I am simply indifferent to the whole thing. It has nothing to do with me.'

'Alan, I entreat you. Think of the position I am in. Just before you came I almost fainted with terror. You may know terror yourself some day. No! don't think of that. Look at the matter purely from the scientific point of view. You don't inquire where the dead things on which you experiment come from. Don't inquire now. I have told you too much as it is. But I beg of you to do this. We were friends once, Alan.'

'Don't speak about those days, Dorian: they are dead.'

'The dead linger sometimes. The man upstairs will not go away. He is sitting at the table with bowed head and outstretched arms. Alan! Alan! if you don't come to my assistance I am ruined.

Why, they will hang me, Alan! Don't you understand? They will hang me for what I have done.'

'There is no good in prolonging this scene. I absolutely refuse to do anything in the matter. It is insane of you to ask me.'

'You refuse?'

'Yes.'

'I entreat you, Alan.'

'It is useless.'

The same look of pity came into Dorian Gray's eyes. Then he stretched out his hand, took a piece of paper, and wrote something on it. He read it over twice, folded it carefully, and pushed it across the table. Having done this, he got up and went over to the window.

Campbell looked at him in surprise, and then took up the paper, and opened it. As he read it, his face became ghastly pale, and he fell back in his chair. A horrible sense of sickness came over him. He felt as if his heart was beating itself to death in some empty hollow.

After two or three minutes of terrible silence, Dorian turned round, and came and stood behind him, putting his hand upon his shoulder.

'I am so sorry for you, Alan,' he murmured, 'but you leave me no alternative. I have a letter written already. Here it is. You see the address. If you don't help me, I must send it. If you don't help me, I will send it. You know what the result will be. But you are going to help me. It is impossible for you to refuse now. I tried to spare you. You will do me the justice to admit that. You were stern, harsh, offensive. You treated me as no man has ever dared to treat me—no living man, at any rate. I bore it all. Now it is for me to dictate terms.'

Campbell buried his face in his hands, and a shudder passed through him.

'Yes, it is my turn to dictate terms, Alan. You know what they are. The thing is quite simple. Come, don't work yourself into this fever. The thing has to be done. Face it, and do it.'

A groan broke from Campbell's lips, and he shivered all over. The ticking of the clock on the mantelpiece seemed to him to be dividing Time into separate atoms of agony, each of which was too terrible to be borne. He felt as if an iron ring was being slowly tightened round his forehead, as if the disgrace with which he was threatened had already come upon him. The hand upon his shoulder weighed like a hand of lead. It was intolerable. It seemed to crush him.

'Come, Alan, you must decide at once.'

'I cannot do it,' he said, mechanically, as though words could alter things.

'You must. You have no choice. Don't delay.'

He hesitated a moment. 'Is there a fire in the room upstairs?'

'Yes, there is a gas-fire[167] with asbestos.'

'I shall have to go home and get some things from the laboratory.'

'No, Alan, you must not leave the house. Write out on a sheet of note-paper[168] what you want, and my servant will take a cab and bring the things back to you.'

Campbell scrawled a few lines, blotted them, and addressed an envelope to his assistant. Dorian took the note up and read it carefully. Then he rang the bell, and gave it to his valet, with orders to return as soon as possible, and to bring the things with him.

As the hall door shut, Campbell started nervously, and, having got up from the chair, went over to the chimney-piece[169]. He was shivering with a kind of ague. For nearly twenty minutes, neither of the men spoke. A fly buzzed noisily about the room, and the ticking of the clock was like the beat of a hammer.

As the chime struck one, Campbell turned round, and, looking at Dorian Gray, saw that his eyes were filled with tears. There was something in the purity and refinement of that sad face that seemed to enrage him. 'You are infamous, absolutely infamous!' he muttered.

'Hush, Alan: you have saved my life,' said Dorian.

'Your life? Good heavens! what a life that is! You have gone from corruption to corruption, and now you have culminated in crime. In doing what I am going to do, what you force me to do, it is not of your life that I am thinking.'

'Ah, Alan,' murmured Dorian with a sigh, 'I wish you had a thousandth part of the pity for me that I have for you.' He turned away as he spoke, and stood looking out at the garden. Campbell made no answer.

After about ten minutes a knock came to the door, and the servant entered, carrying a large mahogany chest of chemicals, with a long coil of steel and platinum wire and two rather curiously-shaped iron clamps.

'Shall I leave the things here, sir?' he asked Campbell.

'Yes,' said Dorian. 'And I am afraid, Francis, that I have another errand for you. What is the name of the man at Richmond who supplies Selby with orchids?'

'Harden, sir.'

'Yes—Harden. You must go down to Richmond at once, see

Harden personally, and tell him to send twice as many orchids as I ordered, and to have as few white ones as possible. In fact, I don't want any white ones. It is a lovely day, Francis, and Richmond is a very pretty place, otherwise I wouldn't bother you about it.'

'No trouble, sir. At what time shall I be back?'

Dorian looked at Campbell. 'How long will your experiment take, Alan?' he said in a calm, indifferent voice. The presence of a third person in the room seemed to give him extraordinary courage.

Campbell frowned, and bit his lip. 'It will take about five hours,' he answered.

'It will be time enough, then, if you are back at half-past seven, Francis. Or stay: just leave my things out for dressing. You can have the evening to yourself. I am not dining at home, so I shall not want you.'

'Thank you, sir,' said the man, leaving the room.

'Now, Alan, there is not a moment to be lost. How heavy this chest is! I'll take it for you. You bring the other things.' He spoke rapidly, and in an authoritative manner. Campbell felt dominated by him. They left the room together.

When they reached the top landing, Dorian took out the key and turned it in the lock. Then he stopped, and a troubled look came into his eyes. He shuddered. 'I don't think I can go in, Alan,' he murmured.

'It is nothing to me. I don't require you,' said Campbell, coldly.

Dorian half opened the door. As he did so, he saw the face of his portrait leering in the sunlight. On the floor in front of it the torn curtain was lying. He remembered that the night before he had forgotten, for the first time in his life, to hide the fatal canvas, and was about to rush forward, when he drew back with a shudder.

What was that loathsome red dew that gleamed, wet and glistening, on one of the hands, as though the canvas had sweated blood? How horrible it was! —more horrible, it seemed to him for the moment, than the silent thing that he knew was stretched across the table, the thing whose grotesque misshapen shadow on the spotted carpet showed him that it had not stirred, but was still there, as he had left it.

He heaved a deep breath, opened the door a little wider, and with half-closed eyes and averted head walked quickly in, determined that he would not look even once upon the dead man. Then, stooping down, and taking up the gold-and-purple hanging, he flung it right over the picture.

There he stopped, feeling afraid to turn round, and his eyes fixed themselves on the intricacies of the pattern before him. He heard Campbell bringing in the heavy chest, and the irons, and the other things that he had required for his dreadful work. He began to wonder if he and Basil Hallward had ever met, and, if so, what they had thought of each other.

'Leave me now,' said a stern voice behind him.

He turned and hurried out, just conscious that the dead man had been thrust back into the chair, and that Campbell was gazing into a glistening yellow face. As he was going downstairs he heard the key being turned in the lock.

It was long after seven when Campbell came back into the library. He was pale, but absolutely calm. 'I have done what you asked me to do,' he muttered. 'And now, good-bye. Let us never see each other again.'

'You have saved me from ruin, Alan. I cannot forget that,' said Dorian, simply.

As soon as Campbell had left, he went upstairs. There was a horrible smell of nitric acid in the room. But the thing that had been sitting at the table was gone.

Chapter 15

That evening, at eight-thirty, exquisitely dressed, and wearing a large buttonhole of Parma violets, Dorian Gray was ushered into Lady Narborough's drawing-room[170] by bowing servants. His forehead was throbbing with maddened nerves, and he felt wildly excited, but his manner as he bent over his hostess's hand was as easy and graceful as ever. Perhaps one never seems so much at one's ease as when one has to play a part. Certainly no one looking at Dorian Gray that night could have believed that he had passed through a tragedy as horrible as any tragedy of our age. Those finely-shaped fingers could never have clutched a knife for sin, nor those smiling lips have cried out on God and goodness. He himself could not help wondering at the calm of his demeanour, and for a moment felt keenly the terrible pleasure of a double life.

It was a small party, got up rather in a hurry by Lady Narborough, who was a very clever woman, with what Lord Henry used to describe as the remains of really remarkable ugliness. She had proved an excellent wife to one of our most tedious ambassadors, and having buried her husband properly in a marble mausoleum, which she had herself designed, and married off her daughters to some rich, rather elderly men, she devoted herself now to the pleasures of French fiction, French cookery, and French *esprit* when she could get it.

Dorian was one of her especial favourites, and she always told him that she was extremely glad she had not met him in early life. 'I know, my dear, I should have fallen madly in love with you,' she used to say, 'and thrown my bonnet right over the mills for your sake. It is most fortunate that you were not thought of at the time. As it was, our bonnets were so unbecoming, and the mills were so occupied in trying to raise the wind, that I never had even a flirtation with anybody. However, that was all Narborough's fault. He was dreadfully short-sighted, and there is no pleasure in taking in a husband who never sees anything.'

Her guests this evening were rather tedious. The fact was, as she explained to Dorian, behind a very shabby fan, one of her married daughters had come up quite suddenly to stay with her, and, to make matters worse, had actually brought her husband with her. 'I think it is most unkind of her, my dear,' she whispered. 'Of course I go and stay with them every summer after I come from Homburg, but then an old woman like me must have fresh air sometimes, and besides, I really wake them up. You don't know what an existence they lead down there. It is pure unadulterated country life. They get up early, because they have so much to do, and go to bed early, because they have so little to think about. There has not been a scandal in the neighbourhood since the time of Queen Elizabeth, and consequently they all fall asleep after dinner. You sha'n't sit next either of them. You shall sit by me, and amuse me.'

Dorian murmured a graceful compliment, and looked round the room. Yes: it was certainly a tedious party. Two of the people he had never seen before, and the others consisted of Ernest Harrowden, one of those middle-aged mediocrities so common in London clubs who have no enemies, but are thoroughly disliked by their friends; Lady Roxton, an overdressed woman of forty-seven, with a hooked nose, who was always trying to get herself compromised, but was so peculiarly plain that to her great disappointment no one would ever believe anything against her; Mrs Erlynne, a pushing nobody, with a delightful lisp, and Venetian-red hair; Lady Alice Chapman, his hostess's daughter, a dowdy dull girl, with one of those characteristic British faces, that, once seen, are never remembered; and her husband, a red-cheeked, white-whiskered creature who, like so many of his class, was under the impression that inordinate joviality can atone for an entire lack of ideas.

He was rather sorry he had come, till Lady Narborough, looking at the great ormolu gilt clock that sprawled in gaudy curves on the mauve-draped mantelshelf, exclaimed, 'How horrid of Henry Wotton to be so late! I sent round to him this morning on chance, and he promised faithfully not to disappoint me.'

It was some consolation that Harry was to be there, and when the door opened and he heard his slow musical voice lending charm to some insincere apology, he ceased to feel bored.

But at dinner he could not eat anything. Plate after plate went away untasted. Lady Narborough kept scolding him for what she called 'an insult to poor Adolphe, who invented the *menu* specially for you', and now and then Lord Henry looked across at him, wondering at his silence and abstracted manner. From time to time the butler filled his glass with champagne. He drank eagerly, and his thirst seemed to increase.

'Dorian,' said Lord Henry, at last, as the *chaud-froid*[171] was being handed round, 'what is the matter with you to-night? You are quite out of sorts.'

'I believe he is in love,' cried Lady Narborough, 'and that he is afraid to tell me for fear I should be jealous. He is quite right. I certainly should.'

'Dear Lady Narborough,' murmured Dorian, smiling, 'I have not been in love for a whole week—not, in fact, since Madame de Ferrol left town.'

'How you men can fall in love with that woman!' exclaimed the old lady. 'I really cannot understand it.'

'It is simply because she remembers you when you were a little girl, Lady Narborough,' said Lord Henry. 'She is the one link between us and your short frocks.'

'She does not remember my short frocks at all, Lord Henry. But I remember her very well at Vienna thirty years ago, and how *décolletée* she was then.'

'She is still *décolletée*,' he answered, taking an olive in his long fingers; 'and when she is in a very smart gown she looks like an édition de luxe[172] of a bad French novel. She is really wonderful, and full of surprises. Her capacity for family affection is extraordinary. When her third husband died, her hair turned quite gold from grief.'

'How can you, Harry!' cried Dorian.

'It is a most romantic explanation,' laughed the hostess. 'But her third husband, Lord Henry! You don't mean to say Ferrol is the fourth?'

'Certainly, Lady Narborough.'

'I don't believe a word of it.'

'Well, ask Mr Gray. He is one of her most intimate friends.'

'Is it true, Mr Gray?'

'She assures me so, Lady Narborough,' said Dorian. 'I asked her whether, like Marguerite de Navarre, she had their hearts embalmed and hung at her girdle. She told me she didn't, because none of them had had any hearts at all.'

'Four husbands! Upon my word that is *trop de zèle*[173].'

'*Trop d' audace*[174], I tell her,' said Dorian.

'Oh! she[175] is audacious enough for anything, my dear. And what is Ferrol like? I don't know him.'

'The husbands of very beautiful women belong to the criminal classes,' said Lord Henry, sipping his wine.

Lady Narborough hit him with her fan. 'Lord Henry, I am not at all surprised that the world says that you are extremely wicked.'

'But what world says that?' asked Lord Henry, elevating his eyebrows. 'It can only be the next world. This world and I are on excellent terms.'

'Everybody I know says you are very wicked,' cried the old lady, shaking her head.

Lord Henry looked serious for some moments. 'It is perfectly monstrous,' he said, at last, 'the way people go about nowadays saying things against one behind one's back that are absolutely and entirely true.'

'Isn't he incorrigible?' cried Dorian, leaning forward in his chair.

'I hope so,' said his hostess, laughing. 'But really, if you all worship Madame de Ferrol in this ridiculous way, I shall have to marry again so as to be in the fashion.'

'You will never marry again, Lady Narborough,' broke in Lord Henry. 'You were far too happy. When a woman marries again, it is because she detested her first husband. When a man marries again, it is because he adored his first wife. Women try their luck; men risk theirs.'

'Narborough wasn't perfect,' cried the old lady.

'If he had been, you would not have loved him, my dear lady,' was the rejoinder. 'Women love us for our defects. If we have enough of them they will forgive us everything, even our intellects. You will never ask me to dinner again after saying this, I am afraid, Lady Narborough; but it is quite true.'

'Of course it is true, Lord Henry. If we women did not love you for your defects, where would you all be? Not one of you would ever be married. You would be a set of unfortunate bachelors. Not, however, that that would alter you much. Nowadays all the married men live like bachelors, and all the bachelors like married men.'

'*Fin de siècle*[176],' murmured Lord Henry.

'*Fin du globe*[177],' answered his hostess.

'I wish it were *fin du globe*,' said Dorian, with a sigh. 'Life is a great disappointment.'

'Ah, my dear,' cried Lady Narborough, putting on her gloves, 'don't tell me that you have exhausted Life. When a man says that one knows that Life has exhausted him. Lord Henry is very wicked, and I sometimes wish that I had been; but you are made to be good—you look so good. I must find you a nice wife. Lord Henry, don't you think that Mr Gray should get married?'

'I am always telling him so, Lady Narborough,' said Lord Henry, with a bow.

'Well, we must look out for a suitable match for him. I shall go through Debrett carefully to-night, and draw out a list of all the eligible young ladies.'

'With their ages, Lady Narborough?' asked Dorian.

'Of course, with their ages, slightly edited. But nothing must be done in a hurry. I want it to be what *The Morning Post* calls a suitable alliance, and I want you both to be happy.'

'What nonsense people talk about happy marriages!' exclaimed Lord Henry. 'A man can be happy with any woman, as long as he does not love her.'

'Ah! what a cynic you are!' cried the old lady, pushing back her chair and nodding to Lady Ruxton. 'You must come and dine with me soon again. You are really an admirable tonic, much better than what Sir Andrew prescribes for me. You must tell me what people you would like to meet, though. I want it to be a delightful gathering.'

'I like men who have a future, and women who have a past,' he answered. 'Or do you think that would make it a petticoat party?'

'I fear so,' she said, laughing, as she stood up. 'A thousand pardons, my dear Lady Ruxton,' she added, 'I didn't see you hadn't finished your cigarette.'

'Never mind, Lady Narborough. I smoke a great deal too much. I am going to limit myself, for the future.'

'Pray don't, Lady Ruxton,' said Lord Henry. 'Moderation is a fatal thing. Enough is as bad as a meal. More than enough is as good as a feast.'

Lady Ruxton glanced at him curiously. 'You must come and explain that to me some afternoon, Lord Henry. It sounds a fascinating theory,' she murmured, as she swept out of the room.

'Now, mind you don't stay too long over your politics and scandal,' cried Lady Narborough from the door. 'If you do, we are sure to squabble upstairs.'

The men laughed, and Mr Chapman got up solemnly from the foot of the table and came up to the top. Dorian Gray changed his seat, and went and sat by Lord Henry. Mr Chapman began to talk in a loud voice about the situation in the House of Commons. He guffawed at his adversaries. The word *doctrinaire*—word full of terror to the British mind—reappeared from time to time between his explosions. An alliterative prefix served as an ornament of oratory. He hoisted the Union Jack on the pinnacles of Thought. The inherited stupidity of the race—sound English common sense he jovially termed it—was shown to be the proper bulwark for Society.

A smile curved Lord Henry's lips, and he turned round and looked at Dorian.

'Are you better, my dear fellow?' he asked. 'You seemed rather out of sorts at dinner.'

'I am quite well, Harry. I am tired. That is all.'

'You were charming last night. The little Duchess is quite devoted to you. She tells me she is going down to Selby.'

'She has promised to come on the twentieth.'

'Is Monmouth to be there too?'

'Oh, yes, Harry.'

'He bores me dreadfully, almost as much as he bores her. She is very clever, too clever for a woman. She lacks the indefinable charm of weakness. It is the feet of clay that make the gold of the image precious. Her feet are very pretty, but they are not feet of clay. White porcelain feet, if you like. They have been through the fire, and what fire does not destroy, it hardens. She has had experiences.'

'How long has she been married?' asked Dorian.

'An eternity, she tells me. I believe, according to the peerage, it is ten years, but ten years with Monmouth must have been like eternity, with time thrown in. Who else is coming?'

'Oh, the Willoughbys, Lord Rugby and his wife, our hostess, Geoffrey Clouston, the usual set. I have asked Lord Grotrian.'

'I like him,' said Lord Henry. 'A great many people don't, but I find him charming. He atones for being occasionally somewhat over-dressed, by being always absolutely over-educated. He is a very modern type.'

'I don't know if he will be able to come, Harry. He may have to go to Monte Carlo with his father.'

'Ah! what a nuisance people's people are! Try and make him come. By the way, Dorian, you ran off very early last night. You left before eleven. What did you do afterwards? Did you go straight home?'

Dorian glanced at him hurriedly, and frowned. 'No, Harry,' he said at last, 'I did not get home till nearly three.'

'Did you go to the club?'

'Yes,' he answered. Then he bit his lip. 'No, I don't mean that. I didn't go to the club. I walked about. I forget what I did....How inquisitive you are, Harry! You always want to know what one has been doing. I always want to forget what I have been doing. I came in at half-past two, if you wish to know the exact time. I had left my latchkey at home, and my servant had to let me in. If you want any corroborative evidence on the subject you can ask him.'

Lord Henry shrugged his shoulders. 'My dear fellow, as if I cared! Let us go up to the drawing-room. No sherry, thank you, Mr Chapman. Something has happened to you, Dorian. Tell me what it is. You are not yourself to-night.'

'Don't mind me, Harry. I am irritable, and out of temper. I shall come round and see you to-morrow, or next day. Make my excuses to Lady Narborough. I shan't go upstairs. I shall go home. I must go home.'

'All right, Dorian. I dare say I shall see you to-morrow at tea-time[178]. The Duchess is coming.'

'I will try to be there, Harry,' he said, leaving the room. As he drove back to his own house he was conscious that the sense of terror he thought he had strangled had come back to him. Lord Henry's casual questioning had made him lose his nerve for the moment, and he wanted his nerve still. Things that were dangerous had to be destroyed. He winced. He hated the idea of even touching them.

Yet it had to be done. He realised that, and when he had locked the door of his library, he opened the secret press into which he had thrust Basil Hallward's coat and bag. A huge fire was blazing. He piled another log on it. The smell of the singeing clothes and burning leather was horrible. It took him three-quarters of an hour to consume everything. At the end he felt faint and sick, and having lit some Algerian pastilles in a pierced copper brazier, he bathed his hands and forehead with a cool musk-scented vinegar.

Suddenly he started. His eyes grew strangely bright, and he gnawed nervously at his under-lip. Between two of the windows stood a large Florentine cabinet, made out of ebony, and inlaid with ivory and blue lapis. He watched it as though it were a thing that could fascinate and make afraid, as though it held something that he longed for and yet almost loathed. His breath quickened. A mad craving came over him. He lit a cigarette and then threw it away. His eyelids drooped till the long fringed lashes almost touched his cheek. But he still watched the cabinet. At last he got up from the sofa on which he had been lying, went over to it, and, having unlocked it, touched some hidden spring. A triangular drawer passed slowly out. His fingers moved instinctively towards it, dipped in, and closed on something. It was a small Chinese box of black and gold-dust lacquer, elaborately wrought, the sides patterned with curved waves, and the silken cords hung with round crystals and tasselled in plaited metal threads. He opened it. Inside was a green paste waxy in lustre, the odour curiously heavy and persistent.

He hesitated for some moments, with a strangely immobile smile upon his face. Then shivering, though the atmosphere of the room was terribly hot, he drew himself up, and glanced at the clock. It was twenty minutes to twelve. He put the box back, shutting the cabinet doors as he did so, and went into his bedroom.

As midnight was striking bronze blows upon the dusky air,

Dorian Gray, dressed commonly, and with a muffler wrapped round his throat, crept quietly out of his house. In Bond Street he found a hansom with a good horse. He hailed it, and in a low voice gave the driver an address.

The man shook his head. 'It is too far for me,' he muttered.

'Here is a sovereign for you,' said Dorian. 'You shall have another if you drive fast.'

'All right, sir,' answered the man, 'you will be there in an hour,' and after his fare had got in he turned his horse round, and drove rapidly towards the river.

Chapter 16

A cold rain began to fall, and the blurred street-lamps[179] looked ghastly in the dripping mist. The public-houses[180] were just closing, and dim men and women were clustering in broken groups round their doors. From some of the bars came the sound of horrible laughter. In others, drunkards brawled and screamed.

Lying back in the hansom, with his hat pulled over his forehead, Dorian Gray watched with listless eyes the sordid shame of the great city, and now and then he repeated to himself the words that Lord Henry had said to him on the first day they had met, 'To cure the soul by means of the senses, and the senses by means of the soul.' Yes, that was the secret. He had often tried it, and would try it again now. There were opium-dens[181], where one could buy oblivion, dens of horror where the memory of old sins could be destroyed by the madness of sins that were new.

The moon hung low in the sky like a yellow skull. From time to time a huge misshapen cloud stretched a long arm across and hid it. The gas-lamps grew fewer, and the streets more narrow and gloomy. Once the man lost his way, and had to drive back half a mile. A steam rose from the horse as it splashed up the puddles. The side-windows[182] of the hansom were clogged with a grey-flannel mist.

'To cure the soul by means of the senses, and the senses by means of the soul!' How the words rang in his ears! His soul, certainly, was sick to death. Was it true that the senses could cure it? Innocent blood had been spilt. What could atone for that? Ah! for[183] that there was no atonement; but though forgiveness was impossible, forgetfulness was possible still, and he was determined to forget, to stamp the thing out, to crush it as one would crush the adder that had stung one. Indeed, what right had Basil to have spoken to him as he had done? Who had made him a judge over others? He had said things that were dreadful, horrible, not to be endured.

On and on plodded the hansom, going slower, it seemed to him, at each step. He thrust up the trap, and called to the man to drive faster. The hideous hunger for opium began to gnaw at him. His throat burned, and his delicate hands twitched nervously together. He struck at the horse madly with his stick. The driver laughed, and whipped up. He laughed in answer, and the man was silent.

The way seemed interminable, and the streets like the black web of some sprawling spider. The monotony became unbearable, and, as the mist thickened, he felt afraid.

Then they passed by lonely brickfields. The fog was lighter here, and he could see the strange bottle-shaped kilns with their orange fan-like tongues of fire. A dog barked as they went by, and far away in the darkness some wandering seagull screamed. The horse stumbled in a rut, then swerved aside, and broke into a gallop.

After some time they left the clay road, and rattled again over rough-paven streets. Most of the windows were dark, but now and then fantastic shadows were silhouetted against some lamp-lit blind. He watched them curiously. They moved like monstrous marionettes, and made gestures like live things. He hated them. A dull rage was in his heart. As they turned a corner a woman yelled something at them from an open door, and two men ran after the hansom for about a hundred yards. The driver beat at them with his whip.

It is said that passion makes one think in a circle. Certainly with hideous iteration the bitten lips of Dorian Gray shaped and reshaped those subtle words that dealt with soul and sense, till he had found in them the full expression, as it were, of his mood, and justified, by intellectual approval, passions that without such justification would still have dominated his temper. From cell to cell of his brain crept the one thought; and the wild desire to live, most terrible of all man's appetites, quickened into force each trembling nerve and fibre. Ugliness that had once been hateful to him because it made things real, became dear to him now for that very reason. Ugliness was the one reality. The coarse brawl, the loathsome den, the crude violence of disordered life, the very vileness of thief and outcast, were more vivid, in their intense actuality of impression, than all the gracious shapes of Art, the dreamy shadows of Song. They were what he needed for forgetfulness. In three days he would be free.

Suddenly the man drew up with a jerk at the top of a dark lane. Over the low roofs and jagged chimney-stacks of the houses rose the black masts of ships. Wreaths of white mist clung like ghostly sails to the yards.

'Somewhere about here, sir, ain't it?' he asked huskily through the trap.

Dorian started, and peered round. 'This will do,' he answered, and, having got out hastily, and given the driver the extra fare he had promised him, he walked quickly in the direction of the quay. Here and there a lantern gleamed at the stern of some huge merchantman. The light shook and splintered in the puddles. A red glare came from an outward-bound steamer that was coaling. The slimy pavement looked like a wet mackintosh.

He hurried on towards the left, glancing back now and then to see if he was being followed. In about seven or eight minutes he reached a small shabby house, that was wedged in between two gaunt factories. In one of the top-windows[194] stood a lamp. He stopped, and gave a peculiar knock.

After a little time he heard steps in the passage, and the chain being unhooked. The door opened quietly, and he went in without saying a word to the squat misshapen figure that flattened itself into the shadow as he passed. At the end of the hall hung a tattered green curtain that swayed and shook in the gusty wind which had followed him in from the street. He dragged it aside, and entered a long, low room which looked as if it had once been a third-rate dancing-saloon. Shrill flaring gas-jets, dulled and distorted in the fly-blown mirrors that faced them, were ranged round the walls. Greasy reflectors of ribbed tin backed them, making quivering disks of light. The floor was covered with ochre-coloured sawdust, trampled here and there into mud, and stained with dark rings of spilt liquor. Some Malays were crouching by a little charcoal stove playing with bone counters, and showing their white teeth as they chattered. In one corner with his head buried in his arms, a sailor sprawled over a table, and by the tawdrily-painted bar that ran across one complete side stood two haggard women mocking an old man who was brushing the sleeves of his coat with an expression of disgust. 'He thinks he's got red ants on him,' laughed one of them, as Dorian passed by. The man looked at her in terror, and began to whimper.

At the end of the room there was a little staircase, leading to a darkened chamber. As Dorian hurried up its three rickety steps, the heavy odour of opium met him. He heaved a deep breath, and his nostrils quivered with pleasure. When he entered, a young man with smooth yellow hair, who was bending over a lamp lighting a long thin pipe, looked up at him, and nodded in a hesitating manner.

'You here, Adrian?' muttered Dorian.

'Where else should I be?' he answered, listlessly. 'None of the chaps will speak to me now.'

'I thought you had left England.'

'Darlington is not going to do anything. My brother paid the bill at last. George doesn't speak to me either....I don't care,' he added, with a sigh. 'As long as one has this stuff, one doesn't want friends. I think I have had too many friends.'

Dorian winced, and looked round at the grotesque things that lay in such fantastic postures on the ragged mattresses. The twisted limbs, the gaping mouths, the staring lustreless eyes, fascinated him. He knew in what strange heavens they were suffering, and what dull hells were teaching them the secret of some new joy. They were better off than he was. He was prisoned in thought. Memory, like a horrible malady, was eating his soul away. From time to time he seemed to see the eyes of Basil Hallward looking at him. Yet he felt he could not stay. The presence of Adrian Singleton troubled him. He wanted to be where no one would know who he was. He wanted to escape from himself.

'I am going on to the other place,' he said, after a pause.

'On the wharf?'

'Yes.'

'That mad-cat is sure to be there. They won't have her in this place now.'

Dorian shrugged his shoulders. 'I am sick of women who love one. Women who hate one are much more interesting. Besides, the stuff is better.'

'Much the same.'

'I like it better. Come and have something to drink. I must have something.'

'I don't want anything,' murmured the young man.

'Never mind.'

Adrian Singleton rose up wearily, and followed Dorian to the bar. A half-caste, in a ragged turban and a shabby ulster, grinned a hideous greeting as he thrust a bottle of brandy and two tumblers in front of them. The women sidled up, and began to chatter. Dorian turned his back on them, and said something in a low voice to Adrian Singleton.

A crooked smile, like a Malay crease, writhed across the face of one of the women. 'We are very proud to-night,' she sneered.

'For God's sake don't talk to me,' cried Dorian, stamping his foot on the ground. 'What do you want? Money? Here it is. Don't ever talk to me again.'

Two red sparks flashed for a moment in the woman's sodden eyes, then flickered out, and left them dull and glazed. She tossed her head, and raked the coins off the counter with greedy fingers. Her companion watched her enviously.

'It's no use,' sighed Adrian Singleton. 'I don't care to go back. What does it matter? I am quite happy here.'

'You will write to me if you want anything, won't you?' said Dorian, after a pause.

'Perhaps.'

'Good-night, then.'

'Good-night,' answered the young man, passing up the steps, and wiping his parched mouth with a handkerchief.

Dorian walked to the door with a look of pain in his face. As he drew the curtain aside a hideous laugh broke from the painted lips of the woman who had taken his money. 'There goes the devil's bargain!' she hiccoughed, in a hoarse voice.

'Curse you!' he answered, 'don't call me that.'

She snapped her fingers. 'Prince Charming is what you like to be called, ain't it?' she yelled after him.

The drowsy sailor leaped to his feet as she spoke, and looked wildly round. The sound of the shutting of the hall door fell on his ear. He rushed out as if in pursuit.

Dorian Gray hurried along the quay through the drizzling rain. His meeting with Adrian Singleton had strangely moved him, and he wondered if the ruin of that young life was really to be laid at his door, as Basil Hallward had said to him with such infamy of insult. He bit his lip, and for a few seconds his eyes grew sad. Yet, after all, what did it matter to him? One's days were too brief to take the burden of another's errors on one's shoulders. Each man lived his own life, and paid his own price for living it. The only pity was one had to pay so often for a single fault. One had to pay over and over again, indeed. In her dealings with man Destiny never closed her accounts.

There are moments, psychologists tell us, when the passion for sin, or for what the world calls sin, so dominates a nature, that every fibre of the body, as every cell of the brain, seems to be instinct with fearful impulses. Men and women at such moments lose the freedom of their will. They move to their terrible end as automatons move. Choice is taken from them, and conscience is either killed, or, if it lives at all, lives but to give rebellion its fascination, and disobedience its charm. For all sins, as theologians weary not of reminding us, are sins of disobedience. When that high spirit, that morning-star[185] of evil, fell from heaven, it was as a rebel that he fell.

Callous, concentrated on evil, with stained mind, and soul hungry for rebellion, Dorian Gray hastened on, quickening his step as he went, but as he darted aside into a dim archway, that had served him often as a short cut to the ill-famed place where he was going, he felt himself suddenly seized from behind, and before he had time to defend himself, he was thrust back against the wall, with a brutal hand round his throat.

He struggled madly for life, and by a terrible effort wrenched the tightening fingers away. In a second he heard the click of a revolver, and saw the gleam of a polished barrel pointing straight at his head, and the dusky form of a short thick-set man facing him.

'What do you want?' he gasped.

'Keep quiet,' said the man. 'If you stir, I shoot you.'

'You are mad. What have I done to you?'

'You wrecked the life of Sibyl Vane,' was the answer, 'and Sibyl Vane was my sister. She killed herself. I know it. Her death is at your door. I swore I would kill you in return. For years I have sought you. I had no clue, no trace. The two people who could have described you were dead. I knew nothing of you but the pet name she used to call you. I heard it to-night by chance. Make your peace with God, for to-night you are going to die.'

Dorian Gray grew sick with fear. 'I never knew her,' he stammered. 'I never heard of her. You are mad.'

'You had better confess your sin, for as sure as I am James Vane, you are going to die.' There was a horrible moment. Dorian did not know what to say or do. 'Down on your knees!' growled the man. 'I give you one minute to make your peace—no more. I go on board to-night for India, and I must do my job first. One minute. That's all.'

Dorian's arms fell to his side. Paralyzed with terror, he did not know what to do. Suddenly a wild hope flashed across his brain. 'Stop,' he cried. 'How long ago is it since your sister died? Quick, tell me!'

'Eighteen years,' said the man. 'Why do you ask me? What do years matter?'

'Eighteen years,' laughed Dorian Gray, with a touch of triumph in his voice. 'Eighteen years! Set me under the lamp and look at my face!'

James Vane hesitated for a moment, not understanding what was meant. Then he seized Dorian Gray and dragged him from the archway.

Dim and wavering as was the windblown light, yet it served to show him the hideous error, as it seemed, into which he had fallen, for the face of the man he had sought to kill had all the bloom of boyhood, all the unstained purity of youth. He seemed little more than a lad of twenty summers, hardly older, if older indeed at all, than his sister had been when they had parted so many years ago. It was obvious that this was not the man who had destroyed her life.

He loosened his hold and reeled back. 'My God! my God!' he cried, 'and I would have murdered you!'

Dorian Gray drew a long breath. 'You have been on the brink of committing a terrible crime, my man,' he said, looking at him sternly. 'Let this be a warning to you not to take vengeance into your own hands.'

'Forgive me, sir,' muttered James Vane. 'I was deceived. A chance word I heard in that damned den set me on the wrong track.'

'You had better go home, and put that pistol away, or you may get into trouble,' said Dorian, turning on his heel, and going slowly down the street.

James Vane stood on the pavement in horror. He was trembling from head to foot. After a little while a black shadow that had been creeping along the dripping wall, moved out into the light and came close to him with stealthy footsteps. He felt a hand laid on his arm and looked round with a start. It was one of the women who had been drinking at the bar.

'Why didn't you kill him?' she hissed out, putting her haggard face quite close to his. 'I knew you were following him when you rushed out from Daly's. You fool! You should have killed him. He has lots of money, and he's as bad as bad.'

'He is not the man I am looking for,' he answered, 'and I want no man's money. I want a man's life. The man whose life I want must be nearly forty now. This one is little more than a boy. Thank God, I have not got his blood upon my hands.'

The woman gave a bitter laugh. 'Little more than a boy!' she sneered. 'Why, man, it's nigh on eighteen years since Prince Charming made me what I am.'

'You lie!' cried James Vane.

She raised her hand up to heaven. 'Before God I am telling the truth,' she cried.

'Before God?'

'Strike me dumb if it ain't so. He is the worst one that comes here. They say he has sold himself to the devil for a pretty face. It's nigh on eighteen years since I met him. He hasn't changed much since then. I have though,' she added, with a sickly leer.

'You swear this?'

'I swear it,' came in hoarse echo from her flat mouth. 'But don't give me away to him,' she whined; 'I am afraid of him. Let me have some money for my night's lodging.'

He broke from her with an oath, and rushed to the corner of the street, but Dorian Gray had disappeared. When he looked back, the woman had vanished also.

Chapter 17

A week later Dorian Gray was sitting in the conservatory at Selby Royal talking to the pretty Duchess of Monmouth, who with her husband, a jaded-looking man of sixty, was amongst his guests. It was tea-time, and the mellow light of the huge, lace-covered lamp that stood on the table lit up the delicate china and hammered silver of the service at which the Duchess was presiding. Her white hands were moving daintily among the cups, and her full red lips were smiling at something that Dorian had whispered to her. Lord Henry was lying back in a silk-draped wicker chair, looking at them. On a peach-coloured divan sat Lady Narborough pretending to listen to the Duke's description of the last Brazilian beetle that he had added to his collection. Three young men in elaborate smoking-suits were handing tea-cakes[186] to some of the women. The house-party[187] consisted of twelve people, and there were more expected to arrive on the next day.

'What are you two talking about?' said Lord Henry, strolling over to the table, and putting his cup down. 'I hope Dorian has told you about my plan for rechristening everything, Gladys. It is a delightful idea.'

'But I don't want to be rechristened, Harry,' rejoined the Duchess, looking up at him with her wonderful eyes. 'I am quite satisfied with my own name, and I am sure Mr Gray should be satisfied with his.'

'My dear Gladys, I would not alter either name for the world. They are both perfect. I was thinking chiefly of flowers. Yesterday I cut an orchid, for my buttonhole. It was a marvellous spotted thing, as effective as the seven deadly sins. In a thoughtless moment I asked one of the gardeners what it was called. He told me it was a fine specimen of *Robinsoniana*, or something dreadful of that kind. It is a sad truth, but we have lost the faculty of giving lovely names to things. Names are everything. I never quarrel with actions. My one quarrel is with words. That is the reason I hate vulgar realism in literature. The man who could call a spade a spade should be compelled to use one. It is the only thing he is fit for.'

'Then what should we call you, Harry?' she asked.

'His name is Prince Paradox,' said Dorian.

'I recognize him in a flash,' exclaimed the Duchess.

'I won't hear of it,' laughed Lord Henry, sinking into a chair. 'From a label there is no escape! I refuse the title.'

'Royalties may not abdicate,' fell as a warning from pretty lips.

'You wish me to defend my throne, then?'

'Yes.'

'I give the truths of to-morrow.'

'I prefer the mistakes of to-day,' she answered.

'You disarm me, Gladys,' he cried, catching the wilfulness of her mood.

'Of your shield, Harry: not of your spear.'

'I never tilt against Beauty,' he said, with a wave of his hand.

'That is your error, Harry, believe me. You value beauty far too much.'

'How can you say that? I admit that I think that it is better to be beautiful than to be good. But on the other hand no one is more ready than I am to acknowledge that it is better to be good than to be ugly.'

'Ugliness is one of the seven deadly sins, then?' cried the Duchess. 'What becomes of your simile about the orchid?'

'Ugliness is one of the seven deadly virtues, Gladys. You, as a good Tory, must not underrate them. Beer, the Bible, and the seven deadly virtues have made our England what she is.'

'You don't like your country, then?' she asked.

'I live in it.'

'That you may censure it the better.'

'Would you have me take the verdict of Europe on it?' he enquired.

'What do they say of us?'

'That Tartuffe[188] has emigrated to England and opened a shop.'

'Is that yours, Harry?'

'I give it to you.'

'I could not use it. It is too true.'

'You need not be afraid. Our countrymen never recognize a description.'

'They are practical.'

'They are more cunning than practical. When they make up their ledger, they balance stupidity by wealth, and vice by hypocrisy.'

'Still, we have done great things.'

'Great things have been thrust on us, Gladys.'

'We have carried their burden.'

'Only as far as the Stock Exchange.'

She shook her head. 'I believe in the race,' she cried.

'It represents the survival of the pushing.'

'It has development.'

'Decay fascinates me more.'

'What of Art?' she asked.

'It is a malady.'

'Love?'

'An illusion.'

'Religion?'

'The fashionable substitute for Belief.'

'You are a sceptic.'

'Never! Scepticism is the beginning of Faith.'

'What are you?'

'To define is to limit.'

'Give me a clue.'

'Threads snap. You would lose your way in the labyrinth.'

'You bewilder me. Let us talk of some one else.'

'Our host is a delightful topic. Years ago he was christened Prince Charming.'

'Ah! don't remind me of that,' cried Dorian Gray.

'Our host is rather horrid this evening,' answered the Duchess, colouring. 'I believe he thinks that Monmouth married me on purely scientific principles as the best specimen he could find of a modern butterfly.'

'Well, I hope he won't stick pins into you, Duchess,' laughed Dorian.

'Oh! my maid does that already, Mr Gray, when she is annoyed with me.'

'And what does she get annoyed with you about, Duchess?'

'For the most trivial things, Mr Gray, I assure you. Usually because I come in at ten minutes to nine and tell her that I must be dressed by half-past eight.'

'How unreasonable of her! You should give her warning.'

'I daren't, Mr Gray. Why, she invents hats for me. You remember the one I wore at Lady Hilstone's garden-party[189]? You don't, but it is nice of you to pretend that you do. Well, she made it out of nothing. All good hats are made out of nothing.'

'Like all good reputations, Gladys,' interrupted Lord Henry. 'Every effect that one produces gives one an enemy. To be popular one must be a mediocrity.'

'Not with women,' said the Duchess, shaking her head; 'and women rule the world. I assure you we can't bear mediocrities. We women, as some one says, love with our ears, just as you men love with your eyes, if you ever love at all.'

'It seems to me that we never do anything else,' murmured Dorian.

'Ah! then[190], you never really love, Mr Gray,' answered the Duchess, with mock sadness.

'My dear Gladys!' cried Lord Henry. 'How can you say that? Romance lives by repetition, and repetition converts an appetite into an art. Besides, each time that one loves is the only time one has ever loved. Difference of object does not alter singleness of passion. It merely intensifies it. We can have in life but one great experience at best, and the secret of life is to reproduce that experience as often as possible.'

'Even when one has been wounded by it, Harry?' asked the Duchess, after a pause.

'Especially when one has been wounded by it,' answered Lord Henry.

The Duchess turned and looked at Dorian Gray with a curious expression in her eyes. 'What do you say to that, Mr Gray?' she enquired.

Dorian hesitated for a moment. Then he threw his head back and laughed. 'I always agree with Harry, Duchess.'

'Even when he is wrong?'

'Harry is never wrong, Duchess.'

'And does his philosophy make you happy?'

'I have never searched for happiness. Who wants happiness? I have searched for pleasure.'

'And found it, Mr Gray?'

'Often. Too often.'

The duchess sighed. 'I am searching for peace,' she said, 'and if I don't go and dress, I shall have none this evening.'

'Let me get you some orchids, Duchess,' cried Dorian, starting to his feet and walking down the conservatory.

'You are flirting disgracefully with him,' said Lord Henry to his cousin. 'You had better take care. He is very fascinating.'

'If he were not, there would be no battle.'

'Greek meets Greek, then?'

'I am on the side of the Trojans. They fought for a woman.'

'They were defeated.'

'There are worse things than capture,' she answered.

'You gallop with a loose rein.'

'Pace gives life,' was the *riposte*.

'I shall write it in my diary to-night.'

'What?'

'That a burnt child loves the fire.'

'I am not even singed. My wings are untouched.'

'You use them for everything, except flight.'

'Courage has passed from men to women. It is a new experience for us.'

'You have a rival.'

'Who?'

He laughed. 'Lady Narborough,' he whispered. 'She perfectly adores him.'

'You fill me with apprehension. The appeal to Antiquity is fatal to us who are romanticists.'

'Romanticists! You have all the methods of science.'

'Men have educated us.'

'But not explained you.'

'Describe us as a sex,' was her challenge.

'Sphinxes without secrets.'

She looked at him, smiling. 'How long Mr Gray is!' she said. 'Let us go and help him. I have not yet told him the colour of my frock.'

'Ah! you must suit your frock to his flowers, Gladys.'

'That would be a premature surrender.'

'Romantic Art begins with its climax.'

'I must keep an opportunity for retreat.'

'In the Parthian manner?'

'They found safety in the desert. I could not do that.'

'Women are not always allowed a choice,' he answered, but hardly had he finished the sentence before from the far end of the conservatory came a stifled groan, followed by the dull sound of a heavy fall. Everybody started up. The Duchess stood motionless in horror. And with fear in his eyes Lord Henry rushed through the flapping palms, to find Dorian Gray lying face downwards on the tiled floor in a death-like swoon.

He was carried at once into the blue drawing-room, and laid upon one of the sofas. After a short time, he came to himself, and looked round with a dazed expression.

'What has happened?' he asked. 'Oh! I remember. Am I safe here, Harry?' He began to tremble.

'My dear Dorian,' answered Lord Henry, 'you merely fainted. That was all. You must have overtired yourself. You had better not come down to dinner. I will take your place.'

'No, I will come down,' he said, struggling to his feet. 'I would rather come down. I must not be alone.'

He went to his room and dressed. There was a wild recklessness of gaiety in his manner as he sat at table, but now and then a thrill of terror ran through him when he remembered that, pressed against the window of the conservatory, like a white handkerchief, he had seen the face of James Vane watching him.

Chapter 18

The next day he did not leave the house, and, indeed, spent most of the time in his own room, sick with a wild terror of dying, and yet indifferent to life itself. The consciousness of being hunted, snared, tracked down, had begun to dominate him. If the tapestry did but tremble in the wind, he shook. The dead leaves that were blown against the leaded panes seemed to him like his own wasted resolutions and wild regrets. When he closed his eyes, he saw again the sailor's face peering through the mist-stained glass, and horror seemed once more to lay its hand upon his heart.

But perhaps it had been only his fancy that had called vengeance out of the night, and set the hideous shapes of punishment before him. Actual life was chaos, but there was something terribly logical in the imagination. It was the imagination that set remorse to dog the feet of sin. It was the imagination that made each crime bear its misshapen brood. In the common world of fact the wicked were not punished, nor the good rewarded. Success was given to the strong, failure thrust upon the weak. That was all. Besides, had any stranger been prowling round the house he would have been seen by the servants or the keepers. Had any footmarks been found on the flower-beds[191], the gardeners would have reported it. Yes: it had been merely fancy. Sibyl Vane's brother had not come back to kill him. He had sailed away in his ship to founder in some winter sea. From him, at any rate, he was safe. Why, the man did not know who he was, could not know who he was. The mask of youth had saved him.

And yet if it had been merely an illusion, how terrible it was to think that conscience could raise such fearful phantoms, and give them visible form, and make them move before one! What sort of life would his be if, day and night, shadows of his crime were to peer at him from silent corners, to mock him from secret places, to whisper in his ear as he sat at the feast, to wake him with icy fingers as he lay asleep! As the thought crept through his brain, he grew pale with terror, and the air seemed to him to have become suddenly colder. Oh! in[192] what a wild hour of madness he had killed his friend! How ghastly the mere memory of the scene! He saw it all again. Each hideous detail came back to him with added horror. Out of the black cave of Time, terrible and swathed in scarlet, rose the image of his sin. When Lord Henry came in at six o'clock, he found him crying as one whose heart will break.

It was not till the third day that he ventured to go out. There was something in the clear, pine-scented air of that winter morning that seemed to bring him back his joyousness and his ardour for life. But it was not merely the physical conditions of environment that had caused the change. His own nature had revolted against the excess of anguish that had sought to maim and mar the perfection of its calm. With subtle and finely-wrought temperaments it is always so. Their strong passions must either bruise or bend. They either slay the man, or themselves die. Shallow sorrows and shallow loves live on. The loves and sorrows that are great are destroyed by their own plenitude. Besides, he had convinced himself that he had been the victim of a terror-stricken imagination, and looked back now on his fears with something of pity and not a little of contempt.

After breakfast he walked with the Duchess for an hour in the garden, and then drove across the park to join the shooting-party[193]. The crisp frost lay like salt upon the grass. The sky was an inverted cup of blue metal. A thin film of ice bordered the flat reed-grown lake.

At the corner of the pine-wood[194] he caught sight of Sir Geoffrey Clouston, the Duchess's brother, jerking two spent cartridges out of his gun. He jumped from the cart, and having told the groom to take the mare home, made his way towards his guest through the withered bracken and rough undergrowth.

'Have you had good sport, Geoffrey?' he asked.

'Not very good, Dorian. I think most of the birds have gone to the open. I dare say it will be better after lunch, when we get to new ground.'

Dorian strolled along by his side. The keen aromatic air, the brown and red lights that glimmered in the wood, the hoarse cries of the beaters ringing out from time to time, and the sharp snaps of the guns that followed, fascinated him, and filled him with a sense of delightful freedom. He was dominated by the carelessness of happiness, by the high indifference of joy.

Suddenly from a lumpy tussock of old grass, some twenty yards in front of them, with black-tipped ears erect, and long hinder limbs throwing it forward, started a hare. It bolted for a thicket of alders. Sir Geoffrey put his gun to his shoulder, but there was something in the animal's grace of movement that strangely charmed Dorian Gray, and he cried out at once, 'Don't shoot it, Geoffrey. Let it live.'

'What nonsense, Dorian!' laughed his companion, and as the hare bounded into the thicket he fired. There were two cries heard, the cry of a hare in pain, which is dreadful, the cry of a man in agony, which is worse.

'Good heavens! I have hit a beater!' exclaimed Sir Geoffrey. 'What an ass the man was to get in front of the guns! Stop shooting there!' he called out at the top of his voice. 'A man is hurt.'

The head-keeper came running up with a stick in his hand.

'Where, sir? Where is he?' he shouted. At the same time, the firing ceased along the line.

'Here,' answered Sir Geoffrey, angrily, hurrying towards the thicket. 'Why on earth don't you keep your men back? Spoiled my shooting for the day.'

Dorian watched them as they plunged into the alder-clump, brushing the lithe, swinging branches aside. In a few moments they emerged, dragging a body after them into the sunlight. He turned away in horror. It seemed to him that misfortune followed wherever he went. He heard Sir Geoffrey ask if the man was really dead, and the affirmative answer of the keeper. The wood seemed to him to have become suddenly alive with faces. There was the trampling of myriad feet, and the low buzz of voices. A great copper-breasted pheasant came beating through the boughs overhead.

After a few moments, that were to him, in his perturbed state, like endless hours of pain, he felt a hand laid on his shoulder. He started, and looked round.

'Dorian,' said Lord Henry, 'I had better tell them that the shooting is stopped for to-day. It would not look well to go on.'

'I wish it were stopped for ever, Harry,' he answered, bitterly. 'The whole thing is hideous and cruel. Is the man...?'

He could not finish the sentence.

'I am afraid so,' rejoined Lord Henry. 'He got the whole charge of shot in his chest. He must have died almost instantaneously. Come; let us go home.'

They walked side by side in the direction of the avenue for nearly fifty yards without speaking. Then Dorian looked at Lord Henry, and said, with a heavy sigh, 'It is a bad omen, Harry, a very bad omen.'

'What is?' asked Lord Henry. 'Oh! this accident, I suppose. My dear fellow, it can't be helped. It was the man's own fault. Why did he get in front of the guns? Besides, it is nothing to us. It is rather awkward for Geoffrey, of course. It does not do to pepper beaters. It makes people think that one is a wild shot. And Geoffrey is not; he shoots very straight. But there is no use talking about the matter.'

Dorian shook his head. 'It is a bad omen, Harry. I feel as if something horrible were going to happen to some of us. To myself, perhaps,' he added, passing his hand over his eyes, with a gesture of pain.

The elder man laughed. 'The only horrible thing in the world is *ennui*, Dorian. That is the one sin for which there is no forgiveness. But we are not likely to suffer from it, unless these fellows keep chattering about this thing at dinner. I must tell them that the subject is to be tabooed. As for omens, there is no such thing as an omen. Destiny does not send us heralds. She is too wise or too cruel for that. Besides, what on earth could happen to you, Dorian? You have everything in the world that a man can want. There is no one who would not be delighted to change places with you.'

'There is no one with whom I would not change places, Harry. Don't laugh like that. I am telling you the truth. The wretched peasant who has just died is better off than I am. I have no terror of Death. It is the coming of Death that terrifies me. Its monstrous wings seem to wheel in the leaden air around me. Good heavens! don't you see a man moving behind the trees there, watching me, waiting for me?'

Lord Henry looked in the direction in which the trembling gloved hand was pointing. 'Yes,' he said, smiling, 'I see the gardener waiting for you. I suppose he wants to ask you what flowers you wish to have on the table to-night. How absurdly nervous you are, my dear fellow! You must come and see my doctor, when we get back to town.'

Dorian heaved a sigh of relief as he saw the gardener approaching. The man touched his hat, glanced for a moment at Lord Henry in a hesitating manner, and then produced a letter, which he handed to his master. 'Her Grace told me to wait for an answer,' he murmured.

Dorian put the letter into his pocket. 'Tell her Grace that I am coming in,' he said, coldly. The man turned round, and went rapidly in the direction of the house.

'How fond women are of doing dangerous things!' laughed Lord Henry. 'It is one of the qualities in them that I admire most. A woman will flirt with anybody in the world as long as other people are looking on.'

'How fond you are of saying dangerous things, Harry! In the present instance you are quite astray. I like the Duchess very much, but I don't love her.'

'And the Duchess loves you very much, but she likes you less, so you are excellently matched.'

'You are talking scandal, Harry, and there is never any basis for scandal.'

'The basis of every scandal is an immoral certainty,' said Lord Henry, lighting a cigarette.

'You would sacrifice anybody, Harry, for the sake of an epigram.'

'The world goes to the altar of its own accord,' was the answer.

'I wish I could love,' cried Dorian Gray, with a deep note of pathos in his voice. 'But I seem to have lost the passion, and forgotten the desire. I am too much concentrated on myself. My own personality has become a burden to me. I want to escape, to go away, to forget. It was silly of me to come down here at all. I think I shall send a wire to Harvey to have the yacht got ready. On a yacht one is safe.'

'Safe from what, Dorian? You are in some trouble. Why not tell me what it is? You know I would help you.'

'I can't tell you, Harry,' he answered, sadly. 'And I dare say it is only a fancy of mine. This unfortunate accident has upset me. I have a horrible presentiment that something of the kind may happen to me.'

'What nonsense!'

'I hope it is, but I can't help feeling it. Ah! here[195] is the

Duchess, looking like Artemis[196] in a tailor-made gown. You see we have come back, Duchess.'

'I have heard all about it, Mr Gray,' she answered. 'Poor Geoffrey is terribly upset. And it seems that you asked him not to shoot the hare. How curious!'

'Yes, it was very curious. I don't know what made me say it. Some whim, I suppose. It looked the loveliest of little live things. But I am sorry they told you about the man. It is a hideous subject.'

'It is an annoying subject,' broke in Lord Henry. 'It has no psychological value at all. Now if Geoffrey had done the thing on purpose, how interesting he would be! I should like to know some one who had committed a real murder.'

'How horrid of you, Harry!' cried the Duchess. 'Isn't it, Mr Gray? Harry, Mr Gray is ill again. He is going to faint.'

Dorian drew himself up with an effort, and smiled. 'It is nothing, Duchess,' he murmured; 'my nerves are dreadfully out of order. That is all. I am afraid I walked too far this morning. I didn't hear what Harry said. Was it very bad? You must tell me some other time. I think I must go and lie down. You will excuse me, won't you?'

They had reached the great flight of steps that led from the conservatory on to the terrace. As the glass door closed behind Dorian, Lord Henry turned and looked at the Duchess with his slumberous eyes. 'Are you very much in love with him?' he asked.

She did not answer for some time, but stood gazing at the landscape. 'I wish I knew,' she said at last.

He shook his head. 'Knowledge would be fatal. It is the uncertainty that charms one. A mist makes things wonderful.'

'One may lose one's way.'

'All ways end at the same point, my dear Gladys.'

'What is that?'

'Disillusion.'

'It was my *début* in life,' she sighed.

'It came to you crowned.'

'I am tired of strawberry leaves.'

'They become you.'

'Only in public.'

'You would miss them,' said Lord Henry.

'I will not part with a petal.'

'Monmouth has ears.'

'Old age is dull of hearing.'

'Has he never been jealous?'

'I wish he had been.'

He glanced about as if in search of something. 'What are you looking for?' she enquired.

'The button from your foil,' he answered. 'You have dropped it.'

She laughed. 'I have still the mask.'

'It makes your eyes lovelier,' was his reply.

She laughed again. Her teeth showed like white seeds in a scarlet fruit.

Upstairs, in his own room, Dorian Gray was lying on a sofa, with terror in every tingling fibre of his body. Life had suddenly become too hideous a burden for him to bear. The dreadful death of the unlucky beater, shot in the thicket like a wild animal, had seemed to him to prefigure death for himself also. He had nearly swooned at what Lord Henry had said in a chance mood of cynical jesting.

At five o'clock he rang his bell for his servant and gave him orders to pack his things for the night-express to town, and to have the brougham at the door by eight-thirty. He was determined not to sleep another night at Selby Royal. It was an ill-omened place. Death walked there in the sunlight. The grass of the forest had been spotted with blood.

Then he wrote a note to Lord Henry, telling him that he was going up to town to consult his doctor, and asking him to entertain his guests in his absence. As he was putting it into the envelope, a knock came to the door, and his valet informed him that the head-keeper wished to see him. He frowned, and bit his lip. 'Send him in,' he muttered, after some moments' hesitation.

As soon as the man entered Dorian pulled his cheque-book[197] out of a drawer, and spread it out before him.

'I suppose you have come about the unfortunate accident of this morning, Thornton?' he said, taking up a pen.

'Yes, sir,' answered the gamekeeper.

'Was the poor fellow married? Had he any people dependent on him?' asked Dorian, looking bored. 'If so, I should not like them to be left in want, and will send them any sum of money you may think necessary.'

'We don't know who he is, sir. That is what I took the liberty of coming to you about.'

'Don't know who he is?' said Dorian, listlessly. 'What do you mean? Wasn't he one of your men?'

'No, sir. Never saw him before. Seems like a sailor, sir.'

The pen dropped from Dorian Gray's hand, and he felt as if his heart had suddenly stopped beating. 'A sailor?' he cried out. 'Did you say a sailor?'

'Yes, sir. He looks as if he had been a sort of sailor; tattooed on both arms, and that kind of thing.'

'Was there anything found on him?' said Dorian, leaning forward and looking at the man with startled eyes. 'Anything that would tell his name?'

'Some money, sir—not much, and a six-shooter. There was no name of any kind. A decent-looking man, sir, but rough-like. A sort of sailor we think.'

Dorian started to his feet. A terrible hope fluttered past him. He clutched at it madly. 'Where is the body?' he exclaimed. 'Quick! I must see it at once.'

'It is in an empty stable in the Home Farm, sir. The folk don't like to have that sort of thing in their houses. They say a corpse brings bad luck.'

'The Home Farm! Go there at once and meet me. Tell one of the grooms to bring my horse round. No. Never mind. I'll go to the stables myself. It will save time.'

In less than a quarter of an hour Dorian Gray was galloping down the long avenue as hard as he could go. The trees seemed to sweep past him in spectral procession, and wild shadows to fling themselves across his path. Once the mare swerved at a white gate-post[198] and nearly threw him. He lashed her across the neck with his crop. She cleft the dusky air like an arrow. The stones flew from her hoofs.

At last he reached the Home Farm. Two men were loitering in the yard. He leaped from the saddle and threw the reins to one of them. In the farthest stable a light was glimmering. Something seemed to tell him that the body was there, and he hurried to the door, and put his hand upon the latch.

There he paused for a moment, feeling that he was on the brink of a discovery that would either make or mar his life. Then he thrust the door open, and entered.

On a heap of sacking in the far corner was lying the dead body of a man dressed in a coarse shirt and a pair of blue trousers. A spotted handkerchief had been placed over the face. A coarse candle, stuck in a bottle, sputtered beside it.

Dorian Gray shuddered. He felt that his could not be the hand to take the handkerchief away, and called out to one of the farm-servants[199] to come to him.

'Take that thing off the face. I wish to see it,' he said, clutching at the doorpost for support.

When the farm-servant had done so, he stepped forward. A cry of joy broke from his lips. The man who had been shot in the thicket was James Vane.

He stood there for some minutes looking at the dead body. As he rode home, his eyes were full of tears, for he knew he was safe.

Chapter 19

'There is no use your telling me that you are going to be good,' cried Lord Henry, dipping his white fingers into a red copper bowl filled with rose-water. 'You are quite perfect. Pray, don't change.'

Dorian Gray shook his head. 'No, Harry, I have done too many dreadful things in my life. I am not going to do any more. I began my good actions yesterday.'

'Where were you yesterday?'

'In the country, Harry. I was staying at a little inn by myself.'

'My dear boy,' said Lord Henry, smiling, 'anybody can be good in the country. There are no temptations there. That is the reason why people who live out of town are so absolutely uncivilized. Civilization is not by any means an easy thing to attain to. There are only two ways by which man can reach it. One is by being cultured, the other by being corrupt. Country people have no opportunity of being either, so they stagnate.'

'Culture and corruption,' echoed Dorian. 'I have known something of both. It seems terrible to me now that they should ever be found together. For I have a new ideal, Harry. I am going to alter. I think I have altered.'

'You have not yet told me what your good action was. Or did you say you had done more than one?' asked his companion, as he spilt into his plate a little crimson pyramid of seeded strawberries, and through a perforated shell-shaped spoon snowed white sugar upon them.

'I can tell you, Harry. It is not a story I could tell to any one else. I spared somebody. It sounds vain, but you understand what I mean. She was quite beautiful, and wonderfully like Sibyl Vane. I think it was that which first attracted me to her. You remember Sibyl, don't you? How long ago that seems! Well, Hetty was not one of our own class, of course. She was simply a girl in a village. But I really loved her. I am quite sure that I loved her. All during this wonderful May that we have been having, I used to run down and see her two or three times a week. Yesterday she met me in a little orchard. The apple-blossoms[200] kept tumbling down on her hair, and she was laughing. We were to have gone away together this morning at dawn. Suddenly I determined to leave her as flower-like as I had found her.'

'I should think the novelty of the emotion must have given you a thrill of real pleasure, Dorian,' interrupted Lord Henry. 'But I can finish your idyll for you. You gave her good advice, and broke her heart. That was the beginning of your reformation.'

'Harry, you are horrible! You mustn't say these dreadful things. Hetty's heart is not broken. Of course she cried, and all that. But there is no disgrace upon her. She can live, like Perdita, in her garden of mint and marigold.'

'And weep over a faithless Florizel,' said Lord Henry, laughing, as he leant back in his chair. 'My dear Dorian, you have the most curiously boyish moods. Do you think this girl will ever be really contented now with any one of her own rank? I suppose she will be married some day to a rough carter or a grinning ploughman.

Well, the fact of having met you, and loved you, will teach her to despise her husband, and she will be wretched. From a moral point of view, I cannot say that I think much of your great renunciation. Even as a beginning, it is poor. Besides, how do you know that Hetty isn't floating at the present moment in some star-lit mill-pond[201], with lovely water-lilies[202] round her, like Ophelia?'

'I can't bear this, Harry! You mock at everything, and then suggest the most serious tragedies. I am sorry I told you now. I don't care what you say to me. I know I was right in acting as I did. Poor Hetty! As I rode past the farm this morning, I saw her white face at the window, like a spray of jasmine. Don't let us talk about it any more, and don't try to persuade me that the first good action I have done for years, the first little bit of self-sacrifice I have ever known, is really a sort of sin. I want to be better. I am going to be better. Tell me something about yourself. What is going on it town? I have not been to the club for days.'

'The people are still discussing poor Basil's disappearance.'

'I should have thought they had got tired of that by this time,' said Dorian, pouring himself out some wine, and frowning slightly.

'My dear boy, they have only been talking about it for six weeks, and the British public are really not equal to the mental strain of having more than one topic every three months. They have been very fortunate lately, however. They have had my own divorce-case[203], and Alan Campbell's suicide. Now they have got the mysterious disappearance of an artist. Scotland Yard still insists that the man in the grey ulster who left for Paris by the midnight train on the ninth of November was poor Basil, and the French police declare that Basil never arrived in Paris at all. I suppose in about a fortnight we shall be told that he has been seen in San

Francisco. It is an odd thing, but every one who disappears is said to be seen at San Francisco. It must be a delightful city, and possess all the attractions of the next world.'

'What do you think has happened to Basil?' asked Dorian, holding up his Burgundy against the light, and wondering how it was that he could discuss the matter so calmly.

'I have not the slightest idea. If Basil chooses to hide himself, it is no business of mine. If he is dead, I don't want to think about him. Death is the only thing that ever terrifies me. I hate it.'

'Why?' said the younger man, wearily.

'Because,' said Lord Henry, passing beneath his nostrils the gilt trellis of an open vinaigrette box, 'one can survive everything nowadays except that. Death and vulgarity are the only two facts in the nineteenth century that one cannot explain away. Let us have our coffee in the music-room[204], Dorian. You must play Chopin to me. The man with whom my wife ran away played Chopin exquisitely. Poor Victoria! I was very fond of her. The house is rather lonely without her. Of course married life is merely a habit, a bad habit. But then one regrets the loss even of one's worst habits. Perhaps one regrets them the most. They are such an essential part of one's personality.'

Dorian said nothing, but rose from the table, and, passing into the next room, sat down to the piano and let his fingers stray across the white and black ivory of the keys. After the coffee had been brought in, he stopped, and, looking over at Lord Henry, said, 'Harry, did it ever occur to you that Basil was murdered?'

Lord Henry yawned. 'Basil was very popular, and always wore a Waterbury watch. Why should he have been murdered? He was not clever enough to have enemies. Of course he had a wonderful genius for painting. But a man can paint like Velasquez and yet be as dull as possible. Basil was really rather dull. He only interested me once, and that was when he told me, years ago, that he had a wild adoration for you, and that you were the dominant motive of his art.'

'I was very fond of Basil,' said Dorian, with a note of sadness in his voice. 'But don't people say that he was murdered?'

'Oh, some of the papers do. It does not seem to me to be at all probable. I know there are dreadful places in Paris, but Basil was not the sort of man to have gone to them. He had no curiosity. It was his chief defect.'

'What would you say, Harry, if I told you that I had murdered Basil?' said the younger man. He watched him intently after he had spoken.

'I would say, my dear fellow, that you were posing for a character that doesn't suit you. All crime is vulgar, just as all vulgarity is crime. It is not in you, Dorian, to commit a murder. I am sorry if I hurt your vanity by saying so, but I assure you it is true. Crime belongs exclusively to the lower orders. I don't blame them in the smallest degree. I should fancy that crime was to them what art is to us, simply a method of procuring extraordinary sensations.'

'A method of procuring sensations? Do you think, then, that a man who has once committed a murder could possibly do the same crime again? Don't tell me that.'

'Oh! anything[205] becomes a pleasure if one does it too often,' cried Lord Henry, laughing. 'That is one of the most important secrets of life. I should fancy, however, that murder is always a mistake. One should never do anything that one cannot talk about after dinner. But let us pass from poor Basil. I wish I could believe that he had come to such a really romantic end as you suggest; but I can't. I dare say he fell into the Seine off an omnibus, and that the conductor hushed up the scandal. Yes: I should fancy that was his end. I see him lying now on his back under those dull-green waters with the heavy barges floating over him, and long weeds catching in his hair. Do you know, I don't think he would have done much more good work. During the last ten years his painting had gone off very much.'

Dorian heaved a sigh, and Lord Henry strolled across the room and began to stroke the head of a curious Java parrot, a large grey-plumaged bird, with pink crest and tail, that was balancing itself upon a bamboo perch. As his pointed fingers touched it, it dropped the white scurf of crinkled lids over black glass-like eyes, and began to sway backwards and forwards.

'Yes,' he continued, turning round, and taking his handkerchief out of his pocket; 'his painting had quite gone off. It seemed to me to have lost something. It had lost an ideal. When you and he ceased to be great friends, he ceased to be a great artist. What was it separated you? I suppose he bored you. If so, he never forgave you. It's a habit bores have. By the way, what has become of that wonderful portrait he did of you? I don't think I have ever seen it since he finished it. Oh! I remember your telling me years ago that you had sent it down to Selby, and that it had got mislaid or stolen on the way. You never got it back? What a pity! It was really a masterpiece. I remember I wanted to buy it. I wish I had now. It belonged to Basil's best period. Since then, his work was that curious mixture of bad painting and good intentions that always entitles a man to be called a representative British artist. Did you advertise for it? You should.'

'I forget,' said Dorian. 'I suppose I did. But I never really liked it. I am sorry I sat for it. The memory of the thing is hateful to me. Why do you talk of it? It used to remind me of those curious lines in some play—*Hamlet*, I think—how do they run?—

Like the painting of a sorrow,

A face without a heart.

Yes: that is what it was like.'

Lord Henry laughed. 'If a man treats life artistically, his brain is his heart,' he answered, sinking into an arm-chair.

Dorian Gray shook his head, and struck some soft chords on the piano. ' "Like the painting of a sorrow," ' he repeated, ' "a face without a heart." '

The elder man lay back and looked at him with half-closed eyes. 'By the way, Dorian,' he said, after a pause, ' "what does it profit a man if he gain the whole world and lose—how does the quotation run?—his own soul"?'

The music jarred and Dorian Gray started, and stared at his friend. 'Why do you ask me that, Harry?'

'My dear fellow,' said Lord Henry, elevating his eyebrows in surprise, 'I asked you because I thought you might be able to give me an answer. That is all. I was going through the Park last Sunday, and close by the Marble Arch there stood a little crowd of shabby-looking people listening to some vulgar street-preacher. As I passed by, I heard the man yelling out that question to his audience. It struck me as being rather dramatic. London is very rich in curious effects of that kind. A wet Sunday, an uncouth Christian in a mackintosh, a ring of sickly white faces under a broken roof of dripping umbrellas, and a wonderful phrase flung into the air by shrill, hysterical lips—it was really very good in its way, quite a suggestion. I thought of telling the prophet that Art had a soul, but that man had not. I am afraid, however, he would not have understood me.'

'Don't, Harry. The soul is a terrible reality. It can be bought, and sold, and bartered away. It can be poisoned, or made perfect. There is a soul in each one of us. I know it.'

'Do you feel quite sure of that, Dorian?'

'Quite sure.'

'Ah! then it must be an illusion. The things one feels absolutely certain about are never true. That is the fatality of Faith, and the lesson of Romance. How grave you are! Don't be so serious. What have you or I to do with the superstitions of our age? No: we have given up our belief in the soul. Play me something. Play me a nocturne, Dorian, and, as you play, tell me, in a low voice, how you have kept your youth. You must have some secret. I am only ten years older than you are, and I am wrinkled, and worn, and yellow. You are really wonderful, Dorian. You have never looked more charming than you do to-night. You remind me of the day I saw you first. You were rather cheeky, very shy, and absolutely extraordinary. You have changed, of course, but not in appearance. I wish you would tell me your secret. To get back my youth I would do anything in the world, except take exercise, get up early, or be respectable. Youth! There is nothing like it. It's absurd to talk of the ignorance of youth. The only people to whose opinions I listen now with any respect are people much younger than myself. They seem in front of me. Life has revealed to them her latest wonder. As for the aged, I always contradict the aged. I do it on principle. If you ask them their opinion on something that happened yesterday, they solemnly give you the opinions current in 1820, when people wore high stocks, believed in everything, and knew absolutely nothing. How lovely that thing you are playing is! I wonder, did Chopin write it at Majorca, with the sea weeping round the villa, and the salt spray dashing against the panes? It is marvellously romantic. What a blessing it is that there is one art left to us that is not imitative! Don't stop. I want music to-night. It seems to me that you are the young Apollo, and that I am Marsyas[206] listening to you. I have sorrows, Dorian, of my own, that even you know nothing of. The tragedy of old age is not that one is old, but that one is young. I am amazed sometimes at my own sincerity. Ah, Dorian, how happy you are! What an exquisite life you have had! You have drunk deeply of everything. You have crushed the grapes against your palate. Nothing has been hidden from you. And it has all been to you no more than the sound of music. It has not marred you. You are still the same.'

'I am not the same, Harry.'

'Yes, you are the same. I wonder what the rest of your life will be. Don't spoil it by renunciations. At present you are a perfect type. Don't make yourself incomplete. You are quite flawless now. You need not shake your head: you know you are. Besides, Dorian, don't deceive yourself. Life is not governed by will or intention. Life is a question of nerves, and fibres, and slowly built-up cells in which thought hides itself and passion has its dreams. You may fancy yourself safe, and think yourself strong. But a chance tone of colour in a room or a morning sky, a particular perfume that you had once loved and that brings subtle memories with it, a line from a forgotten poem that you had come across again, a cadence from a piece of music that you had ceased to play—I tell you, Dorian, that it is on things like these that our lives depend. Browning writes about that somewhere; but our own senses will imagine them for us. There are moments when the odour of *lilas blanc*[207] passes suddenly across me, and I have to live the strangest month of my life over again. I wish I could change places with you, Dorian. The world has cried out against us both, but it has always worshipped you. It always will worship you. You are the type of what the age is searching for, and what it is afraid it has found. I am so glad that you have never done anything, never carved a statue, or painted a picture, or produced anything outside of yourself! Life has been your art. You have set yourself to music. Your days are your sonnets.'

Dorian rose up from the piano, and passed his hand through his hair. 'Yes, life has been exquisite,' he murmured, 'but I am not going to have the same life, Harry. And you must not say these extravagant things to me. You don't know everything about me. I think that if you did, even you would turn from me. You laugh. Don't laugh.'

'Why have you stopped playing, Dorian? Go back and give me the nocturne over again. Look at that great, honey-coloured moon that hangs in the dusky air. She is waiting for you to charm her, and if you play she will come closer to the earth. You won't? Let us go to the club, then. It has been a charming evening, and we must end it charmingly. There is some one at White's who wants immensely to know you—young Lord Poole, Bournemouth's eldest son. He has already copied your neckties, and has begged me to introduce him to you. He is quite delightful, and rather reminds me of you.'

'I hope not,' said Dorian with a sad look in his eyes. 'But I am tired to-night, Harry. I sha'n't go to the club. It is nearly eleven, and I want to go to bed early.'

'Do stay. You have never played so well as to-night. There was something in your touch that was wonderful. It had more expression than I had ever heard from it before.'

'It is because I am going to be good,' he answered, smiling. 'I am a little changed already.'

'You cannot change to me, Dorian,' said Lord Henry. 'You and I will always be friends.'

'Yet you poisoned me with a book once. I should not forgive that. Harry, promise me that you will never lend that book to any one. It does harm.'

'My dear boy, you are really beginning to moralize. You will soon be going about like the converted, and the revivalist, warning people against all the sins of which you have grown tired. You are much too delightful to do that. Besides, it is no use. You and I are what we are, and will be what we will be. As for being poisoned by a book, there is no such thing as that. Art has no influence upon action. It annihilates the desire to act. It is superbly sterile. The books that the world calls immoral are books that show the world its own shame. That is all. But we won't discuss literature. Come round to-morrow. I am going to ride at eleven. We might go together, and I will take you to lunch afterwards with Lady Branksome. She is a charming woman, and wants to consult you about some tapestries she is thinking of buying. Mind you come. Or shall we lunch with our little Duchess? She says she never sees you now. Perhaps you are tired of Gladys? I thought you would be. Her clever tongue gets on one's nerves. Well, in any case, be here at eleven.'

'Must I really come, Harry?'

'Certainly. The Park is quite lovely now. I don't think there have been such lilacs since the year I met you.'

'Very well. I shall be here at eleven,' said Dorian. 'Good-night, Harry.' As he reached the door he hesitated for a moment, as if he had something more to say. Then he sighed and went out.

Chapter 20

It was a lovely night, so warm that he threw his coat over his arm, and did not even put his silk scarf round his throat. As he strolled home, smoking his cigarette, two young men in evening dress passed him. He heard one of them whisper to the other, 'That is Dorian Gray.' He remembered how pleased he used to be when he was pointed out, or stared at, or talked about. He was tired of hearing his own name now. Half the charm of the little village where he had been so often lately was that no one knew who he was. He had often told the girl whom he had lured to love him that he was poor, and she had believed him. He had told her once that he was wicked, and she had laughed at him, and answered that wicked people were always very old and very ugly. What a laugh she had!—just like a thrush singing. And how pretty she had been in her cotton dresses and her large hats! She knew nothing, but she had everything that he had lost.

When he reached home, he found his servant waiting up for him. He sent him to bed, and threw himself down on the sofa in the library, and began to think over some of the things that Lord Henry had said to him.

Was it really true that one could never change? He felt a wild longing for the unstained purity of his boyhood—his rose-white boyhood, as Lord Henry had once called it. He knew that he had tarnished himself, filled his mind with corruption and given horror to his fancy; that he had been an evil influence to others, and had experienced a terrible joy in being so; and that of the lives that had crossed his own it had been the fairest and the most full of promise that he had brought to shame. But was it all irretrievable? Was there no hope for him?

Ah! in what a monstrous moment of pride and passion he had prayed that the portrait should bear the burden of his days, and he keep the unsullied splendour of eternal youth! All his failure had been due to that. Better for him that each sin of his life had brought its sure, swift penalty along with it. There was purification in punishment. Not 'Forgive us our sins,' but 'Smite us for our iniquities,' should be the prayer of man to a most just God.

The curiously-carved mirror that Lord Henry had given to him, so many years ago now, was standing on the table, and the white-limbed Cupids laughed round as of old. He took it up, as he had done on that night of horror, when he had first noted the change in the fatal picture, and with wild tear-dimmed eyes looked into its polished shield. Once, some one who had terribly loved him, had written to him a mad letter, ending with these idolatrous words: 'The world is changed because you are made of ivory and gold. The curves of your lips rewrite history.' The phrases came back to his memory, and he repeated them over and over to himself. Then he loathed his own beauty, and flinging the mirror on the floor crushed it into silver splinters beneath his heel. It was his beauty that had ruined him, his beauty and the youth that he had prayed for. But for those two things, his life might have been free from stain. His beauty had been to him but a mask, his youth but a mockery. What was youth at best? A green, an unripe time, a time of shallow moods, and sickly thoughts. Why had he worn its livery? Youth had spoiled him.

It was better not to think of the past. Nothing could alter that. It was of himself, and of his own future, that he had to think. James Vane was hidden in a nameless grave in Selby churchyard. Alan Campbell had shot himself one night in his laboratory, but had not revealed the secret that he had been forced to know. The excitement, such as it was, over Basil Hallward's disappearance would soon pass away. It was already waning. He was perfectly safe there. Nor, indeed, was it the death of Basil Hallward that weighed most upon his mind. It was the living death of his own soul that troubled him. Basil had painted the portrait that had marred his life. He could not forgive him that. It was the portrait that had done everything. Basil had said things to him that were unbearable, and that he had yet borne with patience. The murder had been simply the madness of a moment. As for Alan Campbell, his suicide had been his own act. He had chosen to do it. It was nothing to him.

A new life! That was what he wanted. That was what he was waiting for. Surely he had begun it already. He had spared one innocent thing, at any rate. He would never again tempt innocence. He would be good.

As he thought of Hetty Merton, he began to wonder if the portrait in the locked room had changed. Surely it was not still so horrible as it had been? Perhaps if his life became pure, he would be able to expel every sign of evil passion from the face. Perhaps the signs of evil had already gone away. He would go and look.

He took the lamp from the table and crept upstairs. As he unbarred the door, a smile of joy flitted across his strangely young-looking face and lingered for a moment about his lips. Yes, he would be good, and the hideous thing that he had hidden away would no longer be a terror to him. He felt as if the load had been lifted from him already.

He went in quietly, locking the door behind him, as was his custom, and dragged the purple hanging from the portrait. A cry of pain and indignation broke from him. He could see no change, save that in the eyes there was a look of cunning, and in the mouth the curved wrinkle of the hypocrite. The thing was still loathsome—more loathsome, if possible, than before—and the scarlet dew that spotted the hand seemed brighter, and more like blood newly spilt. Then he trembled. Had it been merely vanity that had made him do his one good deed? Or the desire for a new sensation, as Lord Henry had hinted, with his mocking laugh? Or that passion to act a part that sometimes makes us do things finer than we are ourselves? Or, perhaps, all these? And why was the red stain larger than it had been? It seemed to have crept like a horrible disease over the wrinkled fingers. There was blood on the painted feet, as though the thing had dripped—blood even on the hand that had not held the knife. Confess? Did it mean that he was to confess? To give himself up, and be put to death? He laughed. He felt that the idea was monstrous. Besides, even if he did confess, who would believe him? There was no trace of the murdered man anywhere. Everything belonging to him had been destroyed. He himself had burned what had been below-stairs[208]. The world would simply say that he was mad. They would shut him up if he persisted in his story....Yet it was his duty to confess, to suffer public shame, and to make public atonement. There was a God who called upon men to tell their sins to earth as well as to heaven. Nothing that he could do would cleanse him till he had told his own sin. His sin? He shrugged his shoulders. The death of Basil Hallward seemed very little to him. He was thinking of Hetty Merton. For it was an unjust mirror, this mirror of his soul that he was looking at. Vanity? Curiosity? Hypocrisy? Had there been nothing more in his renunciation than that? There had been something more. At least he thought so. But who could tell?...No. There had been nothing more. Through vanity he had spared her. In hypocrisy he had worn the mask of goodness. For curiosity's sake he had tried the denial of self. He recognized that now.

But this murder—was it to dog him all his life? Was he always to be burdened by his past? Was he really to confess? Never. There was only one bit of evidence left against him. The picture itself—that was evidence. He would destroy it. Why had he kept it so long? Once it had given him pleasure to watch it changing and growing old. Of late he had felt no such pleasure. It had kept him awake at night. When he had been away, he had been filled with terror lest other eyes should look upon it. It had brought melancholy across his passions. Its mere memory had marred many moments of joy. It had been like conscience to him. Yes, it had been conscience. He would destroy it.

He looked round, and saw the knife that had stabbed Basil Hallward. He had cleaned it many times, till there was no stain left upon it. It was bright, and glistened. As it had killed the painter, so it would kill the painter's work, and all that that meant. It would kill the past, and when that was dead, he would be free. It would kill this monstrous soul-life, and without its hideous warnings, he would be at peace. He seized the thing, and stabbed the picture with it.

There was a cry heard, and a crash. The cry was so horrible in its agony that the frightened servants woke, and crept out of their rooms. Two gentlemen, who were passing in the Square below, stopped, and looked up at the great house. They walked on till they met a policeman, and brought him back. The man rang the bell several times, but there was no answer. Except for a light in one of the top windows, the house was all dark. After a time, he went away, and stood in an adjoining portico and watched.

'Whose house is that, constable?' asked the elder of the two gentlemen.

'Mr Dorian Gray's, sir,' answered the policeman.

They looked at each other, as they walked away, and sneered. One of them was Sir Henry Ashton's uncle.

Inside, in the servants' part of the house, the half-clad domestics were talking in low whispers to each other. Old Mrs Leaf was crying, and wringing her hands. Francis was as pale as death.

After about a quarter of an hour, he got the coachman and one of the footmen and crept upstairs. They knocked, but there was no reply. They called out. Everything was still. Finally, after vainly trying to force the door, they got on the roof, and dropped down on to the balcony. The windows yielded easily: their bolts were old.

When they entered, they found hanging upon the wall a splendid portrait of their master as they had last seen him, in all the wonder of his exquisite youth and beauty. Lying on the floor was a dead man, in evening dress, with a knife in his heart. He was withered, wrinkled, and loathsome of visage. It was not till they had examined the rings that they recognized who it was.

THE END

Notes

1   subject matter
2   Tokyo
3   anyone
4   dragonfly
5   stockbroker
6   someone
7   halfway
8   trade name
9   everyone
10 Antinous
11 If
12 bric-a-brac
13 lodging houses
14 today
15 cigarette case
16 daydreams
17 You
18 lilac blossoms
19 When
20 Realise
21 lifelong
22 armchair
23 the Greek god of merchants and thieves; the messenger of the other gods
24 a Greek demigod with goat's legs and horns
25 painting table
26 palette knife
27 This
28 tea tray
29 tonight
30 dress clothes
31 colour element
32 tea table
33 tomorrow

34 Blue Book; official parliamentary papers

35 The

36 Tell

37 sonnet sequence

38 dining room

39 good nature

40 hymnbook

41 But

42 tightrope

43 a female follower of Bacchus, the Roman god of wine

44 a tutor and companion of Bacchus

45 grape juice

46 That

47 parrot tulips

48 paper knife

49 debut

50 gas jets

51 playbills

52 drop scene

53 dress circle

54 ginger beer

55 Grandfathers are always wrong.

56 beer barrel

57 low comedian

58 oboe

59 garden scene

60 the heroine in Shakespeare's *As You Like It*

61 the heroine in Shakespeare's *Cymbeline*

62 tea parties

63 Why

64 hiding place

65 art instinct

66 high tea

67 sitting room

68 Foolish

69 parrot phrase

70 Let

71 Mother

72 stage player

73 thickset

74 windowpane

75 My

76 supercargo

77 gold fields

78 barrooms

79 sheep farmer

80 heartsick

81 race instinct

82 stage door

83 hunting crop

84 underlip

85 How

86 springtime

87 tulip beds

88 orris root

89 To

90 orange bitters

91 the third wife of the Roman emperor Claudius; a byword of promiscuity

92 Don't

93 fine champagne

94 the daughter to Prospero in Shakespeare's *The Tempest*

95 a monster and a slave of Prospero in Shakespeare's *The Tempest*

96 opera glass

97 Charming

98 You

99 have

100 schoolgirl

101 you

102 does

103 Before

104 Can't

105 the heroine in Shakespeare's *The Merchant of Venice*

106 the heroine in Shakespeare's *Much Ado About Nothing*
107 the heroine in Shakespeare's *King Lear*
108 coffee house
109 carthorses
110 toilet set
111 moneylender
112 dressing gown
113 dressing room
114 love letter
115 a symbol of death
116 a section of the Ancient Greek underworld
117 tragedians at the time of James I
118 No
119 heartbroken
120 Is
121 the consolation of the arts
122 turning point
123 a Parisian gallery
124 boar spear
125 lotus blossoms
126 writing table
127 playroom
128 shan't
129 pencil mark
130 world spirit
131 Symbolists
132 morning room
133 cinnamon stones
134 sea monster
135 turquoise stones
136 skull cap
137 hawk glove
138 table napkins
139 Madam, I am quite happy
140 mourning bed
141 fleurs-de-lys

142 seed pearls

143 acanthus leaves

144 goldthread

145 chalice veils

146 flute player

147 a list of depraved Roman emperors

148 latchkey

149 lamplight

150 soda water

151 dinner tables

152 byword

153 It

154 brushwork

155 What

156 gas lamps

157 a society directory

158 scarfpin

159 title page

160 not cleansed from torment

161 fingers of the faun

162 To see, her bosom covered o'er
     With pearls, her body suave,
     The Adriatic Venus soar
     On sound's chromatic wave.
     The domes that on the water dwell
     Pursue the melody
     In clear drawn cadences, and swell
     Like breasts of love that sigh.
     My chains around a pillar cast
     I land before a fair
     And rosy-pale façade at last,
     Upon a marble stair.
     (Taken from *The Works of Théophile Gautier*, trans. Agnes Lee, 1903)

163 sweet monster

164 porphyry room

165 deadhouses

166 dissecting room
167 gas fire
168 notepaper
169 chimneypiece
170 drawing room
171 chaudfroid
172 deluxe edition
173 overzealous
174 Too audacious
175 She
176 End of century
177 End of world
178 teatime
179 streetlamps
180 public houses
181 opium dens
182 side windows
183 For
184 top windows
185 morning star
186 teacakes
187 house party
188 a hypocritical character in Molière's *The Hypocrite*
189 garden party
190 Then
191 flower beds
192 In
193 shooting party
194 pinewood
195 Here
196 the Greek goddess of hunting
197 chequebook
198 gatepost
199 farm servants
200 apple blossoms
201 millpond

202 water lilies
203 divorce case
204 music room
205 Anything
206 a satyr who was flayed as a result of losing to Apollo in a music contest
207 white lilac
208 below stairs

道林・格雷的畫像

Preface to the Chinese Translation
中文譯本序

"既像玩雜耍，又像變戲法；剛剛讓它滑過去，隨即又把它抓回來；忽而用想像的虹彩把它點綴得五色繽紛，忽而又給它插上悖論的翅膀任其翱翔。"

—— 王爾德《道林·格雷的畫像》第三章

"創作藝術作品依然是我的目的所在。你覺得我的處理精巧且具有藝術價值，我實在欣喜萬分。我覺得報上的那些文章好像出自那些荒淫無恥的市儈之手。我實在無法理解，他們怎麼可以將《道林·格雷的畫像》(下稱《畫像》) 當作不道德的作品呢。"[1]

以上摘自王爾德 1891 年 4 月寫給柯南·道爾的一封信中的幾句話，包含着讀者會感興趣的內容主要有二。收信人確實就是那位創造了大偵探夏洛克·福爾摩斯及其助手約翰·華生醫生的小說家。阿瑟·柯南·道爾 (1859-1930) 比王爾德小五歲，二人應美國出版商斯托達特的邀請與之共進晚餐。席間，兩位作家接受斯托達特的約稿，為《利平科特月刊》(*Lippincott's Monthly Magazine*) 各寫一部小說。柯南·道爾在 1924 年出版的《回憶錄及冒險史》一書中述及："王爾德送去的是《畫像》，那是一本有很高道德水平的書；而我則寫了《四個神祕的簽名》"[2]，此為其一。其二是，最早評論《畫像》的一些文章，卻與柯南·道爾的看法大相徑庭，認為此書公開侮辱了上流社會的價值觀，因而直接斥之為"不道德"。事情的緣由還得從頭說起。

十九世紀末葉，歐洲處於社會大變動的前夜，人心浮動，知識界分化的趨勢加劇。在這個被稱為"世紀末"的時期，歐洲文藝界一些富有才華的代表人物經歷着深刻的思想危機。他們對於自己所屬的階層有相當透徹的了解和頗為強烈的憎恨。為了給自己的創作尋找出路，開闢施展才能的新天地，他們中有些人率先走向唯美主義的殿堂，在文學方面倡導"為藝術的藝術"（Art for Art's Sake），認為"不是藝術反映生活，而是生活模仿藝術"。王爾德曾經寫下這樣一段話："在這動盪和紛亂的時代，在這紛爭和絕望的可怕時刻，只有美的無憂殿堂可以使人忘卻，使人歡樂。我們不去往美的殿堂，還能去往何方呢？只能到一部古代意大利異教經典稱作 citta divana（聖城）的地方去，在那裏一個人至少可以暫時擺脫塵世的紛擾與恐怖，也可以暫時逃避世俗的選擇。"[3]

奧斯卡‧芬格爾‧奧弗萊赫蒂‧威利斯‧王爾德 1854 年 10 月 16 日生於愛爾蘭首府都柏林。他的家世雖不算顯赫，但他父親是眼科名醫，曾給瑞典國王奧斯卡做過治療白內障的手術，並在 1864 年被維多利亞女王冊封為爵士（倒並非因為手術，而是在人口統計方面有突出貢獻，此對於次子的命名也許有影響）。母親是一位富有民族主義精神的詩人（筆名 Speranza —— 拉丁文"希望"），參加過號召愛爾蘭人奮起衝擊都柏林城堡的"青年愛爾蘭"運動。奧斯卡自幼受到文學氛圍很濃的家庭熏陶，深愛古典文化，曾因古希臘文成績優異在都柏林聖三一學院獲授予金質獎章，1874 年得到獎學金進入牛津大學莫德林學院。1805 年，以收藏文物著稱的英國議員羅傑‧紐迪吉特爵士設立了一項以他本人姓氏命名的詩歌獎。儘管王爾德在大學時代就為自己起了詩名，1878 年還以《拉文納》一詩獲紐迪吉特獎，卻未能成為接受獎學金的研究生，遂於同年從牛津畢業。孰料上天給這位躊躇滿志的才子留下的時間已不到一半了。

王爾德的文學活動領域十分寬廣。他既是詩人（1881 年就有他的詩集問世），又寫小說和童話（包括《快樂王子》、《石榴之家》、《阿瑟・薩維爾勛爵的罪行》三個書集，以及他唯一的長篇小說《畫像》，以上四本作品除《快樂王子及其他童話》於 1888 年成書外，其餘三本均於 1891 年出版）。他還寫過不少評論和隨筆（較重要的有他自己選編的《意圖集》和《社會主義制度下人的靈魂》，均刊行於 1891 年）。但為他贏得最輝煌成功的要數 1892 至 1895 年間前後在倫敦西區舞台上首演的社會諷刺喜劇《溫德米爾夫人的扇子》、《一個無足輕重的女人》、《一個理想的丈夫》和《認真的重要》。1891 年王爾德根據聖經故事用法文寫下了獨幕劇《莎樂美》。這個見於《新約・馬太福音》第十四章和《新約・馬可福音》第六章的故事，已在十九世紀經過多位法國作家和畫家的詮釋，特別是以神話和宗教題材作色情畫聞名的象徵派畫家居斯塔夫・莫羅（1826–1898）所作的油畫《莎樂美之舞》，為後來者作了鋪墊。儘管如此，到了王爾德筆下還是給人無比強烈的衝擊，難怪英國內務大臣以藉口「任何以聖經人物為角色的劇目都不准在英國上演」，拒絕給此劇頒發演出許可證。[4] 德國作曲家理查・斯特勞斯在 1905 年把王爾德的原劇譜寫成歌劇，只是由拉赫曼譯成德文的唱詞代替了法文台詞。這位晚期浪漫主義作曲家在《莎樂美》和他的另一部歌劇《厄勒克特拉》(1909) 中完成了向表現主義的過渡。理查・斯特勞斯的歌劇《莎樂美》被選為 1998

年 2 月香港藝術節的揭幕之作,其中的《七重紗之舞》更是二十世紀以來許多指揮家和交響樂隊展示瑰奇多變的管弦樂色彩效果的熱門曲目。

王爾德總共寫過九部戲劇,但另外四部劇作已被遺忘。真正令他名利雙收的那幾部社會諷刺喜劇全都集中在九十年代前期,可想見他在十九世紀末英國戲劇界是何等舉足輕重。本文起首處引用的一段文字,寫的是對道林·格雷的道德淪喪負有很大責任的亨利·沃登勛爵在上流社會餐桌旁口若懸河、妙語迭出的精彩表演。從作者津津樂道的口吻可以看出,王爾德無疑是在顧影自憐,因為他自己正是這樣的表演高手,而他在社交圈中越練越"酷"的口才,在他的社會喜劇中發揮得淋漓盡致,令觀眾如癡如醉,以致當時的劇場頂替了教堂在社會中的地位(蕭伯納語)。然而正當王爾德身為劇作家的好運如日中天之際,一場醜聞官司卻把他從九霄雲端一下子直摔進了萬丈深淵。

1895 年 2 月 14 日,王爾德最後一部,也是他才華機智達到巔峯狀態的劇作《認真的重要》在聖詹姆斯劇院首演,觀眾如潮,盛況空前。兩週後,王爾德在阿爾比馬爾俱樂部收到昆斯伯里侯爵約翰·道格拉斯 (John Sholto Douglas, Marquis of Queensberry, 1844–1900) 留下的名片,上面寫着:"致裝模作樣的好男色者奧斯卡·王爾德。"王爾德從 1891 年開始便與比他小十六歲的阿爾弗雷德·道格拉斯(侯爵之子,當時還在上牛津大學)有不正當關係,而且經常"儷影雙雙"地出現在倫敦的公共場所,並一起旅遊,令侯爵十分反感。侯爵對自己的兒子毫無辦法,而阿爾弗雷德也不斷挑戰父親的權威。1894 年 4 月,兒子還曾打電報侮辱其父；6 月，侯爵亦曾到切爾西泰特街王爾德的寓所羞辱後者遭逐，故在大半年後有這次留名片之舉。王爾德與年輕男性的同性戀行為遭人物議不自此時始。前面提到過譴責《畫像》的評論家中就有一位是查爾斯·惠布里，他在《蘇格蘭觀察家報》上撰文稱："奧斯卡·王爾德先生又開始寫那等還是不寫為妙的貨色了。"其中的"又"字暗示王爾德於 1889 年發表的《W. H. 先生的畫像》一文。要說這篇東西是小說、散文或學術考據都不像，又都像，內容是通過分析研究莎士比亞的十四行詩提出一種觀點：莎翁這些詩篇奉獻和讚美的對象 W. H. 先生乃是一個名叫威利·休斯的小男旦（莎士比亞時代戲劇中的少女角色往往由少男扮演）。惠布里顯然認為王爾德有拉莎翁為自己"好男色"壯膽之嫌疑。評論接着指出："……除了那些不法貴族和變態的電報投送員，沒人要看他寫的東西。"這裏更是毫不含糊地重提發生在 1889 年的一椿同性戀醜聞，那件事曾使經常光顧克利夫蘭街上一家變童妓院的亞瑟·薩默賽特勛爵和一批郵局僱員名譽掃地。[5] 但是到了 1895 年，王爾德居然向一貫百般嘲弄他的作品和生活方式的維多利亞時代英國法律和社會求助，以誹謗罪把昆斯伯里侯爵告上法庭。兩年後，王爾德沉痛地承認自己做了"一生中最可恥、最無法原諒、最可鄙的事"。1895 年 4 月 3 日，法院開庭審理王爾德訴昆斯伯里侯爵誹謗案（王爾德自幼渴望的倒是能在"女王訴王爾德"的官司中出庭），被告輕而易舉地反證原告確是"好男色者"，從而推翻誹謗的指控。4 月 5 日，侯爵無罪獲釋，王爾德反因涉嫌"與其他男子發生有傷風化的肉體關係"被捕後保釋候審。又經過兩次審訊，5 月 25 日，倫敦中央刑事法院根據 1885 年通過針對男子同性戀的刑法修正案判處王爾德兩年勞役刑罰，先後囚於紐蓋特、彭頓韋爾和萬茲沃斯監獄，11 月 20 日又移至雷丁監獄服滿刑期。這位折翼的悖論大師從此一蹶不振。[6]

　　1897 年 5 月，王爾德刑滿釋放後立即流亡法國，化名塞巴斯蒂安·梅爾莫斯。三個月後，他完成了長詩《雷丁監獄之歌》，1898 年在倫敦出書，十六個月內就印至第七版。這是他的天鵝之歌，也是身為詩人的王爾德的最高成就。1897 年 9 月，他在法國魯昂與道格拉斯重逢，兩人還於 10 月同赴意大利的卡布里島旅遊，但終於在次年斷交。1898 年 4 月，康斯坦絲去世。1900 年 11 月 30 日，王爾德因患腦膜炎病逝於巴黎阿爾薩斯旅館，臨終時由羅斯請來了神父為他施洗，實現了逝者皈依天主教的遺願。

　　在王爾德去世之日與這個譯本出版之時中間隔着整整一個二十世紀，還得掛上二十一世紀的肇始。一百多年來，這個"臭名昭著的牛津聖奧斯卡、詩人、殉道者"（他逝世前不久為自己想好的永久稱號），一直是文壇最有爭議的人物之一。不過，讚美也罷，唾罵也罷，若此公泉下有靈，應該不會感到寂寞和悲哀，因為他有一句名言："世上唯一比被人議論更糟糕的，就是無人議論。"上世紀末了的那幾年，英美兩國掀起了一場王爾德熱潮。1995 年 2 月，為紀念《認真的重要》上演一百週年，英國政府在西敏寺詩人角設彩色櫥窗，展覽王爾德的生平和創作，倫敦和都柏林分別舉行王爾德紀念牌揭幕式；4 月，BBC 播放紀念王爾德的專題片；同年，新月書局印行了最新版的《王爾德全集》。1997 年是王爾德刑滿出獄一百週年，倫敦和紐約各地紛紛重排上演《認真的重要》、《溫德米爾夫人的扇子》等名劇，巴黎出版了法文多卷本《王爾德文集》。英國小說家、電影名演員史蒂芬·佛萊 (Stephen Fry) 在《星期日泰晤士報》上撰文指出，王爾德再度崛起，成為繼莎士比亞之後，在歐洲被閱讀最多、被譯成語種最多的英國作家。在為數可觀的傳記中，被認為最客觀和公允的名作是理查德·埃曼所著的《奧斯卡·王爾德》。此書由佛萊改編和主演，並由布萊恩·吉爾伯特執導搬上銀幕。佛萊甚至認為："對於那些近來方有合法同性戀地位且需要英雄和殉道者的人們，他是一個聖人；……稱王爾德為救世主，聽上去有些過分誇張……但與基督的一生比較，相似之處明顯存在。"在 1998 年 3 月 5 日《紐約書評》上發表《預言家》一文的傑森·愛普斯坦寫道："……王爾德用他的花花公子面貌和極端的唯美主義來挑戰的不單單是維多利亞時代的虛偽。他所挑戰的是英國歷史上最為頑固的禮法。"

當然，對於如此興師動眾、頂禮膜拜的紀念活動也有人持強烈反對態度。1998 年 5 月 18 日的《紐約客》週刊發表了阿當·戈普尼克的文章《發明奧斯卡·王爾德》。作者認為"批評家、電影家和劇作家在把維多利亞的傳統敵人王爾德當成同性戀殉道者來紀念。他們全都弄錯了"。戈普尼克引用王爾德生前所言"凡是企圖證明甚麼的書都不值得閱讀"，斷言目前所有與之有關的書，王爾德肯定都不會去讀。[7]

其實，不同觀點的交鋒應該是正常和有益的。一百多年前《畫像》剛問世便遭到強烈譴責，同樣也不意味着當時只有一片討伐聲。除了本文開頭提到的柯南·道爾外，愛爾蘭詩人、劇作家威廉・葉芝（William Yeats, 1865–1939）稱《畫像》是"一本奇妙的書"，沃爾特・佩特用"真正有活力的"來概括它的特點。也許可以公平地說，只要不是把維多利亞時代的道德觀奉為金科玉律的人，都能從中發現不少可供欣賞和值得讚歎的東西。意味深長的是，當初北美洲對此書的評論就比它的原產地好得多。王爾德本人剛從在英國遭到迎頭痛擊的震盪中緩過神來，便開始努力捍衛這部小說的生存權。他在大量書簡和文章（尤其是《從深處》）中提到《畫像》所流露的深情，是他對自己其他作品所不能比擬的。出獄後不久，他在給出版商倫納德・史密瑟斯的信中寫道："我只知道《畫像》是部經典作品，而且堪稱經典作品。"[8]

和任何經典作品一樣，《畫像》也是在其他經典的基礎上寫出來的。探究其淵源，不難想到巴爾札克的《驢皮記》、哥提耶的《莫班小姐》等等。當然，浮士德博士為窮究生命意義用自己的靈魂換取魔鬼梅菲斯特的幫助這筆交易，無疑為道林・格雷表達那個致命的願望——讓畫像變老變醜作為自己永葆青春的代價——提供了一份"合約樣本"。作為《人間喜劇・哲學研究》系列中影響最大的一部作品，《驢皮記》顯然比其他作品與《畫像》有更近的親緣關係。巴爾札克筆下的瓦朗坦因慾望得不到滿足而日夜受着煎熬，只想求得一天的快樂，哪怕用生命去換取也在所不惜。處在這種心態的瓦朗坦，遇到一個老古董商送給他一張有東方文字符籙的驢皮，但須用他的生命作代價。驢皮象徵着持有者的壽限，它將與所滿足的慾望強度和次數成正比同步收縮。瓦朗坦毫不猶豫地接受下來。然而他每次實現自己的願望後感受到的卻不是快樂，而是恐怖，因為眼看着驢皮越縮越小，他清楚地意識到死亡離自己越來越近，最後在一次縱慾中結束了生命。

這裏不能不提到《畫像》第十章末段亨利勛爵帶給道林的一本黃封面的書。這本沒有直接點明的書乃是法國作家若利斯・卡爾・於斯曼（Joris Karl Huysmans, 1848–1907）所寫的《逆流》(*A Rebours*)。它的主人公德艾薩特反抗社會的態度近乎德薩德侯爵（Marquis de Sade, 1740-1814，"性施虐狂"或泛指任何虐待狂的 sadism 一詞，即由其姓氏得名，此人也因而"不朽"）。王爾德並不掩飾自己對此書有一定程度的欣賞，但也毫不含糊地指出"這是一本有毒的書"。上述那些作品的回聲在《畫像》中時有所聞，但王爾德不是一個一邊公開抄襲他人，一邊猶抱琵琶半遮面的人，只要有正當理由，他也不怕抄襲。他曾告訴一名記者，那本毒害了道林・格雷的奇書應該是《逆流》的一個奇幻變種。但是，用過於肯定的方式斷言王爾德與其他作家的相似性或與其他書籍的師承關係，難免會流於輕率。1895 年王爾德在接受一次採訪時說過："撇開希臘文和拉丁文作者的散文和詩歌不說，影響過我的只有約翰・濟慈、古斯塔夫・福樓拜和華特・佩特，而在我與之相會前，我已迎着他們走了一大半路程。"上述三位作家中有兩個是英國人，所以阿瑟・蘭瑟姆認定《畫像》是"用英文寫成的第一部法國小說"這一說法，稍稍有些熱心過頭。[9]

王爾德是個非常迷信的人，《畫像》從一開始便讓人感到宿命和厄運的壓力。請看第一章畫家霍爾渥德對亨利勛爵說的話："才貌出眾的人多半在劫難逃……你有身分和財產，亨利；我有頭腦和才能，且不管它們價值如何；道林・格雷有美麗的容貌。我們都將為上帝賜給我們的這些東西付出代價，付出可怕的代價。"當王爾德自己被關在雷丁監獄的囚室內付出他所說的可怕的代價時，曾在《從深處》中提到"厄運像一條紫線貫穿《畫像》那件金衣"。小說第十二章一開始交代了道林殺死霍爾渥德那天是前者三十八歲生日的前夕,但在《利平科特月刊》上發表的最早版本卻是三十二歲生日的前夕,這不是甚麼無關宏旨的細節。王爾德最初因靈感文思如泉湧而寫得太快,沒有意識到這年齡會洩露天機(王爾德初涉同性戀泥淖時年三十有二),但他把此事與道林謀殺畫家的罪惡聯繫起來,恰恰說明王爾德並不是一個真正隨心所欲、完全蔑視禮法的人。他的負罪感一直令他對自己身上墮落的一面覺得如芒刺在背,但在作者和他筆下的人物之間劃上等號未免過於簡單。王爾德自己 1894 年 2 月 12 日在致拉爾夫‧佩恩的信中寫道:"這本書會造成毒害,或者促成完美,道林‧格雷並不存在……貝澤爾‧霍爾渥德是我認為的個人寫照;亨利勛爵在外界看來就是我;道林是我願意成為的那類人 —— 可能在別的時代。" [10] 在文情斐然的字裏行間未必不能發現道德家尖刻審視的目光,甚至在他唯美派或花花公子的面具後面潛伏着一個天生的清教徒也難說。他喜歡他所創造的那個光輝燦爛的世界,但也可以讓這個世界隨着道林‧格雷臨死前極度恐怖的一聲慘叫訇然倒塌。說到底,通過《畫像》呈現在讀者面前的王爾德,首先是一個小說家,而不是哲學家,也不是文化史家,對小說本身也只能從這一角度來評判。即使不用現今比一百年前"開明"得多的尺度加以衡量,《道林‧格雷的畫像》也不該被詆為一本不道德的書。

榮如德

註解

1 引自《王爾德全集》中國文學出版社中文版第 5 卷（書信卷上）第 495 頁。

2 同上。

3 引自《王爾德全集》中國文學出版社中文版第 4 卷（評論隨筆卷）第 27 頁。

4 參見王爾德之子維維安·霍蘭為《王爾德全集》英文版所寫的序，載《王爾德全集》中文版第 1 卷第 39 頁。

5 Peter Ackroyd, *Introduction to Oscar Wilde's The Picture of Dorian Gray* (Penguin Classics), p.vii.

6 參見《王爾德全集》中文版第 1 卷中文版序第 8–10 頁及第 6 卷王爾德年表。

7 參見趙武平：《世紀末的王爾德——全集編後記》，載《王爾德全集》中文版第 6 卷第 821–834 頁。

8 此信譯文參見《王爾德全集》中文版第 6 卷第 465 頁。

9 Peter Ackroyd, *Introduction*, pp.xi-xii.

10 引自《王爾德全集》中文版第 5 卷（書信卷上）第 606 頁。

自序

$\mathbf{藝}$術家是美的作品的創造者。

藝術的宗旨是展示藝術本身，同時把藝術家隱藏起來。

批評家應能把他對美的作品的印象用另一種樣式或新的材料表達出來。

自傳體是批評的最高形式，也是最低形式。

在美的作品中發現醜惡含義的人是墮落的，而且墮落得一無可愛之處。這是一種罪過。

在美的作品中發現美的含義的人是有教養的。這種人有希望。

認為美的作品僅僅意味着美的人，才是精英中的精英。

書無所謂道德的或不道德的。書有寫得好的或寫得糟的。僅此而已。

十九世紀對現實主義的憎惡，猶如從鏡子裏照不見自己面孔的卡利班的狂怒。

十九世紀對浪漫主義的憎惡，猶如從鏡子裏照不見自己面孔的卡利班的狂怒。

人的精神生活只是藝術家創作題材的一部分，藝術的道德則在於完美地運用並不完美的手段。

藝術家並不祈求證明任何事情。即使那些天經地義的事情也是可以證明的。

藝術家沒有倫理上的好惡。藝術家如在倫理上有所臧否，那是不可原諒的矯揉造作。

　　藝術家從來沒有病態。藝術家可以表現一切。

　　思想和語言是藝術家藝術創作的手段。

　　邪惡與美德是藝術家藝術創作的素材。

　　從形式着眼，音樂家的藝術是各種藝術的典型。從感覺着眼，演員的技藝是典型。

　　一切藝術同時既有外觀，又有象徵。

　　有人要鑽到外觀底下去，那由他自己負責。

　　有人要解讀象徵意義，那由他自己負責。

　　其實，藝術這面鏡子反映的是照鏡者，而不是生活。

　　對一件藝術品的看法不一，說明這作品新穎、複雜、重要。

　　批評家盡可意見分歧，藝術家不會自相矛盾。

　　一個人做了有用的東西可以原諒，只要他不自鳴得意。一個人做了無用的東西，只要他視若至寶，也可寬宥。

　　一切藝術都是毫無用處的。

　　　　　　　　　　　　　　　　奧斯卡・王爾德

第一章

畫室裏彌漫着濃郁的玫瑰花香，每當夏天的微風在花園的樹叢中流動，從開着的門外還會飄進來紫丁香的芬芳或嫩紅色山楂花的幽香。

亨利·沃登勛爵躺在用波斯氈子作面的無靠背長沙發上，照例接連不斷地抽着無數支的煙捲。他從放沙發的那個角落只能望見一叢芳甜如蜜、色也如蜜的金鏈花的疏影，它那顫巍巍的枝條看起來載不動這般絢麗燦爛的花朵；間或，飛鳥奇異的影子掠過垂在大窗前的柞蠶絲綢長簾，造成一刹那的日本情調，使他聯想起一些面色蒼白的東京畫家，他們力求通過一種本身只能是靜止的藝術手段，來表現迅捷和運動的感覺。蜜蜂，有的在尚未割除的長草中間為自己開路，有的繞着枝葉散漫、花粉零落的金色長筒狀金銀花固執地打轉，它們沉悶的嗡嗡聲似乎使凝滯的空氣顯得更加難以忍受。倫敦的市聲，猶如遠處傳來的管風琴的低音，隱約可聞。

畫室中央的豎式畫架上放着一幅全身肖像，畫的是一個俊美出奇的青年。一小段距離外，坐在它前面的就是畫像的作者貝澤爾·霍爾渥德。若干年前他突然不知去向，一度鬧得滿城風雨，引起許多離奇的猜測。

畫家看着作品中風姿秀逸的形象，反映出他精湛的技巧，臉上浮起了滿意的笑容，這笑容彷彿要再多停留一會。可是他霍地站起身來，閉上眼睛，用手指按住眼瞼，彷彿要把一個奇異的夢境羈留在腦際，生怕自己從中醒了過來。

「這是你最好的作品，貝澤爾，在你所有的作品當中，這是最出色的。」亨利勛爵懶洋洋地說。「你明年一定要把這幅畫送到格羅夫納畫廊。皇家藝術學院太大了，而且太庸俗。我每次去到那裏，要不人太多看不見畫作，那很可怕，要不畫作太多看不見人——那更糟糕。格羅夫納畫廊是你唯一能送去的地方。」

「我不想把它送到任何地方去，」他回答時腦袋朝後一仰的獨特姿勢，當年在牛津常常被同學們取笑。「不，我哪兒也不送。」

亨利勛爵揚起眉毛，透過一個個淡藍色的煙圈詫異地望着畫家。他抽的那種摻有鴉片的烈性煙捲中冒出的煙，正盤成奇形怪狀的螺環裊裊上升。「哪兒也不送去？我親愛的朋友，這是為甚麼？究竟是甚麼原因？你們這些畫家真是怪人！你們為了成名甚麼都做。一旦出了名，又覺得是個負擔。你這個傻瓜，世上比被人議論更糟糕的事情只有一種，那就是根本沒有人議論你。這幅畫像可以使你凌駕於英國所有的年輕人之上，並且使老頭們十分妒忌，如果老頭們還能激動的話。」

「我知道你會笑我，」他答道，「可是我確實不能把它拿去展出。我在這裏頭傾注了太多自己的東西。」

亨利勛爵在沙發上伸了個懶腰，放聲大笑。

「是的，我知道你會笑的，反正事情確確實實是這樣。」

「傾注了太多的東西在裏面！我發誓：親愛的貝澤爾，我不知道你還如此虛榮。我實在看不出你和畫像之間有何相似之處。你面孔粗糙僵硬，頭髮黑得像煤，而這個年輕的阿多尼斯，看起來像用象牙和玫瑰蕊製成的。啊,我親愛的貝澤爾,他是納西瑟斯,而你……好吧,當然,你有理智的神情,以及諸如此類的東西。但是美,真正的美恰恰終結於理智神情出現的那一刻。理智本身就是一種誇張的形式,會破壞臉部的和諧。人一旦坐下來思考,就變得只有鼻子或只有額頭,或者某種可怕的東西。看看那些需要高深學識行業中的成功人士,他們真是讓人極其討厭!不過在教堂裏的神職人員除外,因為他們不用動腦筋,一位八十歲的主教,一直說着他十八歲時人們教他說的話,結果,他自然而然總是令人極其愉悦。你那神祕的年輕朋友,你從未告訴過我他的名字,但他的畫像可真令我神魂顛倒。他從不思考,對此我深信不疑。他就是相貌迷人、頭腦空白的那一類人。冬天時我們無花可看,他就該一直待在這兒;夏天時我們也需要某種東西來清醒我們的理智。別太自鳴得意了,貝澤爾,你跟他完全不相像。"

"你不懂得我的意思,亨利,"畫家說。"我當然不像他。這一點我非常清楚。其實我也不願意像他。你不以為然嗎?我對你說的是真話。才貌出眾的人多半在劫難逃,這樣的劫數好像總是尾隨着古今帝王的跟蹌的腳步。普普通通的人倒更安全些。在這個世界上總是醜人和笨蛋最幸運。他們可以舒舒服服地坐在那裏看別人表演。縱使他們不知道甚麼是勝利,至少不必領略失敗的滋味。他們的日子本是我們大家應該過的那種日子:安穩太平,無所用心,沒有煩惱。他們既不算計別人,也不會遭仇人暗害。你有身分和財產,亨利;我有頭腦和才能,且不管它們價值如何;道林·格雷有美麗的容貌。我們都將為上帝賜給我們的這些東西付出代價,付出可怕的代價。"

"道林·格雷？這就是他的名字？"亨利勛爵問，同時從畫室的一端向貝澤爾·霍爾渥德走過去。

"是的，這就是他的名字。我本來不打算告訴你的。"

"那又為甚麼呢？"

"哦，我說不出來。我如果非常非常地喜歡誰，我就從來不把他們的名字告訴任何人。這有點像把他們的一部分出讓。我現在變得喜歡祕密行事了。這大概是能夠使現代生活在我們心目中變得神祕莫測的唯一辦法。哪怕是最平常的事情，只要你把它隱瞞起來，就顯得饒有趣味。現在我要是離開倫敦，我決不會告訴家裏人上哪兒去。我要是告訴了，我就會覺得索然無味。這也許是一種愚蠢的習慣，但不知怎麼的好像能使一個人的生活平添許多浪漫的氣氛。你大概覺得我這種行為荒唐透頂吧？"

"一點也不，"亨利勛爵回答說，"一點也不，我親愛的貝澤爾。你好像忘了我是個已經結婚的人，而結婚的唯一美妙之處，就是雙方都絕對需要靠撒謊過日子。我從來不知道我的妻子在甚麼地方，我的妻子也從來不知道我在做甚麼。我們見面的時候，比如一起在別處吃飯，或者到某一公爵府去拜訪，反正就是偶爾見面的時候，我們總是相互編造種種再荒謬不過的假話，而面部表情卻是再正經不過的。在這方面，我的妻子很高明，實在比我高明得多。她從來不會把日期顛三倒四，而我卻常常如此。不過她即使識破我的謊話，也從不吵鬧。有時我巴不得她吵鬧一場，可她只是把我取笑一番了事。"

"我討厭你這樣談你的家庭生活，亨利，"貝澤爾·霍爾渥德一面說，一面往通向花園的門那邊踱去。"我相信你實際上是個很好的丈夫，不過你硬是以自己的美德為恥辱。你是個怪人。你從來不説正經話，你也從來不做不正經的事。你的玩世不恭無非是裝腔作勢。"

"保持本色才是裝腔作勢，而且是我所知道最令人討厭的裝腔作勢，"亨利勛爵笑着高聲説。這兩個年輕人一同走到了花園裏，在一叢高大的月桂樹的遮蔭下面一張長竹凳上坐定。陽光從光滑的樹葉上溜過。一些白色的雛菊在草叢中搖曳。

在一陣沉默之後，亨利勛爵掏出他的錶來。"我恐怕該走了，貝澤爾，"他喃喃地説，"在我走之前，我還是要你回答剛才我向你提的那個問題。"

"甚麼問題？"畫家問，眼睛仍盯着地上。

"你明明知道。"

"我不知道，亨利。"

"好吧，我告訴你我指的是甚麼。我要你向我解釋，你為甚麼不願意展出道林·格雷的肖像。我要知道真實的原因。"

"我已經把真實的原因對你説了。"

"不，你沒有説。你説因為那裏有太多你自己的東西。這完全是孩子氣的説法。"

"亨利，"貝澤爾凝視着他的臉説："凡是懷着感情畫的肖像，每一幅都是作者的肖像，而不是模特兒的肖像。模特兒僅僅是偶然因素。畫家用油彩在畫布上表現的並不是模特兒，應該説是畫家自己。我不願展出這幅像，是因為我擔心它會泄露我自己靈魂的祕密。"

亨利勛爵笑了起來。"那是甚麼祕密？"他問。

"我來告訴你吧，"霍爾渥德說，但是他臉上現出了困惑的表情。

"我等着聽呢，貝澤爾，"亨利勛爵向他看了一眼敦促道。

"哦，其實也沒有甚麼可談的，亨利，"畫家說，"恐怕你未必能理解。很可能你不會相信。"

亨利勛爵微微一笑，俯身從草叢中摘下一枝粉紅花瓣的雛菊，拿來細心觀看。"我確信我能理解，"他說，一面凝視着那個像是用白羽毛鑲邊的小金盤，"至於信與不信，我可以相信任何事情，只要那是完全難以置信的。"

一陣風從樹上吹落了幾朵花，沉甸甸的星狀紫丁香花簇在重而靜止的空氣中晃去搖來。牆根旁有一隻草蜢開始歌唱，一隻細長的蜻蜓張開棕色的透明翅膀一閃而過，好像劃下一條藍色的線。亨利勛爵幾乎能聽見貝澤爾·霍爾渥德的心跳，但不知下文究竟如何。

"事情的經過很簡單，"畫家稍微沉吟後說。"兩個月前，我去參加布蘭登夫人舉辦的一個晚會。你要知道，我們這些窮畫家有時不得不在社交界露露面，至少是要讓人們知道我們不是野蠻人。有一次你對我說過，只要穿上晚禮服，打着白領結，哪怕一個股票經紀也可以博得文明人的名聲。我在客廳裏跟一些打扮得嚇人的貴族遺孀和乏味透頂的皇家美術學院院士聊了約十分鐘，忽然覺得有人在瞧着我。我轉過頭去，就這樣第一次看見了道林·格雷。當我們的視線碰在一起的時候，我發覺自己的臉色在變白。一陣莫名其妙的恐懼向我襲來。我明白自己面對面遇上了這樣一個人，單是他的容貌就有那麼大的魅力。如果我任其擺佈的話，我整個人，整個靈魂，連同我的藝術本身，通通都要被吞噬掉。我在自己的生活中素來不需要任何外來的影響。你也知道，亨利，我有着怎樣的獨立性格。我一直是自己的主人，至少在我遇見道林·格雷之前一直如此。可現在……我不知道怎麼對你說好。好像有一個聲音告訴我，我正面臨着平生最可怕的危機。我有一種奇怪的感覺，覺得命運為我準備着異乎尋常的快樂和異乎尋常的痛苦。當時我愈想愈害怕，就轉身打算走出客廳。驅使我這樣做的並不是良心，而是膽怯。我不想把打算逃跑說成是我的光榮。"

"良心和膽怯其實是一碼事，貝澤爾。良心不過是膽怯的商標罷了。"

"我不信這種說法，亨利，我想你也不信。不管是甚麼驅使着我，可能是自尊心，因為我一向自尊心很強，反正我竭力往門外擠。偏偏在門口撞見布蘭登夫人。'你這麼早就想逃跑嗎，霍爾渥德先生？'她發出了尖叫。你知道她的嗓子有多尖！"

"她在哪方面都像一隻孔雀，可就是不如孔雀那麼美。"亨利勛爵說着，用他細長的手指神經質地把雛菊扯成碎片。

"我沒法把她甩掉。她把我引薦給皇親國戚、達官貴人和那些頭戴巨大頭飾、長着鸚鵡鼻子的老太婆。她對人說我是她最好的朋友。我以前明明只見過她一回，可她認定我就是她們名流圈子中的一員。誠然，我有一幅畫當時曾獲得很大的成功，至少幾張小報對它鼓噪過一陣子——這是十九世紀名垂不朽的標準。突然，我跟那個使我奇怪地激動起來的年輕人打了個照面。我們靠得很近，幾乎碰着了。我們的視線再次相遇。我竟冒冒失失地請布蘭登夫人給我們介紹一下。也許這並不算太冒失，而且恐怕是無法避免的。即使沒有人介紹，我們也會互相攀談起來。我相信準會這樣。道林事後也對我這樣說過。他也感覺到我們是命中注定要互相認識的。"

"布蘭登夫人是怎樣介紹這位奇妙的年輕人呢？"亨利勛爵問。"我知道她喜歡對每一個客人作急口令式的鑒定。我記得，有一次她把我介紹給一個勛綏滿胸、一臉兇相的紅面孔老頭。我們向他走過去的時候，她湊在我耳邊講有關那老頭的種種駭人聽聞的私隱，她像說悄悄話那樣，但可惜客廳裏人人都聽得一清二楚。我立刻逃之夭夭。我喜歡憑自己的眼光去看人，可是布蘭登夫人介紹她的客人如同拍賣行裏介紹商品一模一樣。她要麼胡亂搪塞，要麼說上好多廢話，可就是沒有你想知道的事。"

"可憐的布蘭登夫人！你把她形容得太過分了，亨利！"霍爾渥德沒精打采地說。

"我的老弟，她打算辦一間沙龍，事實上只是開了一家飯館。這叫我怎麼能為她喝采呢？你還是告訴我吧，關於道林·格雷她是怎麼說的？"

"哦，大概是這麼幾句：'這孩子真可愛……當年我跟他那可憐的媽媽真是形影不離。他做甚麼我可全忘了……恐怕沒有做甚麼……噢，對了，會彈鋼琴，也許是拉小提琴吧，親愛的格雷先生？'我和道林都忍不住笑了起來，我們立刻做了朋友。"

"笑對於交朋友倒是個不壞的開端，要是以笑告終那就更好，"年輕的勛爵說着，又摘下一枝雛菊。

霍爾渥德搖了搖頭。"你不懂甚麼是友誼，亨利，"他嘀咕着說，"你也不懂得甚麼是仇恨。你甚麼人都喜歡，那就是說你對甚麼人都無所謂。"

"你太不公平了！"亨利勛爵嚷着。他把帽子往後一推，抬頭望着像一團團閃光的絹絲在夏天的碧空中飄浮的白雲。"是的，太不公平了。我對人的態度大有區別。我與相貌美的人交朋友，與品格好的人做相識，與頭腦靈的人做對頭。在挑選敵人的時候，再小心也不為過。我的敵人沒有一個是笨蛋。他們的智力都很發達，所以他們都很賞識我。我大概是自命不凡吧？我想是的。"

"我覺得是這樣，亨利。按照你的標準，想必我只是一個相識。"

"我親愛的貝澤爾，你遠遠超過一個相識。"

"但也遠遠算不上朋友。我猜想大概類似一個兄弟。"

"噢，兄弟！我才不在乎我的兄弟。我的哥哥怎樣也不死，而我的幾個弟弟卻總是找死。"

"亨利！"霍爾渥德皺眉喝住他。

"親愛的，你不要太認真。不過我實在討厭我的親屬。大概原因在於我們誰也忍受不了和我們有同樣毛病的人。英國的民主派對於他們所謂的上層階級的劣根性深惡痛絕，我也頗有同感。老百姓把酗酒、愚昧和道德敗壞視為他們所專有，如果我們中間有誰出這種洋相，就被認為侵犯他們的權利。當可憐的索思沃克鬧離婚時，老百姓的憤怒簡直無與倫比。可是我不敢說有百分之十的無產者是循規蹈矩的。"

"你這番話我半句也不同意，不但如此，亨利，我肯定你自己也不相信。"

亨利勳爵捋捋他的棕色尖鬍鬚，用帶流蘇的烏木手杖在漆皮鞋上敲敲。"你是個地道的英國人，貝澤爾！你這是第二次發表這樣的評語了。向一個徹頭徹尾的英國人說出某種想法總是一件欠考慮的事情，因為他從來不去分析這個想法是對是錯。他認為唯一重要的是對方自己相信不相信。實際上，一種想法是否有價值，與說出這個想法的人是否出於真心毫無關係。事實多半是這樣：說的人愈不是真的相信，那個想法就愈顯得有道理，因為這樣才不夾雜他個人的需要、個人的願望或個人的成見。不過我不打算跟你討論政治、社會學或形而上學。我喜歡人多過喜歡原則，我喜歡無原則的人多過喜歡其餘的一切。你多給我講講道林·格雷先生的事吧。你跟他常見面嗎？"

"天天見面。要是一天不見，我就很不高興。我絕對少不了他。"

"稀奇事！我一直以為你除了自己的藝術外，對甚麼都不感興趣。"

"他現在就是我全部的藝術，"畫家一臉嚴肅地說，"有時候我想，亨利，在世界歷史上，只有兩個重要的時代。第一個是出現新藝術手段的時代，而第二個是出現新藝術人格的時代。正如油畫的發明之於威尼斯人的價值，安提諾烏斯的臉孔之於晚期希臘雕塑的價值，將來某一天道林·格雷的容貌之於我，也具有同樣的價值。我不僅僅是照着他畫畫、素描、速寫。當然，這些我全做過，但他對我來說不僅僅是個模特兒或被畫的人。我不想告訴你，我不滿意自己畫的所有道林·格雷的畫像，或者說，藝術不能表現出他的美。沒有甚麼是藝術表現不了的，而我也知道，自從遇到道林·格雷，我的作品都很好，都是我至今為止最好的作品。但我不知道你是否能理解，他的人格魅力以某種奇怪的方式向我展示了一種全新的藝術形式、全新的風格模式。我看事物的方式不同了，思考的方式也不同了。我現在可以用以前看不到的方式重塑生活。'在思想的白晝，實現形式之夢'，我忘了這是誰說過的話，但這正是道林·格雷之於我的價值。只要這個小夥子出現在我眼前 —— 在我看來他只是個小夥子，儘管他實際上已經二十多歲了 —— 只要他出現在我眼前……啊！我不知道你是否明白那意味着甚麼，在不知不覺間，他就為我定義了一個新流派的線條，這個流派包含了浪漫精神的所有激情，以及希臘精神的一切無瑕。靈魂和肉體的和諧是多麼重要啊！而我們卻瘋狂地把兩者分離，創造出一種粗俗的現實主義和一個空洞的理想。亨利！要是你知道道林·格雷對我而言是多麼重要就好了！你記得我那幅風景畫嗎？阿格紐畫商給我開出了很高的價格，但我仍不肯賣出的那幅，那是我畫過其中一幅最好的作品。為甚麼會畫得這麼好呢？因為當我作這幅畫時，道林·格雷就坐在我的旁邊。某種微妙的影響透過他傳給了我，我平生第一次在樸實無華的樹林中，看到了自己總是在尋找又總是錯過的奇跡。"

"貝澤爾，這的確不平常！我要見一見道林·格雷。"

霍爾渥德從長凳站起來，在花園裏踱了幾個來回，又回到長凳前。"亨利，"他說，"道林·格雷無非是我的創作主題。你在他身上看不出甚麼來。而我甚麼都看得出來。在我沒有把他畫進去的作品中可以更強烈地感到他的存在。我剛才說過，他啟示了一種新的技法。我可以在某些線條的折曲、某些色彩的動人微妙處發現他。事情就是這樣。"

"那你為甚麼不願展出他的肖像呢？"亨利勛爵問。

"因為我不知不覺地在裏邊傾注了一個畫家的全部崇拜之情；這是非常奇怪的感情，當然，我從來沒有告訴過他。他一點也不知道。他永遠也不會知道。但是世人可能猜得到，我不願意暴露我的靈魂，讓那些好奇的凡夫俗子瞧個沒完。我的心決不放到他們的顯微鏡下面去。這幅畫像有太多我自己的東西了，亨利，實在太多了。"

"詩人們可不像你這樣躲躲閃閃。他們懂得描寫激情的東西在出版方面是有利可圖的。時下最暢銷的書多半是破碎的心之類。"

"所以我討厭詩人，"霍爾渥德緊接着說。"藝術家應當創造美的作品，但不應當把個人生活中的任何東西放進去。在我們這個時代，人們彷彿把藝術看待為自傳的一種形式。我們喪失了抽象的美感。有朝一日我要讓世人知道甚麼是抽象的美感；為了這個緣故，世人將永遠看不到我給道林‧格雷畫的肖像。"

"我認為你說得不對，貝澤爾，不過我不想跟你辯論。只有完全喪失理智的人才喜歡辯論。告訴我，道林‧格雷是不是很喜歡你？"

畫家思索了一會，然後回答："他喜歡我，我知道他喜歡我。當然，我對他奉承得很厲害。有些話我明明知道講了會後悔，可是我覺得向他講這些話有一種奇妙的樂趣。他對我通常是很親切的，我們兩個坐在畫室裏海闊天空甚麼都談。然而有時候，他麻木不仁得可怕，而且大有以我的痛苦為樂的樣子。那時，亨利，我覺得我把自己的整個心靈都給了一個人，這個人卻把它當作插在上衣鈕孔上的一朵花，當作一件滿足虛榮心的裝飾品對待，只供夏天一日之用。"

"夏天日長，貝澤爾，"亨利勛爵咕噥着。"也許你將比他更早生厭。想起來未免悲哀，但天才無疑要比美耐久些。我們大家拼命想多長點學問，原因就在於此。在激烈的生存競爭中，我們需要有些耐久的東西，所以我們儘量把各種垃圾和事實往腦袋裏裝，妄想保住自己的一席地位。現代的理想人物就是無所不曉的人。而無所不曉的人的頭腦是很可怕的。它像一家古董鋪子，裏邊全是古靈精怪的玩意，到處都是灰塵，每一件東西的標價都大大超過它本身的價值。不管怎樣，我還是認為你將先感到厭倦。總有一天，你看着你的朋友，會覺得他好像不那麼勻稱，或會不喜歡他的膚色或者別的甚麼。你會在心底裏狠狠地責備他，並且當真地認為他非常對不起你。下次他再來，你就對他十分冷淡了。這將是件很大的憾事，你將會被改變。你剛才告訴我的故事的確很浪漫，可以說是一段藝術的浪漫史，而任何浪漫史最壞的後果，是叫人變得沒有絲毫浪漫的氣息。"

"亨利，不要這樣說。只要我一天活着，道林・格雷就永遠是我的主宰。我的感受你是體會不到的。你太多變了。"

"啊，我親愛的貝澤爾，恰恰因為如此，我才能體會你的感受。不變心的人只能體會愛的庸俗的一面，唯有變心的人知道愛的酸辛。"亨利勛爵用精美的銀質煙匣打火，點了一支煙抽起來，那神態似乎因為茫茫世事被自己一語道破而得意。幾隻麻雀在常春藤碧油油的葉片中吱吱喳喳，藍色的雲影像一羣燕子在草上掠過。待在花園裏真愉快！人們的感情真有意思！他覺得，比他們的思想有意思多了。自身的靈魂和朋友的情愛，這是生活中最迷人的。他暗自高興地想像着因他在貝澤爾・霍爾渥德這裏耽擱太久而錯過的那頓無聊的午餐。如果他到了姑媽家去吃飯，準會在那裏碰見古德博迪勛爵，話題反正跳不出給貧民施食，以及設立模範寄宿所的必要性。每個階級都要宣揚那些他們自己無須實行的美德是如何重要。有錢人大講節約的好處，遊手好閒的人口若懸河地談論勞動之偉大。這一切今天都不必奉陪了，真開心！他想到姑媽的時候，一下子若有所悟。他轉向霍爾渥德說道："老弟，我剛想起來了。"

"想起了甚麼，亨利？"

"我在哪兒聽到過道林·格雷的名字。"

"在哪兒？"霍爾渥德問，眉頭略略皺了一下。

"別這麼生氣，貝澤爾。是在我姑媽阿加莎那兒。她告訴我找到了一個很好的年輕人，可以幫忙做些東區的工作，他的名字叫道林·格雷。我肯定她從來沒跟我說起他長得很漂亮。女人不會欣賞好看的長相，至少好女人是這樣。她說他很真誠，稟性很好。我立刻想像出一個戴眼鏡的傢伙，頭髮平直，滿臉雀斑，邁着一雙大腳。但願我當時知道他是你的朋友。"

"我很高興你當時不知道，亨利。"

"為甚麼？"

"我不希望你跟他相識。"

"你不希望我跟他相識？"

"對。"

"先生，道林·格雷先生來了，在畫室裏，"管家到花園裏來通報。

"這下你只好給我介紹了，"亨利勛爵高聲笑道。

畫家轉向站在陽光下睜不開眼睛的僕人，說："帕克，請格雷先生稍待，我一會就來。"僕人鞠了一躬，沿着小路走回去。

這時他對亨利勛爵看了一眼。"道林·格雷是我最好的朋友，"他説。"他心地純潔而善良。你姑母對他的評語一點也不錯。不要毀了他。不要去影響他。你的影響好不了。世界大得很，出色的人物多的是。不要把他從我身邊奪走，唯獨他才能使我的藝術具有目前的那種魅力。我的藝術家生涯全在他手裏。記住，亨利，我相信你。"他説得很慢，這些話幾乎是違背他的意志硬擠出來的。

"你扯到哪兒去了！"亨利勛爵笑容可掬地説着，抓住霍爾渥德的胳膊，連扶帶拽地和他一起回到屋裏。

第二章

他們一進門，就看到了道林・格雷。他正背對着他們，坐在鋼琴邊，翻閱着舒曼的《森林情景》樂譜。"你要把它借給我，貝澤爾，"他喊道，"我想學這些迷人至極的樂章。"

"這完全取決於你今天的姿勢擺得好不好，道林。"

"哦，我可擺膩了，我不要這種跟我一樣大的等身圖像！"那少年任性地鬧着在琴櫈上轉過身來。他看到亨利勛爵，臉上刷地升起一陣淡淡的紅暈，連忙站了起來。"請原諒，貝澤爾，我不知道你有客人。"

"這位是亨利・沃登勛爵，我在牛津時的老朋友。我剛告訴他，你是個多麼好的模特兒，可現在你把事情給弄糟了。"

"一點也沒有弄糟，見到你我很高興，格雷先生，"亨利勛爵說着，走上前去並伸出手。"我姑媽常常跟我談起你。你是她特別喜愛的人，而且我擔心，你也是她其中一個受害者。"

"現在我被列入阿加莎夫人的黑名冊，"道林回答，露出滑稽的懺悔表情。"上星期二，我答應跟她一起去白教堂。說真的，我完全忘記了。我們本來要一起表演二重唱……我想是三段二重唱。不知道她會怎樣說我，我嚇得不敢去見她了。"

"放心，我會使你和我姑媽和解的。她非常疼你。我想，你沒有參加演出也無所謂。聽眾很可能以為那是二重奏。因為阿加莎姑媽彈起鋼琴來音量特別大，一個頂兩個綽綽有餘。"

"這樣的評語對她太不恭敬，對我也不算讚揚，"道林笑着說。

亨利勛爵望着他。是啊，他確實美得出奇：鮮紅的嘴唇輪廓雅致，湛藍的眼睛目光坦然，還長着一頭金色的鬈髮。他的眉宇間有一股叫人一下子就信得過的吸引力。青春的率真、純潔的熱情一覽無遺。你會感覺到，他還沒有被這濁世所玷污。怪不得貝澤爾‧霍爾渥德對他如此崇拜。

"格雷先生，你太可愛了，不適合做慈善，完全不適合。"亨利勛爵說着，在沙發上躺下，打開他的煙匣。

畫家忙着調色和準備畫筆。他似乎顯得心煩意亂，當聽到亨利勛爵末了那句話，便抬頭向他瞥了一眼，猶豫了一下，然後說："亨利，我想今天把這幅畫像完工。我要是請你走，你不會覺得我太不禮貌吧？"

亨利勛爵粲然一笑，向道林‧格雷瞧了瞧，問道："你說我該不該走，格雷先生？"

"哦，請不要走，亨利勛爵。我看貝澤爾今天情緒不好，我最討厭他這副樣子。再說，我希望你告訴我，為甚麼我不適合做慈善。"

"我不知道這事會由我來告訴你，格雷先生。這話題過於沉悶，非得一本正經來談不可。不過既然你要我留下，我一定不走。貝澤爾，你不介意吧？你對我講過好幾次，說你喜歡有人和你的模特兒聊聊。"

霍爾渥德咬了咬嘴唇。"既然道林要這樣，你當然得留下。道林的怪脾氣任何人都得遷就，除了他自己。"

亨利勛爵拿起他的禮帽和手套。"貝澤爾，儘管你誠意相留，我看我還是得走。我跟一個人約好在奧爾良飯店見面。再見，格雷先生。改天下午請到柯曾街舍間來玩。我五點鐘幾乎總是在家。你來之前請寫信告訴我。萬一讓你撲空，我將非常遺憾。"

"貝澤爾，"道林·格雷嚷了起來，"如果亨利·沃登勛爵要走，我也走。你畫畫的時候始終不開口，讓我站在墊腳台上裝出一副快樂的傻相，多無聊啊！請他留下吧。我一定要把他留下。"

"別走了，亨利，看在道林的份上，這也是幫我的忙，"霍爾渥德說時凝神端詳他的作品。"一點不假，我工作的時候從來不開口，也從不聽別人說話，想來我不幸的模特兒一定悶得受不了。我請求你留下。"

"那我在奧爾良約好的人怎麼辦？"

畫家笑了起來。"我想不會有甚麼問題。重新坐下吧，亨利。道林，現在你站到畫台上去，不要挪動得太厲害，也不要把亨利勛爵說的話當作一回事。他所有的朋友都受到他極壞的影響，只有我一個人例外。"

道林·格雷帶着一副年輕的希臘殉道者的表情站到畫台上，他向亨利勛爵做了一個不滿意的怪相，但心裏卻十分喜歡他。他跟貝澤爾大不一樣，兩人形成很有趣的對照。他的聲音非常好聽。不久，道林·格雷對他說："你真的給人極壞的影響嗎，亨利勛爵？貝澤爾是不是言過其實？"

"根本沒有好的影響，格雷先生。任何影響都是不道德的，從科學觀點來看就是如此。"

"為甚麼？"

"因為影響他人就是把自己的靈魂強加於人。對方就不再用自己天賦的頭腦來思想，不再受天賦的慾念所支配。他的美德並不真正是他自己的。他的罪惡也是剽竊來的——如果有罪惡的話。他變成了別人的樂曲的回聲，像一個演員扮演並非為他寫的角色。人生的目的是自我發展。充分表現一個人的本性，就是我們每一個人活在世上的目的。如今的人們害怕自己。他們忘了那種高於一切的義務，就是對自己承擔的義務。當然，他們都有好心腸。他們給飢者施食，給乞丐施衣。可是他們的靈魂卻在捱餓，而且赤裸裸毫無遮蔽。勇氣已經離開了人類。也許我們從未真正有過勇氣。對社會的畏懼、對上帝的畏懼，就是這二者統治着我們。前者是道德的基礎，後者是宗教的祕密。不過……"

"道林，好孩子，把頭向右邊稍微轉過去一點，"畫家說。他全神貫注在工作上，只感覺到這少年的臉上出現了一種前所未有的神采。

"然而，"亨利勛爵接着說，聲音低緩動聽，手優雅地揮動着，這是他在伊頓公學讀書時就有的招牌動作，"我相信，如果一個人能充分地、完整地活着，表現出每一種感情，表達出每一種思想，實現每一種夢想……我相信，世界會獲得一種新鮮的喜悅，會因此使我們忘掉中世紀時代的所有弊病，重回希臘的理想，可能是某種比希臘理想更美好、更豐饒的東西。但我們之中最勇敢的人也害怕自己。野蠻人的那種殘缺，不幸地殘存着自我否定，而這種否定會毀壞我們的生活。我們因為自我否定而受到懲罰。我們竭力壓制住的每一種衝動都在頭腦中孕育着，並毒害着我們。肉體只要犯了罪，就與罪孽無關了，因為行動是淨化的一種方式。除了快樂的回憶，或奢侈的悔恨，就甚麼都沒有了。擺脫誘惑的唯一方法就是屈服於誘惑。若抵制它，你的靈魂就會渴望被禁止的東西，就會渴求那些被可怕的法律弄得可怕和非法的東西。這樣，你的靈魂就會得病。據説，世間諸般大事都發生在頭腦裏。世間的大惡就在頭腦裏，只是在頭腦裏孕育。你，格雷先生，就拿你來説吧，紅玫瑰般的青年時光，白玫瑰般的少年歲月，你曾擁有讓自己感到害怕的激情，那些讓自己備受恐懼折磨的念頭，那些白天黑夜做過的夢讓你一想起就滿臉羞愧⋯⋯"

"等——等一下！"格雷結結巴巴地説，"等一下！你把我搞糊塗了。我不知道説甚麽好。我應該有話回答你，可我找不出話來。不要説了。讓我想一想。不，還是不要讓我想的好。"

約莫十分鐘，他站在那兒一動也不動，嘴唇微微張開，眼睛異樣地發亮。他隱約意識到，一些全新的思緒開始在他身上萌動。不過他覺得那是從他自己心底湧出來的。貝澤爾的朋友對他説的幾句話無疑是信口開河，並不乏刻意的悖論，卻觸動了某一根祕密的心弦。這根弦以前從未被觸及，可是現在已開始振動和奇怪地搏動。

音樂也曾這樣使他激動。音樂也曾多次擾亂他的心。但音樂不是那麽清楚明白的。它在我們身上造成的不是一個新世界，而只是另外的一團糟。然而這是言語！光這麽幾句話就夠可怕了！那是多麽清楚、鮮明，而又殘酷的啊！叫你無處躲避。那裏又有着多麽難以捉摸的魔力啊！言語似乎能使輪廓模糊的事物具備可塑的形態，有它自己像詩琴和古提琴般悦耳的音樂。光這麽幾句話！還有甚麽比得上言語那樣實在嗎？

是啊，在他的少年時代有些事情他不明白。現在他明白了。生活一下子向他閃耀出火紅的色彩。他覺得自己好像在烈焰中行走。他過去怎麼不知道呢？

亨利勛爵帶着一絲淡淡的笑意觀察他。他把握得住，在怎樣的心理時刻應該保持沉默。他產生了強烈的好奇心。他沒料到自己的話竟會給人如此深刻的印象，回想起自己十六歲那年看過的一本書，向他揭示了許多以前不知道的事情，他思量着，道林·格雷是否正在經歷類似的階段？他不經意地向空中射了一箭，難道竟中了靶心！這個少年真迷人！

霍爾渥德的筆在畫布上汪洋恣肆地揮灑自如，這種真正洗練和恰到好處的筆觸只可能來自驚人的才力，至少在藝術上是這樣。畫家沒有察覺到對話出現了冷場。

"貝澤爾，我站膩了，"道林·格雷忽然叫嚷起來。"我要到花園裏去坐一會。這兒悶得要命！"

"親愛的，我很抱歉。我畫畫的時候考慮不到其他事情。不過你的姿勢從來沒有這樣好。你簡直一動也不動。我把握住了所需要的效果：微微張開的嘴唇、閃閃發亮的眼睛。我不知道亨利對你說了些甚麼，但他確實使你表現出最奇妙的表情。他大概對你說了許多恭維話。他的話你半句也信不得。"

"他一點也沒有恭維我。也許正因為這樣，我完全不相信他所說的話。"

"你明明每一句都相信了，"亨利勛爵說着，有氣無力地向他看了看。"我跟你一起到花園裏去。畫室裏熱得可怕。貝澤爾，給我們來一些冷飲，加上點草莓。"

"完全可以，亨利。請你按一下鈴叫帕克進來，我會把你要的東西告訴他。我還得把襯景畫好，過一會我再來。你不要讓道林

328

耽擱太久。我從來也沒有像今天畫得這樣順手。這幅肖像將是我的傑作。它現在就已經是我的傑作了。"

亨利勛爵走到花園裏，發現道林·格雷把臉埋在一大簇陰涼的紫丁香中，連續不停吸着花香，彷彿這就是美酒。他走到道林跟前，一隻手攔在他肩上。"你做得完全正確，"他輕輕說道。"除了感官，甚麼也不能治療靈魂的創痛，同樣，感官的飢渴也只有靈魂解除得了。"

那少年嚇了一跳，連忙退後一步。他沒戴帽子，綴滿葉片的枝條挑起了他那不聽話的鬈髮，把一綹綹金絲扯得凌亂不堪。他目光驚恐，好像一個人被猛然叫醒。他那秀氣的鼻翼微微顫動，一陣內心的緊張使他鮮紅的嘴唇抖個不停。

"是啊，"亨利勛爵繼續說，"通過感官治療靈魂的創痛，通過靈魂解除感官的飢渴，那是人生的一大祕密。你是上帝創造的一個奇跡。你知道的比你認為知道的多，但比你想要知道的少。"

道林·格雷皺起眉頭，轉過臉去。他無法不喜歡站在他身旁的這個修長而瀟灑的青年男子。亨利勛爵浪漫的橄欖色面孔和疲憊的表情引起了他的興趣。他那低沉慵懶的音調有一種了不起的吸引力。甚至他那雙冰涼、白淨、花一般的手也出奇地動人。他說話時，這雙手的動作像音樂般流動，似乎化為一種獨特的語言。但是道林有點怕他，並且為此感到羞慚。為甚麼要讓一個陌生人來啟發他認識自己？他認識貝澤爾·霍爾渥德有好幾個月了，但他們之間的友誼沒有使他發生任何變化。忽然有一個人出現在他的生活道路上，向他揭示人生的奧祕。但其實，有甚麼可怕？他又不是小學生或者小女孩。要是害怕才可笑呢。

"我們到背陰的地方去坐坐，"亨利勛爵說。"帕克已經把冷飲端出來了，你要是再在陽光下烤，會把自己毀壞，貝澤爾就不再給你畫像了。你千萬不能曬傷。那樣就不好看了。"

"那有甚麼要緊？"道林·格雷笑着說道，同時在花園盡頭的凳子上坐下。

"這對你極其重要，格雷先生。"

"為甚麼？"

"因為你擁有無比美麗的青春，而青春是值得珍惜的。"

"我感覺不到，亨利勛爵。"

"對，你現在感覺不到。一旦你變得又老又醜，皮膚鬆垂，思想在你額上刻滿了皺紋，慾望的毒焰烤焦了你的嘴唇，那時你會強烈地感覺到。現在，不論你走到哪兒，大家都被你迷住。但是能永久這樣嗎？你有一張驚人的漂亮面孔，格雷先生。別皺眉頭。你確實如此。美是天才的一種形式，實際上還高於天才，因為美不需要解釋。美屬於世界上偉大的現象，如同陽光，如同春天，如同我們稱作月亮的銀色貝殼在黑沉沉的水中反射的倒影一樣。那是無可爭議的。美有它神聖的統治權。誰有了它，誰就是王子。你在笑？啊！將來你失去它的時候，你就不笑了……人們往往說美只是表面的。也許如此。但它至少不像思想那樣表面。對我來說，美是奇跡中的奇跡。只有淺薄之輩才不根據外貌作判斷。世界上真正的奧祕是有形的，不是無形的……是啊，格雷先生，你得天獨厚。但是神所賜予的不久就要收回。你只有有限的歲月可以真正地、完全地、充分地享受生活。等你的青春逝去，你的美貌也將隨之消失，那時你會突然發現，留待你去奪取的勝利已不復存在，或者你只得滿足於一些微不足道的勝利，回首當年，這些勝利要比失敗的滋味更苦。每過一個月，你就向這可怕的前景走近一步。時光妒忌你，向你臉上的百合花和玫瑰花不斷進攻。你的面色會發黃，兩頰會凹陷，眼神會變暗。你會痛苦不堪……啊！要及時享用你的青春。不要浪費寶貴的光陰去恭聽沉悶的說教，去挽救不可挽救的失敗，去把自己的生命用在愚昧、平淡和庸俗的事情上。這些都是我們時代中病態的目的、虛妄的思想。生活吧！讓你身上美妙的生命之花怒放吧！甚麼也不要放過。要不斷探索新的感覺。甚麼也不要怕……一種新的快樂論——這是我們時代的需要。你可以成為它有形的象徵。憑你的個性，你沒有辦不到的事情。有一小段時間，世界是屬於你的……在我遇見你的一剎那，我就看出你完全不了解你自己，完全不知道你能成為一個怎樣的人。你身上有那麼多吸引我的地方，我覺得我必須使你認識一下你自己。我想，你要是白白浪費掉自己，那太可悲了。要知道，你的青春所能維持的時間是很短很短的。普通的山花謝了還會再開。金鏈花到明年六月又將是黃燦燦的，和現在一樣。一個月後，鐵線蓮上將綴滿紫色的花朵，年復一年，它的葉片總像綠色的夜空襯托着紫色的星星。可是我們的青春卻有去無還。二十歲時在我們身上跳動的快樂的脈搏將緩慢下來。我們的肢體將失去彈性，我們的感覺將變得遲鈍。我們將退化為面目可憎的玩偶，整日回憶那些我們怕得要命的慾念和不敢屈從的異常的誘惑。青春！青春！除了青春，世上的一切毫無價值！”

道林·格雷聽着，眼睛睜大，驚訝不迭。一枝小丁香從他手裏跌落在鋪碎石的地上。一隻毛茸茸的蜜蜂飛過來，繞着那枝丁香噴噴地轉了一陣子。然後它開始爬遍放射形橢圓花球上的每一顆小星。道林異常專心致志地觀察着蜜蜂的動靜。我們有時也會這樣把注意力集中在微不足道的事情上，因為不敢去想真正重要的事情，或者被無法表達的新奇感受弄得心煩，或者某種令人不寒而慄的念頭突然向我們的腦子發動襲擊，逼使我們屈服。過了一會，蜜蜂飛走了。道林看見它鑽進一朵旋花的斑駁小喇叭。那花兒似乎先是顫動了一下，然後開始來回搖曳。

畫家忽然出現在畫室門口，使勁招呼他們回去。亨利勛爵與道林相顧而笑。

"我等着，"畫家喊道。"快來。現在光線正合適，你們可以把冷飲帶來。"

他們站起來，一起順着小徑慢悠悠地走去，兩隻綠白色的蝴蝶在他們旁邊飛過，花園角上一棵梨樹中有一隻畫眉鳥開始歌唱。

"遇見我，你覺得高興嗎，格雷先生？"亨利勛爵瞧着他問。

"是的，現在我是高興的。但不知道我能不能永遠高興？"

"永遠！這是個可怕的字眼。我聽見這個詞就會發抖。女人特別喜歡用這個詞。她們竭力想把每一段浪漫史沒完沒了地延長下去，結果總是大煞風景。其實，'永遠'這個詞沒有甚麼意義。反覆無常和終生的愛之間的唯一差別就在於前者更持久一些。"

他們走進畫室時，道林‧格雷一隻手按住亨利勛爵的胳膊。"那我們就算是反覆無常的朋友吧，"他低聲說，同時為自己的大膽而臉紅，然後站到畫台上去擺姿勢。

亨利勛爵在一張大柳條椅裏舒舒坦坦地坐下來觀看。畫筆刷在畫布上沙沙作響，這是劃破沉寂的唯一聲音。霍爾渥德時而退後幾步，站遠一點看看他的這件作品。陽光從開着的門外射進來，金色的灰塵在這一束斜線中飛舞。到處好像洋溢着醉人的玫瑰花香。

大約過了十五分鐘，霍爾渥德不再畫了。他向道林・格雷看了好長時間，然後又向畫像看了好長時間，咬着那支大畫筆的筆桿，眉頭皺緊，最後大聲宣告："完工了。"說罷俯下身去，在畫布的左角用朱紅色的瘦長字體簽上自己的姓名。

亨利勛爵走過來，仔細看着那幅畫像。這無疑是一件罕見的藝術品，那種惟妙惟肖的程度也是罕見的。

"親愛的朋友，我向你表示最熱烈的祝賀，"他說。"這是當代最傑出的肖像畫。格雷先生，請過來看看你自己。"

少年像從夢裏驚醒似地驀地一震。"真的完工了嗎？"他說着，從畫台上下來。

"真的完工了，"畫家說。"你今天的姿勢擺得極好。我萬分感謝你。"

"這完全是我的功勞，"亨利勛爵插進來說。"可不是嗎，格雷先生？"

道林沒有答話，只是漫不經心地從畫像前走過。他回過頭來一看，不禁倒退一步，兩腮頃刻間泛起欣喜的紅潮。他的眼睛裏閃現出愉快的火花，彷彿是第一次認出了自己。他驚訝地一動不動站在那裏出神，模模糊糊意識到霍爾渥德正在向他說話，但捉摸不住他的話的意思。對自己的美貌的認識在他是一大發現。這一點他過去從來沒有感覺到。貝澤爾・霍爾渥德的誇獎，他固然覺得悅耳，但只當作出於友好的溢美之辭。這些話他聽了，也笑了，過後就忘了，對他本人沒有產生影響。如今亨利·沃登勛爵來發表了一大篇讚美青春的怪論，就青春易逝提出了危言聳聽的警告。這番話立刻打動了他的心，現在他站在畫架前端詳自己風姿的寫照時，亨利勛爵所描繪的前景十分真切地掠過他的心頭。是的，總有一天他的容顏會起皺、憔悴，他的眼睛會暗淡、褪色，他的體態會拱曲、變形。鮮紅的色彩將從他的嘴唇脫落，金黃的光澤將從他的髮絲消失。生命本當造就他的靈魂，結果把他的肉體破壞了。他將變為一個毫無風度可言的醜八怪。

想到這裏，一陣劇痛像刀子捅穿他的胸膛，使他的每一根細微的神經都為之顫動。他的眼睛由淡轉深，變成了紫晶色，並且蒙上了一層淚水。他覺得彷彿有一隻冰冷的手壓在他心上。

"你不喜歡它？"霍爾渥德終於問道。他不理解道林的沉默是甚麼意思，因而略微有些不悅。

"他當然喜歡，"亨利勛爵說。"誰能不喜歡這幅畫像？這是現代美術中最偉大的作品之一。不論你開價多少，我都願意要它。我一定要把它買下來。"

"它並不屬於我，亨利。"

"屬於誰？"

"當然屬於道林，"畫家回答。

"他真是天之驕子。"

"太可悲了！"道林·格雷兩眼盯着他本人的肖像喃喃自語。"太可悲了！我會變得又老又醜，可是這幅畫像卻能永葆青春。它永遠不會比六月的這一天年齡稍大……要是倒過來該多好！如果我能夠永葆青春，而讓這幅畫像變老，要甚麼我都給！是的，任何代價我都願意付！我願意拿我的靈魂換取青春！」

「你大概不會同意這樣的安排，貝澤爾，」亨利勛爵呵呵笑着說。「否則，你作品的命運豈不是太慘了？」

「我會強烈反對這樣的安排，亨利。」霍爾渥德說。

道林·格雷轉過身來望着他。「我相信你會反對，貝澤爾。你愛你的藝術多過愛你的朋友。我在你心目中不會比一件青銅小雕像更有價值。也許還不如，我敢說。」

畫家目瞪口呆地看着他。這完全不像道林說的話。到底是怎麼回事？看來他十分生氣。他的臉漲得通紅，兩腮在發熱。

「是的，」道林繼續說，「我在你心目中還比不上你的象牙信使神或你的銀質牧羊神。你將永遠喜歡祂們。可是你能喜歡我多久呢？大概頂多到我臉上出現第一道皺紋時為止。現在我懂了，不管一個人原本有多美，只要一旦失去美貌，這個人也就失去了一切。這是你的畫告訴我的。亨利·沃登勛爵說得完全正確。青春是唯一可寶貴的東西。當我發現我年華漸逝而變老的時候，我將自殺。」

霍爾渥德頓時臉色煞白，急忙抓住他的手。「道林！道林！」他叫了起來，「不要這樣說。我從來沒有過像你這樣的好朋友，我也將永遠不會再有這樣的朋友。你是不會妒忌沒有生命的東西的，是吧？你比一切東西都美呢！」

「我妒忌一切永不消逝的美。我妒忌你給我畫的肖像。為甚麼它可以保存我必定會失去的東西？每一寸光陰都從我這裏拿走一點東西去給它。哦，要是反過來多好啊！要是畫像會起變化，而我永遠跟現在一樣，那該多好！貝澤爾，你為甚麼要畫這幅像啊？將來它會嘲弄我——狠狠嘲弄我！"熱淚如泉水般湧上道林的眼眶，他掙脱了貝澤爾的手，撲倒在沙發上，臉埋在靠墊裏，就像是在祈禱。

"這是你做的好事，亨利，"畫家痛心地説。

亨利勛爵聳聳肩膀説："這才是真正的道林·格雷，如此而已。"

"這不是。"

"既然不是，跟我有甚麼相干？"

"剛才我要求你走的時候你應當走，"他埋怨道。

"我是應你的要求留下的，"亨利勛爵這樣回答。

"亨利，我不能一下子跟兩個好朋友鬧翻。可是你們兩個使我痛恨我最好的作品，我決心把它毀掉。這不過是一塊抹了油彩的畫布。我不願讓它在我們三人中間作梗，鬧得大家日子不好過。"

道林·格雷從靠墊上抬起長着金髮的腦袋，仰起蒼白的面孔，以迷惘的淚眼望着畫家走到垂着綢簾的窗邊一張松木畫桌跟前。他在那兒做甚麼？他的手在一堆亂七八糟的錫管和乾畫筆中間摸索，在尋找甚麼東西。對了，他在找一把刃面薄而柔軟的長柄調色刀。終於給他找到了。他想要刮破畫布。

道林·格雷抽噎着從沙發上跳起來，衝到霍爾渥德跟前，把刀子從他手裏奪下來扔到畫室的角落裏。"不許這樣，貝澤爾，不許這樣！"他嚷道。"這等於謀殺！"

"我很高興你總算賞識我的作品，道林，"畫家從驚愕中定下神來，冷冷地説。"我本來已經不抱這樣的希望了。"

"賞識它？我愛上了它，貝澤爾。它是我的一部分。我有這樣的感覺。"

「好吧，等你乾了之後，給你塗上油光漆，配好框子，然後送你回家。那時你愛怎樣處置就怎樣處置你自己吧。」他走到畫室的另一頭去按鈴，吩咐僕人送茶進來。「道林，你一定會喝茶，是不是？你喝不喝，亨利？你不反對這點簡單的樂趣吧？」

「我最愛簡單的樂趣，」亨利勛爵說。「對於心理複雜的人，這是最後的避風港。可是我不愛看又哭又鬧的場面，除非在舞台上。你們一對都是逗趣可笑！我不知道是誰下了人是理性動物的定義。這樣的定義下得太早了。人身上甚麼都有，就是缺乏理性。其實，缺乏理性也好，不過我希望你們不要為這幅畫像爭吵。貝澤爾，你還是把它給我吧。這個傻孩子並不真正想要，我是真的想要。」

「貝澤爾，除我以外，你如果把它給任何人，我永遠不會原諒你！」道林‧格雷大聲抗議。「我也不許別人叫我傻孩子。」

「你知道這畫像是屬於你的，道林。在它誕生之前我就把它給了你。」

「你得承認你的表現是有點傻，格雷先生。説你太年輕，你不會真的在意。」

「今天早晨要是有人這樣説，我定必討厭，亨利勛爵。」

「啊，今天早晨！現在你跟那時候大不相同了。」

管家敲門進來，把裝得滿滿的茶盤放在一張日式小桌子上。杯子、碟子叮叮噹噹，一個有凹槽的喬治亞時代茶壺嘶嘶作聲。一名僮僕端進來兩隻球形的瓷缸。道林‧格雷走過去倒茶。貝澤爾和亨利勛爵慢騰騰地走到小桌前，揭開蓋子看瓷缸裏是甚麼東西。

"今天晚上我們去看戲吧，"亨利勛爵説。"一定有甚麼地方在上演好戲。我答應了人家在懷特俱樂部吃晚飯，不過反正是一個老朋友，我可以打電報告訴他我病了，或者説我另有約會不能來。我想這是一個挺好的理由，這樣坦率一定能大大出人意表。"

"穿晚禮服實在是件煩人的事情，"霍爾渥德嘟囔着。"而且，穿上了之後又難看得要命。"

"是啊，"亨利勛爵心不在焉地説，"十九世紀的服裝可惡至極。色調是那麼陰暗沉悶。現代生活中剩下的唯一真正鮮明的色彩就是罪惡。"

"亨利，你不應當在道林面前這樣説話。"

"你指的是哪一個？是那個在給我們倒茶的道林，還是畫上的道林？"

"兩個都是。"

"我想跟你一起去看戲，亨利勛爵，"道林説。

"好極了。貝澤爾，你也去好不好？"

"不行，真的不行。我還是不去的好。我有許多工作要做。"

"那我就跟你兩個人去，格雷先生。"

"我真高興。"

畫家咬了咬嘴唇，手裏拿着茶走到肖像跟前。"我要留下來給真正的道林做伴，"他的聲調悽愴。

"你説這是真正的道林？"肖像的原型激動地問，一邊向畫家走過去。"我真的像它嗎？"

"是的，你跟它一模一樣。"

"多好啊，貝澤爾！"

"至少你在外貌上像它。但它是永遠不變的，"霍爾渥德發出一聲喟歎。"這畢竟是差別。"

"甚麼不變啦、忠誠啦，都是小題大做！"亨利勛爵說。"老實說，即使是愛情，這也純粹是個生理學的問題，根本不依我們的意志。年輕人想要忠誠，結果都變心；老年人想要變心，已無能為力。事情就是這樣。"

"道林，今天晚上不要去看戲了，"霍爾渥德說。"還是留下來和我一起吃晚飯吧。"

"我不能，貝澤爾。"

"為甚麼？"

"因為我答應了亨利・沃登勛爵跟他一起去。"

"他不會因為你信守諾言而更喜歡你。他自己老是說話不算數。我請求你別去了。"

道林・格雷笑着搖搖頭。

"我懇求你，"畫家說。

道林左右為難，望了望笑眯眯的亨利・沃登。這時勛爵正從茶桌那邊觀察他們，覺得煞是有趣。

"我一定要去，貝澤爾，"道林最後答道。

"那好吧，"說完，霍爾渥德走過去把茶杯放在盤子裏。"時間已經不早了，你們還得換裝，不要耽擱了。再見，亨利。再見，道林。希望你很快來看我。明天就來。"

"一定。"

"你不會忘記吧？"

"當然不會，"道林說。

“那麼……亨利……”

“怎麼樣，貝澤爾？”

“請你記住今天早晨我們在花園裏的時候我向你提出的要求。”

“我已經忘了。”

“我相信你。”

“但願我能相信我自己，”亨利勛爵哈哈笑道。“走吧，格雷先生，我的雙人馬車在門口，我可以送你到府上。再見，貝澤爾。今天我們度過了一個極有意思的下午。”

等他們走了出去，門關上之後，畫家頹然倒在沙發上，臉上現出十分痛楚的表情。

第三章

第二天十二點半，亨利·沃登勛爵從柯曾街漫步來到阿爾本尼街，拜訪他舅舅費莫爾勛爵。他是一個性情隨和，舉止有些粗俗的老單身漢。外界都說他自私，因為沒有人從他那兒撈到甚麼特別的好處。但上流社會卻認為他很慷慨，因為他款待着一批使他開心的人。他的父親曾是英國駐馬德里大使，那時候伊莎貝拉還年輕，而普林則默默無聞。但後來他一氣之下離開了外交界，原因是他沒有被派到巴黎當大使。他認為，憑他的出身、懶散的性格、寫快報那一手好英語，以及縱情作樂的派頭，這個職務非他莫屬。他的兒子原是他的祕書，這時候也與上司一起辭職，儘管人家都認為這樣做有點愚蠢。幾個月後，兒子繼承了爵位，開始專心致志地研究貴族的偉大藝術——無所事事。他有兩幢市區的大房子，為了省心，卻寧願住在單人套間裏，並大多在俱樂部裏吃飯。他也花了些心血，管理英國中部諸郡的煤礦，還為自己經營這種敗壞的工業找到了藉口，說是煤的好處是能讓紳士體面地在壁爐裏燒木柴。他在政治上屬於保守黨，只不過保守黨執政的時候，他大罵保守黨人是一批激進分子。在侍從面前他是個英雄，儘管會受他們欺負；在親戚面前他讓人聞之膽寒，倒過來去欺負人家。也只有英國才能造就這樣的人物，而他總是說這個國家快要完蛋了。他的原則已經過時，卻自有一大套理由為自己的偏見辯護。

亨利勛爵走進房間時，他的舅舅身穿粗呢獵裝，抽着方頭雪茄，正在看《泰晤士報》，一邊嘀嘀咕咕自言自語。"你好，亨利，"老紳士說，"有甚麼要事使你這麼早從家裏出來？我知道你們這些公子哥兒照例下午兩點前起不了牀，五點前見不到人。"

　　"喬治舅舅，請相信我，我上這兒來純粹是出於親屬情誼。我想從你這兒搞到一些東西。"

　　"我想一定是錢，"費莫爾勛爵皺起眉頭說。"坐下談吧。如今的年輕人以為有了錢就有了一切。"

　　"嗯，"亨利勛爵含糊地應道，整了整插在外套鈕孔裏的花。"隨着年齡的增長他們更有體會。不過我今天不要錢。只有要付賬的人需要錢，喬治舅舅，我從來不付賬。一個人如果不是長子，他就靠賒賬過日子，而且可以過得挺舒服。何況，我經常跟達特穆爾那邊的零售商打交道，所以他們從不找我的麻煩。我今天是來要情報：當然不是有用的情報，而是無用的情報。"

　　"凡是英國藍皮書裏所寫的，我都可以告訴你，亨利，雖然那些傢伙如今只會寫一堆廢話。我在外交部任職的時候，情況還好些。我聽說如今能經過考試進入外交界，那樣的話你還能指望甚麼呢？考試，純粹是不折不扣的騙局。如果他是一位紳士，他所知自然綽綽有餘；如果他不是紳士，無論他知道甚麼，對其都有害無益。"

　　"道林·格雷先生不會在藍皮書上的，喬治舅舅，"亨利勛爵懶洋洋地說。

　　"道林·格雷先生？他是誰？"費莫爾勛爵問道，他兩道灰白的濃眉打起了結。

"我來就是打聽這件事，喬治舅舅。應當說，我知道他是誰。他是最後一位克爾索勛爵的外孫。他的母親是瑪嘉烈·德弗羅夫人。我要你告訴我他母親的情況。她是甚麼模樣？她嫁給了一個怎樣的人？你那個時代的人你差不多全認識，你可能也認識她。目前我對格雷先生感到極大的興趣。我剛認識他不久。"

"克爾索的外孫！"老紳士重複着，"克爾索的外孫！⋯⋯當然⋯⋯他母親的事我很清楚。我記得還參加過她的洗禮。她——瑪嘉烈·德弗羅——是個絕色的美人，她做了一件使所有的男人都發瘋的事情：跟一個不名一文的年輕人私奔了。那男的甚麼地位也沒有，大概只是在步兵團裏當一名少尉。對了，對了。這件事我原原本本都記得，就像昨天發生的一樣。婚後幾個月，那個窮小子就在斯帕跟人決鬥時被殺死了。這中間有一個很不體面的故事。據說克爾索買通了一個比利時流氓，叫他當眾侮辱他的女婿，是僱他做的，那流氓用劍把他捅了個窟窿，就像叉鴿子一樣。事情好歹算是遮蓋過去，可是此後有相當長一個時期，克爾索只得孤零零一個人在俱樂部裏吃煎牛排。我聽說他把女兒領了回來，可是她再也沒跟父親說一句話。是啊，這是一件很不體面的事情。瑪嘉烈不到一年也死了。你說她留下一個兒子，是嗎？我已經忘了。那孩子是甚麼模樣？如果他像母親的話，一定是個漂亮的小夥子。"

"他的確很漂亮，"亨利勛爵插了一句。

"我希望他不要落在歹人手裏，"老人繼續說。"如果克爾索在遺囑中不虧待他的話，將來有一大筆錢等着他繼承。他母親也有錢。她外祖父的塞爾比莊園的全部財產都歸了她。她的外祖父恨透了克爾索，罵他吝嗇鬼。確實是這樣。有一次他到馬德里去，當時我在那裏。天啊，我真為他害臊。女王幾次問我，那個老是為了車錢跟馬車夫吵架的英國貴族是誰。那裏關於他的故事有一大堆。我足足一個月不敢在宮廷中露臉。我希望他對待自己的外孫不至於像對待出租馬車的車夫那樣刻薄。"

"這可不知道，"亨利勛爵說。"我想這小夥子會有錢的。現在他還未成年。我知道塞爾比已經歸他。這是他自己告訴我的。你說……他母親很漂亮？"

"亨利，瑪嘉烈·德弗羅是我見到過最可愛的一個美人。我怎麼也不明白，是甚麼促使她做出這樣的事來。她可以嫁給任何一個她看中的人。卡林頓曾經為她神魂顛倒。不過，她的氣質很浪漫。這一家的女人都是這樣。這一家的男人全是庸才；可是女人，說真的，都呱呱叫。卡林頓向瑪嘉烈下過跪。這是他自己告訴我的。瑪嘉烈把他嗤笑了一通，而當時倫敦沒有一個女孩子不對卡林頓傾心。哦，說起莫名其妙的婚姻，亨利，我要問你，你爸爸告訴我，達特穆爾要跟一個美國女子結婚，這不是莫名其妙嗎？難道英國女子都配不上他？"

"喬治舅舅，如今娶美國女人非常時髦。"

"亨利，我看好英國女人，我可以跟全世界打賭！"費莫爾勛爵說着，用拳頭敲了一下桌子。

"現在賭注都下在美國女人那一邊。"

"聽人家說她們的後勁不行，"舅舅不以為然。

"打持久戰她們耗不起，不過參加障礙賽非常出色。她們的爆發力特強。我認為達特穆爾沒有希望。"

"那女的親人是誰？"老紳士沒好氣地問。"她有沒有親人？"

亨利勛爵搖搖頭。"美國女人在隱瞞父母的身份這方面和英國女人隱瞞自己的過去一樣巧妙。"說罷，他起身準備告辭。

"她的上一代恐怕是豬肉包裝批發商吧？"

"喬治舅舅，為達特穆爾着想，但願如此。聽說，豬肉包裝批發業在美國是僅次於政治的賺錢生意。"

"她長得怎麼樣？"

"她擺出一副美人的樣子。美國女人大都如此。這是她們迷人的訣竅。"

"這些美國女人為甚麼不留在自己國內？我們整天聽人家說那裏是女人的樂園。"

"的確是這樣。正因為如此，她們才像夏娃一樣拼命要離開那兒，"亨利勛爵說。"再見，喬治舅舅。再不走我吃午飯要遲到了。謝謝你提供了我所需要的情報。我總是喜歡了解新朋友的各種情況，而不想知道舊相識的任何事情。"

"你上哪兒去吃午飯？"

"阿加莎姑媽家。我要她請我和格雷先生吃飯。道林·格雷是她最新的寵兒。"

"嗯！亨利，告訴你的阿加莎姑媽，再也不要為募捐的事來找我的麻煩。簡直把我煩死了！這位女善士大概以為，我除了開支票贊助她的蠢主意就沒事做了。"

"好吧，喬治舅舅，我去告訴她。不過這不起任何作用。慈善家就是缺乏為他人着想的博愛精神。這是他們的顯著特徵。"

老紳士嘟嘟囔囔表示同意，然後按鈴叫他的僕人。亨利勛爵穿過低矮的拱廊走上柏林頓街，再折向巴克利廣場。

　　這就是道林・格雷父母的故事。故事雖然說的很粗略，但當中暗含一段奇異且近乎現代的浪漫情事打動了他。一個漂亮女人，為了追求瘋狂的戀情而冒上了一切。幸福的時光僅過了幾週，被一樁醜惡陰險的罪行打斷了。又經過數月無言的痛苦折磨之後，一個嬰孩在痛苦中出生。死亡奪走了母親的生命，而把男孩留給了孤苦和一個專橫無情的老人。是啊，這個背景很有趣。它成為這個男孩的襯托，使他更完美，就如每一件精美之物的背後，總是存在着某種悲劇那樣。即使最微不足觀的小花要綻開，世界也會經歷痛苦。昨夜在俱樂部的晚餐上，道林・格雷驚恐的目光、半開的雙唇是多麼的迷人啊。他坐在亨利勳爵對面，沉浸於驚喜之中，紅色的燭罩映照着他那讓人驚豔的面孔，像一朵嫣然怒放的玫瑰。與他交談，就像拉一把精製的小提琴，琴弦的每一次拉動和抖動，都會得到回應……能對人施以影響真是讓人無比興奮，沒有甚麼能與之相比。把自己的靈魂投入到某個優雅的形體，並讓它在裏面逗留一會兒；聽到自己睿智的見解得到回應，並伴隨着一切激情和青春的樂章；把自己的精神才情，像一種妙不可言的流體或一股奇異的香氣般，澆灌進另一種精神才情。這都讓人獲得真正的快樂。在這個如我們自身一樣狹隘、庸俗的時代，這個縱情聲色、缺乏大志的時代，這可能是我們所能獲得最愜意的快樂了。機緣巧合，與這個小夥子在貝澤爾的畫室偶遇，他真是極妙的類型，或者說至少可以裝扮成極妙的類型。他優雅，具有少年一塵不染的純潔，以及古希臘大理石雕像的美。你想把他怎麼樣，他就儘可怎麼樣，可以把他塑做成巨神泰坦，或者做成小玩具。可惜啊，這樣的美竟注定要凋零！⋯⋯可貝澤爾呢？從心理學角度看，他多有意思啊！只是因為看到眼前這個人的出現，奇特地啟發了新的藝術風格和觀察生活的模式，而這個人對此竟渾然不覺。如同住在昏暗林地裏的精靈，靜默地在空闊的曠野裏走來走去，突然就像樹林女神德律那樣顯露倩影，而且一點不驚懼。因為畫家一直尋覓着她，他的靈魂裏已經喚起了一幅奇妙的情景，而只有在那裏，奇妙的東西才能顯形。東西的形狀和圖案都似乎變得優雅了，並獲得了一種象徵性的價值，好像它們本身就是另一種東西的圖案，有更完美的形式，它們的影子變成了實體。這一切是多麼奇怪啊！他記得歷史上曾有類似的情況。難道不是那位思想界的藝術家柏拉圖首次對此加以剖析嗎？ 難道不是米高安哲羅曾將它刻在寫有十四行組詩的彩色大理石上嗎？但在我們這個世紀，人們卻覺得這不可理喻⋯⋯是呀，就像他竭力要去影響道林·格雷，就像道林·格雷在不知不覺中影響了畫家，讓他創作出精妙的畫像。他要設法去主導他，實際上他已經成功了一半。他要把那個奇妙的精靈收歸己有，這個愛情和死亡之子身上有種迷人的東西。

他突然停住腳步，看看附近的房屋。他發現已經過了姑媽家好長一段了，自己也覺得好笑，便往回頭走。他走進半明不暗的門廳，管家告訴他，賓主已經入席了。他把帽子和手杖交給一名聽差，然後步入餐廳。

"你又遲到了，亨利，"他姑媽大聲埋怨道，一邊對他搖頭。

他信口編造了一個理由，就在她旁邊一個空位子上坐了下來，隨後他向四周掃了一眼，看看席上有哪些人。道林從桌子的一端向他覷睞地點點頭，臉上徐徐泛起高興的紅潮。對面坐着哈里公爵夫人，凡是認識她的都喜歡這位心地好、脾氣也好的夫人；她的體態豐滿，這在當代的歷史學家筆下會被描寫為肥胖，如果對象不是公爵夫人的話。她右邊坐着托馬斯‧柏登爵士，一位激進黨議員。他的公開言行緊跟本黨的領袖，而在私生活中專去有高明廚師的地方，奉行的是眾所周知的明智信條：吃飯和保守黨在一起，思想與自由黨相一致。坐在哈里公爵夫人左邊的是屈萊德里的厄斯金先生，一位相當可愛、頗有教養的老紳士，不過已養成沉默寡言的壞習慣；有一次他向阿加莎夫人解釋，他在三十歲之前已經把要說的話都說完了。亨利自己的鄰座是范德勒太太，阿加莎姑媽多年的老朋友，一位完全的女聖人，可是她的打扮粗俗不堪，好像一本裝訂得非常彆腳的讚美詩歌集。也算他運氣好，范德勒太太的另一邊坐着福德爾爵士，一個滿腹經綸的中年庸才，他的禿頂可與內閣大臣在下議院所作報告的內容相媲美。范德勒太太與他交談時那副一本正經的神態，據福德爾爵士自己說，是所有真正的好人都犯的一種不可原諒的毛病，而且沒有一個人完全擺脫得了。

"亨利勛爵，我們正在議論可憐的達特穆爾，"公爵夫人高聲說，同時隔着餐桌向他點頭致意。"你說他是不是當真要娶那個迷人的年輕女人？"

"公爵夫人，我相信她已拿定主意向達特穆爾求婚。"

"太可怕了！"阿加莎夫人發出驚歎。"應該有人出面干涉！"

"根據絕對可靠的消息，她父親是開美國乾貨舖的，"托馬斯‧柏登爵士帶着不屑的表情說。

"我舅舅認為他是做豬肉包裝批發生意的，托馬斯爵士。"

"乾貨！美國乾貨究竟是甚麼？"公爵夫人問道，她向上伸出兩隻多肉的手，表示不解，並特意強調那個"是"字。

"就是美國小說。"亨利勛爵說着，自己取鵪鶉來吃。

公爵夫人給弄得莫名其妙。

"別理他，親愛的，"阿加莎夫人向她低聲說。"他從來不說正經話。"

"美洲剛被發現時……"激進黨議員開始講一連串乏味的事實。他好像盡一切努力把話匣子全部倒空的人一樣，總是連聽者的耐心也全部耗盡。公爵夫人歎一口氣，決定行使她的特權打斷話題。"我倒希望美洲還是根本沒被發現為好！"她感慨地說。"如今搞得我們的女孩子的機會全被剝奪了。這太不公平。"

"也許，美洲還根本沒有被發現呢，"厄斯金先生說。"我個人認為它只是僅僅被察覺罷了。"

"哦！不過我見過一些美國女人，"公爵夫人換上捉摸不定的口氣說。"應當承認，她們大多是挺可愛的。而且穿着都很漂亮。她們的衣服都是從巴黎買來。我也希望能這樣闊綽。"

"據說，體面的美國人死後都到巴黎去，"托馬斯爵士咯咯地笑着說，他有一肚子老掉了牙的俏皮話。

"真的嗎？那麼不體面的美國人死後到哪裏去呢？"公爵夫人問。

"到美國去，"亨利勛爵說。

托馬斯爵士皺起眉頭。"我看令姪對這個偉大的國家抱有成見，"他向阿加莎夫人說。"我曾經走遍那個國家，旅程中的車輛都有專人安排，他們在這方面非常周到。你可以相信我，到那裏遊歷可以長不少見識。"

"難道為了長見識就得去芝加哥？"厄斯金先生傷心地問。"我可受不了長途跋涉。"

托馬斯搖搖手。"屈萊德里的厄斯金先生的世界都在他的書架上。我們講究實事的人喜歡親眼去看，不喜歡讀書本上的介紹。美國人是個非常有意思的民族，他們的頭腦絕對清醒。我認為這是他們的特色。是的，厄斯金先生，這是一個極其明智的民族。我敢説美國人從來不做蠢事。"

"多可怕！"亨利勛爵叫了起來。"赤裸裸的暴力我還受得了，可是赤裸裸的明智我完全不能忍受。這樣運用頭腦不夠光明正大。這是對理性的暗算。"

"我不明白你的意思，"托馬斯爵士滿臉通紅地説。

"我明白，亨利勛爵，"厄斯金先生微笑着説。

"奇談怪論自然是很風趣……"那位準男爵想要反駁。

"這是奇談怪論？"厄斯金先生問。"我可沒這樣想過。也許是。不過事物本來的面目正像奇談怪論那樣。要檢驗事實真相必須把它放在繃緊的鋼絲繩上。等真理變成了走鋼絲的雜技藝人，我們才能作出判斷。"

"我的天！"阿加莎夫人説，"你們男人總愛鬥嘴！説實在的，我從來也鬧不清你們在説甚麼。哦，亨利！我非常生你的氣。你為甚麼要勸我們可愛的道林·格雷先生撇下東區的工作不管？要知道，他在那邊能發揮不可估量的作用。他們一定會喜歡聽他的演奏。"

"我要他演奏給我聽，"亨利勛爵面帶笑容說。他向餐桌盡頭掃了一眼，遇到了迎着他投過來閃亮亮的目光。

"可是白教堂那裏的人很可憐的，"阿加莎夫人仍不死心。

"我同情一切，就是不同情疾苦，"亨利勛爵聳聳肩膀說。"我不能同情疾苦。那實在太醜惡、太可怕、太悲慘。那種趕時髦的同情疾苦有一種非常不健康的味道。人的感情應當傾注在生活的色彩、生活的美、生活的樂趣之中。生活的瘡疤少碰為妙。"

"不過，東區的狀況是個極為重要的問題，"托馬斯爵士說，鄭重其事地搖搖頭。

"一點也不錯，"年輕的勛爵答道。"這是個奴隸問題，而我們居然想用提供娛樂給奴隸的辦法來解決這個問題。"

那位政治家盯着他問："那你另有甚麼能改變局面的高見呢？"

亨利勛爵放聲大笑。"除了天氣，我不打算改變英國的任何事情，"他回答道。"我完全滿足於哲理性的沉思默想。但是，既然十九世紀因為揮霍同情而破了產，看來我們要扭轉頹勢只得求助於科學。感情的好處是把我們引入歧途，而科學的好處是不感情用事。"

"可是我們肩上的責任是那麼重，"范德勒太太鼓足勇氣插進來說。

"是啊，重極了。"阿加莎夫人附和着。

亨利勛爵朝厄斯金先生看了一眼。"人類過於鄭重其事了，這是世界的原罪。要是洞穴人當初懂得放聲大笑，歷史就完全不一樣。"

"你很善於讓人寬心，"公爵夫人發出鳥鳴似的顫音，"過去，我每次來看你親愛的姑媽，心裏總是內疚得很，因為我一點也不關心東區的事。往後我正眼看她就不必臉紅了。"

　　"臉紅是挺好看的，公爵夫人，"亨利勛爵説。

　　"那只有在年輕的時候，"她笑道。"要是像我這樣的老太婆臉紅，可不是好兆。啊，亨利勛爵！希望你告訴我有甚麼辦法恢復青春。"

　　他想了想，然後隔着餐桌眼望着她問道："公爵夫人，你能不能記起自己年輕時犯過甚麼大錯誤？"

　　"恐怕多得很。"她喊道。

　　"那就重新再犯，"他鄭重其事地説。"一個人想恢復青春，只消重演過去做過的蠢事就夠了。"

　　"多妙的理論！"她驚歎道。"我一定會付諸行動。"

　　"危險的理論！"這是從托馬斯爵士牙縫裏擠出來的評語。阿加莎夫人頻頻搖頭，但也覺得有趣。厄斯金先生一直聽着。

　　"是的，"亨利勛爵繼續説，"這是人生的一大祕密。如今大多數人死於戰戰兢兢的思想方式，等到發現唯一不後悔的是自己所犯的錯誤時，已經太晚了。"

　　舉座為之大笑。

　　他把玩着這個想法，變得任性自恃起來，既像玩雜耍，又像變戲法；剛剛讓它滑過去，隨即又把它抓回來；忽而用想像的虹彩把它點綴得五色繽紛，忽而又給它插上悖論的翅膀任其翱翔。他這麼玩着玩着，對愚蠢的讚頌竟幻化成一種哲學，而哲學自己則變得年輕起來，如我們能想像的，穿上酒跡斑斑的長袍，戴上常青藤花冠，踏着瘋狂的歡快樂曲，像酒神的女祭司那樣，在生命的小山上跳起舞來，嘲笑遲鈍的西勒努斯依然清醒。事實猶如受驚的森林動物，在她面前紛紛逃走了。她那白皙的腳，踩着巨大的榨酒機，機上坐着智者奧默。她踩了又踩，直到沸騰的葡萄汁泛起一陣陣紫色的泡沫，湧到她光腳的周圍，或者紅色的酒泡溢出，滴在黑色傾斜的桶腰上。這是一件非凡的即興之作。他覺得道林‧格雷正目不轉睛地看着他。由於意識到自己希望迷住聽眾中某個人的心，他的才思更加敏捷，他的想像更富有色彩。他才華橫溢，浮想聯翩，毫無顧忌。他使聽者為之傾倒。他們跟着他的風笛笑個不停。道林‧格雷始終盯着他，着了魔似地坐着，陣陣微笑掠過嘴唇，漸漸暗淡的眼神裏出現越來越驚訝的表情。

最後，現實披着時裝，走進了餐廳：一名僕人進來稟報公爵夫人，她的馬車已在等候。"真掃興！"她一邊假裝失望，一邊擰着手說。"我必須告辭了。我得上俱樂部去接丈夫到威利斯會堂去參加一個無聊的集會，他要在會上當主席。我要是去晚了，他定會大發脾氣，我戴着這頂帽子沒法吵架。這帽子簡直碰不起，說一句重話都能把它震掉。不行，我不奉陪了，親愛的阿加莎。再見，亨利勛爵，你確實討人喜歡，但你敗壞道德的影響大得嚇人。對你的宏論我簡直不知道說甚麼好。改天請你一定要來跟我們一起吃晚飯。星期二，怎麼樣？你有約會嗎？"

"為了你，公爵夫人，我可以對任何人失約，"亨利勛爵說着，鞠了一躬。

"啊，你真是太好了，也太壞了，"她說。"可不要忘記呀。"她大搖大擺地走出餐廳，阿加莎夫人和女客們也跟着出去。

亨利勳爵重新坐下後，厄斯金先生移動身軀，過來坐在緊挨着他的一把椅子上，一隻手按住他的臂膀。

"聽君一席話，勝讀十年書，"厄斯金先生説。"你為甚麼不寫一本書呢？"

"我太喜歡看書了，所以不願寫書，厄斯金先生。我當然樂於寫小説，寫得像波斯地毯一樣美麗，一樣不真實。可是英國讀者除了報紙、入門書和百科全書，甚麼都不看。世上所有的民族就數英國人對文學的美感最差。"

"恐怕你的話有道理，"厄斯金先生應道。"我自己也曾有寫作的雄心，不過很久以前就打了退堂鼓。現在，我親愛的年輕朋友，如果你不反對我這樣稱呼你，我想請問，你在吃飯時對我們説的那些話是否真是你的想法？"

"我説了些甚麼全忘了，"亨利勳爵微微一笑。"我的話要不得嗎？"

"完全要不得。總之，我認為你是個非常危險的人物，如果我們善良的公爵夫人發生甚麼事情，我們將一致認定你是罪魁禍首。不過我還是樂於跟你談談生活。我所屬的一代人都很乏味。有朝一日你在倫敦待膩了，不妨請到屈萊德里來。你可以向我闡述你的享樂哲學，同時嚐嚐我有幸買到的上等勃艮第紅酒。"

"一定領情。我能拜訪屈萊德里是莫大的榮幸。那裏有再好不過的主人，有再好不過的圖書室。"

"你的光臨將使蓬蓽生輝，"老紳士説着，彬彬有禮地鞠了一躬。"現在我要去向卓越的令姑母告辭。我得去文藝俱樂部去。這個時候我們照例要在那邊打瞌睡。"

"全體都到嗎，厄斯金先生？"

"四十個人，坐在四十把扶手椅裏。我們這是在準備當英國文學院的院士。"

亨利勛爵笑了笑，隨後站起來說道，"我現在到海德公園去。"

他正要走出門的時候，道林·格雷在他胳膊上碰了一下。"我想跟你一起去，"他輕輕地說。

"你不是答應貝澤爾·霍爾渥德今天去看他嗎？"亨利勛爵問。

"我更喜歡和你在一起。是的，我覺得應該和你一起走。讓我跟你去吧。你能不能答應一直不停地對我說話？沒有人能講得像你那樣動聽。"

"啊！今天我講得夠了，"亨利勛爵微笑着說道。"現在我只想做一個生活的旁觀者。你可以和我一起旁觀，如果你願意的話。"

第四章

　　個月後，某一天下午，在亨利勛爵位於梅菲爾家中的小書房裏，道林·格雷正斜靠在豪華扶手椅上。書房本身很迷人，牆面鑲有橄欖色橡木壁板、奶油色的牆頂飾帶，刻有浮雕的灰泥天花板。磚粉色的毛氈地毯上，鋪着綴有長長絲綢流蘇的波斯小毛毯。在一張椴木小桌上，放着一個出自克洛迪翁之手的小雕像，旁邊有一部《百篇小說集》，是克洛維斯·伊夫為瑪嘉烈皇后裝訂的，封面上飾有塗金雛菊，是皇后專為自己挑選的圖案。壁爐架上擺着一些大青瓷罐子和鸚鵡鬱金香。倫敦夏日的陽光閃爍着杏黃色，穿過鑲嵌着細小鉛條的小窗，照進書房。

　　亨利勛爵還沒有到達書房，他總是按自己的原則遲到，認為準時是時間的小偷。因此道林·格雷看上去一臉不快。他沒精打采地一頁頁翻開插圖精美的《曼儂·萊斯科》，這本書是他從其中一個書櫃上找到的。路易十四時代的時鐘一板一眼地發出單調的滴答聲，令他感到煩嫌，他想過一兩次離開這裏。

　　終於他聽到門外的腳步聲，門隨即打開了。"你太遲了，亨利！"他抱怨。

　　"可惜不是亨利，格雷先生，"回答的是一把尖利的聲音。

　　他急忙轉過頭去，站起身來。"對不起。我還以為……"

　　"你以為是我丈夫回來了，結果卻是他的妻子。請允許我自我介紹。我已經從照片上認識你好久了。我丈夫大約有十七張你的照片。"

"不是十七張吧，亨利夫人？"

"不是十七，就是十八張。前不久一個晚上我還看見你和他一起在歌劇院。"她發出帶點神經質的笑聲説，一邊用毋忘我似的藍眼睛漫不經意地望着他。這是個奇怪的女人，她的服裝永遠給人這樣的印象：彷彿是在狂怒中設計出來，在暴風雨中穿上身的。她照例熱戀着甚麼人，由於這種愛情始終是單方面的，她的幻想一個也沒有破滅。她力圖顯得新穎別致，然而所達到的只是雜亂無章。她名叫維多利亞，她有上教堂的癖好，甚至到了狂熱的地步。

"我記得是在演《羅恩格林》，對吧？亨利夫人。"

"是的，正是在演可愛的《羅恩格林》。我喜愛華格納的音樂超過任何別的作曲家。他的音樂特別響，你可以不停地説話而不必擔心給旁人聽見。這是一大好處，你説對不對，格雷先生？"

又一陣急促而略帶神經質的笑聲從她的薄嘴唇裏冒出來，她的手指開始擺弄一把長長的玳瑁柄裁紙刀。

道林微笑着搖搖頭説："我不敢苟同，亨利夫人。聽音樂的時候我從來不説話，至少聽優美音樂的時候如此。如果是蹩腳的音樂，那就應當把它淹沒在談話聲中。"

"啊！這正是亨利其中一種觀點，可不是嗎，格雷先生？我總是從亨利的朋友那裏聽到亨利的觀點。這是我了解他的觀點的唯一途徑。不過你不要以為我不喜歡好的音樂。我酷愛好的音樂，可是我又怕聽。好的音樂使我變得過於浪漫。我對鋼琴家簡直拜倒在地，有時候一下子就愛上兩個，這是亨利説的。我不知道他們身上有甚麼魔力。也許因為他們是外國人。他們都是外國人，對不對？即使在英國出生，過一陣子也就成了外國人，可不是嗎？他們這辦法十分聰明，能使他們的藝術生色不少，成為世界性十足的藝術，是不是？你還從來沒有參加過一次我的晚會吧，格雷先生？你一定得來。我買不起蘭花，可是在外國人身上花錢我不心疼。有他們在座，真是滿室生春。哦，亨利來了！亨利，我來找你想問你一件事，甚麼事我已經忘了。我發現格雷先生在這兒。我們挺愉快地聊了一陣子音樂。我們的想法完全一致。不，我認為我們的想法大不一樣。不過跟他聊聊非常愉快，我很高興能認識他。"

"很好，親愛的，好極了，"亨利勛爵說着，抬起他那月牙形的濃眉，笑容可掬地望着他們。"對不起，道林，讓你久等了。我到沃多爾街去物色一塊古老的錦緞，花了好幾個小時講價。現在人們甚麼東西的價錢都知道，可是卻不知道它們的真正價值。"

"很抱歉，我該走了，"亨利夫人以一陣莫名其妙的笑聲打破了難堪的冷場。"我答應了陪公爵夫人去兜風。再見，格雷先生。再見，亨利。你今天不在家吃晚飯吧？我也是。也許我們會在桑柏里夫人那兒見面。"

"很可能，親愛的，"亨利勛爵說。等到維多利亞夫人像一隻淋了一夜雨的天堂鳥從屋裏飛了出去，留下一縷赤素馨花的幽香，亨利勛爵把門關上，然後點上一支煙，在沙發上躺下。

"道林，千萬不要跟麥稈色頭髮的女人結婚，"他抽了幾口煙之後說。

"為甚麼，亨利？"

"因為她們感情太豐富。"

"我就是喜歡感情豐富的人。"

"最好是乾脆別結婚，道林。男人結婚是由於厭倦，女人結婚是出於好奇。結果雙方都大失所望。"

"我恐怕不大會結婚的，亨利。我在戀愛中陷得太深了。這是你的格言之一。我要把它貫徹到行動中去，就像我照你所說的去做每一件事那樣。"

"你跟誰戀愛了？"亨利勛爵沉吟半晌後問。

"跟一個演員，"道林·格雷漲紅了臉說。

亨利勛爵聳聳肩膀。"如此初戀實在不怎麼樣。"

"你要是見過她，就不會這樣說了，亨利。"

"她是誰？"

"她叫西碧兒·韋恩。"

"從來沒聽說過。"

"誰也沒聽說過。不過總有一天人們會聽到她的名字。她是個天才。"

"我的老弟，女人沒有一個是天才。女人是一種裝飾用的性別。她們從來沒有甚麼話要講，可講起來就是娓娓動聽。女人代表着物質對精神的勝利，正像男人代表着精神對道德的勝利一樣。"

"亨利，你怎麼能這樣說？"

"我親愛的道林，這是千真萬確的。目前我正在研究女人，所以我不可能不知道。這個題目並不像我原先想的那樣深奧。我發現，說到底，女人總共只有兩類：本色的和上了色的。本色的女人很有用處。如果你想博取一個正人君子的名聲，你只需要請她們吃晚飯。另一類女人非常可愛。不過她們通常犯一個錯誤：她們為了要顯得年輕而塗脂抹粉。我們祖母一輩的女人塗脂抹粉是要顯示犀利的談鋒。胭脂與機智當年是相輔相成的。如今全都變了樣。一個女人只要能比自己的女兒看起來年輕十歲，她就心滿意足。至於談鋒，全倫敦只有五個女人值得與之一談，而且其中兩個是不容於上流社會的。不管怎樣，你把你那位天才的事情講給我聽聽。你認識她多久啦？"

"啊！亨利，你的論點使我害怕。"

"先不去管它。你認識她多久啦？"

"大約有三個星期。"

"你在哪裏見到她的？"

"讓我告訴你，亨利。不過你可不能潑冷水。事實上，我要是不跟你認識，這件事根本不會發生。你激起了我強烈的慾望去了解有關生活的一切。自從我認識你之後，有好多天總好像有甚麼東西在我的血管裏脈動。不論在公園散步，或是沿着畢卡狄利大街閒逛，我都留神觀察在我身邊經過的每一個人，懷着狂熱的好奇心猜測他們過着怎樣的生活。有些人吸引着我。另一些人使我害怕。空氣裏像是有一種誘人的毒素。我渴望着新奇的感覺……一天晚上，大約七點鐘，我決定出去尋找某種奇遇。我覺得，我們這個灰色的龐然大物——倫敦——有的是數不清的居民，有的是極卑劣的罪人和了不起的罪惡，就像你有一次說的那樣，它應當能為我提供些甚麼。千百種稀奇古怪的事情在我的想像中出現。光是可能遇到的危險就給予我快感。我記着我們第一次一起吃飯的那個奇妙的晚上你對我說的話：人生真正的祕密在於尋找美。我不知道自己期待着甚麼，反正我出了家門往東走，不久就掉進了骯髒的街巷和沒有草木的陰暗空地的迷宮裏。八點半左右，我走過一家可憐巴巴的小劇場，外面的煤氣燈通明，照着俗不可耐的海報。一個面目可憎的猶太人，穿着我從未見過的可笑的背心，站在門口抽蹩腳雪茄。他的頭髮油膩膩的，鬈曲成一個個圈圈，污漬斑斑的襯衫上點綴着一顆極大的鑽石。'爵爺，要包廂嗎？'他看到了我就問，同時脫下帽子，露出巴結的神色。亨利，那個人身上有某種東西使我很感興趣。他是個醜八怪。我知道你會笑我，不過我確實進去了，足足花了一個堅尼租了台邊的一個包廂。直到今天我仍舊不明白當時為甚麼這樣做。但要是我不這樣，親愛的亨利，要是我不進去，我會錯過我一生中最了不起的一段浪漫史。我看得出你在笑。你太可惡了！"

"我不是在笑，道林，至少不是在笑你。不過你不應當說這是你一生中最了不起的浪漫史。你應當說這是你一生中第一段浪漫史。你將永遠被人所愛，你將永遠在戀愛中。多情是無所事事者的特權。這是一個國家的有閒階級的一大本領。別害怕，等着你去體驗的新奇事情多着呢。這僅僅是開始。"

"你把我這個人看得這樣淺薄？"道林‧格雷怒衝衝地嚷道。

"不，我認為你很深情。"

"這怎麼講？"

"我的老弟，一生中只戀愛一次的人才真正是淺薄的。他們稱做忠誠、堅貞的品質，我認為是習慣的懶散病或想像力的缺乏。情感生活中的忠實就同理性生活中的一貫性一樣，無非是承認失敗。忠實！將來我要對它作一番研究。這種感情包藏着佔有慾。我們本來可以扔掉許多東西，如果不怕別人撿去的話。不過我不想打斷你的話。把你的故事講下去。"

"好吧。我發現自己坐進了一個可怕的私人小包廂,一塊粗俗不堪的幕布對着我的面前。我從幕布後往外看去,俯視了一下劇院。劇院簡直庸俗至極,到處是丘比特和豐裕之角的圖案,好像一個低檔的結婚蛋糕。頂層和正廳後座區幾乎滿座,但昏暗的前兩排卻空無一人,而在我猜想他們稱之為'花樓'的樓廳前座,也幾乎不見人影。女人拿着橘子和薑汁汽水走來走去,很多人在大吃堅果。"

"那肯定像是英國戲劇全盛時期的場景。"

"想必正是這樣,那氣氛委實叫人受不了。我坐在那裏,不知怎樣才好,這時我的視線落在海報上。亨利,你猜那天演甚麼呢?"

"八成是《笨蛋或無辜的啞巴》。我相信我們的祖先愛看這類戲。道林,我活得愈久,就愈是強烈地感到:我們的父輩滿意的東西已不能使我們滿意。在文藝方面和在政治方面一樣,老祖宗總是不對的。"

"這齣戲對我們來說夠好了,亨利,是《羅密歐與茱麗葉》。我必須承認,一想到要在這個齷齪不堪的地方看莎士比亞的劇,我就挺惱火。可是我仍然抱有某種興趣,因此決定等待第一幕上演。那樂隊非常糟糕,我差點就被那個彈着刺耳鋼琴聲的年輕猶太指揮嚇跑,但最終幕布被拉起,戲劇要開演了。飾演羅密歐的是一個壯碩的老人,一雙眉毛攢在一起,聲音嘶啞淒慘,體型像一個啤酒桶似的。飾演莫枯修也一樣差勁,他就像一個三流的喜劇演員,說着自己的笑話,跟後座的觀眾打成一片。他們就像佈景一樣可笑,似乎是來自鄉下戲班。但茱麗葉!亨利,試想像一個不足十七歲的女子,有着鮮花一樣的小臉,小巧的希臘式腦袋上盤着一圈圈深棕色的髮辮，她的眼睛像一口注滿熱情的紫羅蘭色深井，她的嘴唇好像玫瑰花瓣。她是我人生中見過最可愛的女孩。你曾經對我說過，你對悲情無動於衷，但美，純粹的美能令你熱淚盈眶。我告訴你，亨利，我眼裏的淚水讓我幾乎看不清這個女孩。而她的聲音——我從未聽過這樣的聲音——它起初低沉而醇厚，像是流進你的耳裏；然後聲量稍微大了一點，聽上去像是長笛或高音雙簧管在遠處演奏。在花園的那一場戲，音調裏有一種只能在天亮前夜鶯歌唱時才能聽到的顫慄狂喜。接着的幾個瞬間，她的聲音又擁有小提琴的狂野熱情。你知道聲音能撩動一個人。你和西碧兒・韋恩的聲音是我一輩子也忘不了的。當我閉上雙眼，我聽見這兩把聲音，各自表達不同的東西，我不知道該聽哪邊的好。我怎能不愛她呢？亨利，我確實愛她，她是我生命中的一切。每晚每夜我都去看她的演出。這夜她是羅瑟琳，那夜她是伊摩琴。我看過她吸着愛人唇上的毒藥，死在意大利陰暗的墓穴；我見過她裝扮成一個漂亮的男孩，穿着長統襪與緊身上衣，頭戴精緻的帽子，在阿登森林裏漫步。她曾是個瘋子，走到有罪的國王前，讓他戴上芸香和吃苦菜；她又曾是個純潔的人，被妒忌的黑手掐斷了蘆葦般的脖子。我見過她演過不同年齡的角色，穿過各式各樣的戲服。普通的女人難以激發人們的想像，因為她們受自己時代所局限，甚至連魅力也無法使她們改變。她們的頭腦像帽子般顯而易見，你總是可以看得清清楚楚，裏面沒有任何祕密。她們早上在公園騎馬，下午在茶會上聊天。她們的笑容一成不變，她們的舉止非常時髦，她們很淺薄直露。但是演員全然不同！亨利！你為甚麼不告訴我最值得愛的是演員呢？”

"因為我愛過許許多多女演員，道林。"

"哦，那都是些染頭髮、塗脂粉的怪物。"

"不要挖苦染頭髮、塗脂粉的女人。有時候她們也有一種異乎尋常的迷人之處，"亨利勛爵說。

"我真後悔把西碧兒・韋恩的事告訴你。"

"你遲早會告訴我的，道林。你這一輩子甚麼事情都會對我說。"

"是的，亨利，我相信會這樣。我忍不住要告訴你種種事情。你對我有一種說不出的影響力。即使我犯了甚麼罪，我也會來向你供認。你會了解我的。"

"道林，你是生活中的任性而快活的人，像你這樣的人不會去犯罪。不過你對我的恭維還是使我感到榮幸。現在你告訴我 ── 請把火柴遞給我，好孩子，謝謝！── 你跟西碧兒・韋恩現在究竟是怎樣的關係？"

道林・格雷霍地跳了起來，兩腮通紅，雙目怒睜。"亨利，西碧兒・韋恩是神聖的！"

"只有神聖的東西才值得去碰，道林，"亨利勛爵的聲調出人意料地稍帶幾分激昂。"你何必發火呢？我料想她總有一天會屬於你。戀愛中的人總是先欺騙自己，最後欺騙別人。這就是大家所說的浪漫史。我想，你至少已經跟她認識了吧？"

"當然。我第一次進那個劇場的晚上，那個面目可憎的老猶太人在演出結束後來到包廂，他表示願意領我到後台去，將我介紹給她。當時我對他大發雷霆，我說茱麗葉已經死了幾百年，她的屍體躺在維羅納的大理石墓穴裏。我從他目瞪口呆的樣子看出，他大概以為我喝了太多香檳或別的甚麼。"

"完全可能。"

"接着他問我是否給哪家報紙寫稿。我告訴他,我從不看報。他聽了好像大失所望,並向我透露,說所有的劇評家都跟他過不去,他們個個都是可以收買的。"

"我認為他這話說得極有道理。不過,話得說回來,從那些劇評家的外貌來看,其中絕大多數身價都不高。"

"他大概以為自己僱不起他們,"道林笑了起來。"當時劇場開始關燈,我得走了。他要我試試某種他竭力推薦的雪茄,我謝絕了。第二天晚上,我自然又到那裏去。他看見我的時候,對我深深鞠了一躬,稱頌我是慷慨的藝術保護者。他是個非常討厭的傢伙,不過對莎士比亞崇拜得五體投地。有一次他以自豪的口氣告訴我,他先後五次破產完全是為了這位'彈唱詩人'── 他堅持這樣稱呼莎士比亞。看來他認為這是很光榮的事。"

"這的確光榮,我親愛的道林,極其光榮。大多數人破產是因為在平庸的生活中投資過猛。為富有詩意的事業破產是一種榮譽。那麼,你第一次跟西碧兒·韋恩小姐交談在甚麼時候?"

"第三天晚上。那天她扮演羅瑟琳。我終於忍不住走了過去。我向她拋了一些花,她看了我一眼,至少我以為她看了我一眼。老猶太人把我纏得很緊。他大概拿定主意要帶我到後台去,我同意了。我不急於去跟她結交,你不覺得奇怪嗎?"

"不,我不覺得奇怪。"

"為甚麼,我親愛的亨利?"

"改天我再告訴你。現在我想知道那個女孩子的情況。"

"西碧兒?哦,她是那麼怕羞,那麼文靜。她身上還有一些孩子氣。當我向她說出我對她的演技的看法時，她的眼睛睜得大大，那驚訝的神情妙不可言。看來她對自己的才能一點也不自覺。我想當時我和她都很激動。老猶太人咧着嘴站在滿是灰塵的化裝室門口，對我們兩個說了一大堆天花亂墜的恭維話，而我們站在那裏，像小孩子那樣你看着我，我瞧着你。老猶太人張口就稱我'爵爺'，使我不得不向西碧兒聲明，我甚麼爵也不是。她很天真地對我說：'你看起來挺像王子。我要把你叫做迷人王子。'"

"道林，我敢擔保，西碧兒小姐很會說恭維話。"

"你不了解她，亨利。她僅僅把我看作戲裏的人物。她對人生一無所知。她和她的母親——一個芳華已逝的憔悴婦人——一起生活，那婦人在第一天晚上裏着一件品紅色晨袍，扮演茱麗葉的母親凱普萊特夫人，看樣子當年也出過風頭。"

"我知道那種樣子，看了叫人難受，"亨利勛爵嘀咕着，反覆察看自己手上的指環。

"那猶太人要向我講她的故事，我說我不感興趣。"

"你做得很對。聽別人的悲慘故事是很卑劣的。"

"我感興趣的只是西碧兒本人。她的出身跟我有甚麼相干？從她嬌小的頭到嬌小的腳，她是絕對神聖、十全十美的。我每天晚上去看她演出，覺得她一天比一天更令人驚豔。"

"怪不得這一陣子你沒跟我在一起吃晚飯。我猜想你多半正發展一段奇妙的浪漫史。果然如此，不過和我的預想不完全一樣。"

"我親愛的亨利，我每天和你在一起不是吃午飯就是吃宵夜，我還和你一起去過幾次歌劇院呢，"道林睜大了一雙碧眼說。

"你每次都很晚才到。"

"是啊,我不能不去看西碧兒演出,"他説着,"哪怕看一幕也好。我變得如飢似渴地想看見她;每當想起那藏在牙雕般嬌小身軀裏的神奇靈魂,我心中就充滿誠惶誠恐的感覺。"

"今天晚上你能和我一起吃飯嗎,道林?"

他搖搖頭説:"今晚她是伊摩琴,明晚她是茱麗葉。"

"那她甚麼時候是西碧兒·韋恩呢?"

"甚麼時候也不是。"

"我祝賀你。"

"你真可惡!要知道,所有戲裏了不起的女主角都集於她一身。她不是一個個體。儘管你認為可笑,我還是要説,她是個天才。我愛她,而且我一定要使她也愛我。你深知人生的奧祕,應當告訴我怎樣吸引西碧兒·韋恩愛上我!我要使羅密歐吃醋。我要讓世上為愛犧牲的有情人聽到我們的笑聲而自歎命薄。我要讓我們愛情的熱浪驚動他們的骸骨,喚醒他們的痛感。天啊,亨利,我是多麼崇拜她啊!"他説這番話的時候在室內不停地走來走去,兩頰泛起朵朵紅暈,像病人的潮熱。他處於極度亢奮之中。

亨利勛爵瞧着他,心中暗暗高興。記得他們在貝澤爾·霍爾渥德畫室裏初次見面的時候,他還是一個靦腆膽怯的孩子,現在同那時已判若兩人!他的本性已像蓓蕾怒放,開出嫣紅的花朵。他的靈魂剛從隱蔽的暗角探出身來,慾望立即迎上前去。

"下一步你打算怎麼辦?"亨利勛爵終於問。

"我希望找天晚上你和貝澤爾跟我一起去看她演出。我對於可能產生的效果一百個放心。你們定能賞識她的天才。然後我們必須把她從猶太人手中弄出來。西碧兒和他訂有三年合約，從現在算起，至少還有兩年零八個月。當然我要付一筆錢給猶太人。這一切辦妥之後，我要找一家西區的劇院讓她一顯身手。她一定能使全世界同我一樣如醉如狂。”

“怕不可能吧，我的老弟？”

“沒問題，她行。她不僅具有完美的藝術直覺，她的個性也了不起，你時常對我説，左右時代的是人，而不是原則。”

“好吧。我們哪一天去呢？”

“讓我想一想。今天是星期二。就定在明天吧。明天她演茱麗葉。”

“一言為定。八點鐘在布里斯托飯店見面，貝澤爾由我去接。”

“八點鐘太晚了，亨利。六點半吧。我們必須在開場前到。你們必須看她怎樣在第一幕中與羅密歐初次相會。”

“六點半！太早了！那是進茶點或看英國小説的時候。七點鐘吧。沒有一個體面的人在七點鐘前吃晚飯。在這段時間裏，你還要跟貝澤爾見面嗎？要不要我寫信給他？”

“可憐的貝澤爾！我已經有一個星期沒去看過他。我太不應該了，他派人把我的畫像給我送來，配上他特地設計的精美框子。雖然我有點妒忌那幅畫像比我年輕整整一個月，我得承認我還是喜歡它。也許你寫信約他更好。我不想單獨見他。他講的話我聽着心煩。他老是向我提出忠告。”

亨利勛爵微微一笑。“人們總喜歡把自己最需要的東西送給別人。我認為這才叫做慷慨到了頂。”

“哦，貝澤爾是個再好不過的人，可我覺得他有那麼一點迂腐。亨利，自從我和你認識之後，我有這樣的感覺。”

"老弟，貝澤爾把他身上全部可愛的氣質都放到創作中。結果他為生活留下的就只有他的偏見、原則和大道理。我所認識的藝術家中討人喜歡的都是不成器的。有才氣的藝術家只存在於他們的創作中，而他們本人都是索然無味的。一個偉大的詩人，一個真正偉大的詩人，是最沒有詩意的人。但是等而下之的詩人卻極其討人喜歡。他們的詩寫得愈糟糕，他們的外貌就愈是生動。如果一個詩人出版了一本二三流的十四行詩集，此人一定具有不可抗拒的魅力。他把寫不出來的詩都在生活中實現了。而另一類詩人卻把他們不敢身體力行的意境都寫成了詩。"

"我不知道事實是否真是這樣，亨利，"道林·格雷說着，從放在桌子上的一隻金塞子大瓶裏往手帕上灑了些香水。"既然你如此說，那一定是這樣。現在我該走了。伊摩琴在等我呢。明天可別忘了。再見。"

等他離開了書齋，亨利勛爵合上沉重的眼皮，開始思量起來。誠然，很少有人像道林·格雷那樣吸引他，但這少年瘋狂地熱戀着另一個人，卻絲毫沒有引起他的不快或妒意。他反而感到高興。這令他成為了一個更加饒有興味的研究課題。亨利勛爵一向醉心於自然科學的方法，但是自然科學的一般研究對象在他看來卻是乏味的、微不足道的。於是他始而解剖自己，繼而解剖別人。在他心目中唯一值得加以研究的就是人生。與此相比，任何別的東西都毫無價值。確實，你要觀察人生在痛苦與歡樂的奇特熔爐中的冶煉過程，不能戴上玻璃面罩，也免不了被硫磺味熏昏頭腦，弄得想像中盡是牛鬼蛇神、噩夢凶兆。有些毒物很難捉摸，你要了解它們的特性，非得先中毒不可。有些病症非常奇怪，你要弄清它們的根源，非得先患病不可。然而，你得到的回報將是

不可估量的！整個世界在你心目中將變得無比奇妙！探明高度嚴
謹的情慾邏輯和塗上感情色彩的理性生活，觀察它們何處相遇，
何處分離，在哪一點上協調，在哪一點上不諧——真是其樂無
窮！至於要花多大的代價，又何必操心？為了得到新的感受，無
論付出怎樣的代價也劃得來。

亨利勛爵意識到，是他的話，是那些用悠揚語調說出來的動
聽的話使道林‧格雷的靈魂轉向那個純潔的女子，使道林拜倒
在她的面前。想到這裏，亨利勛爵棕瑪瑙色的眼睛露出得意的目
光。在很大程度上，現在的道林‧格雷是他的創作。是他催熟了
這個少年。這是值得一提的。普通人總是等待生活向他們展示生
活自身的奧祕。但是對於少數精英中的精英來說，生活的祕密在
帷幕揭開之前即已透露。有時候這份功勞應歸於藝術，主要是直
接訴諸情感和理性的文學。不過藝術的職能間或由某個不簡單的
人物取而代之，而這個人本身也是一件地地道道的藝術品，因為
生活如同詩歌、雕塑、繪畫一樣有它自己的傑作。

是的，那少年被催熟了。他在春天便已經在收穫了。青春的
活力和熱情正在他身上搏動，但他已開始自覺。觀察他的變化是
一種享受。憑他那美麗的容顏和靈魂，他稱得上一個奇跡。這一
切將以甚麼告終，或者注定以甚麼告終，則無關緊要。他就像盛
會或戲劇中那些色藝雙絕的名角，他們的歡樂與我們不相干，但
他們的悲哀能激起我們的美感，他們的創傷更像殷紅的玫瑰。

靈魂與肉體，肉體與靈魂，它們是多麼神祕呀！靈魂包含着
獸性，肉體有靈性的瞬間。感覺會昇華，理智會墮落。誰能說出
肉體的衝動在何處終結，或者說靈魂的衝動在何處起始？平庸心

理學家的武斷定義是多麼淺薄！而要在不同學派的主張之間決定取捨，又何等困難！難道靈魂是坐在罪惡之屋中的影子？或者真如焦爾達諾・布魯諾所想，肉體在靈魂裏？精神與物質的分離是一個謎，精神和物質的結合也是一個謎。

亨利勳爵開始思考，人們能否在將來把心理學建成一門絕對精密的科學，使生命中每一次微小的搏動都瞞不過我們？事實上，我們常常誤解自己，也很少了解別人。經驗沒有倫理上的價值。經驗只不過是人們給他們的錯誤定的名稱。道德家照例認為經驗是一種警告，聲稱它對性格的形成能起一定的倫理效用，頌揚經驗能教我們遵循甚麼、避免甚麼。但是，經驗沒有動力。它和意識本身一樣缺乏能動性。它實質上僅僅表明我們的未來將與我們的過去一樣，我們一度強抑着內心的反感犯過的罪惡，我們還要重複多次，而且將引以為樂。

他很清楚，只有通過實驗才能對慾念作出科學分析，而道林・格雷無疑是他手頭現成的對象，並且看來會結出豐碩的成果。他對西碧兒・韋恩一下子就如火如荼的狂戀是一種不可小看的心理現象。可以肯定，從中起了很大作用的是好奇心和對新奇感受的渴望。然而，這不是一種簡單的情慾，它要複雜得多。在少年時期的純粹感官本能，在想像的運作下已變成道林心目中遠遠超出感官的東西，正因為如此就更危險。被我們誤解了本原的那些慾念，恰恰最牢固地控制着我們。而我們能意識到其本質的感情，卻是我們最脆弱的感情。我們以為是在別人身上做實驗，其實往往是在自己身上做實驗。

亨利勳爵正坐在那裏冥思遐想，他的侍從敲門進來提醒他，該換裝準備吃晚飯了。亨利勛爵站起來向街上望了望。夕陽把從金色中透出血紅的餘暉灑在對面一排房屋的上層窗戶上，玻璃像一片片燒紅的金屬閃閃發光。天空呈現着玫瑰凋謝的顏色。他思量着他的朋友正處於火紅的青春期的生命，不知道這一切將如何了結。

他在午夜十二點半回到家裏，看到門廳裏桌上放着一份電報。拆開一看，原來是道林‧格雷打來的。電文通知説，他已經和西碧兒‧韋恩訂婚了。

第五章

"媽媽，我好開心啊！"女孩悄悄地說着，她的臉偎在一個韶光不再、形容憔悴的婦人膝頭上；母親背向刺眼的光線，坐在不甚潔淨的客廳內唯一一張扶手椅上。"我好開心啊！"女兒還在說，"你也一定很開心！"

韋恩太太的身子一縮，一雙瘦瘦的、因久施鉛華而變得蒼白的手撫摸着女兒的頭。"開心！"她應聲道，"西碧兒，我只有在看你演出的時候才開心。除了演戲，你不應該想別的事情。艾薩克斯先生對我們很好，我們還欠他錢呢。"

女孩仰起頭來，嘟着一張嘴。"你說甚麼，媽媽？錢？"她大聲問道。"錢算得上甚麼？愛情比錢更重要。"

"艾薩克斯先生預支我們五十鎊，讓我們還債，給詹姆士置備行裝。你不能忘了這件事，西碧兒。五十鎊是很大筆款項。艾薩克斯先生對我們很照顧。"

"他不是個上等人，媽媽，我討厭他跟我講話的樣子，"女孩說着，站起來走到窗前去。

"要不是他幫忙，我不知道我們有甚麼辦法，"中年婦人像在埋怨女兒不懂事。

西碧兒把頭一揚，放聲大笑。"媽媽，我們再也不用他幫忙了。今後我們的生活有迷人王子安排。"她突然住了口，她的血液起了波動，兩頰浮起玫瑰色的暈影。頻促的呼吸使她的嘴唇如花瓣微微張開，輕輕顫動。熱情像一陣南風向她襲來，拂動了她的衣裳上雅致的褶子。"我愛他，"西碧兒天真地說。

"傻孩子！傻孩子！"母親不停地重複着，佐以彎曲的手指戴着贗品首飾扭來擺去的動作，給人一種古怪荒誕的印象。

女孩又笑了，那是籠中鳥的歡樂。她的眼睛和着笑聲的旋律，一閃一閃地呼應着；接着閉上一會，似乎生怕泄露了祕密。當它們重新睜開的時候，已經罩了一層朦朧的幻想。

薄嘴唇的智慧化身坐在破舊的扶手椅上開導女兒，提醒她謹慎行事，一再援引一本借用常識之名的怯懦經典作為依據。西碧兒並沒有聽。她墮入了情網，正在悠然自得。她的王子——迷人王子——和她在一起。她召喚自己的記憶再現他的形象。她派遣自己的靈魂去尋找他，果然把他找來了。她的嘴唇感覺到他熱烈的親吻，她的眼皮再次被他的呼吸所溫暖。

於是，智慧化身改變策略，談到要去調查打聽。那個年輕人可能很有錢。若是如此，這門親事應當考慮。但是，精諳世故的浪頭打在女孩的耳廓上濺成微沫，老謀深算的利箭嗖嗖地飛過，沒有觸動她一根毫毛。她看着那薄嘴唇的翕動，忍不住要笑出來。

忽然她覺得必須開口，母親一個人自言自語的冷場使她悶得發慌。"媽媽，媽媽，"她大聲說。"他那樣愛我是為甚麼？我知道我為甚麼愛他。我愛他是因為他恰恰就像愛情的化身。可是我有甚麼能被他看中呢？我配不上他。不過，我說不上是甚麼道理，儘管我遠遠不如他，我卻不覺得丟臉。我感到驕傲，驕傲得厲害。媽媽，以前你也像我愛迷人王子那樣愛父親嗎？"

透過抹在臉頰上的一層廉價香粉，看得出中年婦人的臉色在變青，乾枯的嘴唇起了一陣痛苦的痙攣。西碧兒撲到她懷裏，摟住她的脖子，連連吻她。"原諒我，媽媽。我知道提起父親會使你傷心，但這正說明你愛他之深。不要這樣悲傷。今天我像你在二十年前一樣開心。啊！但願我永遠開心！"

　　"我的孩子，你年紀太小，不應該考慮戀愛。再說，你對那個年輕人了解些甚麼呢？你連他的姓名也不知道。總之，這件事太不妥了。說真的，詹姆士快要去澳洲，有一大堆事情要我操心。在這樣的時候你應當懂事些。不過，我剛才說了，要是他有錢的話……"

　　"啊，媽媽，媽媽，讓我開心吧！"

　　韋恩太太看看女兒，把她摟在懷裏——這一類不真實的舞台動作常常變成演員的第二本性。這時門開了，一個棕髮蓬亂的少年走進客廳。他身材矮壯，粗手大腳，舉止笨拙。他不像他的姐姐那麼文雅。很難猜到他兩個是姐弟，韋恩太太注視着兒子，臉上的笑容更綻開了些。在她的想像中，兒子已取代全體觀眾的地位。她確實感到這個場面十分動人。

　　"西碧兒，我希望你的吻能留一些給我，"那少年佯作向姐姐發牢騷。

　　"啊！可你不喜歡人家吻你，詹姆士，"她說。"你是一隻討厭的老熊。"她跑過去和他擁抱。

　　詹姆士·韋恩親切地看着姐姐的臉。"我要你和我一起出去走走，西碧兒。我大概再也不會回來這個可惡的倫敦了。我確實不願意再回來。"

"我的孩子，不要説這樣喪氣的話，"韋恩太太低聲道。説着，她歎息一聲，拿起一件俗氣的戲衣開始縫補。她略感掃興的是詹姆士沒有參加合演，否則，這個場面的戲劇效果必定更佳。

"為甚麼不要説，媽媽？我説的是正經話。"

"你使我太傷心了，孩子。我指望你會發了財從澳洲回來，我相信在殖民地沒有上流社會，或任何稱得上是上流社會的東西。所以，等你發了財，你應當回來，在倫敦成家立業。"

"上流社會！"少年沒好氣地説。"我才不想知道甚麼上流社會。我只想賺點錢，讓你和西碧兒離開劇場。我恨這個工作。"

"哦，詹姆士！"西碧兒笑呵呵地説。"你就不會説些親切的話！你真的要我陪你出去走走嗎？那很好！我以為你要去跟你的朋友們告別呢，跟那個送一支怪難看的煙斗給你的湯姆·哈迪，或者跟那個笑你抽煙樣子的聶德·蘭頓。你現在決定跟我在一起度過臨走前的最後一個下午，這太好了。我們上哪兒去呢？上公園吧。"

"我的衣着太寒酸，"他皺着眉頭回答。"上公園散步的都穿得漂漂亮亮。"

"別瞎扯，詹姆士，"她輕輕地説，一邊撫摸着他的上衣袖口。

他猶豫片刻，最後説："好吧，你換衣服可不要花太多功夫。"西碧兒跳跳蹦蹦走出客廳。可以聽到她唱着歌跑上樓去。接着樓板上響起了她的腳步聲。

詹姆士在屋裏踱了兩三個來回，然後他轉向靜靜地坐在椅上的中年婦人問道："媽媽，我的東西都準備好了沒有？"

"都準備好了，詹姆士，"她眼睛盯着縫補的謀生工作回答說。最近幾個月來，當她獨自和這個說話粗聲大氣、神態冷冰冰的兒子在一起的時候，她總覺得很不自在。當他們四目相視，這個淺薄而又懷着鬼胎的婦人心裏就發慌。她每每問自己，兒子是不是生了甚麼疑心。現在詹姆士沒有再說甚麼別的話，更使她悶得受不了。她開始抱怨起來。女人往往以攻為守，而她們如果突然莫名其妙地屈服下來，那一定是在進攻。"詹姆士，希望你過得慣航海生活，"她說。"你必須記住這是你自己選擇的道路。你本來可以進一家法律事務所當文員，律師是很受尊敬的一等人，在鄉下他們經常到最體面的人家去吃飯。"

"我討厭事務所，我也討厭當文員，"他回答說。"不過你說得完全對：是我自己選擇的生活。我只想說一句話：好好照顧西碧兒。不要讓她受任何傷害。媽媽，你一定得把她照顧好。"

"詹姆士，你的話真叫人奇怪。我當然會照顧西碧兒的。"

"我聽說一個有身分的人每天晚上去看戲，還到後台去跟她說話。這是不是真的？這是怎麼回事？"

"這些事你一竅不通，詹姆士。做我們這一行，有人捧場，受人抬舉是常有的事。當年，我也接受過不知多少鮮花。那是表演藝術真正得到賞識的時候。至於西碧兒，我不知道目前她的感情是不是一時的心血來潮。不過那個年輕人確實無疑是有身分的。他對我一直彬彬有禮。再說，看樣子他很有錢，他送的花都是挺可愛的。"

"可是你們連他的姓名也不知道，"少年口氣生硬地說。

"是的，"母親回答時不動聲色。"他還沒有說出他的真名實姓。我認為這是他極其浪漫的風格。他也許還是個貴族。"

詹姆士‧韋恩咬了咬嘴唇。"好好照顧西碧兒，媽媽，"他執着地説，"好好照顧她。"

"詹姆士，你的話使我難受極了，西碧兒一直在我的悉心保護之下。當然，如果那位先生有錢的話，也沒有理由不讓西碧兒和他結婚。我相信他是個貴族子弟。他的一舉一動無不説明這一點。這對西碧兒來説是一門最體面的親事。他兩個真是天造地設的一對。那位先生長得非常漂亮，見過的人都這麼説。"

詹姆士自言自語地不知咕噥了些甚麼，用他粗壯的手指在窗玻璃上彈了幾下，轉過臉來正想説甚麼話，這時西碧兒開門跑了進來。

"你們這樣一本正經地做甚麼？"她問道。"出了甚麼事？"

"沒有甚麼，"詹姆士回答説。"人有時應當嚴肅些。再見，媽媽；我五點鐘回來吃晚飯。除了襯衫，其他行李都已經準備好，你不必操心。"

"再見，我的孩子，"她説着，莊重得不大自然地點點頭。

兒子跟她説話的口氣使她很不痛快，兒子的眼神也叫她提心吊膽。

"親我一下，媽媽，"西碧兒説。花兒般鮮艷的嘴唇觸到了枯槁的面頰，使冰涼的皮膚感到一股暖意。

"我的孩子，我的孩子！"韋恩太太連聲叫着，眼睛望向天花板，尋找想像中的頂層樓座觀眾。

"來，西碧兒，"她弟弟在一旁催促。他討厭母親裝腔作勢的表演。

姐弟兩人出了家門，在時而被風雲遮掩的陽光下順着冷清的尤斯登路走去。這個面帶怒容的粗線條少年，穿着不合身的廉價衣服，竟然同這樣一個秀色可餐的女子在一起走，好比一個庸俗土氣的花匠佩帶着一朵玫瑰，行人見了都感到詫異。

詹姆士每次發覺行人投來好奇的目光，他就皺緊眉頭。他不喜歡人家向他注視，這種性格在天才身上要到晚年才形成，而凡人是永遠擺脫不了的。至於西碧兒，她完全察覺不到自己所引起的讚賞。愛的歡樂在她的笑聲中蕩漾。她在想迷人王子，但為了可以再想他多一些，西碧兒並不提起他，而盡是談即將載着詹姆士去遠航的船，談他一定會找到的金礦，談他將要從紅衫土匪手中救出來的美麗女財主。他當然不會永遠當一名水手、一名貨物管理員或者諸如此類的人。決不！水手生活是很苦的。試想想，被塞在悶得要命的船艙裏，洶湧的浪濤嘶啞地吼叫着，拼命想衝進來，狂風折斷桅杆，船帆被撕成長條嘩啦啦地飄，那是甚麼滋味！但是到了墨爾本，他就要離船上岸，客客氣氣向船長道別，立即出發到金礦去。不出一個星期，他必定會找到一塊碩大的純金塊，這樣大的天然金塊還從來沒有人找到過。然後他把金塊裝上大車，在六名騎警保護下運到岸邊。土匪發動三次襲擊，但經過血戰都被打退。不，不，他還是不要到金礦去為妙。那是很可怕的地方，那裏的人們酗酒、吸毒，在酒吧間裏進行槍戰，用不堪入耳的話罵人。他還是去牧場養羊為好。將來有一天晚上，他騎馬回家的時候，看見一個騎黑馬的強盜正要劫走美麗的女財主。他立刻追上去，把女財主救下來。不用說，他們一定會互相愛慕，然後結成夫婦，一同回來，住在倫敦美侖美奂的豪宅內。是的，許多好事在等着他。不過他一定要好好做，不發脾氣，不亂花錢。西碧兒認為自己雖然比他大一歲，但比他懂事得多。她要弟弟每開一班郵船都寫信給她，還要他每天夜裏臨睡前禱告。上帝很慈悲，一定會保佑他。她也會為他祈禱，不消幾年功夫，他必將發了財高高興興回來。

詹姆士緊繃着臉聽她說，一聲也不吭。離家在即，他心情沉重。

使他悶悶不樂的原因還不單單是這一層。儘管沒有多少經驗，他卻強烈地感覺到西碧兒身處的危險。那個正在追求她的紈袴子弟不會有益於她。他是個有身分的人，詹姆士因此恨他，懷着一種奇怪的族類本能恨他。關於這種本能，詹姆士還說不出其所以然；惟其如此，它在這少年的內心深處處於更牢固的支配地位。同時他也知道他母親淺薄虛榮的性格，意識到這對西碧兒和西碧兒的幸福孕育着極大的危險。子女一開始都愛自己的父母，長大後對父母就有所批評，有時也能加以原諒。

母親啊！有一件事他憋在心裏已好幾個月，一直想問她。一天晚上，他在劇場的後台門口偶然聽到一句話。傳到他耳際的竊竊私議在他頭腦裏激起一連串可怕的推想。他想起這件事，就好像臉上被抽了一鞭。他眉頭緊鎖，眉心上刻下一道楔形的槽。一陣痛苦的抽搐使他咬住下唇。

"詹姆士，你根本不在聽我說話，"西碧兒生氣地說，"我在為你的未來設計最美的藍圖。你說話呀！"

"你要我說甚麼呢？"

"你就說你要好好工作，不忘記我們，"她笑盈盈地說。

詹姆士聳聳肩膀。"倒不是我會忘記你，而是你會忘記我，西碧兒。"

"你這是甚麼意思，詹姆士？"她漲紅了臉問。

"我聽說你新交上一位朋友。他是誰？你為甚麼在我面前不提這件事？他不會給你帶來甚麼好處的。"

"住嘴，詹姆士！"她激動地大聲說。"不許你說他的壞話。我愛他。"

"天啊，你連他的姓名都不知道呢，"詹姆士說，"他是誰？我有權利問你。"

"他叫迷人王子。你不喜歡這個名字嗎？啊！你這個傻孩子！你別忘記這個名字。你如果見到他，就會認為他是世界上最美好的人。總有一天你會見到他，等你從澳洲回來的時候。你會非常喜歡他。每個人都喜歡他，而我……我愛他。我真希望你今晚能來劇院，他將會來看我扮演茱麗葉。啊！我該怎樣演呢？想像一下，詹姆士，在熱戀中扮演茱麗葉！而他就坐在那兒！為了他的快樂而演出！我怕我會嚇壞觀眾，不是嚇壞他們，就是迷住他們。戀愛就是要超越自己。我感覺到，可憐又可怕的艾薩克斯先生會在酒吧裏對着游手好閒的人大叫'天才'，把我當作成教條般宣傳，今晚他將會宣告是他發掘我的。這一切都是歸功於他，只歸功於迷人王子、我美妙的愛人、我優雅的神明。但跟他相比，我很貧窮。貧窮？有甚麼關係？貧窮鑽進門，愛情飛進窗。我們的諺語需要重寫，它們是在冬天寫成的，但現在已是夏天了。對我來說是春天，在藍天下花飛的春天。"

"他是個有身分的人，"詹姆士面色陰沉地說。

"他是王子！"西碧兒幾乎在唱歌。"你還要怎麼樣？"

"他要你做他的奴隸。"

"我一想到自由就會發抖。"

"我要你提防他。"

"看見他就會崇拜他，認識他就會信任他。"

"西碧兒，你被他迷昏了。"

她呵呵笑着勾住弟弟的胳膊。"我親愛的詹姆士，你說話的口氣像是活了一百歲。將來你也會戀愛的。甚麼叫戀愛，那時你就知道了。別這麼愁眉苦臉。你應當高興才是，因為我從來沒有像現在這樣快樂，雖然你即將離家遠行。生活對你我都是不容易的，可以說艱難得可怕。但今後不同了。你要到一個新世界去，我呢，已經找到了一個新世界。這兒有兩個座位，過路的人穿得都很漂亮，我們坐下來看看吧。"

他們坐在一羣旁觀者中間。路那邊花壇上的鬱金香像一團團火焰在顫動。白色的塵埃懸在熱氣騰騰的空中，好似鳶尾根粉末升起的浮雲。色彩鮮豔的遮陽傘像大得出奇的蝴蝶在翩翩飛舞。

她要詹姆士談談他自己，談談他的希望、打算。他說得很慢，很勉強。他們這樣的交談簡直像賭徒付出籌碼一樣無可奈何。西碧兒感到不自在。她未能以自己的歡樂影響弟弟。她得到的唯一反應，只是詹姆士悶悶不樂的嘴角上浮起了一絲幾乎察覺不出的微笑。過了一些時候，她也沉默下來。突然，她瞥見了金色的頭髮和歡笑的嘴唇。原來道林・格雷和兩位女士乘坐一輛摺篷馬車在此經過。

她猝然立起身來。"那就是他！"西碧兒激動地說。

"誰？"詹姆士・韋恩問。

"迷人王子，"她目送着那輛摺篷馬車回答。

詹姆士跳起來，一把抓住她的胳膊。"快指給我看。哪個是他？指給我看。我得認認他！"他嚷道。但在這個時候，貝里克公爵的四駕馬車夾進來，擋住了他們的視線。等到能重新看清楚的時候，那輛摺篷馬車已經駛出了海德公園。

"他走了，"西碧兒憂傷地低聲說。"可惜你沒能看見他。"

"我也希望能看見他，因為他要是敢對不起你，我就要他的命。我對着上帝起誓。"

西碧兒駭然望着他。詹姆士把這番話重複了一遍，字字句句像匕首刺破空氣。旁人開始向他們注目。站在近處的一位女士發出吃吃的笑聲。

"我們走吧，詹姆士，走吧，"西碧兒輕輕地說。詹姆士倔頭倔腦地跟着她穿過人羣。他已達到了一吐為快的目的。

他們一直走到阿基里斯銅像前，西碧兒才轉過臉來。她眼睛裏憐憫的神情終於變為嘴唇上的輕笑。她搖搖頭對弟弟說："你真傻，詹姆士，傻得要命，而且是個脾氣很壞的孩子，這就是我要說的。你怎麼能這樣胡言亂語？你自己也不知道在說些甚麼。你明明心裏妒忌，所以才這樣冷酷。啊！我希望你也愛上個甚麼人。戀愛能使人變得善良，可是你剛才說的話很惡毒。"

"我已經十六歲了，"詹姆士回答她說，"我知道我要做甚麼。媽媽對你毫無幫助。她根本不懂得怎麼照顧你。偏偏在這個時候我要到澳洲去。要不是已經辦好手續，我真想把整個計劃通通取消。"

"哦，不要這樣認真，詹姆士。你好像媽媽最喜歡演的那種無聊情節劇裏的英雄。我不想跟你吵架。我看見了他，這就是最

大的幸福！我們別吵啦。我知道你決不會傷害我所愛的人，你説
是嗎？”

“不過只限於你愛他的時候，”這是他陰鬱的回答。

“我將永遠愛他！”西碧兒熱烈地宣稱。

“那麼他呢？”

“他也將永遠愛我！”

“他最好會。”

西碧兒從他身旁往後一縮。接着她笑了起來，把一隻手攔在
弟弟臂膀上。他還十足是個孩子。

在大理石牌樓附近，他們招了一輛公共馬車，直乘到尤斯登
路他們簡陋的家門口。時間已過五點，西碧兒必須在演出前躺下
休息幾個小時。詹姆士堅持要她這樣做。他説他寧願趁母親不在
場的時候和西碧兒告別。要不然，母親一定又要做戲，而這是詹
姆士所深惡痛絕的。

他們在西碧兒房間裏互相道別。詹姆士滿懷着妒意，他恨那
個陌生人到了勢不兩立的程度，因為那個人是他心目中橫在他們
姐弟之間的障礙。然而，當西碧兒的胳膊摟住他的脖子，手指撫
弄他的頭髮的時候，詹姆士的心軟下來了。他帶着一片真摯的柔
情吻了姐姐。他下樓時眼眶裏噙滿了淚水。

母親在樓下等他。詹姆士走進客廳時，她埋怨兒子不守時
間；詹姆士一聲不吭，坐下來吃很清苦的飯菜。蒼蠅圍着飯桌嗡
嗡地叫，在污漬斑斑的桌布上爬。除了公共馬車的隆隆聲和出租
街車的嘚嘚聲，他只聽到這個嘟嘟囔囔的聲音一分鐘一分鐘地吞
噬着他僅有的一點點時間。

不久，他推開盤子，兩手支住腦袋。他覺得他有權利了解真相。倘若事情果真如他所懷疑的那樣，那就早應當向他講明。母親心懷疑懼注視着兒子。嘮嘮叨叨的話幾乎不自覺地從她嘴裏傾瀉出來。她的手指把一條破破爛爛的花邊手絹揉個不停。等到鐘敲了六下，詹姆士站起來向門口走去。但他又轉過身來看着母親。他們四目對視。兒子從母親眼睛裏看到的是乞求哀憐。他頓時發作起來。

"媽媽，我有件事情要問你，"他說。母親失魂落魄地東張西望。她一語不發。"把實情告訴我。我有權利知道。你和父親究竟有沒有結過婚？"

母親發出一聲深沉的歎息。這是如釋重負的感歎。這個可怕的時刻，這個她日日夜夜為之膽顫心驚了幾星期、幾個月的時刻終於來臨，她反而不覺得害怕了。的確，她甚至有點失望。對於開門見山的問題只得直截了當地回答。這樣扣人心弦的場面竟然沒有逐漸引入，一下子就攤牌，根本不講究層次感。這像是非常草率的排練。

"沒有，"她回答說，心裏對於生活的粗鄙和簡單不勝感慨。

"那麼父親一定是個混蛋！"詹姆士握緊拳頭喊道。

她搖搖頭。"我知道他另有婚約，我們十分相愛。他要是活着，一定能養活我們。不要責罵他，我的孩子。他是你的父親，一個有身分的人。是的，他的門第很高。"

詹姆士發出一聲詛咒。"我自己不在乎，"他憤憤地說，"可是不要讓西碧兒……那個正在和她戀愛或者嘴上說愛她的人，不也是個有身分的人嗎？大概門第也是很高的吧？"

韋恩太太霎時間羞愧得無地自容。她垂着腦袋，用哆嗦的手揉揉眼睛。"西碧兒有母親，"她喃喃地說，"我當時可沒有母親。"

詹姆士的心被打動了。他走到母親跟前，俯身吻了她一下。"如果我問起父親的事傷了你的心，請你原諒我，"他說，"可是我不能不問。現在我該走了。再見。別忘了，如今只有一個孩子要你照顧了。你知道，如果那個人敢對不起姐姐，我一定能打聽到他是誰，說甚麼也要把他找到，像宰狗一樣把他宰了，我起誓。"

一時衝動的誇張恫嚇，佐以憤激的手勢和瘋瘋癲癲的情節劇台詞，反倒使她覺得日子不像此前那麼難熬。她習慣這樣的氣氛。她的呼吸也比較順暢了，幾個月以來她第一次真正讚賞自己的兒子。她頗有意在這樣的情感基調上把這幕戲演下去，但是詹姆士驟然中斷了談話。箱子需要拿下來，圍巾手套不知放到哪兒去了。公寓裏的一個雜役走進走出忙碌不堪。還得跟馬車夫講價錢。時間在一連串瑣事中溜了過去。當她在窗口揮動鑲花邊的破手絹，目送兒子的馬車漸漸去遠時，又重新感到悵然若失。她意識到，一次極其難得的機會已失之交臂。收之桑榆的辦法是對西碧兒說，她覺得生活一定會淒涼寂寞，因為如今只有一個孩子要她照顧了。那句話她很欣賞，所以記住了。至於詹姆士的恫嚇，她隻字不提。這番話說得很動人，頗有戲劇效果。她覺得將來他們回憶起這件事來，大家都會哈哈大笑。

第六章

"貝澤爾，我想你已經聽到新聞了吧？"這天晚上，當霍爾渥德剛由侍者引進布里斯托飯店一間擺着三份餐具的雅座時，亨利勛爵問他這個問題。

"沒有啊，亨利，"畫家一邊回答，一邊把帽子和大衣交給殷勤周到的侍者。"甚麼新聞？但願不是關於政治的。我對政治不感興趣。下議院裏幾乎沒有一個人值得一畫；雖然其中許多人很需要刷新形象。"

"道林·格雷訂婚了，"亨利勛爵說時留神觀察畫家的反應。

霍爾渥德先是一驚，繼而皺眉。"道林訂婚了？"他驚訝地說。"不可能！"

"這是千真萬確的。"

"跟誰？"

"一個小演員。"

"我不信。道林決不是沒頭腦的。"

"道林的確夠聰明，所以免不了偶爾做些蠢事，親愛的貝澤爾。"

"婚姻不是可以偶一為之的兒戲，亨利。"

"除了在美國，"亨利勛爵懶洋洋地說。"我又沒說他結了婚。我是說他跟人訂了婚約。這兩者有很大區別。我清楚記得自己結過婚，可是一點也記不起甚麼時候訂過婚。我傾向於認為自己根本沒有訂過婚。"

"但是，請考慮一下道林的家世、地位和財產。跟一個比他低微得多的人結婚，對他來說簡直是胡鬧。"

"如果你想他娶那名女子，你就對他說這番話，貝澤爾。他肯定會這樣做。一個男人做出荒謬絕倫的事來，總是出於最高尚的動機。"

"我希望那是個好女孩，亨利。我不願看到道林被一個會腐蝕他品性、摧殘他理智的壞人縛住手腳。"

"哦，她長得很美；這是更重要的，"亨利勛爵呷着一杯酸橙苦艾酒含糊地說。"據道林說，她長得很美：他在這類事情上很有眼光。你給他畫的畫像啟發了他如何品評別人的容貌。那幅畫像除了別的意義外，確實有這樣了不起的作用。今晚我們就能看到她，只要道林沒有忘記這次約會。"

"你不是開玩笑吧？"

"我沒有半句不嚴肅的話，貝澤爾。我認為我再也不可能比現在這個時候更嚴肅了。"

"那麼你是否贊成這件事呢，亨利？"畫家問道。他在小室裏來回踱步，牙齒咬住嘴唇。"你萬萬不能贊成。這是昏了頭做的蠢事。"

"我現在不會贊成或反對任何事情，這是一種荒謬的方式來對待生活。我們被送來世上不是為了要發表自己的道德偏見。我從不在意普通人說甚麼，也不干預有魅力的人做甚麼。如果一個人吸引我，那不論他選擇怎樣的表達方式，都同樣討我喜歡。道林·格雷愛上了一個漂亮的茱麗葉演員，並計劃和她結婚。有甚麼不好呢？即使他娶了麥瑟琳娜，他的吸引力也不會減少。你知道我不是婚姻的衛士，婚姻真正的壞處是令人變得無私，而無私的人都是平淡無奇、沒有性格的。當然，婚姻會令某些稟性更加複雜，保留利己主義，以及增加不少其他的自我。人們被逼過着多重生活，變得極有條理。我認為高度有序是人類存在的目的。此外，所有經歷都是有價值的，所以即使他人怎樣反對婚姻，它也是種經歷。我希望道林‧格雷會娶這個女孩為妻，熱情地愛她六個月，然後突然被另一個人迷住。他將會是個奇妙的實驗對像。"

"你的話沒有半句是認真的，亨利；你自己也知道。倘若道林‧格雷的生活搞得一團糟，你會比任何人更感到遺憾。事實上，你比你假裝的形象善良得多。"

亨利勛爵笑了起來。"我們之所以把別人設想得那麼善良，是因為我們害怕自己。樂觀主義的基礎是徹頭徹尾的恐懼。我們把可能對自己有益的美德奉獻給別人，從而自以為慷慨大度。我們讚美銀行家，目的是要他同意我們透支銀行存款；我們恭維攔路搶劫的強盜，無非希望他對我們的錢包手下留情。我說的每一個字都是正經話。我對樂觀主義極為蔑視。說到生活被搞糟，那是不可能的，除非它的發展受到壓制。如果你要破壞一個人的天性，你只消對他加以改造。至於正式結婚，那當然無聊得很，男女之間的關係還有其他更有意思的形式。我絕對鼓勵這類形式。它們自有妙處。哦，道林來了！他會告訴你更多東西，比我知道的更要多。"

"親愛的亨利，親愛的貝澤爾，你們都該向我道喜！"道林‧格雷說着，脫去內襯了緞子的晚裝披風，和兩個朋友一一握手。"我從來沒有這樣快樂過。當然，事情比較突然，就像一切真正的喜事一樣。不過，我覺得這正是我無時無刻都在尋找的奇遇。"
他興高采烈，喜上眉梢，顯得益發俊美。

"我希望你永遠快樂幸福，道林，"霍爾渥德說，"可是我不
能完全原諒你把訂婚的事瞞着我。你只告訴了亨利。"

"我也不能原諒你今天姍姍來遲，"亨利勛爵把一隻手攔在道
林肩膀上，面帶笑容插進來說。"來，我們坐下來品嚐這裏新任
廚師的手藝，然後你再把這件事情原原本本告訴我們。"

"沒有甚麼好說的，"他們在一張小圓桌旁就坐時，道林喊
道，"事情很簡單，當我昨天晚上跟亨利你分開後，我換了裝，
到魯伯特街那間你介紹的意大利小餐館吃晚飯，並在八點到了劇
院。西碧兒在扮演羅瑟琳。當然，佈景很糟糕，而且奧蘭多也很
荒唐可笑。但西碧兒！你們應該去看看她！她穿着男裝出場時非
常動人，她穿着一件棕黃袖子的苔青色絲絨緊身衣，一對咖啡色
的背帶長統襪，戴上一頂精緻的綠色小帽，帽上的一顆寶石繫着
老鷹的羽毛。她還披了一個帶兜帽的暗紅色內襯大衣。在我看
來，她從未如此精緻優雅。她擁有貝澤爾你畫室那尊希臘塔納格
拉小雕像的所有風韻，她的頭髮簇擁着她的臉，就像深色的葉子
擁着淺色的玫瑰。至於她的演技，你們今晚就會看到了。她簡直
是個天生的藝術家，我坐在那個破舊包廂內完全被她迷倒，忘記
了自己身處十九世紀的英國。我和我的愛人在一個人所未見的森
林裏。演出結束後，我走到後台跟她說話。我們坐在一起，她眼
裏突然出現一個我從未看過的神情，我的嘴唇湊向了她的嘴唇，
然後二人就吻了起來。我不能形容我當時的感受，我的全部生活
就像是濃縮成完美的玫瑰色歡愉。她渾身顫抖，像一朵搖曳着的

白水仙，隨後一下子跪倒在地，親吻起我的手來。我覺得我不應該告訴你們這些，但我實在忍不住。當然，我們訂婚的事是祕密，她甚至連母親也沒有告訴。我不知道我的監護人會說些甚麼，瑞德利勛爵肯定勃然大怒，但我不在乎，反正我不到一年後便會成年，到時候我喜歡做甚麼就做甚麼。我做得對吧，貝澤爾？我從詩中取得愛情，在莎士比亞劇中找到妻子。被莎士比亞教會說話的嘴唇，在我耳邊輕聲說着它們的祕密。我擁抱着羅瑟琳，親吻着茱麗葉。

"是啊，道林，依我看，你是對的，"霍爾渥德說得很慢。

"你今天見過她沒有？"亨利勛爵問。

道林·格雷搖搖頭。"我在阿登森林和她分別，我將在維羅納的花園和她重逢。"

亨利勛爵若有所思地呷一口香檳。"你究竟在甚麼情況下提到結婚這兩個字，道林？她又是怎樣回答？你是不是都忘了？"

"親愛的亨利，我沒有把這當作一筆買賣，也沒有任何正式的求婚手續。我對她說我愛她，她說她不配做我的妻子。不配！天啊，在我看來，倒是整個世界都配不上她。"

"女人非常講究實際，"亨利勛爵嘀咕着，"遠遠比我們務實。在這類場合，男人常常忘記說任何有關結婚的話，而女人總會提醒我們。"

霍爾渥德用手按住亨利勛爵的胳臂。"不要這樣說，亨利。你惹得道林生氣了。他不是你說的那種男人，決不會虧待任何人。他稟性善良，做不出那種事來。"

亨利勛爵隔着桌子看看他的朋友。"道林從來不生我的氣，"

他説。"我提這個問題的出發點是再好不過的,那就是出於單純的好奇心;在好奇心驅使下提任何問題都可以原諒。根據我的理論,我認為總是女人向我們求婚,而不是我們向女人求婚。當然,中產階級的一套不在此列。但中產階級那一套已經不時興了。"

道林・格雷仰天大笑。"亨利,你這個人本性難移,但我並不介意。反正沒法生你的氣。你見了西碧兒・韋恩就知道,如果有誰忍心欺負她,那必定是畜生,沒有心肝的畜生。我不明白一個人怎麼能讓他心愛的人蒙受恥辱。我愛西碧兒・韋恩。我要把她供在金壇上,讓全世界崇拜這個屬於我的女人。甚麼叫婚約?就是不可推翻的盟約。你為了這個緣故嘲笑結婚。啊!不要嘲笑。我正是要訂立這樣一個不可推翻的盟約。她的信任能促使我忠貞不渝,她的信心使我成為一個更好的人。當我在她身邊的時候,我對你教給我的一切感到羞愧。我變成另一個人,跟你所知道的我不一樣。只要和西碧兒・韋恩的手一碰,我就會把你和你那些誘人而荒謬、動聽而有毒的理論丟在腦後。"

"哪些理論?"亨利勛爵問道,同時取了一點沙律。

"就是關於人生、戀愛、享樂的理論。反正包括你的全部哲學,亨利。"

"享樂是唯一值得建立理論的主題,"勛爵用他悠揚而舒緩的音調回答説。"不過,恐怕這不能算是我自己創造的理論。它的創造者是天性,不是我。享樂是天性測驗我們的試金石,是天性認可的表徵。我們快樂的時候總是好的。但我們好的時候並不總是快樂的。"

"那麼你説的'好'是指甚麼呢?"貝澤爾・霍爾渥德發問。

"是啊，"道林附和道，他靠在椅背上，目光越過餐桌中央的一大簇紫蝴蝶花投向亨利勛爵，"你説的'好'是指甚麼，亨利？"

"好就是順乎本性，"他回答時用白淨而修得很光潔的手指捏住幼細的酒杯腳。"被逼遷就別人便是違反本性。自己的生活極為重要。至於別人的生活，如果你願意做一個正人君子或清教徒，你可以宣揚自己這方面的道德觀，但別人的生活畢竟不關你的事。此外，個人主義的目的實際上是比較高尚的。所謂現代道德就是接受當代的標準。我認為，讓任何有教養的人接受當代的標準都是最不道德的行為。"

"可是，亨利，人活着如果僅僅為了自己，不是要付出可怕的代價嗎？"畫家提醒他注意。

"不錯，如今我們為任何事情都得付出高昂的代價。依我看，窮人真正的悲劇在於他們甚麼都嫌太貴，唯一付得起的代價就是自我克制。美麗的罪惡和美麗的東西一樣是富人的特權。"

"我説的代價不是指錢，而是其他形式。"

"甚麼形式，貝澤爾？"

"比方説：內疚、苦惱……意識到自身的墮落。"

亨利勛爵聳聳肩膀。"親愛的貝澤爾，中世紀的藝術是動人的，中世紀的感情卻早已過時。當然，在小説中儘可以用上。其實，也只有生活中已經不用的東西才適合用在小説裏。我敢説，文明人享樂從不後悔，而未開化的人從來也不知道甚麼叫享樂。"

"我知道，"道林·格雷大聲説。"崇拜某一個人就是享樂。"

"那當然比受人崇拜好些，"亨利勛爵應道，一面擺弄着桌上的水果。"受人崇拜很討厭。女人對待我們好比人類對待神明。

她們崇拜我們，可老是要我們為她們做這做那。"

"依我看，她們要求得到的已經先給了我們，"道林嚴肅地說。"她們把愛情賦予給我們的天性，自然有理由要求我們以愛相報。"

"完全正確，道林，"霍爾渥德表示讚賞。

"從來沒有甚麼是完全正確的，"亨利勛爵說。

"有的，"道林毅然說。"你得承認，亨利，女人把她們一生的精華都給了男人。"

"也許如此，"亨利勛爵歎了口氣，"但她們一概都要討還，而且總是那麼斤斤計較。麻煩就在這裏。有一位俏皮的法國人說過：女人能激起我們成就大業的願望，可又總是阻撓我們實現這樣的願望。"

"亨利，你真討厭！可我不知道為甚麼這樣喜歡你。"

"你將永遠喜歡我，道林，"他答道。"你們兩位要不要咖啡？侍者，來咖啡，還要上等白蘭地和煙捲。噢，煙捲不要了，我自己有。貝澤爾，我不許你抽雪茄。你來一支煙捲吧。抽煙捲是一種完美類型的完美享受：既給人刺激，又不讓你滿足。還有比這更理想的嗎？是啊，道林，你將永遠喜歡我。我在你眼裏代表着你從來不敢做的一切壞事情。"

"你盡胡說八道，亨利！"道林說着，從侍者放在桌上的一條噴火銀龍口中點了支煙捲。"我們到劇場去吧。只要西碧兒一出台，你們就會有新的生活理想。她將向你們展示你們至今不知道的東西。"

"我甚麼都領教過了，"亨利勛爵説這話時的眼神大有往事不堪回首的意味，"不過我隨時願意嘗試新鮮的感受，儘管這樣的東西恐怕已經不存在，至少對我來説是這樣。可是你那位仙女也許能使我有所觸動。我喜歡看戲。舞台上比生活中真實得多。我們走吧。道林，你跟我坐在一起。很抱歉，貝澤爾，我的車只能坐兩個人，你只好僱一輛街車跟在我們後面。"

他們離座起身，穿上外衣，還站着呷了幾口咖啡。畫家默默無言，心事重重。他有些怏怏然。道林這門親事在他看來大大不妥。但是比起可能發生的其他許多事情來，他又覺得這還不算是最壞的。幾分鐘後，三個人走下樓去。按照事先的安排，霍爾渥德一個人坐一輛街車。眼望着他前面那輛雙座小馬車閃爍不定的燈光，一種若有所失的奇怪感覺油然而生。他意識到，對他來説，道林·格雷已不再是過去那個道林·格雷。生活已把他們分開……霍爾渥德的眼睛漸趨黯然，車水馬龍、燈火輝煌的街道同他如隔一層薄霧。馬車來到劇場門口的時候，他覺得自己老了好幾歲。

第七章

不知甚麼原因，劇院當晚非常擁擠。肥胖的猶太經理在門口堆出一個怯懦的諂笑，迎候他們。他謙虛得誇張地領他們到包廂，揮動他滿是珠飾的肥手，以最大的音量説話。道林・格雷比以往更討厭他，感覺像是前來找米蘭達但碰上卡利班。亨利勛爵反而挺喜歡他，至少嘴上這樣説，並堅持要跟他握手，明確地告訴他自己很榮幸遇見一個發現真正的天才，並為一位詩人破產的人。貝澤爾饒有趣味地看着正廳後座觀眾的一張張臉。空氣非常悶熱，而巨大的射燈就像是一朵巨型大麗花，花瓣發出黃色的火焰。頂層樓座的青年已經把外套和背心脱掉，掛在座位旁邊，與隔得很遠的人交談着，還和鄰座打扮得花俏俗氣的女子一起吃着橘子。有些女人在後座大笑，嗓門尖得刺耳。酒吧裏傳來了開瓶塞的啪啪聲。

"真是一個發現敬慕對象的好地方！"亨利勛爵説。

"不錯！"道林・格雷接口説。"我正是在這裏發現了她，她是高居於一切凡人之上的女神。在她表演的時候，你會把甚麼都忘了。等她出場之後，這些相貌鄙俗、野調無腔的粗人就會變樣。他們會靜靜地坐着看她。她要他們哭就哭，要他們笑就笑。他們會像一把小提琴一樣發出反響。她能喚醒他們的靈魂，你會感到他們都是和你一樣由血肉做成的。"

"一樣的血肉！但願不是這樣！"亨利勛爵説着，用望遠鏡細細觀看頂層樓座的觀眾。

"道林，你別理他，"畫家說。"我理解你的意思，我也相信那個女孩。你愛的人一定不同尋常，你說那女孩有這麼大的吸引力，一定是又漂亮又高尚。喚醒一代人的靈魂是件了不起的事情。如果她能給那些至今渾渾噩噩過日子的人注入精神的活力，如果她能在那些過着卑瑣生活的人身上啟發美感，如果她能促使他們放下自私自利之心，為別人的悲哀一掬同情之淚，那麼，她不僅值得你崇拜，也值得世人敬仰。你跟她結婚完全正確。最初我不這樣想，但現在我明白了。是上帝為你創造了西碧兒·韋恩。沒有她，你將感到殘缺不全。"

"謝謝你，貝澤爾，"道林·格雷緊緊握着他的手說。"我知道你會了解我的。亨利是那麼玩世不恭，他使我害怕。哦，樂隊開始演奏了，簡直聽不得。好在只有五分鐘左右就要開幕，你將看到那個女孩。我準備把整個生命都給她，雖則我身上所有美好的東西都已經給了她。"

十五分鐘後，西碧兒·韋恩在一陣異常嘈雜的喝采聲中出場了。是的，她長得確實可愛，亨利勛爵也認為她非常惹人喜愛。她那嬌羞的情致和驚愕的眼神極為討好。她向滿場熱情的觀眾投了一瞥，雙頰泛起淡淡的紅暈，恰似玫瑰在銀鏡中的映像。她退後幾步，嘴唇似乎顫動了一下。貝澤爾·霍爾渥德站起來開始鼓掌。道林·格雷像在夢中坐着紋絲不動，直勾勾地望着她。亨利勛爵的眼睛貼着望遠鏡，連聲讚歎："真迷人！真迷人！"

舞台上是凱普萊特家的廳堂，羅密歐化裝成朝聖者與默丘西奧等幾個朋友一起進來。那支糟糕的樂隊奏起樂聲，人們開始跳舞。西碧兒·韋恩飄然周旋於一羣動作笨拙、服裝寒傖的演員中間，宛若來自另一個更美好世界的仙子。她跳舞的時候身姿搖曳，猶如一棵植物在水中蕩漾。她頸脖的曲線酷似潔白的百合花，兩條胳臂簡直是用象牙雕成。

但她的表情卻異乎尋常地淡漠。當她的視線停留在羅密歐身上的時候，絲毫沒有欣喜的跡象。她的幾句台詞——

> 信徒，莫把你的手侮辱，
>
> 這樣才是最虔誠的禮敬；
>
> 神明的手本許信徒接觸，
>
> 掌心的密合遠勝如親吻。

以及接下來一段簡短的對白，念得十分做作。她的音色優美，但聲調卻徹底失去了原有的味道。音調既不准，致使詩句的神韻全失，激情變假。

道林·格雷注視着她，臉色愈來愈難看。他窘得要命，坐立不安。他的兩位朋友也不敢對他說一句話。西碧兒·韋恩給他們的印象是完全沒有才能。他們大失所望。

然而他們知道，對於任何演茱麗葉的女伶來說，真正的考驗在第二幕陽台上的一場，所以他們還在等待。如果她也演不好那一場，那就毫無希望了。

西碧兒出現在月光如水的陽台上時十分動人，這是不可否認的。但是她那做作的演技令人難以忍受，而且愈往下愈糟糕。她的動作極不自然，幾乎到了荒謬的程度。她把每一句台詞的語氣都加重過頭。那段精彩的獨白——

> 幸虧黑夜替我罩上了一重面幕，
>
> 否則為了我剛才被你聽去的話，
>
> 你一定可以看見我臉上羞愧的紅暈。

像是一個中學生在彆腳的朗誦教師指導下咬緊牙關背出來的。當她上身探出陽台的欄杆，念到一些才氣橫溢的警句時 ——

> 我雖然喜歡你，
> 卻不喜歡今天晚上的密約；
> 它太倉猝、太輕率、太出人意外了，
> 正像一閃電光，等不及人家開一聲口，
> 已經消隱了下去。好人，再會吧！
> 這一朵愛的蓓蕾，靠着夏天的暖風的吹拂，
> 也許會在我們下次相見的時候，開出鮮豔的花來。

似乎根本不理會其中的涵義。這不是神經緊張所致。她非但不顯得神經緊張，而且絕對不動聲色。這純粹是演技不行。這是一次徹底的失敗。

甚至後排和樓座上沒有受過教育的普通觀眾也對台上的戲失去了興趣。他們變得焦躁不安，開始高聲談話，甚至有人吹口哨。猶太經理站在花樓後跺腳，同時破口大罵。唯一無動於衷的人是西碧兒自己。

第二幕結束時，場內噓聲大作。亨利勛爵離座起身，穿上外衣。"她長得很美，道林，"他說，"但是不會演戲。我們走吧。"

"我要把戲看完，"道林·格雷以倔強沉痛的音調回答。"亨利，我感到萬分抱歉，浪費了你們一個晚上的時間。我請你們兩位原諒。"

"親愛的道林，我想韋恩小姐多半是身體不舒服，"霍爾渥德不讓他說下去。"改天我們再來。"

"她身體不舒服倒也罷了，"道林不以為然。"可是我看她簡

直是麻木不仁。她完全變了。昨晚她明明是個偉大的藝術家，今晚她只是一個平庸的三流戲子。"

"不要這樣談論你所愛的人，道林。愛情比藝術更神聖。"

"這兩者無非都是摹擬的形式，"亨利勳爵說。"好了，我們走吧。道林，你不應當再留在這裏。看拙劣的演出於身心無益。何況將來你不見得要你的妻子繼續演戲。既然如此，即使她把茱麗葉演得像個木偶，又有甚麼關係？她很可愛，要是她對生活也像對演戲一樣不甚了了的話，那倒是一次饒有興味的經歷。真正討人喜歡的人只有兩種：一種是無所不知的人，一種是一無所知的人。老弟，不要這樣哭喪着臉！永葆青春的祕訣在於力戒醜惡的情緒。跟貝澤爾和我一起到俱樂部去吧。我們一邊抽煙，一邊為西碧兒的美貌乾一杯。她是個美人。你還要甚麼呢？"

"你走吧，亨利，"道林煩躁地說。"讓我一個人待一會。貝澤爾，你也走吧。啊！難道你們沒看到我的心都快碎了？"道林說時熱淚盈眶，嘴唇發抖。他退到包廂後部倚牆而立，兩手捂住面孔。

"貝澤爾，我們走吧，"亨利勳爵的語氣出人意料地柔和。這兩位年輕人一起走了出去。

幾分鐘後，腳燈亮了，台幕升起，第三幕開始了。道林·格雷回到座位上。他面色蒼白，神態傲慢而冷淡。戲拖拖拉拉地演下去，像是沒完沒了似的。有一半觀眾在踢踢囊囊的步履聲和嘻嘻哈哈的談笑聲中離開了劇場。這是一次全軍覆沒的慘敗。最後一幕幾乎是演給空場子看的。幕落下時有人吃吃地笑，有人唉聲歎氣。

戲剛一演完，道林就衝到後台去。西碧兒獨自站在候場室裏，臉上的神色頗為得意。她雙目炯炯，幾乎渾身光彩煥發。她略略張開的嘴唇在向着心底的祕密微笑。

　　道林走進去時，西碧兒面帶無限欣喜的表情看着他。"道林，今天我演得很糟糕！"她說。

　　"糟透了！"道林·格雷愕然望着她，進一步說，"簡直可怕！你是不是病了？你根本不知道糟到甚麼程度，也不知道我忍受了多大的痛苦。"

　　西碧兒依然在笑。"道林，"她用唱歌似的聲調徐緩地喚出他的名字，似乎她的兩瓣櫻唇覺得這名字比蜜更甜。"道林，你應該明白的。現在你明白了，是不是？"

　　"明白甚麼？"他氣呼呼地問。

　　"我今天為甚麼演得這樣糟。以後我還是好不了。我再也不能演得像過去那樣。"

　　他聳聳肩膀。"我看，你準是病了。既然你有病，就不該演出，何苦招人恥笑？我的兩個朋友再也坐不住了。我也看不下去。"

　　西碧兒好像不在聽他。她高興得變了樣。幸福使她處在極度亢奮之中。

　　"道林，道林，"她喊道，"我認識你之前，表演是我生活中唯一的真實，我只在劇院生活過，我以為這一切都是真實的。我這天是羅瑟琳，那天是波蒂阿。碧翠斯的歡樂就是我的歡樂；寇蒂莉阿的哀傷就是我的哀傷。我相信這一切，跟我同台演出的普通人都像是神一樣，繪成的佈景就像是我的世界。我除了影子以外都不知道，而我還以為它們是真的。然後你來了。啊，我英俊的愛人！你把我的靈魂從牢獄中釋放，你教會我甚麼是真正的現實。今晚是我人生首次看透了我一直演出的空洞、虛假和愚蠢。今晚是我首次意識到羅密歐是醜陋、年老和虛偽的；意識到果園裏的月光是虛假的；意識到佈景是庸俗的，意識到我念的台詞是不實的，既不是我的話，亦不是我想說的。你帶給我更高尚的東西，一切的藝術都是它的影子。你令我知道真正的愛是甚麼。我的愛！我的愛！迷人王子！生命的王子！我已對影子感到煩厭。對我來說，你勝過所有的藝術。我與劇中的木偶有何關係呢？當我今晚上台，我不明白為甚麼所有東西都離我而去。我原以為我會演得很出色，但卻發現自己無能為力。忽然，我心裏開始明白箇中原因。對我來說，這個感悟好極了。我聽見了他們的噓聲，但一笑置之。他們怎麼能理解我們這樣的愛呢？把我帶走吧，道林。帶我到沒有人打擾我們的地方去。我討厭舞台。我可以模仿一種自己感受不了的激情，但無法模仿在我心中燃燒的激情。啊，道林，道林，現在你明白它的意義了嗎？即使我能做得到，對我來說在戲裏表演熱戀也是一種藝瀆行為。你令我了解這一切。”

道林·格雷頹喪地坐在沙發上，把臉側向一邊。“你扼殺了我的愛情，”他悲不自勝地說出這麼一句話。

西碧兒用詫異的眼光看着他，笑了起來。道林不做聲。西碧兒走到他跟前，用纖細的手指撫摸他的頭髮。她跪下來，把道林的雙手按在她的嘴上。道林全身顫動起來，立刻把手抽回去。

然後他跳起來便向門口走去。“是的，”他喊道，“你扼殺了我的愛情。你曾經喚醒了我的想像，現在你甚至引不起我的興趣。你已經變得可有可無。過去我愛你是因為你不尋常，因為你聰明，有才華，因為你實現了偉大詩人的夢想，使藝術的幻影有了血和肉。現在你把這一切都毀了。原來你淺薄無聊、冥頑不靈。我的天！我會愛上你真是發了瘋！我是多麼愚蠢啊！現在你對我已經不存在。我再也不願看見你，再也不願想到你，再也不願提起你的名字。你不知道你對我曾經意味着甚麼。天啊，那時……哦，想起來我就受不了！我真希望從來沒有見過你！你破壞了我生活中浪漫的情調。你竟然說愛情損害了你的藝術，可見你對愛情是何等無知！你離開了自己的藝術，是毫無價值的。我本想使你成名，一步登天，讓全世界都拜倒在你腳下，讓你冠上我的姓氏。可現在你是個甚麼？一個長着一張漂亮臉蛋的三流女戲子。"

西碧兒面色慘白，全身哆嗦。她把兩隻手扭絞在一起，她的聲音像在喉嚨裏卡住了。"你不是認真的吧，道林？"她說得很輕，"你一定在演戲。"

"演戲！這是你的工作。你演得妙極了，"他刻毒地回答。

她從地上站起來，臉上帶着很可憐的痛苦神情從屋子的盡裏頭走到他跟前。她諦視着道林的眼睛，一隻手按住他的胳臂。道林把她推開。"別碰我！"他叱喝道。

西碧兒發出一聲低沉的悲泣，倒在他的腳下，像一朵花兒遭踐踏。"道林，道林，別離開我！"她輕聲哀告。"我非常後悔沒有演好今天的戲。我的心老是繫在你身上。不過我願意重新試一試……一定再試一試。我對你的愛情發生得太突然了。要不是你吻了我，要不是我們接了吻，我想我決不會產生這樣的感覺。再吻我一下吧，我的愛。不要把我撇下。我弟弟……不，這不要緊。

他不是認真説的。他不過是開開玩笑……可是你，哦！難道你不能原諒我今晚的失常嗎？我一定會下苦功，努力演得好些。不要對我那樣狠心，要知道，我愛你超過世上的一切。歸根到底，我使你不高興也只有這麼一次。當然，你説得很對，道林。我應該表現出更多的藝術家氣質。我太傻了，可我實在沒法控制自己。哦，別離開我。"一陣猛烈的抽噎幾乎使她感到窒息。她像一隻受傷的動物在地上蜷做一團，而道林‧格雷縱然有一雙美麗的眼睛，卻鄙夷地俯視着她，還輕蔑地撇着一張清秀的嘴。對着一個不再為你所愛的人，人的感情往往就是這麼可笑。道林‧格雷認為西碧兒‧韋恩是在演一齣拙劣的情節劇，這女孩的眼淚和抽泣使他反感。

"我要走了，"最後他説，語調平靜，口齒清楚。"我不願做一個不講情義的人，但我不能再看見你。你使我太失望了。"

西碧兒無聲地哭着，一句話也不説，只是爬得更近了些。她伸出一雙小手，像個盲人摸索着他。道林轉身離開了候場室。不一會，他已經走出劇場。

他要到哪裏去，自己也不清楚。事後回憶起來，他曾在幾條燈光暗淡的街上徘徊，經過幾座黑影憧憧的拱門和看起來像凶宅的房屋。一些嗓門嘶啞、笑聲刺耳的女人在後面招呼他。幾個醉漢跟跟蹌蹌地走過，一邊連聲辱罵，或者自言自語，好像醜惡的猿人一樣。他看到一些古怪的孩子擠在台階上，聽到從黑洞洞的院子裏傳來尖聲的叫喊和詛咒。

拂曉時分，他發現自己在柯芬園附近。夜幕升起，露出火紅的微光，天空像是一顆掏空了的完美珍珠。大車載滿搖曳多姿的百合花，隆隆作響，慢悠悠地駛過空曠光潔的街道。空氣裏彌漫着濃郁的花香。對他來說，美麗的花就像是一帖鎮痛劑。他跟着進了市場，看那些人卸貨。一個穿白色罩衫的車夫送了些櫻桃給他，他道了謝，不明白為甚麼那人拒絕收錢，開始無精打采地吃起櫻桃來。櫻桃是半夜裏採摘的，還帶着月色的寒氣。一長列男童，扛着一筐筐紮起來的鬱金香、黃玫瑰和紅玫瑰，在他面前魚貫而過，挨挨擠擠穿過一大堆翠綠的蔬菜。門廊下被太陽曬得褪了色的灰柱子旁邊，有一羣邋遢骯髒、不戴帽子的女孩閒蕩着，正等待拍賣完結。其他人都擠在廣場咖啡屋的旋轉門附近。拉車的大馬打滑，踩在粗糙的石子路上，搖動着馬鈴和馬飾。有些車夫睡在一堆麻袋中間。頸部色彩斑斕、腳呈粉紅色的鴿子跳來跳去，啄着穀物。

過不多久，道林僱了一輛街車回家。他在台階上逗留片刻，環顧靜悄悄的廣場，以及關得嚴嚴實實的窗戶和顯眼的百葉簾。這時天空已是純淨的蛋白石顏色，屋頂在這樣的天幕前閃着銀光。一縷輕煙正從對面的煙囱裏升起，像一條紫色的緞帶在呈珍珠母色澤的空氣中嫋嫋浮動。

寬敞的門廊鑲着橡木嵌板，天花板上垂下一座鍍金的威尼斯大吊燈 —— 大概是從當地某個總督的遊覽船上獵獲的戰利品 —— 其中三個噴口還亮着，閃爍不定的火焰像鑲着白邊的淺藍色花瓣。他關了燈，把帽子和披風往桌上一扔，穿過書齋走向臥室，那是樓下一間八角形的大房間。隨着道林最近對奢華的生活講究起來，他的臥室也剛剛裝潢一新，掛上了幾張珍奇的文藝復興時期的壁毯，那是在塞爾比莊園荒廢的閣樓裏發現的。他正要轉動門把，視線落在貝澤爾・霍爾渥德為他畫的肖像上。道林像受了甚麼驚嚇似地倒退一步。然後他走進臥室，神色顯得迷惑不解。他取下插在上衣鈕孔中的花，猶豫了一會。最後他還是回到書齋裏，走到畫像前細看了一番。光線受阻於乳白色的絲綢百葉簾，不甚明亮。他覺得肖像的面部起了一點變化，神態和原本不大一樣：嘴角流露出些許冷酷。這可是件怪事。

他轉身走到窗前，把簾子拉上去。燦爛的朝陽把整個房間都照亮了，一些莫名其妙的怪影遭此掃蕩，只得瑟瑟發抖地躲在陰暗角落。可是，他在畫像面部發現的些微奇怪的表情非但沒有消失，反而更加明顯。強烈的陽光在畫像上晃動，把嘴角冷酷的線條向他揭示得清清楚楚，彷彿他做了甚麼虧心事後又從鏡子裏照見了自己。

他打了個寒顫，從桌上拿起一面橢圓形鏡子，鏡子的象牙邊框刻有多個丘比特圖案，是亨利勛爵送給他的許多禮物之一。他急忙向光潔的鏡子深處照去，但鮮紅的嘴唇並沒有現出畫像上那樣冷酷的線條。這到底是怎麼回事？

他揉揉眼睛，一直走近畫像前面，重新仔細看了一番。他看不出有任何異樣的變化，然而整個神態無疑起了變化。這不是他的幻覺。事情明明白白擺在那裏，太可怕了。

他在一把椅子上頹然坐下，開始思考。突然，他腦際響起了肖像完工那天自己在貝澤爾・霍爾渥德畫室裏說過的話。是的，他記得十分清楚。當時他發了一個癡願：希望自己能永葆青春，而讓畫像漸漸老去；希望自己的美貌如花開不敗，而讓畫布上的容顏承受他的慾念和罪惡的重荷；畫上的形象即使佈滿痛苦和憂慮的皺紋亦無妨，只要自己能保持住當時他剛剛意識到的年少英俊的翩翩風采。莫非他的願望竟然實現了？這種事情是不可能的。甚至想一想都叫人害怕。可是，畫像明明在他面前，嘴角帶着些許冷酷。

冷酷！他的行為算是冷酷嗎？那要怪西碧兒，不能怪他。他把西碧兒幻想成一個偉大的藝術家，正因為如此而把自己的愛情獻給了她。不料西碧兒使他大失所望。原來她是個俗物，一無可取。不過，他想到西碧兒躺在他腳下像個小孩子似地嗚咽抽泣的情景，禁不住無限懊悔。當時他竟是那樣狠心地看着她。他怎麼成了這樣的一個人？他為何被賦予這樣的一顆靈魂？但是，他不也感到痛苦嗎？演出持續的那三個小時比死更難熬，他有如承受了幾世紀的酷刑和無窮盡的折磨。他生命的價值與西碧兒的一樣。如果説他使西碧兒終生受了傷害，那麼，西碧兒也造成了他一段時間的創痛。何況，女人承受不幸的能力天生比男人強。她們生活在情懷裏，想的也只是她們的感情。她們要情人無非是可以向他哭，向他鬧。這是亨利勛爵告訴他的，而亨利勛爵對女人知之甚深。何苦為西碧兒‧韋恩自尋煩惱呢？在道林的心目中，她已與他無關。

可是那幅肖像的變化又該如何解釋呢？它掌握着他生活的祕密，反映出他的所作所為。它使道林懂得如何鍾愛自己的美貌。難道它還將教他憎恨自己的靈魂不成？他怎麼能再去看自己的畫像？

不，這純粹是思緒紛亂造成的幻覺。他度過了可怕的一夜，無數怪影還在作祟。他驀地想起一個紅色小斑點可以使人發瘋的事。不，畫像沒有起變化。這完全是疑心生暗鬼。

然而，被冷酷的獰笑破壞了美貌的畫中人在注視着他。畫上的金髮在早晨的陽光照耀下熠熠生輝。碧藍的眼睛和他本人的目光相遇。他感到無限惋惜，不是惋惜自己，而是惋惜畫上的形象。它已經變了，而且將變得更厲害。它的金髮將褪成灰色。紅白玫瑰似的容顏將枯萎憔悴。他做的每一件壞事都將在畫布上留下污點，毀壞它美麗的形象。但他不再作惡了。畫像變也罷，不變也罷，對他終究是良心的一面鏡子。他要抗拒誘惑。他再也不跟亨利勛爵往來，至少再也不聽他那些精緻奧妙的有毒謬論。正是這些話在貝澤爾·霍爾渥德的花園裏第一次激起了自己的非非之想。他要回到西碧兒·韋恩身邊，向她賠不是，和她結婚，努力重新愛她。對，他有義務這樣做。她忍受的痛苦遠遠超過他自己。西碧兒對他一度擁有的魅力將恢復過來。他們在一起將幸福快樂。他兩人的共同生活將是美麗而純潔的。

他從椅子站起來，把一道很大的屏風拉到肖像的正前方，但在一瞥畫中人的表情時自己還是打了個寒顫。"真可怕！"他喃喃自語，然後走到窗前，把窗戶打開。他跨到室外的草地上，深深吸了一口氣。早晨清新的空氣似乎驅散了他所有陰暗的思緒。現在，他腦子裏想的只是西碧兒。他一遍又一遍地念着她的名字，心底重新激起愛情微弱的迴響。鳥兒在露水浸潤的花園裏歌唱，像是向花兒細說她的故事。

第八章

他醒來時早已過了中午。他的侍從多次悄悄地進來看他有沒有動靜,對於年輕主人今天這麼晚還睡着很覺詫異。終於,鈴聲響了,維克多用法國塞夫爾產的古老小瓷盤托着一杯茶和一疊信輕輕地進來,把遮在三扇長窗前附有翠藍內襯的橄欖綠緞窗簾拉開。

"先生今天上午睡得好香啊,"他笑嘻嘻地說。

"現在幾點了,維克多?"道林·格雷看來還沒睡夠。

"一點十五分,先生。"

怎麼這麼晚了!他坐起來,呷了幾口茶,翻閱信件。其中一封信是亨利勛爵早上派人送過來的,他猶疑了一會,把信放到一旁,沒精打采地打開其他信件。裏面仍舊是一些賀卡、晚飯的邀請卡、私人畫展的入場票、慈善音樂會的節目單等等,每個時髦的年青人都會在這個季節的每個早上收到這些信件。此外還有一張數額巨大的賬單,用作支付一套路易十五時代風格的銀質鏤空梳妝用具。他還不敢把賬單拿給他的監護人,因為他們非常守舊,並不了解在我們生活的這個時代,不必要的東西才是必需品。還有幾封是傑明街的放債人寫來的,用詞非常謙恭,表示隨時可以最合理的利息提供任何數額的貸款。

大約過了十分鐘,他起身披上一件非常講究的絲繡羊絨晨袍,走進用縞瑪瑙鋪面的浴室。涼水使他從久睡之後清醒過來。

他似乎把昨夜的事全忘了。只有一兩次，他隱約感到自己參與了一件奇怪而不愉快的事情，不過記不真切，像是一場夢。

他穿好衣服，走進書齋，在靠近敞開的窗口的小圓桌旁坐下來，用一餐法式早點。天氣極好，暖和的空氣裏充滿了芳香。一隻蜜蜂飛進來，繞着道林面前插滿黃玫瑰的青龍瓷花盆嗡嗡地打轉，道林的心情十分愉快。

忽然，他的視線落在他用以遮蔽畫像的屏風上，不禁打了個寒顫。

"你冷嗎，先生？"侍從問，同時端上奄列。"要不要關窗？"

道林搖搖頭説："我不冷。"

到底有沒有這樣的事？畫像真的變了，還是純屬他的想像作怪，使他把愉悦看成了獰笑？一塊塗上顏料的畫布總不會改變吧？事情實在不可思議。這件事可以當作奇談改天講給貝澤爾聽。他一定會覺得好笑。

然而，他對整件事情的記憶還歷歷在目！先是在昏暗的微明中，然後又在燦爛的朝陽下，他從扭曲的嘴唇周圍看到了些微的冷酷。他幾乎害怕他的侍從離開這間房間。他知道，那時只剩下他一個人，他又要去察看那幅畫像。他害怕得到證實。當維克多送上咖啡和煙捲轉身要走的時候，道林真想叫他留下。眼看門就要關上，他又把侍從叫回來。維克多站在門口等候吩咐。道林對他看了半晌。"維克多，無論誰來，我一概不見，説我不在家，"他歎一口氣説。侍從鞠了一躬後退下去了。

於是他從桌旁站起來，點了一支煙，在面對屏風的一張鋪着奢華坐墊的榻上躺下。屏風的年代已相當久遠，是用燙金的西班牙皮革製成的，上面刻有花紋，圖案顯示路易十四時代花俏的風格。他懷着好奇的心情凝視着這道屏風，不知它以前是否藏匿過某人的祕密。

要不要把它移走？讓它放在那裏不是挺好嗎？為甚麼一定要知道呢？如果事情是真的，那太可怕了。如果不是真的，又何必自尋煩惱？然而，萬一鬼使神差，有別人向屏風背後窺探，發現了可怕的變化，那怎麼辦？如果貝澤爾・霍爾渥德到這兒來，要看看他自己的作品，又怎麼辦？他肯定會這樣做。不，事情非徹底澄清不可，立刻就澄清。無論結果如何，總比這種疑神疑鬼的狀態好。

他站起來，把兩扇門都鎖上。至少他看到這張記錄着他的醜行的面具時，沒有旁人在場。於是他拉開屏風，面對面看到自己。這是千真萬確的，畫像變了。

事後他一再回想起，而且每次都深感驚訝，他發現自己看這幅肖像時，最初幾乎懷着一種研究科學的興趣。他認為發生這樣的變化是難以置信的，偏偏又是明擺着的事實。畫布上構成輪廓和色彩的化學原子，與他的靈魂之間是否存在着某種難以捉摸的親緣關係？難道靈魂所想的，那些原子會察覺得到？靈魂夢寐以求的，它們會實現？抑或另有某種更可怕的原因？想到這裏，他不寒而慄。他回到榻旁躺下來，強抑着恐懼和噁心，對畫像仔細端詳。

無論怎樣，他知道畫像對他起了作用。它使道林意識到自己對待西碧兒・韋恩是多麼不應該，多麼忍心。這件事還來得及補救。她仍然可以做他的妻子。他的虛偽而自私的愛將接受較崇高的影響，變為較純正的感情，而貝澤爾‧霍爾渥德為他畫的肖像，將成為他終生的嚮導，正如一些人靠聖潔的靈魂，另一些人靠良心，所有的人都靠對上帝的敬畏作嚮導一樣。有些鴉片能麻醉悔恨之心，有些藥物能把道德觀念催眠。但這裏卻有着看得見的墮落的象徵和罪惡的標記。它記錄人把自己的靈魂引向毀滅所留下的永恒足跡。

鐘在三點、四點和四點半敲起來，可是道林‧格雷仍不動彈。他試圖把生活的一根根紅線收集起來織成圖案，試圖找到一條路走出他正徬徨其中的血紅色的慾念之迷宮。他不知道該做甚麼或想甚麼。最後，他走到桌旁，坐下來寫一封充滿激情的信給他愛過的那個女人，祈求她寬恕，痛責自己的瘋狂行為。他寫了一頁又一頁，字字句句表達他深切的悔恨和更深的痛苦。自我譴責是一種奢侈的概念。當我們譴責自己的時候，就覺得別人沒有權利再譴責我們。赦免我們的是懺悔本身，而不是教士。信寫好後，道林覺得自己已經得到寬恕。

忽然有人叩門，接着他聽到亨利勛爵的聲音在門外説："親愛的道林，我一定要見你。快讓我進去。你這樣把自己關起來，我受不了。"

道林起先不作聲，一動也不動。叩門聲還在繼續，而且愈來愈響。對，還是讓他進來的好，道林要向他聲明今後決定重新做人；如有必要，如果勢在必行，甚至不惜跟他鬧翻，大家分道揚鑣。主意既定，道林霍地立起身來，匆匆忙忙用屏風把肖像遮起來，然後去開門上的鎖。

"這件事非常令人遺憾，道林，"亨利勛爵進門就説。"不過你不要太想不開。"

"你是説西碧兒·韋恩嗎？"道林問。

"是的，"亨利勛爵在一把椅子上坐下，慢慢地脱去黄色手套。"從某種角度看來，事情確實很糟糕，但這不能怪你。告訴我，散戲後你是不是到後台去看她了？"

"是的。"

"我想你一定會去。你有沒有同她發生口角？"

"我當時心腸太狠，亨利，太狠心了。不過現在一切都好了。我並不為所發生的事感到後悔。它使我更清楚地認識自己。"

"啊，道林，你能這樣看待這件事，我很高興！我本來擔心會看到你沉浸在悔恨中，使勁扯你自己漂亮的鬓髮。"

"所有這些我都經歷過了，"道林搖搖頭微笑着説。"我現在心情十分愉快。首先，我懂得了甚麼叫做良知。這跟你對我説的不一樣。良知是我們身上最神聖的東西。亨利，再也不要嘲笑它，至少在我面前不要這樣。我要做個好人。我不能眼看自己的靈魂變得醜惡。"

"這倒是倫理學上一套絕妙的藝術基礎，道林！我向你表示祝賀。但是你準備從何做起呢？"

"與西碧兒·韋恩結婚。"

"與西碧兒·韋恩結婚？"亨利勛爵驚呼着站起來，惶惑地看着他。"可是，我親愛的道林……"

"是的，亨利，我知道你要説甚麼。又是發表一通關於婚姻的謬論。別説了，再也不要向我説這類話。兩天前我向西碧兒求了婚。我不打算對她言而無信。她將成為我的妻子。"

"你的妻子！道林……難道你沒有收到我的信？今天上午我寫了一封信給你，是差專人送來的。"

"你的信？噢，是的，我想起來了。我還沒有看，亨利。我擔心裏面又是一些我不愛聽的話。你總是用你的驚人之語來粉碎生活。"

"這麼説，你還完全不知道？"

"你指的是甚麼？"

亨利勛爵從房間的另一頭走過來，靠近道林‧格雷坐下，緊緊握住他的兩隻手，説："道林，你不要驚慌，我寫信是要告訴你，西碧兒‧韋恩死了。"

一聲痛苦的叫喊從道林喉嚨裏衝口而出，他跳起來，使勁抽出被亨利勛爵握住的手。"死了！西碧兒死了！這不是事實！這是駭人聽聞的謠言！你怎麼説這樣的話？"

"這的確是事實，道林，"亨利勛爵鄭重其事地説。"所有的早報都登了。我寫信叫你在我來到之前不要見任何人。當局無疑要驗屍，你不能被捲進去。這類事情在巴黎可以使人出名。可是倫敦人偏見太深。在這裏，剛剛進入社交界就跟醜聞有牽連可要不得。這類事情不妨留待晚年點綴風景。我想劇場裏的人也許不知道你的姓名。如果不知道，那就萬事太平。有沒有人看見你到她的化裝室去？這一點很重要。"

道林半晌沒有回答。他嚇呆了。後來終於用喑啞的嗓音結結巴巴地説："亨利，你説要驗屍？這是甚麼意思？難道西碧兒？哦，亨利，我受不了！⋯⋯快説。快把一切都告訴我。"

"我確信這不是不幸的意外事故，道林。但是必須讓外界得到這樣的印象。從報道看來，午夜十二點半左右，她和她母親一起離開劇場時，她説有甚麼東西忘記在樓上。她母親等了她一段時間，可是她沒有再下來。後來她被發現死在化裝室的地上。她誤吞了劇場裏有毒的化裝用品。我不記得究竟是甚麼，反正裏邊含有氫氰酸或鉛白。想必是氰氫酸，因為她看來是當場斃命的。"

"亨利，亨利，這太可怕了！"道林號叫着。

"沒錯，這當然是非常不幸，但你一定不能捲進去。我從《虎報》上知道她今年十七歲，我原以為她更年輕，她看上去像個孩子，而且不懂得表演。道林，你可不能被此事刺激到，你來和我去吃飯，然後我們去看歌劇。今晚的主演是帕蒂，每個人都會出席。你可以來我妹妹的包廂，她有幾個漂亮的女人和她在一起。"

"所以是我殺死了西碧兒·韋恩，"道林·格雷像是在自言自語，"等於用刀子割破她細細的喉嚨。可是，儘管她死了，玫瑰卻還是那麼嬌豔，鳥兒還是那麼歡快地在我花園裏歌唱。今天晚上我還將同你一起吃飯、上歌劇院，然後多半還要去哪兒吃宵夜。生活是多麼富有戲劇性啊！假如我在書上讀到這一切，亨利，我一定會傷感落淚。現在真的發生了這樣的事，而且發生在我自己身上，簡直令人無法相信，所以流不出眼淚。這裏是我平生寫的第一封熱烈的情書。奇怪的是，我的第一封熱烈的情書竟是寫給一個死去的女人。我不禁要問：被我們稱為死人的那些蒼白沉默的軀體有沒有知覺？西碧兒！她會不會感覺到，會不會知道，會不會聽見？哦，亨利，我一度多麼愛她啊！我覺得這像是好多年前的事。她曾經是我的一切。不料來到了那可怕的夜晚 —— 這難道真的僅僅是昨夜的事？—— 她演得那麼糟糕，簡直使我的心都碎了。事後她向我說明了非常可悲的原因。可是我絲毫不為所動。我認為她淺薄無聊。後來，忽然發生了一件使我毛骨悚然的怪事。我不能告訴你那是怎麼回事，總之是極可怕的。我決定回到西碧兒身邊。我意識到自己做了壞事。可現在她死了。天啊！我的上帝！我該怎麼辦啊，亨利？你不知道我面臨着怎樣的危險，又沒有任何人拉我一把。她本來應當挽救我的。她沒有權利自殺。她這是自私的行為。"

"親愛的道林，"亨利勳爵從煙盒裏取出一支煙捲，用一隻鍍金的火柴匣點了火，一面說，"女人使男人改邪歸正的唯一辦法，就是把男人煩死，煩得我們對生活意興索然。你要是娶了那個女人，可就倒霉了。當然，你會待她很好。誰都可以待完全不感興趣的人很好。但是她不久就會發現你對她毫無感情。女人一旦發現丈夫對她毫無感情，她要麼在衣着上顯得惡俗不堪，要麼開始戴非常漂亮的帽子，不過掏錢的是別的女人的丈夫。且不說這樣門第不相當的婚姻多麼丟人，當然，我也不會讓它成為事實，但我敢擔保，這段婚姻在任何情況下都將以徹底的失敗告終。"

"大概是的，"道林低聲說。他在屋子裏來回走着，面色煞白。"但我覺得這是我的責任。這次不幸的事件阻礙了我盡應盡的責任，這不能怪我。我記得你有一次說過：正當的決心注定沒有好的結果，因為這樣的決心總是下得太晚。我的決心便是這樣。"

"嘗試以正當的決心去抗拒自然法則是徒勞的。其根源純粹是虛榮，其結果絕對是無用。這種決心間或能促使我們的感情來一番華而不實的衝動，頗合意志薄弱者的脾胃。除此以外，便沒有甚麼可談的了。這種決心無非是空頭支票。"

"亨利，"道林·格雷叫了一聲，走過來在他旁邊坐下，"為甚麼這個悲劇對我的打擊不如我希望的那麼厲害？難道我如此薄情？你說呢？"

"最近兩個星期你做了那麼多傻事，肯定沒有資格贏得薄情的美名，道林，"亨利勛爵面帶親切而憂鬱的微笑回答。

道林蹙額說："我不喜歡這樣的解釋，亨利，但我感到安慰，因為你不認為我薄情。我決不是那種人，我知道我不是。不過我得承認，所發生的這件事對我的影響並未達到應該有的程度。在我看來，它只是像一個精彩劇本的精彩結尾。它完全具有希臘悲劇裏可怕的美，我在這齣悲劇裏扮演了一個要角，可是心靈卻沒有受到創傷。"

"這是一個頗有意思的問題，"亨利勛爵說。他逗弄着道林不自覺的自私心理，感到妙不可言，其樂無窮。"一個極有趣味的問題。正確的解釋我認為是這樣：生活中真正的悲劇往往以毫無美感可言的形式出現，這些悲劇一味兒猛狂暴，絕對不合邏輯，無謂到荒唐的程度，而且完全不講章法。它們給我們的影響無異於一切鄙俗的事物。它們給我們的印象只是赤裸裸的暴力，於是我們起來反抗。不過，我們在生活中偶爾也會遇到具有藝術美感成分的悲劇。如果這種美的成分貨真價實，整個事情就會引起我們欣賞戲劇效果的興趣。我們會突然發現自己不再是戲劇中的演員，而是觀眾。或者既是演員又是觀眾。我們開始觀察自己，單是這一奇觀本身就能叫我們着迷。以目前這件事情來說，到底發生了甚麼呢？一個女人因為愛你而自殺了。我真希望自己曾有這樣的經歷。它可以使我從此一輩子愛上愛情。我的崇拜者不太多，但有那麼幾個。在我對她們生膩或者她們對我生膩之後，她們都堅持活下去。她們個個發了福，變得很不知趣，見了我立刻大談其往事。女人回首前塵可不得了！管教你啼笑皆非！她們的記憶暴露出她們的智力完全處於停頓狀態！人應該吸收生活的色彩，但千萬不可記住它的細節。細節總是俗不可耐的。"

"我一定要在花園種些罌粟花，"道林歎息道。

"沒有必要，"亨利勛爵回答，"生命的手中一直掌握着罌粟花。當然，有時候事情總讓人揮之不去。我曾經一整季只戴着紫羅蘭花，希望以這種藝術形式來悼念一段不願逝去的浪漫故事，但最終它還是逝去了。我忘了是由甚麼導致的，我猜是因為她提出要為我犧牲整個世界。那總是個可怕的時刻，令人充滿了對永恆的恐懼。你相信嗎？一星期前，在漢普夏夫人家，我發覺自己坐在那個女人的旁邊，而她執意重溫舊事，翻出歷史，找出未來。我已把浪漫史埋葬在長春花糟裹，而她又將它掘出來，説是我毀了她的生活。我必須指出她在晚宴上吃了很多，因此我不必為她擔心。但她是多麼的失儀！過去的魅力就在於它是過去，但女人永不知道何時落幕，她們總想要第六幕。儘管戲劇中的趣味已蕩然無存，她們還希望戲能繼續演下去。如果按她們的心意行事，每套喜劇都會以悲劇結尾，每套悲劇都會以鬧劇終結。她們造作中帶點吸引力，但卻毫無藝術性。你比我幸運得多了。我向你保證，道林，我遇見的每個女人沒有一個會為我做出西碧兒·韋恩為你做的事。普通的女人經常自我安慰，有些會用感情的色彩來尋求慰藉。千萬不要相信穿淡紫色的女人，不論她是甚麼年齡，或者年過三十五歲卻喜歡粉紅色緞帶的女人。這往往意味着她們有過一段歷史。有的女人會突然發現丈夫的美德而得到極大的安慰，在他人面前炫耀婚姻的美滿，好像它是最迷人的罪孽。宗教也會安慰一些人，它的神祕與調情一樣富有魅力，曾有一個女人這麼告訴我，我深表理解。此外，最值得炫耀的是被説成罪人。

良心把我們都變得自我中心。是的，女人可以在現代生活中找到無窮無盡的安慰。實際上，最重要的安慰我還沒提到呢。"

"甚麼，亨利？"道林心不在焉地問。

"哦，最顯然的安慰就是：在失去自己所愛時，把別人的所愛奪過來。在上流社會中，這個辦法總是可以洗刷女人的名聲。道林，你想想，西碧兒‧韋恩跟所有那些尋常的女人是多麼不一樣！她的死包含着一種我認為非常美的成分。我很高興自己生活在一個出現這種奇跡的時代。這些奇跡使人相信，諸如浪漫、激情、愛情般我們大家都視同兒戲的事情確實存在。"

"我對她實在太狠心。這一點你忘了。"

"很難說。女人最賞識的也許正是狠心，赤裸裸的狠心。她們具有極好的原始本能。我們解放了她們，可是她們仍然像奴隸一樣在尋找主人。她們喜歡受人支配。我相信你當時一定壯美至極。我從來沒有見過你真正大發雷霆，但我可以想像你的神態該是多麼動人。還有，前天你對我說過一段話，當時我覺得純粹是異想天開，但現在看來極有道理，而且正是解釋一切的關鍵所在。"

"我說了甚麼，亨利？"

"你對我說，西碧兒‧韋恩在你的心中代表所有浪漫的女主角，一夜她是苔絲狄蒙娜，另一夜她是奧菲莉亞。她若以茱麗葉的身份死去，便以伊摩琴的身份復活。"

"如今她永遠不會復活了，"道林雙手掩面，悲切地說。

"沒錯，她永遠不會復活，她已經演出了最後的一幕戲了。但你一定要把她在那俗氣的更衣室裏獨自死去，看作詹姆斯一世時期某部悲劇中古怪駭人的片段，想成韋伯斯特、福特、西瑞爾·圖納劇本中的美妙場景。那女孩從未活過，亦從未死去。對你而言，至少她永遠是場夢，一個為莎士比亞劇本添色的幽靈，一支為莎士比亞劇中增添歡快醇厚音樂的豎笛。她接觸現實生活的一瞬間，就毀了現實生活，也被現實生活毀了，她亦因此消逝。要是你願意，可以哀悼奧菲莉亞，可以因寇蒂莉亞被絞死而往頭上撒灰，可以為勃拉班修女兒之死而責問上天。但不要把淚水浪費在西碧兒·韋恩身上，她還沒有比這些角色真實。"

接着是一陣沉默。屋子裏的暮色漸濃。不知不覺間銀色的陰影悄然沒聲地從花園裏潛入室內。各種色彩從它們依附的物體上疲憊地褪去。

頃刻，道林·格雷抬起頭來。"你幫助我認識了我自己，亨利，"他低聲說，好像還鬆了一口氣。"你所說的我也感覺到了，可是我害怕這一切，我又不能向自己講清楚。你多麼了解我啊！不過我們不要再提這件事了。這是一次驚心動魄的經歷，謹是如此。我不知道生活是否還能為我提供這樣驚心動魄的奇遇。"

"生活對你來說一應俱全，道林。憑你這樣出類拔萃的美貌，還怕甚麼事情辦不到？"

"可是，亨利，一旦我容顏憔悴，年華老去，臉上佈滿皺紋，那時會怎麼樣？"

"啊，到那時，"亨利勳爵起身準備告辭，"親愛的道林，到那時你得為爭取每一次勝利而苦戰。目前，勝利會送上門來。不，你必須保持你的美貌。我們所處的時代，讀書太多，把腦子都讀糊塗了，想得太多，把容貌都變醜了。你也不能倖免。而現在你最好還是換了裝跟我一起到俱樂部去吃晚飯。我們已經耽擱很久了。”

“我還是直接上歌劇院去找你，亨利。我累得很，甚麼也吃不下。令妹的包廂是幾號？”

“大概是二十七號。在豪華等級。門上有她的姓名。不過你不跟我一起吃晚飯使我很掃興。”

“我實在力不從心，”道林無精打采地説。“但我非常感謝你對我説的那些話。你確實是我最好的朋友。沒有人像你這樣了解我。”

“我們的友誼剛剛開始呢，道林，”亨利勳爵握着他的手説。“再見，我希望在九點半前再見你。別忘了，今晚帕蒂演出。”

等他走出去把門關上後，道林·格雷搖了一下鈴。不一會，維克多拿着燈進來，把簾子放下。道林不耐煩地等着他出去。那侍從磨磨蹭蹭，好像每一件事情都做得沒完沒了。

維克多一出去，道林急忙走到屏風前把它拉開。不，畫像沒有新的變化。在他自己知道西碧兒·韋恩的死訊之前，畫像已經得悉。在他的生活中發生甚麼事情，肖像立刻能感覺到。使輪廓優美的嘴變得猙惡的冷酷表情，無疑在西碧兒·韋恩仰藥的一剎那就出現了。也許，肖像對於他所作所為的結果不感興趣，而只管他靈魂深處的變化，是不是？不知道有朝一日他是否會眼看着肖像起變化？他希望能看到。但想到這裏，他不由得毛骨悚然。

可憐的西碧兒！這一切是多麼浪漫啊！她經常在舞台上模仿死亡。現在死神真的降臨到她頭上，把她帶走了。那慘烈的最後一場她是怎麼演的？她臨終時詛咒了他沒有？不，西碧兒是為他殉情的，對他來說，愛情將永遠保持神聖。西碧兒用自己的生命作犧牲，已把一切都抵償了。他再也不必去想那可怕的晚上在劇場裏西碧兒使他受到的痛苦。他如果想起西碧兒來，那應該是一個動人的悲劇形象，從天上被送到人間舞台上，就是為了顯示愛情無上的真實性。一個動人的悲劇形象？他回想起西碧兒稚氣十足的臉蛋、憨態可掬的癡情和羞羞答答的韻致，禁不住鼻酸淚湧。他趕緊擦了擦眼睛，重新看着畫像。

他覺得，現在確實到了必須作出抉擇的時刻。也許，他已經作出抉擇了？是的，生活本身以及他自己對生活無限的好奇心已代他做了決定。永不憔悴的青春、無法滿足的慾望、神祕奧妙的享受、如醉如狂的快樂和更加瘋狂的墮落——一切都將為他所有。而他恥辱的重荷將由肖像承擔，就這樣了。

想到畫中人俊美的面貌將被糟蹋得不成樣子，一陣痛楚潛入他的心房。有一次，他出於一股孩子氣效法顧影自憐的納西瑟斯，吻了一下，或只是假裝吻了一下畫上那正向他嬝笑的嘴唇。他天天早晨坐在肖像前欣賞它的風采，有時候甚至覺得自己戀上了它。難道今後這幅肖像就要隨着他對每一次誘惑的屈服而變化？難道它必須變成一件可憎可厭的東西而被鎖起來，避開常常照得它金色的鬈髮熠熠生輝的陽光？多可惜呀！多可惜呀！

有那麼一瞬間，他想祈求自己和肖像之間這種令人膽寒的感應從此停止。肖像正是回應以前的一次祈禱起了變化，那麼它也可能回應另一次祈禱而保持不變。然而，只要對生活有一點了解的人，誰肯放棄永葆青春的機會？儘管這可能是一個大好的機會，或者可能孕育着不堪設想的後果。再說，難道他真的能如此從心所欲？難道真是那次祈禱造成了人與肖像的位置對調？這裏頭會不會有某種奇妙的科學道理？既然思想能影響有生命的機體，難道就不能影響死去的機體或無機體？再者，即使撇開思想或有意識的願望，難道我們身外的事物就不能同我們的情緒和感覺發生共振，像原子與原子在某種神祕的引力或親和力的作用下相互趨附？但道理本身並不重要。反正他再也不想通過祈禱來試驗任何可怕的力量。如果肖像要變，就由它去變。何必刨根問底呢？

觀察這個過程倒是一種真正的享受。他將有可能跟隨自己的思想進入神祕的靈魂深處。這幅肖像將成為他最神奇的一面鏡子。如果說過去這面鏡子映出了他的形體，那麼今後將向他揭示他自己的靈魂。即使將來畫中人面臨寒冬，他本人依舊處在春夏之交。即使將來畫中人臉上紅潤的血色消逝，留下一張死灰色的面具和兩顆暗淡無神的眼珠，他本人仍將保持翩翩少年的風采。他那如花的容顏永遠不會枯萎，他生命的脈搏永遠不會衰竭。他將同希臘的神一樣強壯、敏捷、快樂。畫上的形象發生變化又算得上甚麼？只要他本人青春常在，這是最要緊的。

道林把屏風拉回到它原本在肖像前的位置，面露笑意，然後走進臥室。侍從在那裏等候着他。一小時後，他已坐在歌劇院裏，而亨利勛爵正湊近他的座椅。

第九章

第二天上午，道林·格雷正在進早餐，貝澤爾·霍爾渥德在僕人引領下走了進來。

"總算把你找到了，道林，"畫家沉重地說。"昨天晚上我來找你，他們說你上歌劇院去了。我當然不相信，可是你又沒留下行蹤。我一宿沒好好睡覺，生怕一個不幸引起另一個不幸。我以為，你一得到這個消息，就會打電報把我叫來。我是偶然在俱樂部裏拿起一份剛出版的《環球報》才知道的。我立刻上你這兒來，遺憾的是沒有找到你。我沒法向你表達我為這件事難過到甚麼程度。我知道你一定很痛苦。可是你到底去了哪兒？你是不是看那個女孩的母親去了？有一剎那我想跟你到那裏去。報上有死者的地址。在尤斯登路某一個地方，是不是？但我擔心只會干擾而不能減輕別人的悲痛。可憐的韋恩太太！她該多麼傷心啊！何況這是她唯一的孩子！她說了些甚麼？"

"親愛的貝澤爾，我怎麼知道？"道林·格雷不悅地說着，從一隻威尼斯玻璃杯中啜飲泛着金珠般氣泡的淡黃色美酒，神情頗不耐煩。"我的確在歌劇院，你該上那兒去找我。我第一次見到了亨利的妹妹格溫多林夫人。我們坐在她的包廂裏，她可愛極了。帕蒂唱得也十分出色。不要談那些可怕的話題。事情只要不去提它，就等於從來沒有發生過。亨利曾說過，事物是否確實存在，取決於是否有人談論。我可以告訴你，西碧兒不是那女人唯一的孩子。她還有一個兒子，大概也挺可愛。但他並不演戲。聽說他在船上當水手。好啦，談談你自己吧。最近你在畫甚麼？」

「你上歌劇院去了？」霍爾渥德說得很慢，語氣緊張而沉痛。「西碧兒‧韋恩還躺在髒亂不堪的公寓裏，而你居然上歌劇院去了？曾經為你所愛的女人還沒有入土長眠，你居然向我談論別的女人如何可愛，帕蒂有多麼了不起的歌唱天才？老弟啊，還有好多恐怖景象在等着她嬌小蒼白的軀體呢！」

「別說了，貝澤爾！我不要聽！」道林大聲說着，霍地立起身來。「你不必對我講這些事情。事已至此，往事已經過去了。」

「難道昨天的事對你已經是‘往事’？」

「這與時間的長短遠近沒有關係。淺薄的俗物需要幾年時間才能擺脫某種感情的束縛。有自持力的人結束哀傷就像找到快樂一樣容易。我不想被自己的感情牽着鼻子走。相反，我要利用、享受、支配自己的感情。」

「道林，這太可怕了！顯然有甚麼事情使你變成了另一個人。從外貌看，你還是那個天天到我畫室裏來給我當模特兒的好孩子。但當初你純樸自然，充滿深情。你本來是整個世界上最清白的人。如今，我不知你被甚麼迷住了心竅。你說話好像全無心肝，沒有半點同情。這都是受了亨利的影響。我看得出來。」

道林的臉一下子漲得通紅，他走到窗前，看看花園在陽光下被暑氣蒸得搖曳顫動的一派荽鬱氣象。「貝澤爾，我從亨利獲益的地方，」他終於說，「比從你獲益的地方多得多。你僅僅啟發了我的虛榮心。」

「我已經因此受到懲罰，道林，或者總有一天要受到懲罰。」

"我不明白你的意思，貝澤爾，"他轉過身來說。"我不明白你要甚麼。你到底要甚麼？"

"我要我所畫的那個道林·格雷，"畫家悲切地回答。

"貝澤爾，"道林走過來，把一隻手放到他的肩膀上說，"你來遲了。昨天我得悉西碧兒·韋恩自殺的消息——"

"自殺？天啊！你確信她是自殺的？"霍爾渥德驚駭地抬頭望着道林，失聲叫了起來。

"親愛的貝澤爾！難道你真以為這是一般的意外事故？她當然是自殺的。"

畫家雙手掩面。"多麼可怕！"他說不出別的話來，渾身哆嗦不已。

"不，"道林·格雷說，"這沒甚麼好怕，這是這個時代偉大的愛情悲劇。演員總過着最普通的生活。他們是好丈夫、忠誠的妻子，或是乏味的人。你知道我說甚麼，那些中產階級的美德和其他類似的東西。西碧兒是多麼的與眾不同！她演出了最出色的悲劇，她將永遠是個女主角。她演出的最後一個夜晚，你看到她的那個晚上，她演得那麼糟是因為她已經懂得愛情的現實。當她知道它的虛構，她就像茱麗葉般死去。她重新進入藝術的疆界，身上有種殉道者的味道。她的死亡具有殉道的所有悲哀徒勞，以及所有荒廢的美。但在我說這話的同時，你絕不能以為我沒有受苦。如果你昨天在特定的時間過來，大約是五點半還是五點四十正分，你會看見我在哭泣。即使是為我帶來這個消息的亨利，他雖然在場，也不知道我實際經歷了些甚麼。我極為痛苦，然後痛苦就消散了。我無法重覆一種情感，除了多愁善感的人外，無人能夠。貝澤爾你很不講道理。我很感謝你來這裏安慰我，但當你發現我已得到安慰的時候，你又勃然大怒。這怎麼像有同情心的人！你令我想起一個亨利告訴我的故事，一個慈善家用了二十年時間嘗試伸冤，或是改變某條不公平的法律，我忘記了是哪個。最後他成功了，卻大失所望。他沒有任何事做，幾乎死於無聊，變成了一個確確實實的厭世者。除此之外，我親愛的老朋友貝澤爾，要是你真的想安慰我，那就教我如何忘記已經發生的事，或者教我如何以一個正確的藝術觀點來看待此事。哥提耶不是寫過藝術的慰藉嗎？我記得有一天在你的畫室裏拿起一本牛皮封面的小書，偶然看到那些精彩的句子。我不像那個你在馬洛向我提起的年輕人，他總說黃色緞子能慰藉生活的一切痛苦。我喜歡能夠摸得着、碰得着的美麗東西。不管是古老的錦緞、青銅器、漆器工藝品、象牙雕刻、精美的環境、奢華的陳設，這些東西都使人獲益良多。但對我來說，這些東西所創造或展示的藝術氣質更重要。正如亨利所說，成為自己人生的旁觀者是逃避生活的痛苦。我知道你對我所說的話感到很驚奇，因為你沒有意識到我已經成長了。你認識我的時候，我還是個男生。如今我是個男人，擁有新的激情、新的思想、新的想法。雖然我改變了，但你得跟以前一樣喜歡我。雖然我改變了，但你得永遠是我的朋友。當然我很喜歡亨利，但我知道你是個比他更好的人。你不比他強壯，你太害怕生活，但你是個更好的人。我們以前在一起的時候是多麼的快樂！不要離開我，貝澤爾，不要和我爭吵。我就是我，沒有別的好說了。"

這番話奇怪地打動了畫家的心。他無限鍾愛道林，這個年輕人是他創作道路上一個重大的轉折點。他沒有勇氣再責備他。歸根到底，道林的冷漠也許是一種暫時的情緒。他身上有那麼多善良的成分，有那麼多高尚的品質。

"好吧，道林，"霍爾渥德終於帶着一絲苦笑説。"從今天起，我再也不向你提起這件可怕的事情。但願你不要受到牽連。驗屍定於今天下午舉行。他們有沒有傳召你？"

道林搖搖頭，聽到"驗屍"這兩個字，他臉上顯出一種厭煩的神情。這類事情照例鄙俗而無聊。"他們不知道我的姓名，"他回答説。

"可是那女孩總該知道吧？"

"她只知道我叫道林，不知道我姓甚麼，而且我確信她沒有對任何人説過。有一次她告訴我，人家都想打聽我是何許人，她一概回答説我叫迷人王子。真虧她想得出來。貝澤爾，你得為我畫一張西碧兒的畫像。在我的記憶中，只有幾次親吻和一些悲傷的話語。除此以外，我還想保留一些對她的紀念。"

"那我就試試看，道林，只要你喜歡。不過你必須到畫室裏來再給我當模特兒。我少不了你。""我不能再給你當模特兒，貝澤爾。這辦不到！"他説着，猛然退後兩步。

畫家直勾勾地望着他。"我的老弟，你胡説些甚麼！"他驚問。"你是不是不喜歡我給你畫的肖像？它在哪兒？你為甚麼用屏風把它遮起來？讓我看看它。這是我生平最好的作品。把屏風拉開，道林。這一定是你的傭人做的混賬事，居然把我的作品這樣藏起來。怪不得我進來的時候覺得有些異樣。"

"這跟我的傭人沒有關係，貝澤爾。你以為我能讓傭人做主佈置我的房間？他頂多有時候為我搬動一下花卉。不，屏風是我放在那裏的。因為射在畫像上的光線太強。"

"太強？不見得吧，老弟？那地方非常合適。讓我看看去。"說完，霍爾渥德向房間的那個角落走過去。

一聲驚駭的急叫從道林‧格雷口中衝出來，他搶步上前，站在畫家和屏風之間。"貝澤爾，"他嚇得面如土色，"你看不得。我不要你看。"

"我自己的作品不讓看！你開甚麼玩笑？為甚麼我不能看？"霍爾渥德笑問。

"你要是敢看一眼，貝澤爾，我發誓這輩子再也不跟你說話。我不是開玩笑。我不打算作任何解釋，你甚麼也不要問。但是你得記住：你要是碰一下這道屏風，你我之間就算完了。"

霍爾渥德像捱了當頭一棒。他望着道林‧格雷，呆若木雞。畫家以前從來沒有見過他這個模樣。道林因狂怒而臉色發白。他攥緊兩個拳頭，一對瞳孔射出青光，全身抖個不停。

"道林！"

"住口！"

"你這是怎麼啦？既然你不想我看，我當然不會看，"霍爾渥德相當冷淡地說，並轉身向窗口走去。"不過，說真的，我自己的作品竟不讓我看，這未免太不講理。我還打算秋天把它送到巴黎去展出呢。在這之前，恐怕需要給它重新上一道油光漆，所以我總有一天要看。那麼，為甚麼今天不能看呢？"

"把它送去展出？你要把它展出？"道林‧格雷連聲問道，同時一種詭異的恐怖感潛入他的心房。難道要把他的祕密向世人公開？讓人們飽看他的私隱？這可不行！必須立即採取對策，然而他不知道該怎麼辦。

"是的，對此你大概不會有異議。喬治·珀蒂打算收集我最好的作品，十月初在巴黎賽澤街舉辦一次專題畫展。這幅肖像拿去頂多一個月就送回來。我想你能慨然允諾暫借一段時間，反正那時你不在倫敦。而且，你既然老是用屏風把它遮起來，可見對它興趣不大。"

道林·格雷伸手抹了抹額上的冷汗，覺得自己正面臨着不堪設想的危險。"一個月之前你對我說過，你決不展出這幅肖像，"他氣急敗壞地說。"你為甚麼改變了主意？你們這些人口口聲聲堅定不變，事實上跟別人一樣反覆無常。唯一的區別就是你們的情緒沒有甚麼意義。你曾經極其鄭重地向我保證，無論甚麼都不能誘使你把它送往任何展覽，難道你忘了？你對亨利也講過同樣的話。"他突然頓住，眼睛一下子變得明亮起來。他想起亨利勛爵有一次半認真半玩笑地對他說過："你如果願意度過奇妙的十五分鐘，不妨叫貝澤爾談談他為甚麼不肯展出你的肖像。他跟我談過其中的原因，這對我來說是一大發現。"對，說不定貝澤爾也有自己的祕密。得試探一下。

"貝澤爾，"他走近畫家前面，兩眼直盯着他的臉說。"你我都有自己的祕密。讓我先了解你的祕密，然後我把我的祕密告訴你。你拒絕展出我的肖像，到底是甚麼原因？"

畫家情不自禁地周身為之顫慄。"道林，我要是告訴了你，你會減少對我的好感，而且一定會取笑我。這兩者我都受不了。如果你要我再也不看你的肖像，我同意，反正我隨時可以看着你本人。如果你要把我生平最好的作品藏起來不讓世人看到，我也樂意。你的友誼對我來說比任何名望聲譽更寶貴。"

"不，貝澤爾，你必須告訴我，"道林·格雷堅持要他講。"我認為我有權了解。"他的恐懼已被好奇所取代。他拿定主意要把貝澤爾·霍爾渥德的謎底揭開。

"我們坐下談，道林，"畫家面有難色。"坐下。你先回答我一個問題：你是否發覺畫像有甚麼奇怪的地方？是否有甚麼地方起初也許沒有引起你的注意，可是後來忽然被你發覺了？"

"貝澤爾！"道林驚呼一聲，一雙發抖的手牢牢抓住椅子的扶手，眼睛睜得老大，瞪着霍爾渥德。

"我看出你發覺到了。別說話，先聽我要說的。道林，從我遇見你的一刻，你的人格就對我產生了異於尋常的影響，我的靈魂、腦袋和精力都被你支配。看不見的理想像美夢一樣常在我們藝術家的記憶中縈繞不去，而你在我眼裏已成為這理想可見的化身。我崇拜你，我妒忌所有跟你說話的人，我希望你全屬於我。只有在和你一起的時候，我才會快樂。當你不在我的身邊，你仍然在我的藝術裏……當然我不曾告訴過你，我不可能這樣做，因為你不會理解。我自己也難以理解。我只知道我面對着完美，世界在我眼中變得美好，也許過於美好了，因為這種瘋狂的崇拜存在着失去崇拜物件的風險，並不亞於保持崇拜物件的危險……週復一週，我越來越沉迷於你。然後有了新的發展，我把你畫成身穿精美盔甲的帕里斯，頭戴沉甸甸的蓮花花冠，坐在哈德良國王的船頭，凝視着尼羅河綠色的濁浪；又把你畫成穿着獵人斗篷、手持鋥亮的標槍的阿多尼斯，俯視着希臘森林裏的一汪平靜的湖水，在寂靜的銀鏡中看到了自己驚豔的容顏。這些都是藝術應有的樣子——無意識、理想化、遙不可及。有一天，我有時會想那是致命的一天，我決定要為你畫一幅奇妙的肖像，跟你一模一樣的畫，不是穿着古代服裝，而是在你的時代穿着你自己的服裝。我說不清是因為採用現實主義的畫法，還是因為你毫無掩飾地直接把你純粹的人格魅力呈現在我面前，但我知道我作畫時的每個筆觸、每層顏色都似是透露着我的祕密。我怕別人會知道我的崇拜。道林，我覺得我流露的東西太多了，我把太多自己的東西放進去了，因此我決定絕不會展出這幅畫。你當時有點生氣，但你不明白這一切對我的意義。我和亨利說過此事，他嘲笑我，但我不在意。畫像完成之後，我獨自坐在它旁邊，我覺得自己是正確的……過了幾天，畫像離開了畫室，當我一擺脫畫像存在所產生的難以抗拒的吸引力，就覺得自己很傻，除了你極為漂亮的外表和我作畫的能力外，我竟會臆想自己從中看到了別的東西。直至現在，我還是禁不住覺得，人在創作中感受到的激情會在其作品中真實呈現這個想法是錯誤的。藝術總比我們想像的更抽象，形狀和顏色僅僅代表着形狀和顏色。我常常覺得比起揭露藝術家自身，藝術更能掩飾他。因此當我收到來自巴黎的邀請之後，我就決定把你的畫像作為展覽的主要作品。我從未想到你會拒絕，但我現在明白了，你是對的，這幅畫不能展示。你千萬不能因為我告訴你的事而生我的氣，道林。正如我對亨利說的，你生來是受人崇拜的。

道林·格雷深深地舒了一口氣。他的兩頰恢復了紅潤，嘴唇周圍又泛起微笑。危險過去了。暫時他可以放心。但他禁不住無限憐憫剛才向他作了這番奇怪自白的畫家，心想："我自己會不會這樣拜倒在一個朋友腳下？亨利勛爵的吸引力在於他是個危險人物，但也就到此為止。他過於聰明，過於尖刻，所以不能真正贏得別人的心。有沒有人能激起我崇拜偶像的感情？生活是否也能提供這樣的機會呢？"

"道林，"霍爾渥德說，"你竟從畫像中看出了這一點，我非常驚訝。你真的看到了嗎？"

"我看到了一些東西，"他答道，"一些我覺得很有趣的東西。"

"那麼，現在可不可以讓我看看它。"

道林搖搖頭。"貝澤爾，你不應該提出這個要求。我決不能讓你站在畫像前面。"

"將來總可以吧？"

"永遠不可以。"

"好吧，也許你有道理。我該走了，道林。你是我一生中唯一真正影響了我的創作的人。我的作品如有可取之處，應當歸功於你。啊！你無法想像，剛才我向你說出的那一番話是多麼不容易呵！"

"親愛的貝澤爾，"道林說，"你向我說了些甚麼呀？你只是說你覺得對我的讚賞過了頭。這甚至算不上恭維。"

"我說這話可不是為了恭維你。這是一篇自白。現在我覺得好像失去了甚麼。也許對人的崇拜不應當用言語來表達。"

"這是一篇令人失望的自白。"

"為甚麼？你原先指望聽到甚麼，道林？你是不是從畫像上看到了別的東西？沒有其他東西可看了吧。"

"沒有，別的甚麼也沒有。你別問了。你不要再談甚麼崇拜了，這簡直愚蠢。你我是朋友，貝澤爾，我們應當永遠做朋友。"

"現在你有亨利了，"畫家說着，黯然神傷。

"哦，你說亨利？"道林發出一陣清脆的笑聲。"亨利白天盡說不足信的話，晚上盡做不可能的事。這正是我喜歡的那種生活。不過，萬一我遇到甚麼患難，我大概不會去找亨利。我多半會找你，貝澤爾。"

"你再來給我當模特兒，行嗎？"

"不行！"

"你的拒絕將斷送我的藝術生涯，道林。任何人都不可能遇上兩個理想的形象。一個已經是鳳毛麟角了。"

"我沒法向你解釋，貝澤爾，反正我不能再給你當模特兒。每一幅肖像都連帶着某種致命的因素，都有它自己的生命。我願意到你那裏去跟你一起喝茶，那同樣是挺愉快的。"

"恐怕對你更愉快些，"霍爾渥德不勝惋惜地說。"再見吧，道林。遺憾的是你不讓我再看一眼這幅畫像。這也沒有辦法。你的心情我完全理解。"

他走後，道林・格雷暗暗在笑。可憐的貝澤爾！他完全被蒙在鼓裏！道林非但沒有被逼吐露真情，反而在無意中套出朋友心底的祕密，你說怪不怪！貝澤爾這番不尋常的自白使道林明白了許多事情。畫家幾次莫名其妙的妒意發作、他的一片癡情、他的無比慷慨的諛辭，以及有時候欲言又止的奇怪態度。這一切道林現在全明白了，並為此感到內疚。在他看來，這種帶有浪漫色彩的友誼，包含着悲劇的成分。

他歎息着按了一下鈴。畫像無論如何得藏起來。他不能再冒被發現祕密的風險。除非是瘋子，否則決不能讓肖像繼續放在隨時可能被他的朋友闖進來的房間裏，哪怕一小時也拖延不得。

第十章

侍從進來了，道林目不轉睛地盯着他，心想他有沒有想到向屏風後面偷看一眼。維克多毫無表情地等候吩咐。道林點了一支煙捲，走到鏡子前面，瞧着鏡子，這樣他可以把維克多的面孔看得一清二楚。那是一張不動聲色的順從的面孔。沒有甚麼可擔心。不過道林認為還是要留神提防。

道林一字一句説得很慢，他吩咐維克多先把女管家叫來，然後到畫框店去，要那邊立刻派兩個人來。道林覺得，維克多走出房間的時候曾向屏風那邊瞟了一眼。不過也許這僅僅是他自己多心？

過不多久，女管家黎甫太太身穿黑色絲綢裙子，佈滿皺紋的手戴着老式線手套，急匆匆地走進書齋。道林向她要課室的鑰匙。

"你是説老課室嗎，道林先生？"她驚訝地問。"哎呀，那兒全是灰塵。你要進去的話，我得先把它打掃一下，收拾收拾。現在你去不得。真的，去不得。"

"我不要你收拾，黎甫。你只要把鑰匙給我。"

"不，先生，你走進去一定會蒙上一身蜘蛛網。自從勛爵故去之後，那間屋子差不多有五年沒打開過。"

道林聽到她提起他的外祖父，臉上很不自在。外祖父留給他的回憶是可憎的。"不要緊，"道林對女管家説。"我只要看一下那個地方，沒有其他事。你把鑰匙給我。"

"鑰匙在這裏，先生，"老婦人説着，不聽使喚的手顫巍巍地從一大串鑰匙裏挑揀。"是這把，我馬上就把它從鑰匙串上拿下來。你不是想搬到那裏去住吧，先生？你在這裏挺舒服的。"

"不，不，"道林不耐煩了。"謝謝你，黎甫，沒你的事了。"

女管家還逗留了一會，喋喋不休地説了些家務瑣事。道林歎了一口氣，叫她瞧着辦就是了。黎甫太太滿面堆笑地走了出去。

門關上後，道林把鑰匙放入口袋，向室內四周打量了一番。他的視線落在一張用金線繡得密密麻麻的紫緞大罩布上。這是他外祖父從波隆那附近一座修道院弄來的一件出色的十七世紀晚期威尼斯工藝品。對，就用它來罩那幅可怕的肖像。這幅罩布可能多次蓋過靈柩，現在就讓它來遮蓋一件腐化程度遠較屍體為甚的東西，一件使人為之戰慄而又永遠不會死亡的東西。如同蛆蟲啃蝕屍體一樣，他的罪惡將啃蝕畫中人的形象。他做的壞事將損毀肖像的風采，蠶食它的韻致，把它糟蹋得不成樣子，使它蒙受恥辱。然而肖像本身將繼續存在，永遠活下去。

他打了個哆嗦，有一刻他後悔沒有把藏起畫像的真實原因告訴貝澤爾。貝澤爾會幫助他抵抗亨利勛爵的影響，以及源自於他個性更有害的影響。貝澤爾對他的愛，正因為是真正的愛，沒有一絲不高尚或不知性。這不僅是對肉體美的愛慕，隨感官的亢奮而來，因感官的疲憊而去，而是一種米高安哲羅、蒙田、溫克爾曼以及莎士比亞所感受的愛。是啊，貝澤爾本可以拯救他，但現在已經太遲了。過去總可以以悔恨、否認或遺忘來抹去，但未來是無法避免的。他內心的激情總要找到可怕的出口，夢想總會把罪惡的影子變成現實。

他把罩在榻上的那一大塊金繡紫緞織物取下來，拿着它走到屏風背後。畫中人的面孔是不是更邪惡了？看來還是那樣。然而道林對它的厭惡更強烈了。金色的頭髮、碧藍的眼睛、玫瑰紅的嘴唇都同原本一樣，就是表情變了，冷酷得叫人害怕。與畫中人的非難或申斥相比，剛才貝澤爾為西碧兒‧韋恩的事對他的責備太不足道了！簡直算不上一回事！他自己的靈魂從畫布上逼視着他，責令他接受審判。一片痛苦的陰影浮上道林的面龐，他急忙把富麗的緞罩覆蓋在畫像上。這時有人在敲門。他從屏風背後轉出來時，他的侍從走了進來。

"你要的人已經來了，先生。"

道林思量着，必須立刻把維克多支開。畫像要搬到哪裏去不能讓他知道。這傢伙有點狡猾，那雙眼睛說明他有頭腦和不可信賴。道林在書桌旁坐下，草草寫了封短簡給亨利勛爵，請他帶幾本書來，並提醒他晚上八點十五分見面。

"你要等候回覆，"道林把信交給他，"你把那兩個人帶進來。"

過了兩三分鐘，敲門聲又起。奧德麗南大街上有名的畫框店老闆赫巴德先生親自帶了一個粗眉大眼的年輕夥計走進來。赫巴德先生身材矮小，面色紅潤，蓄着棕紅色的連鬢鬍子。由於他經常與窮愁潦倒的畫家打交道，使他對藝術的熱愛也大為降低。照例他從不離開他的鋪子，總是等主顧上門，但卻隨時樂意為道林‧格雷破例。道林有一種能使任何人產生好感的魔力。只要見到他，本身就是一件樂事。

"有甚麼能幫到你，格雷先生？"他搓着長滿斑的肥手說，"我想我很榮幸能親自到您府上效勞。最近我在大減價的時候買了一個漂亮的畫框，是古佛羅倫斯風格的，我想是來自豐塞爾的，非常適合宗教題材的畫，格雷先生。"

"我很抱歉麻煩你枉駕親臨，赫巴德先生。我一定上寶號去看看那個框子，儘管目前我對宗教藝術的興趣不是很大。不過今天只要給我把一幅畫搬到最高一層樓上去。東西重得很，所以我想請你派兩個人來。"

"一點也不麻煩，格雷先生。我很高興能為你效勞。哪一幅畫，先生？"

"是這一幅，"道林把屏風拉開。"就這樣連蓋着的罩布一起搬，行不行？我怕在上樓的時候給刮壞了。"

"沒問題，先生。"和氣的畫框店老闆說着，在他的夥計幫助下開始動手，把畫從吊住它的銅質長鏈條取下。"格雷先生，往哪兒搬？"

"我給你們引路，赫巴德先生，請跟我來。或者你們走在前面。很抱歉，一直要搬到最頂的一層。我們從正中的樓梯上去，那裏比較寬。"

道林為他們扶着打開的門，他們從書齋進入門廳，開始上樓。極其講究的畫框使這幅畫極之笨重，道林也不時插手進去助一臂之力，儘管赫巴德先生一再客氣地請他不要幫忙。身為一個地道的商人，他認為有身分的紳士親自動手做事是萬萬使不得的。

"是有點重量，先生，"到了頂層的樓梯口，這位小個子老闆氣喘吁吁地說。他擦了擦額上亮晶晶的汗水。

"確實重得厲害，"道林附和着說，他用鑰匙打開了房門，這間屋子將為他保守生命中奇異的祕密，將他的靈魂藏匿起來，不讓世人看到。

他已有四年多沒有到這裏來了。當他是個小孩的時候，他在這裏玩耍；稍長，他就在這裏讀書。這間寬敞的課室是已故的克爾索勛爵造給外孫專用的。由於道林酷肖他的母親，再加上其他原因，克爾索始終嫌棄他的外孫，總是希望他離得遠些。道林覺得課室幾乎沒有甚麼變化。那個着色精美、鍍金緣飾已經黯然失色的意大利大箱櫃還放在那兒，他小時候常常躲在裏邊。一架椴木書櫃塞滿了他摺滿書角的課本。書櫃背後的牆上依舊掛着那張殘舊的佛蘭德斯掛毯，上面褪色的國王和皇后在花園裏對弈，一羣侍從騎馬經過，他們戴着護手套的手腕上蹲着頭套罩子的獵鷹。這一切他都記得很清楚！當他四下環顧的時候，他孤獨的幼年景象又歷歷在目。他回憶起潔白無瑕的童年時代，而現在卻偏偏要把這幅不祥的畫像藏在這個地方，不免使他感到駭然。在那些逝去的歲月裏，他做夢也想不到命運竟會給他作出這樣的安排！

可是屋內沒有別的地方像此處這樣穩當，外人是看不見的。鑰匙由他掌管，誰也進不去。畫中人的面孔可能會在紫色柩罩下變得猙獰、霉爛、不潔。那有甚麼關係？反正沒人看見。他自己也看不見。何必眼睜睜看着自己的靈魂令人作嘔地墮落下去。只要能保住他的青春就夠了。再說，難道他的本性就不能變得好一些嗎？憑甚麼理由斷言未來必定不堪設想？愛情也許會降臨到他的生活，使他洗心革面，摒除似乎已經在他的靈魂與肉體中萌動的邪念。這些尚未被描繪過的邪念，單憑其神祕新奇就具有難以捉摸的吸引力。也許某一天，冷酷的表情會從敏感的猩紅色嘴唇周圍消失，那時他可以讓世人都來欣賞貝澤爾·霍爾渥德的這一傑作。

不，這是不可能的。畫中人將一小時比一小時、一星期比一星期變得蒼老。縱使它能逃避罪惡可怕的烙印，也無法不讓年齡留下無情的標記。兩頰將深陷或鬆垂，暗淡無神的眼睛周圍將佈滿黃色的眼角皺紋，使人望而生厭。頭髮將失去光澤，嘴巴將老是張開或下垂，顯得傻氣愚昧或令人噁心，跟很多老頭的嘴巴沒甚麼兩樣。皮膚皺縮的頸項、青筋暴突的手背、彎曲變形的體態，這就是道林記憶中外祖父的樣子。在道林的少年時代，他對道林的態度始終冷漠而嚴厲。畫像非藏起來不可，除此別無他法。

"請把它搬進來吧，赫巴德先生，"他轉過身來說道，顯得有些倦意。"真對不起，我剛才在想別的事情出了神，讓你久等了。"

"我總是很樂意歇一歇，格雷先生，"畫框店老闆回答，他還沒有喘過氣來。"把它放在哪兒，先生？"

"隨便哪兒都行。就放在這兒吧，行了。我不需要把它掛起來，靠在牆壁上就可以了。謝謝。"

"可以看看這件藝術品嗎，先生？"

道林嚇了一跳。"你不會感興趣的，赫巴德先生，"他盯着畫框店老闆回答說。如果他膽敢揭開藏匿着他個人私隱的華麗緞罩，道林隨時準備撲上去把他打倒在地。"我不想再麻煩你了。這次勞煩你親自來，我非常感激。"

"不客氣，不客氣，格雷先生。我隨時願意為你效勞，先生。"於是，赫巴德先生腳步沉重地走下樓去。跟在後面的夥計回頭向道林瞅了一眼，粗陋的臉上帶着不好意思的驚異神情。他從未見過這樣漂亮的人物。

他們的腳步聲去遠後，道林鎖上房門，把鑰匙放在口袋裏。

現在他放心了。再也沒有人會向這件可怕的東西看一眼。除他以外，他的恥辱不會落在任何別人的眼睛裏了。

回到書齋，他發現時間剛過五點，茶點已經擺好。在一張鑲嵌了不少珍珠母的深色香木茶几上，他看到了亨利勛爵的回信。茶几是他監護人之妻瑞德利夫人送的禮物，她終年忙於為自己治病，去年冬天還在開羅療養。旁邊有一本書，黃色的封面紙稍許有些破損，頁邊也比較髒。茶盤裏放着一份第三版的《聖詹姆士報》。顯然，維克多已經回來。不知畫框店的兩個人出去時有沒有在門廳跟他碰上？他有沒有向這兩個人打聽主人要他們做甚麼？維克多必將發覺畫像不見了。不，在他擺上茶具的時候無疑已經發覺了。屏風沒有放回原處，牆上的一塊空白非常顯眼。説不定某一天夜裏，他會撞見維克多躡手躡腳上樓準備破門進入課室。家裏有密探是件頭痛的事情。他曾聽説有些富人一輩子遭到某個僕人的訛詐，就因為被他看到一封信，或者偷聽到一次對話，或者撿到一張有地址的名片，或者在枕頭底下發現一朵枯萎的花或一綹揉皺的花邊。

道林歎了口氣，他給自己倒了一杯茶，把亨利勛爵的信拆開。信裏邊簡單地寫着，他會給道林帶一份晚報和一本道林也許會感興趣的書，並説他會在八點十五分準時到俱樂部。道林懶洋洋地把《聖詹姆士報》翻了一遍，第五頁上用紅鉛筆標出的地方引起了他的注意。那裏登着一則報道：

女演員驗屍調查完成

今晨，地區驗屍官丹比先生在霍克斯頓路貝爾旅館，對新近就職於霍爾本皇家劇院的年輕女演員西碧兒·韋恩，進行了驗屍調查。驗屍結論為意外死亡。死者母親在作供和比勒爾法醫驗屍時，情緒非常激動，眾人深表同情。

道林緊皺眉頭，把報紙撕成兩半，走到房間的另一端去扔掉。醜惡至極！這貨真價實的醜惡真是太可怕了！他有點生亨利勛爵的氣，不該把這份報紙送來。尤其糊塗的是還用紅鉛筆作了記號。維克多可能已經先看到了。他認得的字足夠看懂這篇報道。

也許他看了之後已開始生疑。不過，那又怎麼樣呢？西碧兒‧韋恩的死跟道林‧格雷有甚麼相干？不用害怕。又不是道林‧格雷殺了她。

他的視線落在亨利勛爵給他帶來的那本黃封面的書上。他不知這是本怎樣的書。他走到珍珠色的八角形茶几前，拿起了那本書，在一張扶手椅上坐下來，開始翻閱。道林總覺得那張茶几好像是由某種神祕的埃及蜜蜂用銀搭製的。幾分鐘後，他被吸引住了。他從來沒有讀過這樣一本奇書。他覺得，彷彿全世界的罪惡都穿上了精美的衣服，在柔美的長笛聲伴奏下默默地從他面前無言地走過。以前他曾迷離恍惚地夢見的事物，一下子都變得十分真實，而他連做夢都沒有想過的事物，也逐漸顯露出形象。

這本小說沒有情節，只有一個角色，單單是研究一個巴黎青年的心理狀況。這個青年用他的一生在十九世紀實現屬於每個世紀而非他身處時代的一切慾望和思想。他想集所有能體現世界精神的情感於一身。他喜歡那種純粹裝模作樣的克制，卻被人愚蠢地稱為美德；他同樣喜歡那種天性的反叛，卻被聰明人稱為罪惡。這本書的寫作風格奇異，生動及晦澀兼具，充滿行話、古語、術語，以及詳細的釋義，擁有某些法國最優秀的象徵主義作品的特徵。書中的比喻如蘭花一樣，形狀古怪，顏色微妙。感官的生活以神祕的哲學語言來描寫，令人弄不清自己在讀某個中世紀聖人的精神極樂，還是一個現代罪人的病態自白。這是一本有毒的書，書頁間濃重的焚香味擾亂大腦。隨他一章章看下去，句子的抑揚頓挫，以及由複雜的疊句和重複的樂章組成微妙單調的音樂，在他的腦海中激起一種幻想，如同得了夢遊症。即使夕陽西下，夜幕低垂，他也毫不自覺。

窗外銅綠色的蒼穹萬里無雲，刺破天幕的唯見孤星一顆。道林在暮色蒼茫中讀着讀着，直到再也無法辨認書上的字句。侍從數次提醒他時間已經不早，道林這才起身走到隔壁房間裏去，把書放在一直在自己牀邊的一張佛羅倫斯小桌子上，開始換上晚裝赴晚餐。

他到俱樂部快九點了，發現亨利勛爵獨坐在休息室裏，神態很不耐煩。

"對不起，亨利，"道林說，"不過這完全是你的過錯。你帶來的那本書把我迷住了，使我忘記了時間。"

"我知道你會喜歡它的，"亨利勛爵從椅子站起來。

"我沒有說我喜歡它，亨利。我是說它把我迷住了。這兩者大有區別。"

"啊，你已經發現了這種區別？"亨利勛爵含糊其辭地說。於是他們一同步入餐室。

第十一章

道林・格雷有好幾年不能擺脫那本書的影響。也許，更確切一點的說法是他自己從未試圖從中擺脫出來。他從巴黎弄到多達九冊該書的初版大開本，並用不同顏色的封面重新裝訂，以便適應他不同的情緒和變化多端的奇想怪癖，而他對這種脾性有時好像已完全失去控制。那個主人公，那個獨特的巴黎青年，身上十分奇怪地糅合着浪漫和科學的氣質，在道林心目中成了他自己的原型。而整本書所講的就好像是他自己一生的故事，只不過他還沒有經歷過便已經寫下來了。

有一點他比小說中古怪的主人公更幸運。那個巴黎青年顯然一度也是十分漂亮的，但突然香消玉殞，所以他從很早的時候起就對鏡子、表面光滑的金屬、平靜的水面產生一種病態的恐懼。這種感覺道林並沒有，也永遠不會產生。這本書的後半部分，作者以真正的悲劇筆法，或許稍帶誇張地，刻畫了一個人的悲哀和絕望，因為他認為自己失去了別人身上以及普天之下最寶貴的品質。道林對這一部分總是懷着幸災樂禍的心情加以欣賞。其實，每一種樂趣和快感可能都含有幸災樂禍的成分，幾乎沒有例外。

看來道林似乎永遠不會失去貝澤爾・霍爾渥德以及其他許多人為之傾倒的稀世美貌。關於他生活方式的種種離奇的流言蜚語已傳遍整個倫敦，成了俱樂部議論不休的話題。但那些人即使聽過極度不利他的壞話，只要一看見他，就無法相信任何有損他名譽的事情。他始終像個身居濁世而出塵不染的人。人們本來在談論穢聞褻事，道林‧格雷一進來，便立即鴉雀無聲。他純潔無邪的面容有一種使人感到內疚的力量。只要他在場，人們就會慨歎他們也曾是無瑕的白璧，但被自己糟蹋了。在他們看來，像他這樣的翩翩美男子，居然能不為人慾橫流的時代所玷污，殊屬罕見。

他經常會神祕地失蹤一段很長的時間，因而在他的朋友以及那些自命為他的朋友中間引起種種奇怪的臆測。每次回到家裏，他總會偷偷地上樓，走向那間鎖着的課室，用始終不離身的鑰匙把門打開，手執一面鏡子，站在貝澤爾‧霍爾渥德為他畫的肖像前，看看畫中人猙獰可惡、愈來愈老的面孔，再看看鏡子裏向他盈盈微笑的英俊臉龐。強烈的對比刺激着他的快感。他變得更加鍾愛自己的美貌，也更加欣賞自己靈魂的墮落。他會懷着殘暴且具病態的樂趣，細細地端詳刻在皺紋累累的前額或簇聚在淫邪的厚嘴唇周圍的醜惡線條，有時他自己也説不上：罪惡的烙印和年齡的標記，究竟哪個更可怕？他把自己白淨的手放在畫像上變得粗糙而浮腫的手旁邊，臉上露出笑容。他嘲笑畫中人形態發生畸變，肢體日益衰敗。

夜晚，當他無眠地躺在自己異香撲鼻的臥室，或者習慣地喬裝化名，在碼頭附近一家聲名狼藉的小酒店的陋室中不能成眠時，他偶爾也會想到自己靈魂的墮落，而且那種懊惱之情因其純粹出於自私而特別強烈。不過，這樣的時刻並不多。道林對生活的好奇心，在一次和亨利勛爵坐在畫家的花園時被對方首次激起，現在似乎因一再得到滿足而更加強烈了。他體驗得愈多，就愈是希望得到更多體驗。他瘋狂的飢餓心理因得到食物而益發不知饜足了。

然而，他也不是真的無所顧忌，至少在處理上流社會關係時。在冬天每個月一兩次，或是在社交季節的每個星期三晚上，他都會向世界敞開他漂亮住宅的大門，邀請當時最有名的音樂家，用奇妙的藝術取悅賓客。亨利勛爵總是幫忙他安排小型宴會，這些宴會因精心挑選的賓客和細心安排的座位而聞名，而非凡的餐桌裝飾品味體現於異國花朵、繡花桌布和金銀古盤微妙而和諧的擺位。實際上，很多人，尤其是年輕人，都從道林身上看到或以為看到他們在伊頓公學或牛津大學時的夢想，看到結合了真正學者的教養與上流人士的所有優雅、名望和完美舉止。在他們的眼中，道林似乎屬於但丁所描繪的那種"以崇拜美來使自己完美"的人，與哥提耶一樣，道林是一個"現實世界為他存在"的人。

　　不言而喻，生活本身對他來說是首要的、最偉大的藝術，而其他各種藝術只不過是為它作準備。當然，他也講究時髦和派頭。時髦能把奇思異想變成風靡一時的習尚，派頭就是要以獨特的方式證明美的絕對現代性。他的服裝式樣、不時變換的新奇作風，對於梅菲爾舞會和佩爾美爾俱樂部的紈袴子弟有顯著的影響。他們亦步亦趨，事事模仿道林。他舉手投足間縱然並非刻意為之的那份瀟灑，也被奉為楷模。

　　雖然他早就準備好接受一成年就會得到的地位，而且實際上，一想到自己對當下的倫敦而言，可能就如同《薩蒂利孔》的作者對於尼祿皇帝統治時期的古羅馬一樣，他就有一絲妙不可言的快感。但是，在內心最深處，他不只渴望做"時尚的權威"，教大家珠寶搭配、領帶繫法和手杖姿勢。他想要建立出一種新的生活方式，含有理性的哲學和有條理的原則，在感官的昇華中達到最高境界。

對感官的崇拜常常遭到頗有道理的責難，因為人們本能地害怕看來要比他們自身更強的嗜慾和知覺，而且他們知道那種嗜慾和知覺在較低等的動物身上也有出現。但在道林‧格雷看來，感覺的真諦之所以至今未被理解，感覺之所以停留在野蠻的獸性狀態，僅僅因為世人力圖用飢餓使之就範，用痛苦加以扼殺，而不是寄望於把感覺造成新精神生活的一部分，愛美的天性將會是這種新精神的主要特徵。每當他回首人類在歷史上所走過的路程，就會痛心地感到損失之大。為了一些微不足道的目的付出了多麼大的代價啊！歷史上不知有多少荒唐而頑固的抵制舉動，有多少奇怪的自我折磨和自我克制，其根源無非是恐懼，其後果則是退化墮落，遠比人們出於無知和想像而竭力逃避的墮落可怕千百倍。試看造物主逐出修道士到荒野去尋找禽獸充飢，讓獸類與隱士作伴，豈非絕妙的諷刺？

　　是啊，誠如亨利勛爵所預言，要有一種新享樂主義來再造生活，使它掙脫那種苛刻的、不合時宜的清教主義。這種清教主義不知怎地如今又出現在我們這個時代。當然，新享樂主義也有借助於理性的地方，但決不接受包含犧牲任何強烈感情體驗的任何理論或體系。因為新享樂主義的目的就是體驗本身，而不是體驗結出的果實，不管它是甜是苦。扼殺感覺的禁慾主義固然與之無緣，麻木感覺的低俗縱慾同樣與之無關。新享樂主義的使命是教人們把精力集中於生活的若干片刻，而生活本身也無非是一瞬間而已。

　　很少人未曾在天亮前醒來，這夜也許是無夢之夜，讓人傾心於死亡，或許是經歷了恐懼和奇異歡樂的夜晚。閃過腦海的幻象比現實更可怕，還具有奇誕地匿藏生動活力的本能。它們會賦予哥德式藝術持久的生命力，令人覺得這種藝術是屬於患有幻想症的藝術家。白色的手指慢慢地伸進窗簾，似乎在抖動。奇形怪狀的黑影靜默地鑽進房間的角落，蜷縮在那兒。外面，鳥兒撥弄着樹葉，或是人們前往工作的聲音鼎沸，或是風從山下來嗚咽歎息着，並在寂靜的房子周圍盤桓，彷彿擔心驚擾了沉睡者，但又必須把睡神從紫色的山洞中喚醒。一層層昏暗的薄紗升起了，萬物漸漸地回復原本的形狀和顏色。我們觀察着黎明以它古老的方式重建世界，暗淡的鏡子又開始它映照事物的一天，熄滅的細蠟燭依舊豎立在原地，旁邊擺着一本看了一半的書，或是在舞會上戴過紮着金屬絲的花，或是一封不敢讀或讀了太多遍的信。在我們看來，似乎甚麼都沒有改變。熟識的現實生活從虛幻的夜影裏回來，我們必須從中斷的地方繼續生活，一種可怕的感覺悄然襲來，我們必須在一成不變、讓人厭倦的習慣中留有繼續的力量。我們或許會狂熱地渴望，早上一睜開眼睛，就看到在黑夜中已為我們量身重建的新世界。萬物都有了新的形狀和色彩，擁有新的祕密。在新世界，過去無足掛齒，即使有立足之地，也不再會有責任或悔恨的意識。愉悅的記憶裏帶着辛酸，享樂的回憶裏也帶有痛苦。

道林・格雷認為，創造那樣的世界才是生活的真正目的或真正目的之一。為了追求既新鮮又愉快，同時含有浪漫要素的奇異感覺，他常常採納明知與自己稟性格格不入的各種思想，沉湎於它們潛移默化的影響。一旦領略了它們的精髓，滿足了自己的求知慾，便毫不猶豫地放棄它們。那種不在乎的態度同熱情奔放的氣質非但並行不悖，某些現代心理學家甚至還認為前者往往是後者的先決條件之一呢。

一度傳言他要加入羅馬天主教教會。的確，羅馬天主教的儀式對他一直有很大的吸引力。每天的獻祭比古代世界的任何祭典都更加可怕，但卻使他為之激動，這種儀式傲然無視明明存在的感情，具有原始的質樸氣息和它所象徵的人類悲劇的亙古悲壯。他喜歡跪在冷冰冰的大理石板上，看身穿硬繃繃的繡花祭衣的神父用蒼白的手慢騰騰地揭開聖龕的帷幔，或端起嵌有寶石的燈籠形狀的聖體匣，這時裏面盛着一塊顏色泛白，且能叫人心悅誠服地相信是"天使的麵包"的硬麵餅。他也喜歡看神父穿上耶穌受難時的裝束，把麵餅掰入聖餐杯，並捶胸痛責自己的罪孽。神態莊重的男孩穿着鑲花邊的猩紅色衣服，把冒煙的香爐像一朵朵大金花似的不斷搖動，讓氤氳的爐煙在空氣中散開，這對他也有一種不可言喻的吸引力。他每次走出教堂，總要向黑洞洞的告解室投去好奇的眼光，渴望能坐在其中一間的幽暗處，偷聽信男信女們隔着殘舊的窗柵低聲訴説他們生活中真實的故事。

但是，如果正式皈依某種信仰或體系，或者錯把只適合在星月無光之夜借宿一宵，乃至把度過幾個小時的旅館當作定居的家園，那就會阻礙他的智力發展，他永遠不會陷入這樣的錯誤。具有化平凡為神奇力量的神祕主義，以及與它形影相隨的唯信仰論，曾經使他熱中於一時。而在另一個時期，他卻傾向於德國達爾文主義運動的唯物主義學説，一心追溯人們的思想和慾念，探究珍珠似的腦細胞或白色神經纖維的活動，興致勃勃地設想精神絕對取決於某些生理條件，不論是病態還是健康，正常還是有病。然而，誠如前面已說過的那樣，他認為任何關於生活的理論與生活本身相比都微不足道。他深切地意識到，一切推理演繹如果脫離了行動和實驗都顯得空洞無比。他知道，就感覺而言，有待揭開的精神奧祕，並不比靈魂少。

因此，他開始研究各種香水及其製作的祕密，把濃郁的香油加以蒸餾，燃點從東方弄來的芳烈的樹脂。他認為任何一種精神狀態都在感官生活中有它的對應物，便下決心探索兩者的真正關係。他想弄清楚：為甚麼乳香使人產生神祕感，龍涎香撩人情慾，紫羅蘭能令人回憶起逝去的浪漫史，麝香能叫人暈頭轉向，金香木使人失去想像？他經常考慮創立一門並非徒具虛名的香水心理學，估算它們的各種影響，包括帶有甜香的根部、授粉期的香花、香油、芳香的深色木頭、使人作嘔的穗甘松、能熏人致瘋的枳棋子，以及據說能驅除愁緒的蘆薈。

另一個時期，他完全醉心於音樂。他有一間以格子裝飾的長方形房間，天花板的朱紅色和金黃色交錯，牆壁則漆成了橄欖綠。他常常在這間房間舉辦奇怪的音樂會，瘋狂的吉卜賽人用細小的齊特琴撕出狂野的音樂，頭戴黃色頭巾的突尼斯人表情嚴肅地拉着巨大的魯特琴上緊繃的弦，咧着嘴笑的黑人單調地擊打着銅鼓，裹着頭巾、身材瘦小的印度人蹲在猩紅墊子上，吹着長長的蘆笛或銅管，迷惑或假裝迷惑大眼鏡蛇和可怕的角蝰蛇。當他對舒伯特的優雅、蕭邦美麗的哀傷、貝多芬強大的和聲都感到麻木時，這些野蠻音樂刺耳的停頓和尖銳的不和諧卻能打動他。他從世界各地收集了各種奇形怪狀的樂器，不是從某個亡國的陵墓，就是從幾個在西方文明下仍然生存的原始部落找來的。他喜歡撫弄和彈奏這些樂器。他擁有黑河流域印第安人的"朱魯帕里斯"，這種神祕的樂器不允許婦女看，年輕男人要等到受齋戒或鞭笞時才能一睹真容。他還藏有能發出鳥兒尖叫聲的祕魯泥罐，以及阿方索·德·奧瓦列在智利聽過的人骨笛子。他在祕魯庫斯科附近發現渾厚的碧玉，可以奏出一個甜美的音調。他還擁有裝滿了卵石的彩繪葫蘆，搖起來嘎嘎作響；墨西哥人的"克拉令"，演奏的方法不是往裏吹，而是朝外吸；阿馬遜部落刺耳的"特克"，由整天坐在大樹上的哨兵吹奏，據說九英里之外也能聽見；一種叫"特龐那斯德利"的樂器，裝有兩片振動的木製簧片，演奏時用塗上乳白色植物黏液的木棒敲擊；一種阿茲特克人的"龍特爾"鈴，像葡萄般成串掛着；一個用巨蟒皮包裹的圓筒形大鼓，貝爾納爾·迪亞斯與科爾特斯一起進入墨西哥神廟時曾經見過這個鼓，他還生動地描繪了那悲涼的鼓聲。這些樂器奇怪的特徵使他着迷，當他想到藝術如自然一樣，有着自己的怪物，外形醜惡，聲音可怕，他便感到奇異的愉悅。但過了一段時間，他就會厭倦這些樂器，走到劇院裏自己的包廂，一個人或是跟亨利勛爵一起，沉醉地聽《唐懷瑟》，並在這部偉大藝術作品的序幕中，觀看自己靈魂的悲劇。

不知從何時起，他對珠寶產生了興趣，曾像法國的海軍將領安·德儒瓦厄斯那樣，穿了一件綴有五百六十顆珍珠的衣服參加化裝舞會。這種嗜好持續了若干年，甚至可以說從來沒有被他拋棄。他常常花一整天玩弄收藏在首飾匣裏的各種寶石，搬來倒去，弄了又弄，包括在燈光下會轉成紅色的橄欖金綠寶石、嵌着銀色紋理的貓眼石、淡黃中微泛綠色的橄欖石、玫瑰紅和黃酒色的黃玉、火紅色並帶有閃亮四角星的紅玉、紅得火辣辣的桂榴石、橘黃色和淡紫色的尖晶石，以及紅藍相間的紫晶。他喜歡日長石的金紅、月長石的珠白、蛋白石的虹暈。他從阿姆斯特丹物色到三顆大得出奇而顏色鮮豔的綠寶石，還有一顆古老的綠松石，是行家無不嘖嘖稱羨的極品。

他還發現了關於珠寶的奇妙故事。在阿方索的《教士規誡》中提到，蛇的眼睛是真正的風信子石。在亞歷山大的浪漫傳說中，依馬提亞的征服者據說在約旦峽谷裏發現了一種蛇，它的"背上長着真實的綠寶石圈"。菲洛斯特拉托斯告訴我們，龍的腦袋裏有一種寶石，只要"出示金色的字母和一件紅袍子"，怪物便會着了魔般沉睡，隨即可將它殺死。按偉大的煉金術士皮埃爾·德·卜尼法斯所說，鑽石可令人隱身，印度的瑪瑙可令人善辯，紅玉髓可消氣，紅鋯石可催眠，紫晶可解酒，石榴石可驅魔，天牛石可使月光失色，透石膏會隨月亮的盈虧而增減光亮，翡翠寶石能識別竊賊，唯有山羊之血可致其失效。列昂納達斯·卡蜜拉斯看過從剛被殺的蟾蜍中取出的白色寶石，它可用作解毒劑。阿拉伯鹿的心臟裏的牛黃石能夠治療瘟疫。根據德謨克利特所言，阿拉伯鳥巢中有一種"阿斯皮萊茨"石頭，戴上它就可免除一切火災。

錫蘭國王在加冕典禮上，會手捧一顆巨大的紅寶石，騎馬穿過城市。約翰牧師大殿的宮門"用瑪瑙做成，鑲嵌着角蛇的角，攜毒者將無法進內"。山牆上放着"兩個金蘋果，蘋果裏有兩塊紅玉"，白天金子閃光，夜晚紅玉發亮；洛奇的浪漫怪談《美洲的一顆珍珠》中提到，在女王的寢宮，可以看到"世界上所有貞潔女子的銀雕塑像，正對着用橄欖石、紅玉、藍寶石和綠寶石做的漂亮鏡子照個不停"。馬可·孛羅曾見過日本國國民把玫瑰色的珍珠放進死者嘴裏。有人潛水採得一顆珍珠，獻給比路斯王，一隻海怪因迷戀這顆珍珠而殺死採珠人，悲悼了七個月。後來匈奴人把比路斯王誘入陷阱，國王扔掉了珍珠，據普羅科匹厄斯所說，儘管阿納斯塔修斯一世為珍珠懸賞五百磅黃金，但再也沒有找到這顆珍珠。馬拉巴爾王曾給某個威尼斯人看過一串共有三百零四顆珍珠的念珠，每顆珍珠代表一個他所崇拜的神。

據布朗托姆所言，亞歷山大六世之子瓦倫提努亞公爵拜見法王路易十二的時候，坐騎披滿金葉，帽子鑲着兩排紅寶石，光芒四射。英王查理的馬鐙掛着四百二十一顆鑽石。理查二世有一件外套，鑲滿淺紅尖晶石，價值相當於三萬馬克。霍爾描寫亨利八世在加冕前前往倫敦塔的路上，身穿"凸金線外套，胸牌上飾有鑽石和其他寶石，頸項有一大塊飾品，綴有巨大的淺紅尖晶石"。詹姆斯一世的女寵都戴着用金絲線綴成的綠寶石耳環。愛德華二世贈予皮爾斯·加韋斯頓一副鑲着紅鋯石的紅金色盔甲、一個金玫瑰嵌綠松石的頸圈，以及一頂佈滿珍珠的頭盔。亨利二世的手套直抵肘部，上面滿佈珠寶。他的一隻獵鷹手套綴有十二顆紅寶石和五十二顆大珍珠。"魯莽的查理"是勃艮第家族中最後一個公爵，他所戴的公爵帽懸掛着梨形珍珠，點綴着藍寶石。

生活曾是多麼講究！那些排場、裝飾多麼富麗堂皇！甚至從書上看看古人的豪華氣派已經是一種享受。

然後他的注意力又轉向刺繡和在北歐寒冷的房間裏當作壁畫的掛毯。他一投入研究這個主題——他總有一種異乎尋常的能力，能一下子極為專注他埋首的事情——就想到時間摧殘美麗和奇妙的東西，因而感到悲哀。而他，至少已經避過了這種命運。

一個又一個夏天過去了，黃色的丁香水仙花開了又謝了幾次，可怕的夜裏仍不斷發生着可恥的事情，但他依然不變。冬天沒有損害他的容顏，或是玷污他如花的青春。時間對物質的東西帶來多麼不同的影響！它們到哪裏去呢？那件由棕皮膚的女子為取悦雅典娜而做，繡有眾神與巨人搏鬥圖案的紫色袍子，它在哪裏呢？那張尼祿皇帝用於蓋着羅馬鬥獸場上空，上面畫有阿波羅在星空下駕着白馬金韁雙輪戰車的巨型紫色風帆，它又在哪裏呢？道林渴望看一看為太陽祭司編織的奇異餐巾，上面繡着盛宴所有的美食與佳餚；希爾佩里克王靈柩上的蓋布，蓋布綴有三百隻金色蜜蜂；那些激怒了龐脱斯主教的奇妙袍子，袍子上畫了"獅子、黑豹、熊、狗、森林、岩石、獵人等畫家所能描摹自然界的一切"；奧爾良的查理一世曾經穿過的外套，袖子上繡着一首歌，起句是"夫人，我欣喜萬分"，配樂的歌詞用金線繡成，當年的音符是方形的，每個音符均由四顆珍珠組成。他讀過勃艮第的約娜皇后在蘭斯皇宮的寢室，裏面裝飾了"一千三百二十一隻刺繡鸚鵡，以及五百六十一隻蝴蝶，鸚鵡身上繪有國王的徽記，每隻蝴蝶的翅膀上則繪了皇后的徽記，全都用金線繡成"；為嘉芙蓮·德·麥地奇皇后特製的靈牀，鋪着有無數新月和太陽的黑絲絨，靈牀的帳幔是錦緞做的，綴有葉圈和花冠，以金銀襯底，邊緣的流蘇上繡有珍珠，靈牀放在掛着一排排皇后紋章的房間裏，紋章用碎黑絲絨繡在銀線底布上拼成；路易十四的寓所裏豎着一根十五英尺高的鍍金女像柱；波蘭國王索別斯基的御牀是用士麥那的金色錦緞鋪成，上面以刻有《古蘭經》經文的綠松石作裝飾，牀柱鍍銀，雕刻精美，嵌滿了搪瓷和寶石圓飾，這張牀是從維也納城前的土耳其營地得來的，當時穆罕默德的軍旗曾立在它顫動的鍍金牀罩之下。

足足有一年功夫，道林到處收集各種最珍奇的織物和繡品。他的收藏有德里的上等薄紗，上面有用金線織成的葉子和虹彩的甲蟲翅膀；有達卡的薄綢，在東方因其透明飄逸被稱為"氣織"、"流水"、"夜露"；有染着奇怪圖案的爪哇花布；有中國精製的黃色簾幔；有用茶色緞子或藍色名綢裝幀的書籍，上面有百合花、飛禽和肖像作裝飾；有匈牙利花邊網繡的面紗；有西西里的錦緞和西班牙的硬絲絨；有繡着小金幣的格魯吉亞工藝品；有日本的帛紗，上面繡有綠色的金線和羽毛鮮豔的鳥類。

他對教會的祭衣亦情有獨鍾，實際上，他對宗教儀式相關的一切都很感興趣。在他房子的西廊，有一排長長的雪松木櫃，裏面收藏了許多罕見而漂亮的"基督的新娘"服飾真品。她們不得不穿上紫色的阿麻布衣服，再戴好珠寶，才能掩蓋那自找的苦難和痛苦所造成蒼白消瘦的身軀。他擁有一件華麗的長袍，用深紅絲綢和金線錦緞做成，六瓣花中鑲嵌着重複排列的金石榴圖案，上面兩側是小珍珠組成的鳳梨圖案。祭衣的飾帶分成一格格，分別描繪了聖母瑪利亞生活中不同的場景，聖母加冕圖則用彩色絲線繡在兜帽上，這是十五世紀意大利的工藝品。另一件綠絲絨祭袍繡着一簇簇心形的莨苕葉子，葉子上長出長柄的白花，銀絲線和彩色水晶襯托出圖案的細節，祭衣的襻扣用金線挑凸了六翼天使頭像的紋飾，飾帶用紅金絲線織成菱形圖案，點綴着聖塞瓦斯蒂安在內眾多聖人和殉道者的頭像。他還有一些無袖長袍，包括琥珀色真絲的、藍色絲綢與金色織錦相間的、黃絲錦緞和金色布料交替的，全都繪有耶穌在十字架上受難的情景，另外還繡有獅子、孔雀和其他徽紋；用白色緞子和粉色絲錦緞造成的祭衣，上面有鬱金香、海豚和百合花圖案；暗紅色絲絨和藍色阿麻布做的祭壇帷簾，以及許多聖餐巾、聖餐杯罩和聖像手帕。那些使用這些衣物和器具的神祕儀式，有某種東西激發起他的想像。

這些珍寶跟他收藏在富麗的宅第裏的每件東西一樣，對他來說是忘懷的手段，可藉以暫時逃避簡直無法忍受的恐懼。在那個他度過了大部分童年時光的上鎖空室中，他親手把畫像掛在牆上，再用紫紅繡金的緞罩當帷幕把畫像遮起來。那幅可怕的畫像不斷變化的面貌向他揭示着他生活腐化墮落的真相。他可以一連幾個星期不到那裏去，把那可惡的畫中人拋在腦後，回復輕鬆愉快、逍遙自在，並且狂熱地沉浸在對生活本身的享受之中。然後，他會突然在某一個夜晚溜出家門，來到藍門郊野附近一些藏垢納污的去處，在那裏一天又一天地待下去，直到被攆走。回到家中，他就去坐在畫像前面，有時對它和對他自己都感到討厭，有時又充滿個人主義的自豪，而罪惡的吸引力大半寓於其中。看着那畸形的影子承受了本該由他本人承擔的惡果，他暗暗得意地露出微笑。

過了幾年，他無法忍受長時間離開英國，因而放棄了他在特魯維爾與亨利勛爵合住的別墅，以及在阿爾及爾帶有圍牆的白色小屋，他們曾在那裏度過不止一個冬天。他不願意離開畫像，因為它已成了他生命的一部分。雖然他已命人裝上牢固的門閂，但依然害怕有人會趁他離開之時闖進去。

他心裏很清楚，即使外人看見了也不知內情。誠然，肖像的面部儘管打上了種種邪惡和醜陋的烙印，仍然保留着與他本人明顯的相似之處。但外人從中又能知道甚麼呢？任何人若想奚落他，他大可嗤之以鼻。又不是他自己畫的，肖像無論怎樣面目可憎，見不得人，跟他有甚麼相干？即使他把真相告訴世人，人家會相信嗎？

然而他還是懼怕。有幾次他到自己在諾丁漢郡的大宅，款待與他身分相當的時髦青年兼好友，其奢侈的生活方式使全郡紳士大為吃驚。可是他竟突然撇下賓客，趕回倫敦去看那扇門有沒有被撬壞，肖像還在不在。萬一它被偷走了怎麼辦？想到這一層，他嚇得手腳冰冷。要知道，那時他的祕密就會暴露在光天化日之下。也許人們已經有所懷疑了。

事實上，儘管他使許多人為之傾倒，但不相信他的人為數也不少。他險些遭到西區某俱樂部抵制，而憑他的出身和社會地位完全有資格當那裏的會員。據說，有一次，當他被一個朋友帶進邱吉爾俱樂部的吸煙室時，貝里克公爵和另一位紳士毫不掩飾地站起身走出去。自從他滿了二十五歲，關於他的離奇故事更是層出不窮。據傳，有人看見他在白教堂偏僻地區的一個下流去處與幾個外國水手對罵。又有謠言說他結交盜賊和偽幣鑄造者，並知道他們那一類工作的內幕。他隔三差五地神祕失蹤早已遭人物議，所以每當他在社交界重新露臉的時候，人們就會在角落竊竊私語，或者在他身旁走過時譏笑他，或者用冷冰冰的眼光審視他，似乎下定了決心要探明他的祕密。

這類傲慢無禮的行為他當然不放在心上。在大多數人看來，他那誠懇溫文的態度、天真可愛的笑容、無限美妙而且像是永不消逝的青春，本身便足以推翻那些造謠中傷，他們把道林的種種傳聞一概稱為造謠中傷。雖然如此，還是可以注意到，某些曾經同他過從甚密的人，後來似乎一個個避開他了。那些以前發瘋般愛過他的女人，曾經為了他不惜置一切輿論責難於不顧，敢於向陳規舊習挑戰，現在她們看到道林‧格雷，也會因羞慚或恐懼而面色頓變。

不過，這些悄悄議論的醜聞在許多人心目中只會增強道林‧格雷奇怪而危險的魅力。他雄厚的財力在相當程度上提供了保障。在社會上，至少在上流社會，人們總是不大願意相信任何有損那些既有錢又可愛的人名譽的話。人們本能地認為，舉止比道德重要得多，再高尚、再可敬的品性也遠不如家有一位好庖廚來得吃香。歸根究底，如果某人請你吃飯的菜餚不佳，或者酒味不純，事後你即使聽說東道主的為人無可非議，也未必就能釋然。有一次在討論到這個題目時，亨利勛爵說過，甚至最偉大的德行也補救不了半冷不熱的主菜。的確，可以舉很多事實為他的觀點佐證。因為上流社會的準則與藝術的準則是相同的，或者應該是相同的。在上流社會，形式極為重要。它應當兼有禮儀的莊重和不真實性，應當把浪漫主義戲劇的虛偽與劇中令人喜愛的機智和美糅合在一起。虛偽有甚麼大不了？我看沒甚麼。這無非是豐富我們個性的一種手段。

至少道林‧格雷就是這樣想。他曾經對那種膚淺的心理學感到納悶，那種心理學認為人的自我是簡單、永久、可靠、本質單一的。對他來說，人是一種具有多重生活、多種感覺、多種形式的複雜生物，內在秉承了思想和激情的奇怪遺產，肉體則沾染上了祖先的可怕疾病。他喜歡在自己鄉間別墅中荒涼冰冷的畫廊漫步，看看那些跟他血脈相同的人的畫像。這是菲利普・赫伯特，弗蘭西斯・奧斯本在《伊利沙伯女王與詹姆斯國王執政回憶》中，把他描繪成一個"因外貌漂亮而得到宮廷寵幸，但美貌並不長久"的人。他有時候過的生活就是年輕赫伯特的生活嗎？難道某種奇怪的毒菌從一個軀體潛入另一個軀體，最後到了他身上？難道是他突然隱約地意識到那種即將毀掉的魅力，才讓他幾乎毫無原因地在貝澤爾・霍爾渥德的畫室瘋狂祈禱，從而令他的人生有極大的改變？這是安東尼・謝拉德，他身穿繡金紅背心和鑲着寶石的外套，皺領和袖口都鑲有金邊，銀黑兩色的盔甲堆在他腳邊。這個男人留下了怎麼樣的遺產？喬安娜皇后在拿坡里的情人有把罪惡和恥辱留給他嗎？他的所作所為只是死人不敢實現的夢想嗎？在這塊褪色畫布上的是伊利沙伯・德芙洛夫人，她微笑着，披着薄紗頭巾，身穿珍珠胸衣，露出粉紅色分叉的手袖。她右手拿着一朵花，左手緊握一個白色搪瓷項圈和大馬士革玫瑰。她身旁的桌子上放着一把曼陀鈴和一個蘋果。她尖尖的小鞋上綴着綠色的玫瑰花飾。道林知道她的故事，還有她情人們的奇聞趣事。他身上有她的脾性嗎？那雙杏眼重重地垂着眼瞼，似乎好奇地望着他。至於這位頭髮塗粉、臉上貼着奇怪裝飾片的喬治・威洛比又怎樣呢？他看上去多邪惡！他的臉孔陰沉黝黑，性感的嘴唇流露出目空一切的扭曲表情，精製的花邊褶袖蓋住了那雙瘦黃的手，手上戴滿了戒指。他是個十八世紀的紈絝子弟，年輕時曾是弗拉爾斯勛爵的朋友。那邊的貝肯漢姆勛爵二世又是一個怎樣的人呢？他是攝政王喬治四世的同伴，陪伴他度過最荒唐的歲月，還見證了他與菲茨赫伯特夫人的祕密婚姻。他當年一頭栗色鬈髮，一副神氣凌人的姿態，顯得多麼傲然英俊！他又傳下了怎樣的激情？世人都認為他聲名狼藉，他帶頭在卡爾頓府縱情狂歡，胸前的嘉德勛章閃爍着星光。他旁邊掛着他妻子的畫像，是一個身穿黑衣、臉色蒼白、薄唇的女人，她的血也在道林身上流動。這一切是多麼不可思議！然後就是他的母親，長着一副漢彌爾登夫人的臉，唇上沾着濕漉漉的酒滴。他知道自己從母親身上得到了甚麼，他得到了她的美，得到了追求他人之美的慾望。她身穿寬大的女祭司服裝，對他笑着，頭髮上有幾條藤葉，紫色的酒從她手中的酒杯灑出。畫中的肉粉色已經褪去，但她美麗的眼睛仍深邃明亮。無論他走到哪裏，那雙眼睛似乎都跟到那裏。

　　然而，人不僅有血統上的祖先，還有文學上的祖先，並且就類型和性情而言，許多文學祖先可能與後代更接近，影響當然也更大。道林・格雷有時候覺得自古至今的歷史無非是他自己一生的記錄，不過記載的不是他實際度過的生活，而是他的想像所創造的、存在於他的腦海和慾念中的生活。那些離奇可怕的人物曾經先後登上世界舞台，他們犯罪也是壯美的，作惡也是精妙的。道林覺得自己與他們都似曾相識，在神祕之中，他們的生活已變成了他的生活。

　　那本奇妙的小說的主角影響了他的生活，令他了解這種古怪的幻想。那個主角在第七章講述自己如何戴上桂冠，避開雷擊，像提貝里烏斯那樣坐在卡普利島裏，讀着愛里芳提斯寫的淫書，侏儒和孔雀神氣地在他身旁走來走去，吹笛者嘲笑着搖動香爐的人；像卡里古拉般，與馬廄裏的綠衣馬夫痛飲一番，又在象牙馬槽裏與頭戴寶石的馬兒共進晚餐；像多米提安那樣，徘徊在掛滿大理石鏡子的走廊，用憔悴的目光，尋找後來了結他性命的匕首的映像，他因為無聊而產生了厭世感，這種厭世感只出現在生活應有盡有的人身上；像尼祿·凱撒一樣，透過一塊晶瑩的綠寶石，觀看競技場上鮮紅的殺戮，隨後坐上以珍珠和紫袍作裝飾的轎車，被有銀色馬蹄鐵的驢子拉着，穿過石榴街到了金宮，沿路聽見人們高叫他的名字；像埃拉伽巴路斯，把臉塗上油彩，在女人中間使用卷線桿，從迦太基那兒請來月亮神，使她與太陽神祕密地結合。

道林重復地讀着這奇妙的章節，以及緊接的兩章。那兩個章節如同某些稀奇的壁毯或精巧的搪瓷，勾畫出那些被罪惡、鮮血和厭倦逼成魔鬼和瘋子的美麗而又可怕的形象。米蘭的菲利浦公爵殺死自己的妻子，並在她唇上塗上鮮紅色的毒藥，令她的情人在吸啜愛人嘴唇時中毒而死；威尼斯人伯多祿·巴爾博，亦即是保羅二世，為了虛榮而想要獲得"福莫蘇斯"的教皇封號，他不惜犯下駭人的罪行來獲取價值二十萬弗羅林的三重冠；吉安·瑪莉亞·維斯康蒂曾派獵犬追咬活人，後來被人謀殺，一個愛過他的妓女在他屍體上撒滿玫瑰；波吉亞騎着白馬，與弗拉特利西德策馬同行，他的披風染着佩洛托的血；佛羅倫斯的年輕紅衣主教皮特洛·里阿尼奧，是西斯科特四世的兒子及其寵臣。他的放蕩與美貌齊名，在一個用紅白兩色的絲綢帳篷中接待了阿拉岡的列昂娜拉，帳篷裏滿是仙女和半人馬，他還在一個男童身上塗金，讓他裝成甘米德或海拉斯，在宴會上充當招待；埃澤林的憂鬱只有在看見死亡的景象時才能得以消解。他嗜血成性，就像別人嗜愛紅酒一樣。據說他是魔鬼的兒子，為了獲得父親的靈魂，不惜在擲骰子時作弊；詹巴迪斯塔·希波出於嘲諷，自稱"教皇依諾增爵"，一位猶太醫生為了救他，在他毫無生氣的血管裏注入了三個青年的血；西吉斯蒙多·馬拉特斯達是伊索達的情人，以及里米尼的君主。由於他被視作上帝和人類的敵人，導致雕像在羅馬被人焚燒。他用餐巾勒死了普里西娜，在吉內弗拉·德埃斯特的綠寶石酒杯中下毒，並為了紀念一段可恥的情慾，而給基督教徒建了一座異教教堂；查理六世瘋狂地愛慕他的嫂嫂，甚至有一個麻瘋病人警告他已精神失常。當他的腦袋變得病態而反常的時候，他只能依靠撒拉森卡牌上愛情、死亡和瘋狂的圖案才可平靜下來；格里芬內托·巴廖尼身穿鑲邊的無袖外套，莨苕般的鬈髮上戴着寶石帽，殺死了阿斯托雷和他的新娘、西蒙納多和他的侍從。但他的容貌清秀，以至當他奄奄一息地躺在佩魯賈的黃色廣場時，那些恨過他的人們也不禁流淚，詛咒過他的阿塔蘭妲也為他祈福。

所有這些人物都有一種可怕的魅力。夜裏，道林夢見他們；白天，他們擾亂他的想像。文藝復興時期有許多下毒的妙法：通過頭盔和點亮的火炬下毒；通過繡花的手套或嵌有珠寶的扇子下毒；通過繡金的香袋和琥珀項鏈下毒。道林·格雷中的毒則是來自一本書。有時候，他乾脆把作惡看成實現他構想的美感的一種方式。

第十二章

事情發生在十一月九日，事後他才一再回憶起來：那天正好是他自己三十八歲生日的前夕。

他在亨利勛爵家裏吃了晚飯，十一點左右從那裏步行回家。夜裏天寒霧濃，他裹着很厚的裘皮大衣。在格羅夫納廣場和奧德麗南大街的轉角，迷霧中有一個人從他身旁經過。那人走得非常快，灰色大衣的領子豎了起來，手拿着一個袋。道林認出那是貝澤爾·霍爾渥德。他感到一陣不可言喻的驚恐，不動聲色地加快腳步，朝着自己家裏的方向走去。

但是霍爾渥德看到了他。道林聽見他先是在行人道上站住，接着急匆匆地跟了上來。很快，他的一隻手已經攔到道林的胳臂上。

"道林！巧極了！我從九點鐘一直在你的書齋等你。後來看到你的侍從實在太累了，就叫他把我送走後自己去睡覺。我要趕午夜的一班火車去巴黎，很想在臨走前跟你見一面。剛才你從我身旁走過，我認出了你，其實應該說認出了你的裘皮大衣。不過我沒有十分把握。你沒有認出我嗎？"

"親愛的貝澤爾，你不想想這霧有多濃！我連格羅夫納廣場都認不清呢。我相信我的家就在此地附近，但是也不敢擔保。真遺憾，你馬上就要遠行，我已經很久沒看見你了。你大概很快就會回來吧？"

"我要離開英國半年左右。我打算在巴黎租一間畫室,把自己關在裏面,直到完成我已構思成熟的一幅偉大的作品為止。不過,我不是想跟你談我自己的事情。瞧,已經到你家門口了。讓我進去坐一會。我有話要對你説。"

"那太好了。可是,會不會耽誤了你上火車?"道林·格雷無精打采地説着,走上台階,用自己的鑰匙開門。

燈光勉強穿破大霧,霍爾渥德看了看錶。"還早呢,"他回答説。"火車十二點十五分開,現在才十一點。剛才碰見你的時候,我正想上俱樂部去找你。你瞧,我也沒有多少行李,重的東西都先送走了。我隨身只帶這一個手提袋,二十分鐘就可以從從容容到達維多利亞車站。"

道林望着他,微微一笑。"瞧你這位名畫家出門旅行的樣子!一個手提袋、一件大衣!快進來,否則霧要鑽到屋裏來了。注意不要談任何嚴肅的問題。如今都沒有甚麼嚴肅的事情,至少不應當讓任何嚴肅的事情發生。"

霍爾渥德搖搖頭進了門,然後跟隨道林走進書齋。書齋的開放式大壁爐裏柴火燒得正旺,燈也亮着。鑲嵌細工的小桌子上放着一個打開的荷蘭銀質酒箱、幾瓶梳打水和幾隻雕花大玻璃杯。

"瞧,你的侍從對我的招待多周到,道林。他給了我所需要的一切東西,包括你最好的金頭煙捲。他非常殷勤好客。我覺得他比你之前那個法國侍從好得多。說起那個法國人,他後來怎麼樣了?"

道林聳聳肩膀。"他大概娶了瑞德利夫人的侍女,在巴黎開了一家英國時裝店。聽說那邊現在時興一股英國熱。法國人也真無聊，可不是嗎？不過，說實在的，維克多倒是個不壞的傭人。可是我從來不喜歡他，儘管對他沒有甚麼可抱怨。一個人往往會憑空想像出毫無根據的事來。其實他對我忠心耿耿，離開時看上去很難過。要不要再來一杯白蘭地梳打？或者混了氣泡水的霍克酒？我自己常喝混了氣泡水的霍克酒，隔壁房間大概找得到。"

"謝謝，我甚麼也不要了，"畫家說着，把帽子和大衣脫下來，往他放在角落裏的手提袋上一扔。"老弟，現在我要跟你嚴肅地談一談。別把眉頭皺得那麼緊，這樣我就很難開口了。"

"關於甚麼的？"道林不耐煩地問，無奈得撲倒在沙發上。"但願與我本人無關。今晚我對自己已經感到膩煩。我很想變成另一個人。"

"這是有關你本人的，"霍爾渥德用深沉嚴肅的聲音說，"我必須把這件事告訴你，只佔用你半個小時。"

道林長歎一聲，點了一支煙。"半個小時！"他咕噥了一句。

"這不能算是不情之請，道林，何況我要說的都是為你着想。我認為應當讓你知道，倫敦流傳着極其可怕的謠言，都是說你的壞話。"

"我一點也不想知道那些事情。我喜歡聽有關別人的醜聞，可是有關我自己的流言蜚語引不起我的興趣，都是些老調。"

"它們一定能引起你的興趣，道林。每位神士都對自己的名聲感興趣。你不會希望他人把你說成邪惡墜落之人。當然你擁有地位、財富諸如此類的東西，但地位和財富不是一切。先告訴你，我完全不相信那些謠言，至少我看見你的時候不相信。罪惡會寫在臉上，不能被掩蓋。人們有時說起祕密犯罪，但根本沒有這種東西。如果一個惡棍犯了罪，罪行就會在他嘴唇的線條、下垂的眼瞼，甚至雙手的形狀上顯露出來。有人——我不提他的名字，反正你也認識他——去年找我幫他作畫。我從未見過他，當時亦沒有聽過他的任何傳言，雖然自那之後就聽到了不少。他給出一個非常可觀的價錢，但我拒絕了他，我很討厭他手指的形狀。現在我知道我對他的想法是正確的，他的人生很糟糕。但道林你純潔明朗、天真爛漫的面容，你無憂無慮、美妙絕倫的青春，令我不能相信任何關於你的壞話。然而我很少見到你，你現在不再到我的畫室了。當我不在你身旁，聽到人們竊竊私語地說你的醜惡謠言，我不知道該說甚麼。道林，為甚麼像貝里克公爵這樣的人看見你進門就離開俱樂部？為甚麼倫敦那麼多紳士從來不去你家，也不邀請你去他們那裏？你曾是斯特夫利爵士的朋友，上星期我吃飯時碰到他，言談之間偶然說起了你，說你把袖珍畫像借給達德利美術館作展覽。斯特夫利撇着嘴說，也許你很有藝術品味，但你這樣的人，純潔的女子都不應和你交往，貞潔的女人都不應與你共處一室。我提醒他我是你的朋友，並問他到底是甚麼意思。他告訴了我，就在所有人面前告訴了我。多可怕！為甚麼你的友誼對年輕男子是那麼致命？那個在皇家禁衛隊的可憐男孩子自殺了，而你曾是他要好的朋友。然後是亨利・艾森頓爵士，他聲名狼藉地離開了英國，而你曾經和他形影不離。至於阿德里安・辛格爾頓和他可怕的下場呢？肯特勛爵的獨生子和他的職業生涯又是怎麼回事？我昨天在聖詹姆士街遇見他的父親，他看上去被恥辱和傷心壓垮了。那年輕的珀斯公爵呢？他現在過的是怎樣的生活？怎樣的紳士會跟他來往？"

"別説了，貝澤爾。你根本不知道你在談論的事，"道林‧格雷咬着嘴唇，聲音充滿無限的輕蔑，"你問我為何貝里克公爵在我進門時就離開，那是因為我清楚他生活的一切，而不是他知道任何關於我的事。血管裏流着那樣的血液，他的身家怎會是清白的呢？你問我關於亨利‧艾森頓以及年輕的珀斯的事，難道是我教唆一人犯罪，另一人放蕩嗎？要是肯特的傻兒子在街上隨便找了個妻子，那跟我有甚麼關係？如果阿德里安‧辛格爾頓在賬單上冒簽了朋友的名字，那我要為他作保證人嗎？我知道在英國是如何議論他人的，中產階級在粗俗的飯桌上發表他們的道德偏見，耳語着比他們優越的人的奢靡生活，嘗試裝作自己也屬於上流社會，跟他們詆毀的人保持密切的關係。在這個國家，只要一個人擁有名聲和智慧，就足以令普通人對他説三道四。而那些道貌岸然的人又過着怎樣的生活呢？老兄，你忘了我們生活在偽君子的祖國。"

　　"道林，"霍爾渥德激動地説，"問題不在這裏。我知道英國糟糕透了，英國社會全是錯誤。正因為如此，所以我希望你潔身自好。但你沒有做到。一個人對他的朋友影響如何，可以據此對他本人作出判斷。你的那些朋友看來已把名譽、品德、清白通通丟在腦後。你向他們灌輸了瘋狂的享樂慾望，使他們掉進深淵。你把他們推下去，是的，是你把他們推下去的，而你居然還在微笑，就像現在這樣。還有比這更壞的呢。我知道你同亨利‧沃登是莫逆之交。且不管別的理由，單是看在這一點上，你就不應該讓他妹妹的名聲成為笑柄。"

　　"留神，貝澤爾，別太放肆了。"

"我必須要説，而你必須要聽。聽着，當你初遇格溫多林夫人的時候，她沒有任何醜聞，但現在倫敦還有清白的女人願意和她在海德公園與她共乘馬車嗎？為甚麼連她的子女也不被允許與她一起生活？還有其他傳言，有人看見你在天亮時溜出那些烏煙瘴氣的房子，又喬裝鑽進倫敦最骯髒的地方。這些傳聞是真的嗎？它們怎麼可能是真的？我第一次聽見的時候，大笑不已。現在我又聽到了，不禁為之震顫。你鄉下的別墅以及在那邊的生活怎樣？道林，你不知道人家説了你些甚麼。我不會對你説我不想説教，我記得亨利曾説過，每個人變成業餘的牧師時，一開口都會説這句話，然後就食言。我真的想對你説教，我希望你能過受人尊敬的生活，我希望你名聲良好和身家清白，我希望你能不再跟那些糟糕的人來往。別那樣聳肩，別那麼冷漠。你有很大的影響力，讓這些影響成為好的，而不是壞的。人們説你帶壞了跟你親密的人，當你一走進房屋，就足以把某種恥辱帶到那裏。我不知道這些是不是真的。我怎能知道？但別人就是這樣説你。我聽到的事似乎是無可懷疑的。格洛斯特勛爵是我在牛津大學很要好的朋友。他給我看了一封信，是他妻子臨終時獨自在門通的別墅寫給他的。這封我所看過的最可怕的懺悔信，提及你的名字。我告訴他這很荒謬，還説我非常了解你，你不可能做出這樣的事情。了解你？我很納悶，難道我真的了解你？在我能回答這個問題之前，我得看一看你的靈魂。"

　　"看我的靈魂！"道林·格雷喃喃地重複了一遍。他從沙發上霍地站起來，幾乎嚇得面無人色。

　　"是的，"霍爾渥德嚴肅地回答説，聲調顯得更加沉痛。"看你的靈魂。但只有上帝能這樣做。"

道林發出一陣刻薄的苦笑。"你也能看到，就在今天夜裏！"他惡狠狠地說着，從桌上抓起了一盞燈。"走，這是你一手造成的，為甚麼不去看看？以後只要你願意，你可以把一切都告訴世人，但誰也不會相信你的話。要是人們相信了，反而會更加喜歡我。我比你更了解這個時代，儘管你談起這個時代來嘮嘮叨叨叫人心煩。來吧。關於腐化墮落你說得夠了。現在你可以面對面看到甚麼叫腐化墮落。"

他說的每一句話都流露出失去理性的傲氣。他像個無理取鬧的孩子頻頻頓足。想到有一個人將分享他的祕密，想到這幅成為他一切恥辱之根源的肖像畫的作者，將因自己做了這樣一件可怕的事而從此抱恨終生，道林簡直按捺不住幸災樂禍的心情。

"是的，"他繼續說着，向畫家走得更近些，同時逼視着貝澤爾嚴厲的眼神，"我要讓你看我的靈魂。你將看到你以為只有上帝看得見的東西。"

霍爾渥德驚恐地倒退一步。"這是褻瀆啊，道林！"他喊道。"你千萬不能這樣說話。這樣的話太可怕，也太荒謬了。"

"是嗎？"又是一陣狂笑。

"確實如此。至於我剛才對你說的話，那都是為你好。你知道我始終是你忠實的朋友。"

"別碰我。把你要講的話都講完。"

一陣痛苦的痙攣在畫家的臉上掠過。他沉默了一會，心中產生一股強烈的同情。歸根究底，他有甚麼權利干預道林·格雷的生活？即使他做的事只及傳聞的十分之一，想必已經夠他自己痛苦了。霍爾渥德定了定神，走到壁爐前，站在那裏看熊熊燃燒的木柴在霜華似的灰燼中吐着晃動不已的火舌。

"我在等你，貝澤爾，"道林以生硬而清晰的聲音説。

霍爾渥德轉過身來。"我要講的就是，關於那些針對你的指控，你必須給我一個答覆。只要你對我説，那些可怕的指控全是徹頭徹尾的捏造，我一定相信你。説吧，道林，快否認吧！你沒看見我在忍受怎樣的折磨？我的天啊！我不願知道你是個墮落、可恥的壞人。"

道林·格雷鄙夷地撇嘴冷笑。"到樓上去，貝澤爾，"他鎮靜地説。"我有一本日記記載着我每天的生活，一直保存在寫日記的那間房間裏。你只要跟我上樓去，我就讓你看。"

"道林，如果你希望的話，我會跟你去。反正我已經誤了我的火車。這沒多大關係，我可以明天再走。不過你可不要叫我在今天夜裏閲讀甚麼東西。我只要你明確地回答我的問題。"

"到樓上會給你答覆。在這裏我不能回答你。你用不着花很多時間去讀。"

第十三章

他走出房門，開始上樓。貝澤爾·霍爾渥德緊跟在後面。他們的腳步很輕，人們在深夜裏走路時總不自覺地這樣做。燈光把奇形怪狀的影子投在牆上和樓梯上。起風了，有幾扇窗戶被搖得格格直響。

他們走到頂層的樓梯口，道林將燈放在地板上，取出鑰匙插入鎖孔。"你仍堅持要知道嗎，貝澤爾？"他壓低了嗓門問道。

"是的。"

"好極了，"他微微一笑，然後又有點嚴厲地説，"你是這個世界上唯一有資格了解我全部底細的人。你跟我生活的關係比你想像的密切得多。"他拿起燈開了門走進去。一股冷氣吹過，使那盞燈霎時間閃起昏橙色的火焰。道林打了個寒噤。"你進來把門關上，"他悄悄地説着，將燈放在桌上。

霍爾渥德四下看看，臉上現出困惑不解的表情。這間房間看起來好多年沒有人住了。一張褪了色的佛蘭德斯掛毯、一幅被遮起來的畫、一個意大利舊箱櫃、一個幾乎空空如也的書櫃，再加上一張椅子和一張桌子，似乎就是裏面的全部陳設。當道林·格雷把壁爐架上半支蠟燭點亮的時候，霍爾渥德發現這裏的一切都封了塵，地毯已有不少窟窿，一隻老鼠在護壁板後面打滾奔跑，屋子裏有一股潮濕的霉味。

"貝澤爾，你以為只有上帝看得見人的靈魂，是不是？你把這罩布揭開，就會看到我的靈魂。"

說這話的聲音陰冷而殘酷。"你一定是瘋子，道林。要不然就是在演戲，"霍爾渥德咕噥着，皺起了眉。

"你不揭開？那我自己來揭，"道林說罷，將罩布從掛杆上扯下來，扔在地上。

霍爾渥德發出一聲恐怖的叫喊，他在昏慘慘的燭光燈影中看到一張可憎可怕的臉從畫布上向他獰笑。畫中人的神態使霍爾渥德充滿了厭惡，簡直令人作嘔。老天爺啊！難道他看到的是道林的臉嗎？不管怎樣，獰惡的表情還沒有完全掩蓋那出類拔萃的美。開始變得稀疏的頭髮還是金黃的，淫邪的嘴唇也還紅得鮮豔。渾濁的眼睛多少保持着原本可愛的碧藍色，清秀的鼻孔和雕塑似的脖子尚未完全喪失典雅的曲線美。是的，這是道林。但是誰把他畫成這樣的呢？霍爾渥德好像認出了自己的手筆，畫框也是他親自設計的。這簡直不可思議。他感到害怕，一下子拿起點亮的蠟燭，舉着它照那幅像。左角分明有他朱紅色瘦長字體的親筆簽名。

這簡直是差勁的仿作，是一種卑劣缺德的諷刺。他從來沒有畫過這樣的東西。然而，這又明明是他的作品。他認出來了，只覺得自己身上的血液一下子從火結成了冰。他的畫像！這是怎麼回事？為甚麼變了樣？他轉過身來，用病人的目光望着道林·格雷。霍爾渥德的嘴抽搐着，敝焦的唇舌說不出話來。他抹一下額頭，發現額上滲出了黏糊糊的汗珠。

道林靠在壁爐架上，帶着異樣的表情觀察霍爾渥德，像是全神貫注地看一位偉大的演員演戲。道林的表情既談不上哀愁，也不算高興。他只抱着一個旁觀者的興趣，也許眼睛裏閃現出勝利的火花。他把外套鈕孔裏的花取下來聞了聞，不過也許只是做做樣子。

"這是怎麼回事？"霍爾渥德終於問道，但聲音是那麼刺耳，他自己也覺得奇怪。

"好多年前，我還是個少年，"道林一面説，一面把那朵花在掌心裏抓碎，"你遇見了我，説了許多恭維我的話，使我懂得了自己的美貌是值得驕傲的。有一天，你把我介紹給你的一個朋友。他向我講解青春有多大的魅力，而你正好完成了我的一幅畫像。那幅畫開了我的眼界，使我看到了美的魅力。在癡迷心竅的一刹那……直到現在我依然不知道自己是否感到後悔，我許了一個願，也許可以説是作了一次祈禱……"

"我記起來了！哦，我記得很清楚！不！那是不可能的。這間屋子潮濕，霉菌侵蝕了畫布；或者，我用的顏料裏含有可惡的有毒礦物質。你説的那種事是不可能的。"

"不可能？"道林沉吟着，走到窗前，把前額貼在冰涼模糊的玻璃上。

"你告訴過我，説你已經把畫像毀掉了。"

"我撒了謊。是畫像把我毀了。"

"我不相信這是我的作品。"

"你從上面看不到自己的理想了，是不是？"道林尖刻地説。

"你所説的我的理想……"

"是你自己説的。"

"這沒有甚麼要不得，沒有甚麼不光彩。我曾經把你看作是再也遇不上第二次的理想。可是這幅畫像上的面孔是一個色情狂的嘴臉。"

"這是我靈魂的面貌。"

"主啊！我崇拜的竟是這樣的東西！它的眼睛完全是魔鬼的眼睛。"

"天堂和地獄都在我們每個人身上，貝澤爾！"道林大聲說，同時做了一個動作幅度很大的手勢以示其絕望。

霍爾渥德又轉過臉來注視着畫像。"我的天！如果這是真的，"他驚呼道，"如果你過的正是這樣的生活，那麼，你甚至要比說你壞話的人所想像的更壞！"他再次舉起蠟燭照着肖像仔細觀看。畫布的表面看來完好無損，與離開他畫室的時候一樣。可怕的變化顯然是從內部發生的。罪惡的菌體透過畫像的內在生命怪異地甦醒起來，慢慢地蠶食着它。在潮濕的墳墓裏腐爛的屍體也沒有這樣可怕。

他的手開始發抖，蠟燭從燭台跌落下來，在地板上發出嘩嘩啪啪的聲音。霍爾渥德把它踩熄了，然後頹然坐在桌旁一張東歪西倒的椅子上，兩手捂住面孔。

"老天啊，道林，多麼可怕的教訓！這是多麼可怕的教訓！"道林沒有回答。但他聽見他在窗前抽噎。"祈禱吧，道林，祈禱吧，"他低聲說。"小時候大人是怎麼教我們的？'不要讓我們墮入魔障，寬恕我們的罪過，洗滌我們的惡行。'讓我們一起來念。你逞一時驕氣所作的祈禱應驗了，你表示懺悔的祈禱也會應驗的。我對你的崇拜太過分了，為此我受到了懲罰。你對自己的崇拜也太過分了。我們都受到了懲罰。"

道林・格雷慢慢轉過身來，淚眼迷茫地望着他。"現在已經太晚了，貝澤爾，"他結結巴巴地說。

　　"永遠不會太晚的，道林。讓我們跪下來，試試看能不能背出一段禱文來。好像在哪裏見過這樣的詩句：'哪怕你的罪惡殷紅似血，我也能把它們洗刷得潔白如雪。'"

　　"這些話現在對我毫無意義。"

　　"噓！不要這樣說。你一生作孽已經夠多了。天啊！你沒看到這個該死的東西不懷好意地看着我們嗎？"

　　道林・格雷向畫像瞟了一眼，突然對貝澤爾・霍爾渥德產生一種情不自禁的憎恨，彷彿這是畫中人向他暗示的結果，是那獰笑的嘴唇向他耳語的結果。野獸遭到追捕時的瘋狂開始在他身上游走。此時他憎恨坐在桌旁的那個人，甚至超越他一生中厭惡過的任何事物。他睜大了眼睛四下張望，那個面朝着他的彩繪大箱櫃蓋上，有一件亮閃閃的東西吸引住他的視線。他知道那是前幾天他帶到樓上來割繩子的一把刀，忘了拿下去。他慢慢地朝那邊移動，從霍爾渥德身旁經過。道林剛一繞到他背後，立刻抓起那把刀子，轉過來。霍爾渥德在椅子上挪動了一下身體，好像要站起來。道林向他猛撲過去，把刀子戳進他耳朵後面的大靜脈，接着就把他的腦袋往桌上按下去，又捅了好幾刀。

　　一聲喘不過氣來的呻吟伴隨着某人喉嚨被血堵住的可怕聲響。伸出的兩條胳膊痙攣地往上揮了三下，發僵的指頭在空中做了幾個古怪的動作。道林又刺了他兩刀，但是那個男人已不再動彈了。甚麼東西開始滴滴答答落在地上。道林等了一會，手仍舊按住那顆腦袋。最後他把刀子扔在桌上，側耳細聽。

除了落在磨光露底的地毯上的滴答聲外，聲息全無。他開了房門，走到樓梯口。整幢房屋一片寂靜。沒有任何人走動。他靠在欄杆上俯視着沸騰的黑夜，這樣站了幾秒鐘。然後他從鎖孔中取出鑰匙，回到課室裏，把自己反鎖在裏面。

那東西依然坐在椅子裏，低頭拱背趴在桌上，伸着兩條長胳臂。要不是頸上那邊緣不整齊的紅色裂口，要不是凝成塊狀的黑色血泊在桌上逐漸散開，你還以為這個人睡着了呢。

這一切都完成得多麼俐落！他出奇地冷靜，走到窗前打開窗，走出陽台。風把霧氣吹散，天空就像是一隻巨大孔雀的尾巴，佈滿無數的金色眼睛。他向下望，看見警察在巡邏，把手提燈長長的光束投在寂靜的家門上。一輛來回走動的馬車在街角閃出一個紅點，然後消失了。一個女人正沿着欄杆跟蹌地蠕動，身上的披肩一顫一顫。她時不時停下來，盯着身後。突然，她開始用沙啞的聲線唱歌。警察走過去，跟她説了幾句話。她大聲笑着，跌跌撞撞地走開。一陣刺骨的風吹過廣場，煤氣燈火閃爍不定，變成藍色，光禿禿的樹木來回搖動着黑鐵一樣的樹枝。他打了個寒顫，返回室內，並關上身後的窗。

他走到房門口，轉動鎖孔中的鑰匙把門打開。對那個被他殺死的人，道林甚至沒有看上一眼。他覺得關鍵在於不要去想所發生的事。一個朋友曾經畫了一幅給他帶來這麼多苦難的可怕肖像，現在這個朋友從他的生活中消失了。如此而已。

這時他想起了帶上樓來的燈。那是北非摩爾人製作的啞光銀器，嵌有阿拉伯風格的拋光鋼鐵花紋，還點綴着好幾顆粗糙的綠松石，相當罕見。他的侍從也許會發現少了這盞燈，難免要查問。

道林猶豫了一會，還是回到桌子旁邊去拿這盞燈。他不由自主地看了一下那具屍體。它還是紋風不動！兩條長長的胳臂是那樣慘白！它就像一座蠟像，令人毛骨悚然。

道林鎖好房門，開始輕手輕腳地下樓。木樓梯嘰嘰嘎嘎地叫，像在痛苦中呼號。他幾次停下來靜聽。不，沒有任何動靜，除了他自己的腳步聲。

他走進書齋，看到了角落裏有一個手提袋和一件大衣。這些東西必須藏起來。他用鑰匙打開一個藏有他各種偽裝衣服的祕密衣櫃，把手提袋和大衣放進去。之後他可以輕而易舉地把它們燒毀掉。他掏出錶來看看時間，一點四十分。

他坐下來尋思。在英國，每一年，不，幾乎每一個月，都有人因為做了剛才他所做的事被處絞刑。時下流行着一股殺戮的狂熱。大概是某一顆火紅的星星太靠近地球了……得想一想，有沒有不利於他的證據？貝澤爾・霍爾渥德是十一點鐘離開這裏的。沒有人看見他第二次再來。大部分傭人都在塞爾比莊園。他的貼身侍從已經睡了……巴黎！對了。貝澤爾按原計劃坐午夜的火車到巴黎去。這位畫家素來孤僻成性，幾個月之內他無聲無息，也不會引起任何懷疑。幾個月！這麼長的時間定能把一切痕跡都消滅乾淨。

忽然他想出一個主意，立刻穿上裘皮大衣，戴上帽子，走到門廳裏。他在那兒停下來，聽警察踏着緩慢而沉重的腳步在門外的街上走過，看窗上映出巡捕燈一閃一閃的發光。他屏住呼吸等着。

頃刻，他拔去門閂溜到外面，輕輕地把門關上。然後，他開始按門鈴。約莫過了五分鐘，他的侍從一邊穿衣服，一邊睡眼惺忪地出來開門。

"我很抱歉不得不把你叫醒，弗蘭西斯，"道林進了門説。"我忘了帶鑰匙。現在幾點了？"

"兩點十分，先生，"侍從眨着眼睛看了看鐘説。

"兩點十分？都這麼晚了！上午九點你得把我叫醒。我有工作要做。"

"是，先生。"

"晚上有人來過嗎？"

"霍爾渥德先生來過，先生。他一直等到十一點，後來他走了，説是還要去趕火車。"

"哦！可惜我沒有碰到他。他沒有甚麼話要你轉告嗎？"

"沒有，先生。他只説要是在俱樂部找不到你，他到了巴黎再給你寫信。"

"好吧，弗蘭西斯。別忘了九點鐘叫醒我。"

"不會忘記的，先生。"

侍從趿拉着拖鞋從走廊退了下去。

道林把他的帽子和大衣扔在桌上，走進書齋。有十五分鐘他一直在屋子裏踱來踱去，咬着嘴唇反覆思量。然後他從書架上取下一本社會名人錄，開始翻查。"艾倫·坎貝爾，梅菲爾市赫特福德街一百五十二號"。對，這正是他需要的那個人。

第十四章

翌晨九點鐘，他的侍從用盤子托着一杯巧克力進來，把遮窗板拉開。道林身體向右側臥，一隻手壓在臉頰下，睡得正香。他看起來像個玩得十分疲倦或用功過度的孩子。

侍從在道林肩膀上碰了兩下，他才醒來。他睜開眼睛的時候，嘴上浮起一絲淡淡的笑意，彷彿剛剛離開甜蜜的夢鄉。實際上他根本沒有做夢。這一夜沒有任何幻象打擾他，不管是愉快的還是痛苦的。青春的笑往往無緣無故，這是它其中一個主要的魅力。

他翻過身來，用胳膊肘支住上身，開始啜飲那杯巧克力。十一月柔和的陽光照進房間。天色明亮，空氣裏有一股舒適的暖意，簡直就像五月的早晨。

漸漸地，昨夜發生的事情無聲無息而血跡斑斑地潛入他的腦海，清晰得令人膽寒地在那裏一一重演。回憶起自己經歷的那一切，他立即緊鎖雙眉。對貝澤爾莫名其妙的厭惡，驅使道林把坐在椅子上的他殺死，現在這種厭惡感又甦醒過來，使道林從心裏開始冷遍全身。那死人還坐在那裏，這時正被陽光照耀着。這太可怕了！這種討厭的東西只能讓黑夜把它遮蓋起來，不能暴露在光天化日之下。

他感到，要是細想自己的經歷，就非生病或發瘋不可。有些罪惡事後回味比實行更有意思。有些不尋常的勝利所滿足的，與其說是慾念，不如說是虛榮心。這種勝利對思想所起的興奮作用，大於給感官帶來或可能帶來的快樂。但這個罪惡不屬於那一類，應當把它從記憶裏趕出去，用鴉片加以麻醉，扼殺它，否則它會把你扼殺掉。

鐘在九點半敲起來，道林用手抹了抹前額，然後急忙起牀。他比平時更講究穿着，在挑選領帶和領帶夾時着實費了點功夫，戒指也再三更換。他還在早餐上花了不少時間，品嚐各種早點，跟侍從說他打算給塞爾比莊園的傭人做新制服，還瀏覽一遍收到的信件。有幾封信使他露出會心的微笑。有三封信他覺得討厭。其中一封他讀了好幾遍，臉上略帶心煩的表情，最後把它撕了。"女人的記性真是要命的玩意！"他想起亨利勛爵有一次說過這樣的話。

他喝完一杯黑咖啡，慢慢地用餐巾抹了抹嘴，示意他的侍從等一下，自己走到桌旁坐下來寫了兩封信。一封放在自己的口袋裏，另一封交給侍從。

"弗蘭西斯，把這封信送到赫特福德街一百五十二號去。如果坎貝爾先生不在倫敦，你打聽一下他在甚麼地方。"

等到他獨自一人的時候，他點了一支煙，開始在一張紙上隨手素描，先是畫一些花卉和建築的不同部分，後來畫人的面孔。突然，他發覺自己畫的每一張面孔都很像貝澤爾·霍爾渥德。他皺眉蹙額地站起來，走到書櫃跟前隨便拿了一本書。他決意非到萬不得已，也不去想已經發生的事情。

他在沙發上伸展身體時，看到一本書的扉頁。這是哥提耶的《搪瓷與雕玉》，是夏隴蒂埃的日本紙版本，配以雅克瑪的刻版畫插圖、黃綠色的皮革裝幀，綴有鍍金格子和圓點石榴的圖案。這本書是阿德里安·辛格爾頓送給他的。他一頁一頁地翻着，眼睛聚焦到一首關於拉塞內爾的手的詩。那雙冰冷泛黃的手"殘留着罪惡的痕跡",長滿紅色的毛髮,有"農牧神的手指"。他看了一眼自己白皙尖細的手指,不自禁輕輕地哆嗦了一下。他接着往下翻,看到了幾節描寫威尼斯的可愛的詩:——

> 亞德里亞海的維納斯,
> 從水中露出白裏透紅的身體,
> 在半音音階的陪襯下,
> 胸前灑下粒粒珠璣。
> 碧波砌就的圓穹頂,
> 像豐滿的乳房高高聳起,
> 合着輪廓完美的樂句節奏,
> 頻頻發出愛的歎息。
> 船家把我送到岸邊,
> 柱樁上繫纜停放舟楫。
> 在嫩紅色的正門前,
> 我踏上大理石的階梯。

這些詩句是多麼的精妙!讀着這些詩句,人就像坐在銀色船首的黑色簾垂小船上,在粉紅色珍珠般的城市中的綠色水道上漂浮。一行行的詩句就像破浪駛向利多島時,船後泛起的青藍色直線。詩中閃爍的色彩讓他想起那些彩色脖頸的鳥兒,它們常常在蜂房般的高聳鐘樓周圍盤旋,或是姿態優雅地在沾滿灰塵的昏暗拱門下踱步。他半閉着雙眼,靠在沙發上,一遍遍地吟着:——

在嫩紅色的正門前，
我踏上大理石的階梯。

　　整個威尼斯就在於那兩行詩句中間。他記得在那裏度過了一個秋天，想起了一段令他瘋狂而快樂的美妙愛情。每個地方都有浪漫故事，但威尼斯和牛津一樣，為浪漫留下了背景。而對真正的浪漫而言，背景就是一切，或者說幾乎是一切。貝澤爾跟他度過了一段時間，然後沉迷於丁托列多。可憐的貝澤爾！他死得太慘了！

　　他歎息後重新拿起書，嘗試忘記剛才的回憶。他讀到燕子在士麥那的小咖啡館飛進飛出，朝聖者坐在那兒細數琥珀念珠，裹着頭巾的商人抽着帶有流蘇的長煙桿，嚴肅地交談着；協和廣場的方尖碑流着花崗石的眼淚，哀歎自己孤苦伶仃地被放逐到了這個見不到陽光的地方，恨不得返回遍佈荷花且炎熱的尼羅河去，那裏有獅身人面像，有玫瑰紅色的朱鷺，有長着金黃爪子的白色禿鷹，有眼睛小如綠玉的鱷魚在蒸騰的綠色泥潭中爬行。他開始思索着哥提耶的詩句，在留有吻痕的大理石中聽到了音樂，把奇異雕像比作女低音，“迷人的怪物”現臥於羅浮宮的斑岩廳。但過了一會，書從他手下跌落。他緊張起來，感到一陣強烈的恐懼。如果艾倫・坎貝爾出了國那怎麼辦？等他回來要好幾天。他或許會拒絕過來，到時候要怎麼辦？每分每刻都至關重要。

　　五年前，他和艾倫・坎貝爾曾經是朋友，幾乎形影不離。後來這種親密的關係突告中斷。如今他們在社交場合見面時，只有道林・格雷向他微笑，艾倫・坎貝爾卻毫不動容。

艾倫・坎貝爾是一個極其聰明的青年，雖然他不會欣賞視覺藝術，而且對詩歌的那一點點美感也完全是從道林那兒學來的。他主要把精力放在科學上。就讀劍橋大學時，他把大部分時間都花在實驗室裏，並在他那學年的自然科學榮譽學位考試中取得很好的成績。到現在，他仍然醉心研究化學，還擁有一個實驗室，整天把自己關在裏面，令他的母親很生氣，她一心希望他去競選議員，隱約地認為化學家只是負責開藥方。他也是個出色的音樂人，他的小提琴和鋼琴比大多數的業餘音樂人都要演奏得好。事實上，最初正是音樂把他和道林・格雷拉在一起，應該說是音樂和道林身上難以言喻的吸引力。道林的吸引力似乎能隨意顯現，但實際是他無意識地顯露出來。他們是在伯克希爾夫人家裏認識的，魯賓斯坦當晚在那裏演出。自此之後，他們就經常在歌劇院，或任何有好音樂的地方一起出現。他們度過了十八個月的親密時光。坎貝爾不是在塞爾比莊園，就是在格羅夫納廣場。如同很多人一樣，對他來說，道林・格雷代表着人生中的一切美好奇妙的事物。沒有人知道他們有否爭吵過，但人們突然發現他們見面時幾乎不說話，坎貝爾更似乎提早離開任何道林・格雷在場的聚會。坎貝爾也改變了，有時憂鬱得很奇怪，似乎很討厭聽音樂，更用忙於研究科學，沒有時間練琴為藉口，不再為人演奏。當然這也是事實，他對生物學的興趣似乎日益濃厚，他的名字也有一兩次登上了某些與奇怪實驗相關的科學評論裏。

道林等候的就是這麼一個人。他不時舉目看鐘。時間一分鐘一分鐘地過去，他的情緒愈來愈焦躁。最後他站起來，在房間裏走來走去，像一隻關在籠子裏的美麗動物。他的步伐很大，但是聲息全無。他的手冷得出奇。

道林忍受不了這件事就這麼懸着，他覺得時間像拖着灌鉛的腿那樣在爬行，而他自己正被狂風飛速推向黑洞洞的懸崖絕壁。他知道在那裏等着他的是甚麼，甚至已經看到了那景象。他一邊哆嗦着，一邊用冰涼而潮濕的手擠壓發燙的眼皮，似乎要把大腦的視覺也剝奪掉，把眼珠塞回到眼球去。然而沒有用處。腦袋有自己的營養來源，想像則因恐懼而變得奇怪，像有生命的東西受到痛苦而掙扎扭動，又像污穢的傀儡在台上亂蹦亂跳，戴着活動面具扮出種種怪相。突然，時間為他而停止。是的，那盲目而呼吸緩慢的東西停止爬行了。時間既然死去，恐怖的念頭立刻衝上前來，把無比殘酷的未來從墳墓中拖出，展示在他的眼前。他睜大眼睛看着這個未來，嚇得不能動彈。

　　門終於開了，他的侍從走進來。道林把一雙呆滯的眼睛轉過去望着他。

　　"坎貝爾先生來了，先生，"侍從向他通報。

　　他張開枯焦的嘴唇鬆了一口氣，兩頰恢復了原有的血色。

　　"快請他進來，弗蘭西斯。"他覺得自己又恢復了鎮定。膽怯的情緒已經消失。

　　侍從鞠了一躬退下去。不一會，艾倫・坎貝爾走了進來，他神態嚴峻，在烏黑的頭髮和兩道濃眉的反襯下，面色顯得分外蒼白。

　　"艾倫，你來得太好了。我向你表示感謝。"

　　"我已經立意永遠不進你家的門，格雷。可是你信上說這是一件生死攸關的事。"他掛字酌句地說得很慢，語氣生硬而冷淡。他定睛注視着道林，目光犀利而輕蔑。他的手插在阿斯特拉罕羔皮大衣的口袋裏，並不理會道林歡迎他的姿勢。

“是的，艾倫，這是一件生死攸關的事，而且涉及不止一個人。請坐。”

坎貝爾在桌旁一張椅子上坐下，道林坐在他對面。兩個人四目相遇。道林的眼神流露出無限憐憫。他知道自己打算採取的手段極為狠毒。

在一陣難堪的沉默之後，他湊到對方面前，很沉着地说，同時留神觀察他請來的這個人的臉，看他對每一句話、每一個字有甚麼反應。“艾倫，這幢房屋的頂層有一間鎖着的房間，除了我自己，任何人也進不去。裏面有一個死人坐在桌子旁邊。他死了有十個小時。別緊張，也不要這樣看着我。那個人是誰，他為甚麼死了，怎麼死的，這些跟你都不相干。你要做的只是……”

“住口，格雷。我不願聽下去。你對我说的話是真是假，我也不管。你的事我絕對不插手。把你醜惡的祕密留給自己吧，我對這些把戲再也不感興趣了。”

“艾倫，你不感興趣也不行。這件事你非管不可。我感到萬分抱歉，艾倫，但也是出於無奈。你是唯一能救我的人。我不得不把你拖進來。我沒有別的辦法。艾倫，你是搞科學的，你對化學之類的學問很內行，做過不少實驗。你得把樓上那個東西消滅掉，消滅得乾乾淨淨，不留下一點痕跡。沒有人看見他進來這間房子，目前他應該到巴黎去了。幾個月之內不會有人發覺他失蹤。到人們發覺的時候，這裏決不能找出任何他的痕跡。艾倫，你必須把他以及屬於他的一切變成可以在空中撒開的一撮灰。”

“你瘋了，道林。”

“啊！我就等着你叫我道林。”

"我告訴你，你一定是瘋了。要不，你怎麼能想像我願意盡舉手之勞幫你忙？你怎麼會向我作這番駭人聽聞的自白？不管這到底是怎麼回事，反正我不插手。難道你以為我甘願為你去冒身敗名裂的風險？你在搞甚麼鬼名堂，我根本不想知道！"

"艾倫，他是自殺的。"

"但願如此。可是把他帶上這條路的是誰？我敢說，是你。"

"你是不是仍然拒絕為我做這件事？"

"當然拒絕。我絕對不插手。你出醜與否跟我無關。你出醜也是活該。看到你當眾丟臉，名譽掃地，我不會感到惋惜。你竟敢要我自己往火坑裏跳！為甚麼不找別人，偏偏找到我頭上來？我本以為你比較了解人們的心理。看來，你的朋友亨利·沃登勛爵在心理學方面給你的教益不多，儘管他教會了你其他許多本領。我決不為你出半點力氣。你找錯人了。你該去找你的朋友，不要來找我。"

"艾倫，他是被殺的。是我把他殺了。你不知道他給我帶來了多大的痛苦。不管我過的是怎樣一種生活，在造就或毀壞這種生活上面，他起的作用比可憐的亨利更大。也許這不是他的本意，但結果卻是如此。"

"殺人！我的老天！道林，你竟然走到了這一步？我不會告發你。這不關我的事。何況，即使我不摻和進去，你也一定會被捕。犯下罪行的人沒有不露馬腳的。反正我不參與這件事。"

"你必須參與。等一下，等一下，聽我說，艾倫。我只要求你作一次科學實驗。你經常到醫院和陳屍所去，你不是不受這些可怕的事情影響嗎？假如你在一間令人作嘔的解剖室或臭氣觸鼻的實驗室裏，看到這個人躺在有讓血可以往外流的槽的暗灰色長枱上，你必定單純地把他看作一件有趣的實驗品。你連眉毛也不會動一下。你決不會想到自己在做甚麼壞事。相反，你大概認為你是在造福人類，或者擴大世界的知識寶庫，或者滿足自己的求知慾，諸如此類。我要你做的無非是你過去經常做的事情。其實，消滅一具屍體應當比你做慣的事情好受得多。請你記住，這是唯一對我不利的證據。萬一它被發現，我就完了。你要是不幫我忙的話，它肯定會被發現。"

"我根本不想幫你的忙。我已經說過了，我對這件事完全不感興趣，它跟我毫無關係。"

"艾倫，我懇求你。請設身處地替我想一想。就在你來到這裏之前，我害怕得差點昏倒。將來你自己可能也會嘗到恐怖的滋味。不！還是不要去想這些。你得純粹從科學的角度來看這件事。你從來不問讓你做實驗的死屍是從哪裏來，現在你也不要問。我告訴你的已經太多了。但是我請求你做這件事。我們畢竟一度是朋友，艾倫。"

"不要提過去的事，道林。過去種種已經死去。"

"死去的東西往往死而不去。樓上那個人死了，但就是不去。他坐在桌旁，垂着頭伸出胳臂。艾倫！艾倫！你要是不幫助我，我就完了。我會被絞死，艾倫！你懂嗎？我做了這樣的事，他們非判我絞刑不可。"

"這齣戲再演下去已經沒有意思。我絕對不插手這件事。你一定是神經錯亂了才來求我幫忙。"

"你不幫我？"

"是的。"

"我懇求你，艾倫。"

"這沒有用。"

道林·格雷的眼睛裏又出現了那種憐憫的表情。然後他伸手取過一張紙來，在上面寫了些甚麼。他默默讀了兩遍，把那張紙仔細摺好，隔着桌子推過去。接着他站起來走到窗前去。

坎貝爾驚訝地對他看了看，拿起紙條把它展開。他讀了這張字條，頓時面色煞白，頹然靠在椅背上。他感到噁心，好像他的心臟在一片空虛中怦怦亂跳，眼看着就要破裂。

在兩三分鐘可怕的沉默之後，道林轉身走到桌旁，站在艾倫·坎貝爾背後，把一隻手擱在他肩上。

"我為你感到抱歉，艾倫，"他輕聲説着，"但是你逼得我沒有別的路可走。我已經寫好了一封信，就是這封。你看看上面的地址。你要是不幫忙的話，我只得把這封信寄出去。你不幫忙，我就寄信。你也知道後果，不過你會幫助我的，現在你要拒絕也不可能。我本來不打算對你來這一套，你應當承認我作過這樣的努力，但是你毫不通融，出口傷人。從來沒有人敢像你這樣對待我，至少活着的沒有。我全都忍受下來了。現在該由我來提出條件。"

坎貝爾雙手掩面，一陣顫慄通過他的全身。

"是的，該輪到我提條件了，艾倫。我不提你也知道。事情非常簡單。來吧，不要這樣像發燒似的。事情還是得做。面對現實，動手吧。"

坎貝爾發出一聲呻吟，又打了一個寒戰。對他來説，壁爐架上一座台鐘的滴答聲，正在把時間分裂成痛苦的原子，每一顆都是可怕難熬的折磨。他感到有一圈鐵箍在他前額周圍慢慢地愈收愈緊，彷彿威脅着他的奇恥大辱已經臨頭。擱在他肩上的那隻手像灌了鉛一般沉重，實在受不了。這樣他非被壓得粉碎不可。

「快一點，艾倫，你必須當機立斷。」

「我不能做這種事，」他機械地說着，其實任何言語都改變不了局面。

「你必須得做。你沒有選擇的餘地。不要拖拖拉拉。」

艾倫猶豫了一會。「樓上那間房裏有沒有火爐？」

「有，是一個以石棉隔熱的煤氣爐。」

「我得回家一趟，從實驗室取一些東西。」

「不，艾倫，你不能離開這所房屋。你把所需要的東西寫在便條上，我的僕人會坐車去取來。」

坎貝爾匆匆寫了幾行字，用吸墨水紙吸乾，信封上寫上他助手的姓名。道林接過便條，仔細讀了一遍，這才打鈴。他把信交給進來的侍從，並吩咐他儘快把東西都帶回來。

門廳的門關上時，坎貝爾神經質地全身震了一下。他從椅子站起來，走到壁爐前，像發寒熱似地哆嗦着。有二十分鐘左右，兩個人誰也不開口。一隻蒼蠅在房間裏嗡嗡亂轉，台鐘的滴答聲像一把錘子敲個不停。

鐘在一點敲起來。坎貝爾轉身向道林・格雷一看，見他兩眼滿是淚水。他那充滿哀愁但眉清目秀的臉龐頓使艾倫無名火起。「你真無恥，無恥到了極點！」他咬牙切齒地說。

「噓，艾倫，你救了我的生命，」道林說。

「你的生命？老天爺！那是怎樣的生命啊！你一步步地腐化

墮落，現在索性犯罪。我之所以答應做你強逼我做的那件事，考慮的可不是你的生命。"

"唉，艾倫，"道林歎了口氣嘀咕着，"你要是有我對你千分之一的憐憫就好了。"他邊說邊轉過身去，站着看窗外的花園。坎貝爾並不答理。

過了十分鐘左右，侍從敲門進來。他搬來一個放化學藥品的紅木大箱子、一圈長長的鋼絲和白金絲，還有兩隻形狀很怪的鐵夾鉗。

"這些東西是否放在這裏，先生？"侍從問坎貝爾。

"沒錯，"道林說，"弗蘭西斯，我恐怕還有另一件差事要你幫忙。那個在列治文供應蘭花給塞爾比莊園的男人叫甚麼名字？"

"叫哈登，先生。"

"對，哈登。你立刻去列治文一趟，找哈登本人，告訴他以後送蘭花要比我原本訂的增加一倍。白的儘量少些。最好完全不要白的。今天天氣很好，弗蘭西斯，列治文又是個挺漂亮的地方，否則我不想麻煩你跑這麼遠。"

"沒關係，先生。我甚麼時候該回來？"

道林向坎貝爾望了望。"艾倫，你的實驗需要多少時間？"他用平靜的語調很隨便地問。看來，室內有第三者在場，他就特別膽壯。

坎貝爾皺緊眉頭，咬了咬嘴唇。"大約五個小時，"他回答說。

"時間充裕得很，弗蘭西斯，你可以在七點半回來。等一等，你把我的衣服準備好。晚上你自己安排。我不在家裏吃晚飯，不需要你的幫忙。"

"謝謝，先生，"侍從説着，退了出去。

"艾倫，現在得馬上動手。這箱子重得厲害！我來給你搬，你拿其餘的東西。"他説得很快，一副指揮若定的樣子。坎貝爾不由自主地聽從他的調遣。兩個人一起離開書齋。

他們登上了頂層樓梯口，道林掏出鑰匙來開鎖。這時他停下來，眼睛露出惶惑的神色。他打了個寒戰，囁嚅道："我大概不能進去，艾倫。"

"對我來説無所謂。我不需要你，"坎貝爾冷冷地説。

道林把門打開一半，首先映入他眼簾的是他的肖像上沐着陽光，不懷好意地看着。被扯破的罩布扔在畫像前面的地上。他這才想起昨天夜裏，生平第一次忘記把那幅要命的畫像遮好。他正想衝過去，但立即哆嗦着退了回來。

肖像的一隻手上出現了濕漉漉、亮閃閃的紅色露珠。那是甚麼討厭的東西？難道畫布會冒汗滲血？多可怕啊！霎時間，他覺得這比伸出胳臂趴在桌上毫無動靜的死人更可怕。血跡斑斑的地毯上輪廓奇特的陰影表明，那東西沒有移動過，依舊在道林離開時它所在的地方。

他深深地倒抽一口氣，把門開大些，側着腦袋匆匆走了進去。眼睛不敢完全睜開，拿定主意不向死人看上一眼。然後，他俯身拾起地上紫金色的緞罩，把它直接蓋在畫像上。

他站在那裏，頭也不敢回，眼睛盯着自己面前那緞罩上所繡的細巧花紋。他聽見坎貝爾把沉重的箱子、鐵夾鉗和做這件可怕工作所需的其他用具都搬了進來。道林心想，不知貝澤爾‧霍爾渥德與艾倫·坎貝爾是否認識？要是認識的話，他們現在互相該有何感想？

"現在你可以走了，"一把嚴厲的聲音在道林背後說。

他轉過身去，急急忙忙走出房間，只瞥見那具屍體已被掀翻，靠在椅背上，坎貝爾正凝視着那張油光光的黃臉。道林下樓時，聽見鑰匙在鎖孔中轉動。

等到坎貝爾下樓回到書齋裏時，早已過了七點。他面色蒼白，但十分鎮定。"我完成了你要求我做的事情，"他咕噥着。"現在讓我們分手吧。以後誰也不要再看見誰。"

"你救了我的命，艾倫，我沒齒難忘，"道林只說了這麼一句。

坎貝爾一走，道林立即奔上樓去。那間屋子裏有一股觸鼻的硝酸味，但是原先坐在桌旁椅子上的東西不見了。

第十五章

那天晚上八點半，道林‧格雷衣着講究，鈕扣孔裏插着一大串帕爾馬紫羅蘭，跟隨謙恭的僕人，進入納爾巴勒夫人的客廳。他額頭的神經跳動着，感到異常興奮，但當他俯身親吻女主人的手時，他的舉止如平時一樣從容優雅。也許人在演戲時才表現得最自如。當然，那晚見過道林‧格雷的人不可能會相信他經歷了一場悲劇，一場可怕程度不亞於我們時代的任何一場悲劇。那些纖細的手指不可能拿刀犯罪；那微笑的雙唇，絕不會褻瀆上帝諸神。他也對自己冷靜的行為感到驚訝，並有一瞬間對這種雙面生活感到低劣的快感。

納爾巴勒夫人匆匆忙忙邀集了這個小型宴會。她是一個很聰明的女人，保存着被亨利勛爵形容為"醜得可以"的殘餘。她嫁給我國一位毫無風趣的大使，博得了一位賢德夫人的名聲。大使死後，她按應有的排場把丈夫葬在她親自設計的大理石墓室中。她還把好幾個女兒一一嫁給年紀相當大的有錢人。現在，她一心一意欣賞法國小說、法國烹飪和法式詼諧，只要她能明白這種詼諧的情趣。

道林是她其中一個特別喜歡的人。她常常對他說，她很高興不是在年輕的時候遇見他。"我知道的，親愛的，我會瘋狂地愛上你，"她總是這樣說，"為了你，我會把帽子扔向風車。幸好我當時沒有想起你。但事實上，我們的帽子不好看，而風車又忙於招風，因此我從未跟別人調過情。然而，這全都是納爾巴勒的錯，他眼睛近視得厲害，玩弄一個甚麼都看不見的丈夫，沒有任何樂趣。"

她這天晚上的賓客相當無聊。事實上，納爾巴勒夫人用一把簡陋的扇子擋着臉向道林解釋，她其中一個嫁了人的女兒突然回來跟她一起住，更糟的是，她女兒把丈夫都帶回來。"我覺得她這樣做很不體貼，親愛的，"她小聲地說，"當然，我每年夏天從霍姆堡回來後都住在他們那裏，但像我這樣的老婦人，有時總要一些新鮮空氣。而且我真的需要讓他們清醒一點。你不知道他們在那裏過的是怎樣的生活。那是切切實實的鄉下生活。他們很早起牀，因為他們沒事可做；他們很早睡覺，因為他們沒事好想。從伊利沙伯女王時代以來，鄰里之間沒有任何流言蜚語，所以他們吃完晚飯就睡了。你可不要坐在他們旁邊。你應該坐在我旁邊，哄我開心。"

道林含含糊糊地恭維了一番，向大廳掃視一周。是啊，這羣賓客確實無聊得很。其中兩個人他從未見過，其餘的包括：歐內斯特·哈羅登，倫敦俱樂部裏比比皆是的中年庸才之一，這種人沒有仇敵，但是朋友無不討厭他；臘克斯頓夫人，一個四十七歲還打扮得花裏胡哨的女人，長着一個鷹鉤鼻，老是努力敗壞自己的名聲，但相貌實在太不標致，所以從來沒有人相信她的任何桃色事件，這使她大為懊喪；厄林太太，一個野心勃勃的無名人物，頭髮呈棕紅色，説起話來咬着舌頭，挺可笑的；愛麗絲·切普門夫人，女主人的女兒，一個不懂得如何穿戴、遲鈍的女郎，擁有一張見過一次就再也想不起來的典型英式面孔；還有她的丈夫，兩頰紅潤，蓄着白蒼蒼的連鬢鬍子，他與他階層的許多人一樣，相信無節制的愉悅可以彌補思想的極度空虛。

道林正在後悔來到這裏，但這時納爾巴勒夫人望着用紫紅色絲絨裝飾起來的壁爐架上一座造型鬆散、線條繁複的鍍金台鐘，大聲說道：「亨利·沃登簡直不像話，這麼晚還不來！今天上午我特地派人去過，他表示決不使我掃興，說是以信譽擔保。」

知道亨利要來，道林才稍感寬慰。後來門開了，他聽見亨利悠揚舒緩的聲調言不由衷，但是娓娓動聽地表示歉意，也就不再覺得無聊了。

但在宴席上道林甚麼也吃不下。他面前一道又一道的菜嚐也沒嚐就撤了下去。納爾巴勒夫人不住口地埋怨他，說這「對阿道夫是一種侮辱，可憐他特意為你安排了今天的菜單」。亨利勛爵不時隔着餐桌向他這邊瞭一眼，對他的沉默和心不在焉感到不解。管家頻頻往道林的酒杯裏斟滿香檳。他喝了一杯又一杯，愈喝就愈是渴得難熬。

「道林，」在傳遞野禽肉凍的時候，亨利勛爵終於問道，「今晚你怎麼啦？你好像神思恍惚得厲害。」

「八成是愛上甚麼人了，」納爾巴勒夫人說。「他不敢告訴我，怕我吃醋。他確實應該瞞着我。要不，我非大發醋勁不可。」

「親愛的納爾巴勒夫人，」道林含笑低語道，「說實話，自從費羅爾夫人離開倫敦後，我已經整整一星期沒跟任何人相愛了。」

「你們男人怎麼能愛上這樣一個女人！」上了年紀的女主人驚歎道。「我實在不明白。」

「那純粹是因為她還記得你小女孩時的情景，納爾巴勒夫人，」亨利勛爵說。「她是我們和你連衫短裙的唯一連接。」

"她決不會記得我穿連衫短裙的時代，亨利勛爵。我倒是對她三十年前在維也納裸肩露胸的模樣記得很清楚。"

"她現在還穿裸肩露胸的禮服，"亨利勛爵說着，用細長的指頭拿起一顆橄欖。"她盛裝打扮的時候就像一部蹩腳法國小說的豪華版。她非常有趣，不時忽發奇想做出怪事來。她眷戀家庭的本領真了不起。當她第三個丈夫去世的時候，由於傷心，她的頭髮完全變成了金黃色。"

"你太缺德了，亨利！"道林說。

"這倒是最浪漫的解釋，"女主人笑呵呵地說。"不過，亨利勛爵，你提到她'第三個丈夫'，難道費羅爾已經是第四個了？"

"當然，納爾巴勒夫人。"

"我絕對不信。"

"你可以問格雷。他是她最親密的朋友之一。"

"是真的嗎，格雷先生？"

"她確是這樣跟我說的，納爾巴勒夫人，"道林說，"我問她，她是不是像瑪嘉烈‧德‧納瓦皇后那樣，給每個丈夫的心都塗上防腐劑，然後掛在腰帶上。她說她沒這麼做，因為他們根本沒有心。"

"四個丈夫！未免太賣力了！"

"太勇敢了，我對她這樣表示，"道林說。

"噢！她有足夠的勇氣做任何事情，親愛的。那麼，費羅爾是個怎樣的人物呢？我不認識他。"

"絕色女子的丈夫應該歸入罪犯一類，"亨利勛爵說着，呷一口酒。

納爾巴勒夫人用扇子拍了他一下。"亨利勛爵，怪不得世人説你這個人極度壞透。”

“但你所説的‘世人’究竟是哪個世界上的人呢？”亨利勛爵揚起眉毛問道。“我看必定是來世的。我同今世相處得十分融洽。”

“我認識的人都説你很不正經，”納爾巴勒夫人連連搖頭。

有一會亨利勛爵顯得相當嚴肅，此後他説：“真討厭！如今時興在背後講人家壞話，偏偏這些話都是千真萬確。”

“這個人確實本性難改！”道林從椅子裏探身過去向女主人説。

“我看不改也罷，”納爾巴勒夫人笑道。“説實在的，要是你們都這樣荒唐地崇拜費羅爾夫人，我非得再嫁不可，否則就要落伍了。”

“你永遠不會再嫁，納爾巴勒夫人，”亨利勛爵插進來説。“你太幸福了。女人再嫁是因為恨前夫。男人續娶則是因為愛前妻。女人結婚是碰運氣，男人則是冒風險。”

“納爾巴勒也不是十全十美，”女主人不以為然。

“他如果十全十美，你就不愛他了，尊敬的夫人，”亨利勛爵對答如流。“女人愛的是男人的缺點。我們如果有一大堆缺點，她們甚麼都可以原諒我們，包括我們的才智。我擔心説了這話，你再也不會請我吃飯，納爾巴勒夫人；但事實的確如此。”

“當然是這樣，亨利勛爵。要不是我們女人愛你們的缺點，你們不知會落到怎樣的田地。你們一定誰也娶不到老婆。你們會變成一羣可憐巴巴的光棍。不過，儘管如此，你們也不會有多大改變。如今有家室的人生活都像光棍，而光棍反倒像有家室。”

"這就叫做世紀末，"亨利勛爵咕噥了一句。

"這叫做世界的末日，"女主人作了修正。

"但願是世界的末日，"道林感慨地歎道。"生活太令人失望了。"

"啊，親愛的，"納爾巴勒夫人急忙加以制止，同時戴上她的手套，"可不要説生活對你已變成一口枯井。一個人説這樣的話，那肯定是他知道自己的生活已變成一口枯井。亨利勛爵太不正經，我有時候真希望自己也能這樣；但你生來是一塊做好人的料，你的相貌也端端正正。我一定要給你找一位好太太。亨利勛爵，你説格雷先生是不是該結婚了？"

"我一直就是這麽對他説，納爾巴勒夫人，"亨利勛爵説着，低頭施禮。

"那麽，我們必須為他找頭合適的婚事。我今晚就要去仔細翻閲德布利特的貴族名錄，把所有合格的年輕女子都列出一張名單來。

"是否附上她們的年齡，納爾巴勒夫人？"道林問。

"當然附上，只是要作一番小小的校訂。但不能草率了事。我要把事情辦得門當戶對，像《晨郵報》所説的那樣。我要使雙方都稱心如意。"

"甚麽門當戶對，稱心如意，全是胡扯！"亨利勛爵説。"男人跟任何女人都可以得到快樂，只要男的不愛女的。"

"啊，你這個玩世不恭的厚臉皮！"女主人説着，把自己的椅子往後一推，並向臘克斯頓夫人點頭示意。"亨利勛爵，過幾天你必須再來跟我一起吃飯。你比安得魯爵士處方給我吃的補藥靈得多。不過你得告訴我，你喜歡跟哪些人見面。我要把那次聚會搞得活潑熱鬧。"

"我喜歡擁有未來的男人和擁有過去的女人，"他答道。"不過，這樣恐怕會變成一次清一色的女士聚會吧？"

"恐怕是的，"納爾巴勒夫人笑道，一邊起身離席。"非常抱歉，親愛的臘克斯頓夫人，"她添上一句，"我沒看見你還在抽煙。"

"沒關係，納爾巴勒夫人。我抽得太多了。今後我要克制一下。"

"千萬不要，臘克斯頓夫人，"亨利勛爵說。"克制是最糟糕的事情。適度就好比吃飯充飢一樣令人鬱悶。過量才像豐盛的筵席一樣熱鬧。"

臘克斯頓夫人好奇地看了看他。"改天下午一定請你到舍間來賜教，亨利勛爵。你的道理很吸引人，"她低聲說完後步出大廳。

"注意，你們可不要總是留在這裏談你們的政治和醜聞，"納爾巴勒夫人從門口提出警告。"否則我們在樓上非吵架不可。"

男客們哈哈大笑，切普門先生鄭重其事地從餐桌一端走到另一端。道林·格雷換了個座位，坐到了亨利勛爵旁邊。切普門先生開始就下議院的現狀大發宏論，他以放肆的大笑攻訐他的政敵，笑聲之間不時提到在英國人聽來非常可怕的一個名詞——空論家。這大概算是演講藝術的修辭技巧。他在思想之塔上升起了大不列顛的旗幟，他興致勃勃地把這個民族祖傳的愚鈍叫做英國常識，聲稱這是社會的可靠支柱。

亨利勛爵撇着嘴淡然一笑，掉過臉去向道林看看。

"老弟，你覺得好點了嗎？"他問道。"在席上我看你有些神思恍惚。"

"我沒有甚麼不舒服，亨利。只不過有點累罷了。"

"昨天晚上你很有魅力。那位嬌小的公爵夫人完全被你迷住了。她對我說準備到你的塞爾比莊園去。"

"她答應我二十號來。"

"蒙茂斯是不是也去？"

"是的，亨利。"

"我非常討厭這個人，簡直跟公爵夫人討厭他的程度一樣。公爵夫人很聰明，身為一個女人，也許聰明過頭。她缺少那種妙不可言的柔弱。金身偶像之所以可貴，就在於有一雙泥足。她的腳非常可愛，但不是用黏泥做的，不妨說是用白瓷。這雙腳經過火燒，而凡是經過火燒而無損的，就煉結實了。她很有經驗。"

"她結婚多久了？"道林問。

"據她說已經很久很久。從貴族姓名錄上看，大概是十年，但是和蒙茂斯在一起過十年簡直等於幾輩子。其他還有甚麼人去？"

"威洛比夫婦、臘格比勛爵夫婦、這裏的女主人、傑弗里·克羅斯登，照例是這幾個人。我還邀請了格羅特連勛爵。"

"我喜歡這個人，"亨利勛爵道。"很多人不喜歡他，可是我認為他挺可愛。他偶爾穿得花俏了些，但他的學問淵博極了，足夠彌補這個缺點。他非常合乎時代的潮流。"

"我不知他是否去得成，亨利。他也許得陪他父親到蒙特卡羅去。"

"啊，那些父母家屬真討厭！你想辦法還是叫他到塞爾比去。對了，道林，昨天晚上你一溜煙走得很早，十一點還不到。後來你做甚麼去了？是不是直接回家啦？"

道林急忙向他瞅了一眼，旋即皺起眉頭。"不，亨利，"他終於說，"我差不多三點鐘才回到家裏。"

"你上俱樂部去了？"

"是的，"道林答道。他咬了咬嘴唇。"不，不，我沒有上俱樂部。我是在散步。我忘了我做甚麼去了……你真好奇別人的事，亨利，你老是想知道別人在做甚麼。我老是想忘掉自己做了些甚麼。如果你要知道確切的時間，我可以告訴你，我兩點半回到家裏。我忘了帶鑰匙，只得叫傭人起來開門。你如果需要旁證，可以去問他。"

亨利勛爵聳聳肩膀。"老弟，我才不管這些呢！我們到樓上客廳去吧。謝謝，切普門先生，我不要雪利酒。道林，你大概出了甚麼事。告訴我，是怎麼回事？今晚你的情緒不對頭。"

"不要管我，亨利。我心裏煩得很，情緒不好。明天或者後天，我會去看你。你代我向納爾巴勒夫人打個招呼。我不上樓去了。我這就回家。我得馬上回家去。"

"好吧，道林。明天我等你來喝茶。公爵夫人也會來。"

"我儘可能去，亨利，"他說着，走出大廳。在駕車回家的路上，他意識到原先以為已被他悶死的恐怖感又甦醒了。亨利勛爵無意間問的話使他一時失去了自持力，現在他十分需要鎮定。危險的東西必須銷毀。想到這裏，他禁不住發抖。單是碰一碰那些東西就能叫他噁心。

然而他明白這件事非做不可。到了書齋裏，他用鑰匙把門反鎖起來，便去打開藏着貝澤爾・霍爾渥德的大衣和手提袋的祕密衣櫃。壁爐裏火燒得正旺，道林又添了一根木柴。燒衣服和皮革的焦味非常難聞，他花了四十五分鐘才把所有的東西全部銷毀。最後他覺得頭暈想吐，就在一個有孔的銅盆裏點了一些阿爾及利阿香錠，再用一種麝香味的涼醋洗刷兩手和前額。

　　他驀地全身一震，眼睛變得異樣地明亮，牙齒狠命咬着下唇。在兩扇窗之間放着一個象牙和天青石嵌面的佛羅倫斯烏木櫃子。道林瞪着它發愣，彷彿那個櫃子既吸引着他，又使他害怕；彷彿裏邊藏着甚麼他既嚮往又憎恨的東西。他的呼吸愈來愈急促。一個狂熱的念頭油然而生。他點了一支煙，但旋即扔掉。他的眼皮愈垂愈低，以致流蘇似的睫毛幾乎觸及面頰。他依舊瞪着那個櫃子。最後，他從原本躺着的沙發站起來，走到櫃子跟前，開了鎖，再按動一處彈簧暗門。一個三角形的抽屜慢慢地自動抽出。道林的手本能地向那裏伸進去，摸到了一件東西。那是一個黑漆灑金的中國小匣子，做得十分精巧，外面雕着波狀花紋，絲帶上串着水晶小球和金屬絲編成的辮狀流蘇。他把匣子打開。裏邊放着一團綠色的膏狀物，光澤像蠟，香味濃得出奇，而且經久不散。

　　他猶豫片刻，一絲微笑停留在臉上。接着他打起寒顫來，儘管屋子裏熱得要命。他定一定神，看了看鐘。這時是十一點四十分。他把匣子放回原處，關好櫃子的門，然後走到臥室去。

　　等到古銅的鐘錘在幽暗中敲了十二下，道林・格雷身穿不起眼的尋常服裝，脖子上裹着圍巾，悄悄地溜出公館。他走到邦德街上，看到一輛套着一匹好馬的出租街車，便招呼一聲，壓低了嗓門向馬車夫説出一處地方。

車夫搖搖頭，嘀咕了一句："太遠了。"

"這個金鎊給你，"道林説。"你要是趕得快，再加你一鎊。"

"行，先生，"車夫答應説，"一小時內保證把你送到。"等乘客上了車，他掉轉馬頭，飛快地向河邊駛去。

第十六章

外面下起冷雨來了，昏暗的街燈在雨濛濛的濃霧中透出一派陰森森的鬼氣。酒店正準備打烊，門口聚着一堆堆男人和女人，模模糊糊的看不真切。有幾家小酒店不時傳出放蕩的笑聲，另外幾家則有醉漢在吵架和尖聲喊叫。

道林·格雷斜臥在車座靠背上，帽檐拉到額前，以淡漠的眼光觀察這座大都市見不得人的一面，時而默默地重複着亨利勛爵在與他結識的第一天所説的話："通過感官治療靈魂的創痛，通過靈魂解除感官的飢渴。"對，這是一張祕方，而且屢試不爽，現在他又要試一試。那裏有鴉片館，可以出錢買一個忘乎所以；有罪惡的淵藪，可以不顧死活地做新的壞事來消除記憶中舊的劣跡。

月亮低垂在空中，像一顆黃色的骷髏。一大片形狀古怪的浮雲不時伸出長臂把它遮住。煤氣路燈愈來愈稀，街道愈來愈窄，愈來愈暗。車夫有一段路趕錯了，不得不退回半英里。馬蹄啪嚓啪嚓踩得泥漿四濺，馬背上直冒熱氣。兩邊的車窗被灰色法蘭絨似的大霧遮得嚴嚴實實。

"通過感官治療靈魂的創痛，通過靈魂解除感官的飢渴！"這話為何老是在他耳際迴響？的確，他的靈魂已病入膏肓。感官真的能解救它嗎？無辜的血也流了。怎樣才能抵償呢？這筆債是沒法還的；不過，寬恕雖然辦不到，忘卻還是可能的，所以他決意把這件事忘掉，從記憶中一筆勾銷，像踩死一條咬了他的蝮蛇一樣把它碾得粉碎。確實如此，貝澤爾憑甚麼對他說那些話？誰授予他充當法官審判別人的權利？他說的話是極其可怕、駭人聽聞、不能容忍的。

馬車勉強繼續前進，好像一步比一步走得更慢了。道林推開天窗，催促車夫趕得快些。難熬的鴉片煙癮折磨着他，他的喉嚨乾渴如焚，一雙皮膚柔嫩的手神經質地扭絞在一起。他伸出手杖惡狠狠地抽打馬背。車夫放聲大笑，並且也揮動他的鞭子。道林跟着他笑，那車夫卻又沉默了。

路好像沒有盡頭似的，這一帶的街道宛如一張巨大的黑色蜘蛛網，景色的單調沉悶使人受不了。隨着霧愈來愈濃，他也愈來愈害怕。

馬車經過荒涼的磚廠區。這裏的霧比較薄，道林看得出一座座呈奇怪瓶狀的磚窰吐着橘紅色的扇形火舌。一頭狗向着馬車吠叫，一隻失羣的海鷗在遠處黑暗中尖聲哀鳴。馬在轍槽打了個趔趄，車身向旁邊歪了一下。然後馬車開始快跑。

不久，馬車離開泥路，又哼嗤哼嗤走上高低不平的石子街路。大多數窗子都漆黑無光，但偶爾幾處有燈光的窗簾上映出形形色色的怪影。道林興致勃勃地看着。那些影子像巨大的傀儡晃動着，做着各種手勢。看了一會，他就覺得討厭，心中無名火起。馬車在一處轉角拐彎的時候，有個女人從一扇開着的門口向他們叫罵，兩個男人跟在車後跑了有一百碼，車夫揮動鞭子才把他們趕開。

據說，在強烈的慾望支配下，人的念頭會不停地打轉。果然，道林‧格雷咬得齒痕累累的嘴唇頑固地翻來覆去念叨着關於靈魂與感官的那兩句神祕的話，直到認為這兩句話確已充分表達他的心情，並從理性上承認他的慾望是正當的。其實，即使不承認，慾望照樣主宰着他的情緒。這個念頭從一個腦細胞潛入另一個腦細胞；生存的強烈慾望是人類一切慾念中最可怕的一種，它加速着每一條神經、每一根毫毛的顫動。醜惡的陰暗面因使人面對現實而一度為他所憎恨，如今卻由於同樣的原因而使他感到親切。醜惡的陰暗面是唯一的現實。粗野的辱罵、下流的巢窟、放蕩的生活、卑劣的盜賊和無賴，凡此種種，就其給人鮮明和強烈的印象而言，勝過一切優美的藝術形式，勝過仙樂飄飄所能營造的夢幻意境。這正是他追求忘卻所需要的，三天之內他便將獲得解脫。

車夫突然使勁勒住韁繩，馬車在一條暗沉沉的胡同口停下。這一帶房子低矮的屋頂和破損的煙囪後面高聳着黑色的船桅。一團團白茫茫的霧氣像鬼船的帆貼在桁上。

"是這地方吧，先生？"車夫以沙啞的嗓音向天窗裏問。

道林吃了一驚，向窗外看了看。"對，"說着，急忙下車。他付了向車夫許下的額外車資，便朝碼頭的方向快步走去。有幾條大商船的船尾點着燈。燈光在污水坑裏搖曳閃爍。從正在加煤準備開往國外的一艘輪船射來耀眼的紅光。濘滑的路面猶如一件濕漉漉的雨衣。

他匆匆折向左邊，頻頻回頭看是否有人尾隨。七八分鐘後，他走到夾在兩家可憐巴巴的工場中間的一所又小又髒的房子門前。有一扇窗口點着一盞燈。他停下來用暗號敲門。

一會兒，他聽到走廊上有腳步聲，接着，鏈條的鉤子被拔去。門悄然沒聲地開了，他走進去的時候，一個矮胖臃腫的身影向暗處一縮，道林一句話也沒有說。走廊盡頭掛着一塊破破爛爛的綠色門簾，被一陣跟着他衝進來的勁風吹得飄飄蕩蕩。他把門簾拉開，跨進一間相當長的矮屋子，看樣子過去是一所三等舞廳。靠牆排列着煤氣燈的噴火口，刺目的燈光映在對面滿是蠅卵的鏡子裏，變得昏暗歪斜。燈口後面襯着油膩膩的波紋形鐵皮反光罩，火焰的圓圈在反光罩的反射下不住地顫動。地上鋪着黃褐色的鋸屑，有些地方被踩實了露出泥地，還有潑翻的酒留下的一圈圈深色的痕跡。幾個馬來人蹲在一隻小炭爐旁邊玩骨籌碼，說話時露出很白的牙齒。角落裏有個水手頭枕着胳膊趴在一張桌子上。漆色俗豔的吧台沿着整整一面牆壁排開，兩個骨瘦如柴的女人站在台邊嘲弄一個正在刷大衣袖子的老頭。道林經過那兒時，聽到其中一個女人格格地笑着說："他以為有紅螞蟻爬到他身上吧。"那個老頭驚恐地望着她，竟抽抽搭搭哭起鼻子來。

屋子盡頭有一段小梯通往一間暗室。道林匆匆登上那三級搖搖晃晃的梯階，立刻有一股濃烈的鴉片香味迎面撲來。他深深吸了口氣，鼻翼舒服地翕動着。當他走進暗室時，一個長着滑溜黃髮的青年正弓着腰湊在燈上點一支煙槍。他舉目對道林一看，略帶猶豫地點點頭。

"阿德連，你在這裏？"道林低聲問。

"我還能上哪兒去？"他沒精打采地回答。"過去的朋友現在誰也不理我。"

"我以為你到國外去了呢。"

"達林頓一點不講交情。最後還是我哥哥付的賬。喬治也不睬我……"他歎了一口氣後又説，"我不在乎。只要有這玩意，就不需要朋友。我過去交的朋友也許太多了。"

道林身不由主地一縮，眼睛向周圍那些三分像人、七分像鬼的煙客掃去。他們都以同樣古怪的姿勢躺在破墊子上。他們蜷曲的肢體、呵欠連連的嘴巴、呆滯無光的眼神使他看得出了神。他能體會這些人正在何等特異的天堂忍受煎熬，也知道他們正向何等幽暗的地獄討教領略新奇快感的訣竅。他們的處境比他好。他被思緒纏住了不得脱身。回憶像一種惡疾齧食着他的靈魂。貝澤爾‧霍爾渥德的眼睛不時在冥冥中瞪着他。但他還是不敢留下，因為有阿德連‧辛格爾頓在此地終究不妥。他要找一個沒人認識他的地方。他恨不得連自己的影子也甩掉。

"我要到另一個地方去，"道林沉默片時後説。

"上碼頭？"

"是的。"

"那隻瘋貓八成在那邊。這兒現在不讓她來了。"

道林聳聳肩膀説："我對愛我的女人已經厭倦，倒是恨我的女人有意思得多。再説，那邊的煙土也好些。"

"都是一路貨。"

"我比較喜歡那邊的。我們去喝一杯吧。我很想喝點甚麼。"

"我甚麼也不想喝，"那青年喃喃地説。

"去喝一杯吧。"

阿德連懶洋洋地爬起來，跟着道林向吧台走去。一個纏着破頭巾、身穿破大褂的英印混血兒在醜臉上堆着笑招呼他們，同時把一瓶白蘭地和兩隻平底酒杯放到他們面前。剛才那兩個女人側着身子挨過來搭訕。道林背對着她們,低聲向阿德連‧辛格爾頓説了些甚麼。

一個女人扭動臉上的肌肉作了一個怪笑。"如果今晚我們能有幸,"她用譏誚的口吻説。

"看在上帝份上,別跟我糾纏,"道林把腳一跺嚷道。"你要甚麼?錢?拿去。再也別來纏我。"

那女人一雙直勾勾的眼睛霎時間迸出兩顆紅色的火花,但是一閃即逝,旋又歸於暗淡而呆滯。她腦袋一揚,急忙把幾枚硬幣從櫃檯上耙到貪婪的手裏。她的同伴歆羨地望着她。

"這沒有用,"阿德連‧辛格爾頓歎道。"我不打算回去。回去又怎麼樣?我在這兒挺快活。"

"你如果需要甚麼,就寫信給我,好不好?"道林沉吟半晌後説。

"好吧。"

"那麼,祝你晚安。"

"晚安,"青年回答説,一邊登上梯階,一邊用手帕抹抹枯乾的嘴唇。

道林臉帶痛苦的表情向門口走去。在他掀簾子的時候,剛才拿了他錢的那個女人從塗着口紅的嘴唇上吐出一陣浪笑。"魔鬼撿來的便宜貨走了!"她一面打嗝,一面用難聽的粗嗓子喊着。

"你這個臭婆娘!"道林不甘示弱。"不許這樣叫我。"

那女人打了一個響指。"難道你要人家叫你迷人王子嗎?"她在後面咆哮。

本來想打個盹的那個水手，聽到了這句話，霍地跳起身來，睜大眼睛四下張望。這時，過道門砰然關上的聲音傳到他耳邊，水手立即追出門去。

道林·格雷在毛毛雨中沿着碼頭匆匆地走着。與阿德連·辛格爾頓的不期而遇搞得他心裏亂糟糟。他不禁問自己："這個青年的墮落是否應歸咎於我，像貝澤爾·霍爾渥德毫不留情地指責我那樣？"他咬住嘴唇，有一瞬間兩眼現出悽愴的神情。不，這畢竟不關他的事！人的生命太短促了，犯不着把別人失足的責任攬到自己身上。各人走各人的路，並為此而各自付出代價。唯一可悲的是：僅僅由於偶一失足，卻往往必須沒完沒了地付出代價。命運與人打交道時永遠不肯清賬。

據心理學家說，犯罪的慾望，或者世人稱之為罪惡的慾望，有時候會把一個人緊緊抓住不放，使他體內的每一根血管、腦子的每一個細胞都好像快被可怕的衝動所脹破。男人和女人在這樣的時刻便會失去意志的自控力。他們會像自動機器那樣運轉，走向不堪設想的結局。他們的選擇權已被剝奪，意識也被扼殺，即使還殘留着，也只會給叛逆增添魅力，使反抗更加誘人。因為反抗是萬惡之本，正像神學家不嫌其煩地提醒我們的那樣。高尚的神靈，也就是罪惡的晨星，因叛逆而從天上謫降人間。

道林·格雷麻木不仁，污濁的頭腦裏只有邪念，靈魂渴望着反叛。他急急忙忙加快步伐，折入一條黑洞洞的拱道，正想同往常一樣抄近路前往他要去的那個臭名昭著的地方，突然發覺自己被人從後面揪住。他還來不及自衛，那人已把他向拱道的壁上狠狠地一搡，一隻蠻不講理的手掐住了他的脖子。

道林沒命地掙扎，拼出全身力氣把掐住脖子的手指扳開。但就在這一剎那，他聽到手槍扳機唭嗻的聲響，只見擦得鋥亮的槍筒已對準他的腦袋，一個身材矮壯的人黑糊糊的輪廓站在他面前。

　　"你要做甚麼？"道林嚇得上氣不接下氣。

　　"閉嘴！"那人說。"你要動一動，我就開槍！"

　　"你瘋啦？我招你惹你了？"

　　"你坑害了西碧兒·韋恩。"那人說。"西碧兒·韋恩是我的姐姐。她是自殺的。我知道。她的死由你一手造成。我發誓要殺死你償命。我已經找了你好幾年，但是沒有一點線索，沒有一點蹤跡。只有兩個人說得出你的外貌，可是都死了。我對你一無所知，只曉得西碧兒過去叫你的一個愛稱。剛才碰巧給我聽見了這個名字。現在你向上帝祈禱吧，因為你今夜就要死了。"

　　道林·格雷嚇得魂不附體。"我從來不認識她，"他結結巴巴地否認。"我也從來沒有聽人說起過她。你一定發瘋了。"

　　"你還是老實懺悔的好。因為你必死無疑，否則我就不叫詹姆士·韋恩。"這是驚心動魄的一剎那。道林不知該說甚麼或做甚麼。"跪下！"那人叱喝着。"我給你一分鐘禱告，再多不行。我今夜要上船到印度去，我得先把這件事了結。就只有一分鐘。"

　　道林頹喪地垂下兩條胳膊。他被震懾得不能動彈，不知如何是好。突然，一線絕處逢生的希望在他腦際閃過。"慢着！"他喊道。"你姐姐死了有多久？快告訴我！"

　　"十八年，"那人說。"你問這做麼？死了多少年有甚麼關係？"

　　"十八年，"道林·格雷帶着一點勝利的得意放聲大笑。"十八年！你讓我站到燈光下去，你再看看我的面孔！"

詹姆士・韋恩猶豫了一下，摸不透對方有何用意。他將道林・格雷一把拖出拱道。

風很大，街上的燈光昏暗而不穩。儘管如此，詹姆士・韋恩還是能看清自己犯了個大錯誤。想不到他正要結束其性命的這個人的面貌，竟煥發着純潔無邪的青春光輝。從這張臉看來，此人不過二十多歲，比好多年前他離家時的西碧兒大不了幾歲，簡直不相上下。顯然，這不是摧殘了他姐姐生命的那個人。

他鬆了手，晃晃悠悠地退後幾步。"我的天！我的老天爺！"他連聲說道。"我差點兒把你殺了！"

道林・格雷倒抽了一口冷氣。"老兄，你險些犯下了滔天大罪，"說着，嚴厲地向他瞪了一眼。"但願你記住這次教訓，不要自己動手報仇。"

"請原諒我，先生，"詹姆士・韋恩深表歉意。"我弄錯了。剛才我在那個鬼地方無意中聽到的一句話把我鬧糊塗了。"

"我勸你還是回家去，把手槍放好，免得招麻煩，"說完，道林轉過身去，不慌不忙地沿着街路走開。

詹姆士・韋恩站在行人道上，嚇得從頭到腳抖個不停。不一會，沿着潮濕的牆壁潛行的一個黑影出現在燈光下，踏着無聲的腳步走近他前面。他感到有一隻手按在他臂膀上，慌忙回頭一看。原來是剛才在吧台前喝酒的兩個女人中的其中一個。

"你為甚麼不殺死他？"她把枯瘦的面孔湊到他鼻子前，從牙縫裏發出嘶嘶的聲音說。"我知道你從戴利館中衝出來一定是追他。你這個笨蛋！你應該把他殺掉。他有許多許多錢，又是個十足的壞蛋。"

"他不是我要找的那個人，"詹姆士·韋恩回答，"我也不要任何人的錢。我只要一個人的命。這個人現在該快四十歲了。而剛才那人個差不多還是個孩子。謝天謝地，我的手幸虧沒有沾上他的血。"

那女人發出一陣苦笑。"差不多還是個孩子！"她鼻子裏哼了一聲。"告訴你吧，迷人王子把我害成現在這副模樣大概有十八年了。"

"你撒謊！"詹姆士·韋恩失聲驚呼。

那女人舉起手指着天。"我敢向上帝起誓，我說的句句是真話，"她喊道。

"向上帝起誓？"

"要是我撒謊，叫我變成啞巴！他是上這兒來的人中最壞的一個。據說他把自己出賣給魔鬼，換了一張漂亮的臉孔。我認識他大概有十八年了。從那時到現在，他沒有變怎樣。可是我……"說到這裏，她斜着眼睛，露出一副怪相。

"你敢起誓？"

"我敢起誓，"從她扁平的嘴唇上吐出的像是沙啞的回聲。"不過，可不能讓他知道是我說的，"她哀告着，"我怕他。給我點錢付夜宿費吧。"

詹姆士·韋恩咒罵一聲，拔腿便向街角那邊奔去，但是道林·格雷已杳無蹤影。詹姆士回過頭來一看，那女人也不見了。

第十七章

　　個星期後，道林・格雷坐在塞爾比莊園的溫室裏與漂亮的蒙茂斯公爵夫人聊天。她和她年已花甲、倦容滿面的丈夫一起來到這裏作客。現在正是茶點時間，桌上放着一盞帶花邊罩子的大燈，柔和的燈光照亮了細瓷的和銀質的茶具。主持茶會的是公爵夫人。只見她雪白的雙手在杯盤之間翩翩張羅，豐滿的朱唇微微含笑，大概道林向她説了些甚麼有趣的悄悄話。亨利勛爵靠在有綢套的柳條椅上瞧着他們。納爾巴勒夫人坐在桃紅色的無靠背軟榻上，裝作在聽公爵描述他的收藏中新近增添的一隻巴西甲蟲。三個年輕人穿着精工製作的晚禮服在把點心遞給幾位女客。到塞爾比莊園小住的共有十二人，明天還有幾位客人要來。

　　"你們在談甚麼？"亨利勛爵走到桌邊，放下他的茶杯問道。"格蕾狄絲，道林有沒有把我打算給每一件東西改名的計劃告訴你？這是一個絕妙的主意。"

　　"我可不願改名，亨利，"公爵夫人説時，一雙俏眼睛朝着他往上一瞟。"我對我的名字十分滿意，我想格雷先生對他的名字也挺滿意。"

　　"我親愛的格蕾狄絲，你們的名字都完美無瑕，我絕不會更改。我主要想改的是花的名字。昨天我剪了一朵蘭花，插在鈕扣孔裏。那朵漂亮的花上有斑紋，如七大罪一樣令人印象深刻。沒有多想，我向其中一個園丁問這花的名字，他告訴我這是一個"魯濱遜尼亞"的優良品種，或者是類似的可怕名字。我們已經失去了起動聽名字的能力了，這真是個悲傷的事實。名字就是一切。我從不為行為爭論，只跟語言過不去。這是我討厭庸俗的現實主義出現在文學的原因。一個稱鏟子為鏟子的人，就該逼他去使用鏟子，因為他只適合用這個。"

"那麼我們該稱呼你甚麼呢，亨利？"公爵夫人問。

"他叫悖論王子，"道林說。

"我一聽這名字就知道是他，"公爵夫人表示歡賞。

"我可不願聽到，"亨利勛爵笑道，同時在一張椅子上坐下。"一旦給貼上了標籤就不用想甩掉！敬謝不敏。"

"王位是不能謙讓的，"美麗的嘴唇提出告誡。

"這麼說，你要我維護君權？"

"對。"

"我的話都是明天的真理。"

"我寧可聽今天的謬誤，"她回答。

"你繳了我的武器，格蕾狄絲，"亨利勛爵不禁對她縱情馳騁的機智表示折服。

"我繳了你的盾，亨利，而不是你的矛。"

"我從來不攻擊美，"他說着，擺一擺手，恭敬地行了個禮。

"這就是你的錯誤，亨利。你把美的價值看得太高了。"

"這是甚麼話？的確，我認為美比善更好。但反過來說，我比任何人都樂於承認善比醜更好。"

"難道七大罪惡也包括醜陋？"公爵夫人提出詰問。"可是你剛才把蘭花比作七大罪又怎麼講呢？"

"醜陋是七大美德之一,格蕾狄絲。你身為優秀的保守黨員,絕不能小看它們。啤酒、聖經,以及七大美德造就了我們的英國。"

"這麼說,你不喜歡這個國家?"她問。

"我不是住在這裏嗎?"

"無非是便於你非難它。"

"你是不是要我接受歐洲對它的評價?"亨利勛爵問道。

"歐洲說我們甚麼來着?"

"他們說,偽君子移民到英國,然後開了一家店。"

"這恐怕是你杜撰的吧?"

"我把版權送給你。"

"我要來何用?這話太真實了。"

"你不用害怕。我們的同胞從來認不出自己的寫照。"

"他們注重務實。"

"與其說注重務實,不如說老奸巨猾。他們結賬時總是用財富抵償愚蠢,用偽善抵償邪惡。"

"不過,我們畢竟做過大事業。"

"是大事業強加於我們,格蕾狄絲。"

"可我們還是把擔子挑了起來。"

"可是只挑到證券交易所為止。"

她搖搖頭聲稱:"我相信民族的力量。"

"它代表進取精神的殘餘。"

"它有發展前途。"

"我覺得沒落更可愛。"

"那麼藝術呢?"她問。

"那是一種病。"

"愛情呢?"

"是幻想。"

"宗教呢?"

"信仰的時髦代用品。"

"你是個懷疑論者。"

"完全不是!懷疑是虔誠的開端。"

"那你是甚麼呢?"

"下定義就是定框框。"

"給我一點線索。"

"線會斷的。你會在錯綜複雜的岔路中迷失方向。"

"你把我弄糊塗了。還是談談別的吧。"

"我們的東道主就是個很有趣的話題。若干年前他有一個雅號,叫迷人王子。"

"啊,不要提這個名字,"道林‧格雷叫了起來。

"我們的東道主今晚真討厭,"公爵夫人紅着臉說。"他大概以為蒙茂斯跟我結婚純粹出於科學上的考慮,因為在當代再也找不到比我更好的蝴蝶標本。"

"但願他沒有用針把你釘起來,公爵夫人,"道林笑道。

"哦!我的侍女生我氣的時候已經這樣做了,格雷先生。"

"她怎麼會生你的氣呢,公爵夫人?"

"都是些雞毛蒜皮的小事,格雷先生。比方說,我在八點五十分時對她說:我要在八點半前換好裝。"

"她太沒有道理了!你該把她解僱才對。"

"我不敢，格雷先生。她能為我設計各種帽子。你還記得在希爾斯登夫人的遊園會上我戴的那頂帽子嗎？你忘了，不過你真不錯，裝做記得的樣子。那頂帽子是她用最不值錢的材料做的。其實，所有好看的帽子材料都不值錢。"

"就像所有的好名聲一樣，格蕾狄絲，"亨利勛爵插進來說。"誰要是出人頭地，馬上就會樹敵。要受人歡迎，必須做一個庸才。"

"女人可不是這樣，"公爵夫人不以為然，"而世界是女人統治的。我敢肯定，我們女人決不能容忍庸才。正如某人所說，我們女人是用耳朵來戀愛的，而你們男人卻用眼睛，如果你們曾經愛過的話。"

"我覺得我們除了戀愛從來不做別的事情，"道林說。

"啊！那就是說你從來沒有真正戀愛過，格雷先生，"公爵夫人故作傷感地說。

"親愛的格蕾狄絲！"亨利勛爵提出異議。"你這是甚麼話！浪漫是靠反覆來維持生命的，情慾也要經過反覆才變成藝術。此外，每一次戀愛對於本人都是獨一無二的。對象不同並不意味着愛情就不是獨一無二，這只能使愛情更加熱烈。我們一生頂多只能得到一次偉大的體驗，而生命的祕密就在於重溫這種體驗，儘可能重溫多次。"

"倘若曾受到這種體驗帶來的傷害，是不是也該重溫，亨利？"公爵夫人停頓片刻後問。

"受過傷害更需要重溫，"亨利勛爵答道。

公爵夫人掉過臉去，用異樣的眼神望着道林・格雷。"你有何高見，格雷先生？"她問。

道林遲疑了一下，然後仰天大笑。"公爵夫人，我永遠同意亨利的觀點。"

　　"他錯了你也同意？"

　　"亨利從來不會錯的，公爵夫人。"

　　"他的哲學能給你幸福嗎？"

　　"我從不追求幸福。誰需要幸福？我只追求享受。"

　　"你得到了沒有，格雷先生？"

　　"常常得到。得到的次數太多了。"

　　公爵夫人慨然歎道："我需要的是安寧，如果現在我不去換裝，今晚就別想得到安寧。"

　　"我去給你挑幾朵蘭花，公爵夫人，"道林說着，立起身來就往溫室深處走去。

　　"你跟他調情已經到了不成體統的程度，"亨利勛爵向他的表妹說。"你可要留神一點。他的誘惑力很大。"

　　"假如他沒有誘惑力，戰也就打不起來了。"

　　"這樣說來，你們像是希臘人遇上希臘人，是棋逢敵手？"

　　"我是站在特洛伊人的一邊，他們為一個女人而戰。"

　　"最後他們戰敗了。"

　　"當俘虜並不是最壞的命運，"她說。

　　"你像是放鬆了韁繩騎在馬上快跑。"

　　"跑得快才有樂趣，"她不假思索地說。

　　"我今晚應該把這寫到我的日記去。"

　　"寫甚麼？"

　　"一個燒傷的孩子愛玩火。"

"我可沒有受過火燙。我的翅膀還是好好的。"

"你的翅膀哪兒都用得上，就是不能用來飛。"

"勇氣已經從男人轉移到女人那裏。這對我們來說是新的體驗。"

"有一個人在和你競爭。"

"誰？"

亨利勛爵哈哈大笑，然後悄悄地說："納爾巴勒夫人。她對道林愛得可厲害呢！"

"經你這樣一說，我倒擔心起來了。我們這些熱中於古典的浪漫主義者一定會失敗。"

"浪漫主義者？你們把全套科學方法都用上了，還是浪漫主義者？"

"這是男人教我們的。"

"但是男人始終沒有對你們作出透徹的解釋。"

"那就請把全體女人概括一下吧，"她以挑逗的口吻說。

"無謎可猜的斯芬克斯怪物。"

她微笑着望了望亨利勛爵。"格雷先生怎麼還不來？"她說。"我們去幫他挑選吧。我還沒有告訴他，我要換甚麼顏色的連衣裙。"

"啊！你得用你的連衣裙去配他的花，格蕾狄絲。"

"那豈不是不戰而降？"

"浪漫主義藝術是從高潮開始的。"

"我得給自己留一條退路。"

"像帕提亞人那樣假裝撤退，實為攻擊？"

"帕提亞人可以逃入沙漠。我沒有地方可逃。"

"女人有時候也會弄到沒有選擇的餘地，"他還沒說完，忽然從溫室深處傳來一聲像是閉氣的呻吟，隨後是沉重的倒地聲。大家都驚慌起來。公爵夫人站着嚇呆了。亨利勛爵睜大充滿恐懼的眼睛，撥開棕櫚葉奔過去，發現道林‧格雷臉朝下躺在地磚上不省人事。

他立即被抬到藍色客廳裏的沙發上。過不多久，他甦醒過來，向周圍看看，惑然不解。

"這是怎麼回事？"他問。"噢！我想起來了。我在這裏有沒有危險，亨利？"說着，開始發抖。

"親愛的道林，"亨利勛爵安慰他說，"你不過是暈倒了。別的沒有甚麼。一定是太累的緣故。你不要下樓去吃晚飯吧。我替你招待客人。"

"不，我要下去，"他說着，勉強撐起身子。"我還是下樓去的好。我不能一個人待着。"

他到自己臥室裏去換了裝。在晚餐席上，道林談笑風生，放浪形骸。但只要他一想起剛才看見一張像白手絹似的臉貼在溫室外面的玻璃窗上，窺伺着他，就會渾身發抖。那是詹姆士‧韋恩的臉。

第十八章

第二天，道林足不出戶，大部分時間留在自己的臥室裏，因為怕死而時時刻刻感到芒刺在背，但對生命本身又漠然無動於衷。一種遭到尾隨、追逐、行將落入陷阱的意識開始支配他。只要掛毯被風稍一吹動，他就發抖。枯葉打在鑲鉛條的窗框上，也會使他聯想起自己徒勞的決心和瘋狂的後悔。他一閉上眼睛，又看到蒙着霧氣的玻璃窗外那個水手的面孔，於是恐怖又一次攫住了他的心。

不過，也許僅僅是他的幻覺使復仇神的幽靈從黑夜中現身，使森嚴可怕的報應景象呈現在他面前。現實生活一片混亂，但想像的思路卻有條不紊得可怕。正是想像驅使着悔恨在罪孽後面尾隨不捨。正是想像使每一顆罪惡的種子結出了醜陋畸形的果實。現實世界裏惡人並不遭惡報，好人也沒有好報。成功的永遠是強者，弱者總是倒霉，歷來如此。何況，如果有陌生人在莊園宅子周遭徘徊不去，定會被僕人或獵場看守發覺。花圃上如果發現足印，花匠也會來報告。可見，這純粹是他的幻覺。西碧兒·韋恩的弟弟並沒有回來索命。他隨船出航，也許已經葬身冰冷的大海。無論怎樣，詹姆士·韋恩對他並不構成威脅。那水手根本不知道他是何許人，也不可能知道。青春的面具救了他的命。

雖然這僅僅是幻象，但良心竟會發出如此恐怖的怪影，而且賦以清晰可見的形狀，令其在你面前出沒，想起來真叫人膽寒！

倘若他罪惡的魅影一天到晚從冷僻的角落裏瞅着他，在祕密的地方嘲笑他，在宴席上向他耳語，用冰涼的手指把他從睡夢中觸醒，這樣的日子叫他怎麼過？隨着這個念頭潛入他的腦髓，恐懼使他的臉色愈變愈慘白，空氣對他又驟然變冷了。天啊！他在陷入狂亂的時刻竟把自己的朋友殺了！一想起那幅景象，他就毛骨悚然！可怕的細節在想像中一一重演時更加觸目驚心。他罪行的幽靈陰慘慘、血淋淋地從漆黑的時間洞穴裏冉冉升起。當亨利勛爵六點鐘走進來的時候，他發現道林正哭得心都快碎了。

直到第三天，道林方敢出門。那是一個冬天的早晨，洋溢着松樹清香的新鮮空氣似乎使他恢復了興致和生趣。然而引起這種變化的原因不完全在於自然環境。過多的苦痛企圖徹底摧垮他內心的安寧，結果他自己的天性起來反抗了。稟性敏感、氣質高雅的人往往會這樣。他們強烈的情感不是受傷，就是屈服；不是把人毀滅，就是自己死亡。渺小的憂傷和渺小的愛壽命很長。偉大的愛和偉大的憂傷卻毀於過於強烈的自身。此外，他已使自己確信是疑心生了暗鬼。現在回顧幾天來心驚膽戰的情狀，對自己既有些憐憫，也頗為鄙夷。

早餐已畢，道林同公爵夫人一起在花園裏散了一小時步，然後他坐車穿過林苑去加入打獵的一夥。乾脆的霜花像撒在草上的鹽巴，天空猶如一杯傾覆的藍色金屬溶液，湖面平靜如鏡，蘆葦叢生的岸邊結着一層薄冰。

到了松林邊緣，他看見公爵夫人的弟弟傑弗里·克羅斯登爵士正從獵槍裏拔出兩顆空彈殼。道林縱身下車，吩咐車夫把母馬牽回去，自己穿過枯蕨蔓草和亂草叢向這位客人走去。

"手氣好吧，傑弗里？"他問道。

"不太理想，道林。看來鳥兒大多飛到曠野去了。下午我們換一個地方，估計情況會好些。"

道林在他旁邊走着。空氣中的芳香沁人心脾，棕色和紅色的光斑在樹林裏時隱時現，助獵者不時發出嘶嘎的吆喝驚起鳥獸，接着就響起扳動槍栓的唭嗻聲。這一切吸引着道林，使他充滿了愉快的自由感。他沉浸在無憂無慮、逍遙自在的情緒中。

忽然，從他們前面大約二十碼一個留着殘草的亂草叢那邊，竄出一隻野兔。它支楞起尖端長長的黑毛耳朵，蹬着細長的後腿向一片檟木叢逃去。傑弗里爵士把槍托到肩上。但是，説也奇怪，那隻野兔優美矯捷的動作竟使道林‧格雷為之心動。他急忙喊道："別開槍，傑弗里。饒它一條命吧。"

"你真傻，道林！"傑弗里爵士笑道。就在野兔剛剛溜進樹叢的一剎那，他開了槍。緊接着，同時傳來兩聲號叫：其一是野兔痛苦的哀號；其二是一個人臨死前的慘叫。後者比前者更加慘不忍聞。

"天啊！我打中了一個助獵夫了！"傑弗里爵士驚呼起來。"這頭蠢驢怎麼會跑到槍口前面去的？喂，你們那兒別開槍！"他扯開嗓子大叫。"有人受傷啦！"

獵場看守手裏拿着一根棍子聞聲趕來。

"在哪兒，先生？他在哪兒？"他氣急敗壞地問。這時，整條線上的槍聲都停了下來。

"在這邊，"傑弗里爵士生氣地回答説，自己急忙向樹叢中跑。"你怎麼不叫你手下的人離遠些？把我今天打獵的興致全敗壞了。"

道林看着他們撥開富有彈性的枝條鑽進欅木叢去。隔不多久，他們從那裏出來，把一具屍體拖到陽光下。道林驚駭地掉過臉去。看來，他走到哪裏，厄運就跟到哪裏。他聽傑弗里在問：那人是否確實死了。獵場看守作了肯定的回答。道林覺得樹林一下子活起來了，到處都是面孔。他彷彿聽見億萬人踩腳和嗡嗡地說話的聲音。不知從哪兒飛來一隻古銅色胸脯的大山雞，在頭頂上的樹枝間撲打着翅膀。

　　過了幾分鐘，心亂如麻的道林好像熬過了無數小時的苦痛，他感到有一隻手擱在他肩上。他嚇了一跳，急忙回過頭來。

　　“道林，”亨利勛爵說，“我看還是叫大家今天停止打獵吧。這樣繼續下去也怪沒趣。”

　　“我願意永遠不再打獵，亨利，”他沉痛地回答。“這件事太糟了，也太慘了。那個人難道……”

　　他無法把這句話完全說出口。

　　“是的，很遺憾，”亨利勛爵應道。“整整一發槍彈的火藥正打在他的胸膛，想來幾乎是當場斃命。走，我們回去吧。”

　　他們朝着林蔭道的方向並排而行，默默地走了有五十碼左右。然後道林看看亨利勛爵，長歎一聲，說：“這是一個凶兆，亨利，一個很壞的兆頭。”

　　“你說甚麼？”亨利勛爵問。“哦！你是指這件意外事故嗎？老弟，這是沒有辦法的。是那個人自己不好。誰叫他跑到槍口前面去呢？何況，這也不關我們的事。當然，傑弗里非常懊惱。請助獵夫吃開花彈太不像話。人家還以為他是個亂開槍的射手。其實不然，傑弗里的槍法很準。可是說這話又有甚麼用呢？”

道林搖搖頭。"這是個凶兆，亨利。我覺得將有可怕的事情降臨到我們中某一個人頭上。八成會降臨到我自己頭上，"末了他添上這麼一句，同時深感痛苦地抹了一下眼睛。

亨利勛爵笑了起來。"世上最可怕的事情是無聊，道林。這是不可寬恕的罪過。不過我們大概不會遭到這種厄運，除非那些傢伙在吃晚飯的時候沒完沒了地談這件事。我得告訴他們不准談及這個話題。至於兆頭，根本沒有兆頭。命運女神從來不事先向我們報信。憑她的聰明和殘忍都不會這樣做。再說，你還怕甚麼事情會降臨到自己頭上，道林？凡是一個人可能需要的一切，你都有了。沒有人不樂於同你交換位置。"

"沒有一個人的位置是我不願意和他交換的，亨利。你不要笑，我說的是實話。剛才那個不幸死去的鄉下人比我現在的處境好得多。我對死亡本身並不恐懼，使我恐懼的是死神的即將來臨。它好像已經在我周圍像鉛一樣沉重的空氣舞動巨大的翅膀。天啊！你看，那邊的幾棵樹後面是不是有一個人影在移動，在監視我，在等待着我？"

亨利勛爵朝着道林戴手套的手瑟瑟發抖地所指的方向望去。"是的，"他微笑着說，"那是花匠在等你。他大概要向你請示，今晚餐桌上該插甚麼花。老弟，你的神經太脆弱了！回倫敦之後，你得找我的醫生看看去。"

道林看見花匠走近來，才鬆下一口氣。花匠舉手觸帽行了個禮，猶豫地向亨利勛爵看了一眼，然後掏出一封信交給他的主人。"公爵夫人叫我等候答覆，"他囁嚅着說。

道林把信放進衣袋。"告訴公爵夫人，說我就來，"他冷淡地説。花匠轉身向宅院那邊很快地走去。

"女人總愛做危險的事！"亨利勛爵笑着。"這是她們身上我最為賞識的一種品質。女人會跟任何人調情，只要旁人注意她們。"

"你總愛説危險的話，亨利！這一次你大錯特錯了。我非常喜歡公爵夫人，但是我並不愛她。"

"公爵夫人非常愛你，但是並不怎麼喜歡你，所以你們是天造地設的一對。"

"你不要無中生有，亨利，這裏頭沒有任何製造醜聞的根據。"

"醜聞的根據都是不道德的肯定，"亨利勛爵説着，點了一支煙。

"你為了説一句俏皮話，亨利，不惜用任何人作犧牲。"

"世人是自願走向祭壇的，"這是亨利勛爵的回答。

"我真想能夠愛上甚麼人！"道林・格雷以悽愴的語調歎道。"可是看來我已經心如止水，萬念俱灰。我的心思過於集中在自己身上。我本人已經成了我的累贅。我想逃脱、避開、忘卻。這次我到鄉下來實在愚蠢。我打算給哈維打個電報去，叫他把帆船準備好。在帆船上才能擺脱威脅。"

"你要擺脱甚麼威脅，道林？你有甚麼為難的事？為甚麼不告訴我？你知道我會幫助你的。"

"我不能告訴你，亨利，"他憂鬱地回答。"很可能這完全出於我的胡思亂想。這次不幸的意外把我鬧得心裏煩透了。我有一種可怕的預感，類似的事情將要降臨到我頭上。"

"簡直是夢話！"

"但願如此，可是我確有這樣的感覺。啊！公爵夫人來了，就像一位穿着訂造長袍的狩獵女神。你瞧，我們不是回來了嗎，公爵夫人？"

"那件事我全都聽説了，格雷先生，"她説。"可憐的傑弗里懊喪得不得了。據説你還勸過他不要開槍打那隻野兔。真是件怪事！"

"是啊，真奇怪。我也不知道為甚麼説了這話。大概是心血來潮吧。那隻野兔確實是極可愛的小動物。但是，我很抱歉，他們已經把這件事告訴了你。這件事慘極了。"

"只不過是件不愉快的意外，"亨利勛爵插嘴説。"根本沒有心理研究的價值。要是傑弗里故意做那件事，他這個人倒有意思了！我很想結識一位真正的殺人者。"

"亨利，你簡直全無心肝，"公爵夫人大聲説。"格雷先生，你説是不是？亨利，格雷先生又犯病了。他恐怕馬上就要昏倒。"

道林好不容易把身子站穩，強作笑容。"不要緊，公爵夫人，"他費力地説，"我的神經系統嚴重紊亂。就只是這樣。大概上午路走得太遠了。剛才亨利説了甚麼？我沒聽見。又是甚麼可惡的怪話，是不是？之後你再告訴我。很抱歉，我要去躺一會。失陪了。"

他們走到溫室通往露台的寬闊台階前。等道林進去把玻璃門關上，亨利勛爵轉過臉來，倦眼惺忪地望着公爵夫人，問道："你真的深深地愛上他了嗎？"

公爵夫人半晌沒有作聲，只是站着眺望風景。"我自己也想知道，"她終於説了這麼一句。

亨利勛爵搖搖頭。"知道了就會味同嚼蠟。妙就妙在迷離恍惚。霧裏看花分外有趣。"

“霧裏也會迷路。”

“條條道路都通往同一個終點，親愛的格蕾狄絲。”

“通往哪裏？”

“幻滅。”

“我的生活正是從幻滅開始的，”她不勝感慨。

“你感到幻滅時已經戴上了爵冕。”

“我已厭倦爵冕上的草莓葉。”

“你戴着正相宜。”

“那只是在人前。”

“你少不了它，”亨利勛爵說。

“我不打算捨棄任何一片花瓣。”

“蒙茂斯是有耳朵的。”

“上了年紀的人聽覺不靈。”

“難道他從來不吃醋？”

“我真希望他能生一點醋意。”

亨利勛爵東張西望，像在尋找甚麼。“你找甚麼？”公爵夫人問。

“你劍尖上的保護帽，”他回答，“你把它掉了。”

公爵夫人放聲大笑。“我還戴着面罩呢。”

“這會使你的眼睛格外動人，”亨利勛爵說。

她又笑了起來。她的皓齒像鮮紅的果實中間的白籽。

道林·格雷躺在樓上自己臥室裏的沙發上，恐怖滲透了他身上的每一個細胞。生命一下子變成他無法承受的負擔。那個倒霉的助獵人像一隻野獸在樹叢中飲彈慘死一事，在道林看來預示着他自己的死亡。剛才亨利勛爵脫口而出的一句俏皮怪話差點兒使他暈厥。

五點鐘，他打鈴吩咐侍從整理行裝，讓馬車八點半在門口等，準備趕夜班快車回倫敦去。他決意不在塞爾比莊園上再睡一夜。這個地方處處是凶兆。死神在光天化日下出沒無常，林中草地已經染上斑斑血跡。

他給亨利勛爵寫了一張便條，告訴他要回倫敦去就醫，並要求亨利勛爵代他款待賓客。他正要把便箋裝入信封，他的侍從敲門進來，說獵場看守求見。道林皺起眉頭，咬住嘴唇。"叫他進來，"遲疑片刻後，他相當勉強地說。

獵場看守一進來，道林就從抽屜裏取出一本支票簿，把它翻開了放在自己面前。

"你來大概是為上午那件不幸的意外事故吧，桑頓？"他一面說，一面拿起筆來。

"是的，先生，"獵場看守回答。

"那個可憐的人有沒有成家？有沒有人靠他養活？"道林露出不耐煩的神色問。"如有的話，我願贍養他們。你認為該付多少錢，我就拿出多少錢來。"

"我們不知道那個人是誰，先生。我冒昧求見正是為了這一點。"

"不知道他是誰？"道林心不在焉地問。"你說甚麼？難道他不是你手下的人？"

"不是，先生。我從來沒有見過那個人。他像是個水手，先生。"

筆從道林手中跌落，他覺得自己的心臟突然停止了跳動。"水手？"他失聲驚呼。"你說他是個水手？"

"是的，先生。看樣子他當過水手，兩條胳臂都刺着刺青之類的東西。"

"他身邊有些甚麼東西？"道林上身前傾，瞪着獵場看守問。"從中能不能知道他叫甚麼名字？"

"他身上有一點錢，先生，可是不多，還有一支六響手槍。沒有姓名標記。那個人長相還可以，就是眉目粗些。我們猜想他是個水手。"

道林霍地立起身來。一個可怕的希望在心頭閃起。他發瘋似地抓住這點希望不放。"屍首現在甚麼地方？"他急忙問。"快！我得立刻去看一下。"

"在家用農場的空馬棚裏，先生。大夥都不願把死人擱在家裏，那樣總是會帶來壞運氣的。"

"在家用農場裏？你馬上到那裏去等我。你叫一個馬夫把我的馬帶來。不，不必了。我自己去吧。這樣快些。"

沒過十五分鐘，道林・格雷已經以最快的速度騎馬奔馳在很長的林陰道上。樹木像鬼怪列隊般從他旁邊刷刷地飛掠過去，在他經過的路上投下駭人的魅影。有一次，道林的座騎看到一根白漆門柱，突然向那裏一拐，險些把他摔下馬背。道林在馬脖子上抽了一鞭。那匹馬像一支箭劃破飛揚的塵土向前直奔。石子從馬蹄下被踢起來紛紛濺開。

他終於趕到農場。兩個僱工在院子閒蕩。道林翻身下了馬鞍，把韁繩扔給其中一個僱工。在最遠的一座馬棚裏有燈光露出來。他下意識地感到屍體就在那邊，便三腳兩步跑到門前，準備拔閂開門。

這時他立停片刻，覺得自己正站在打開悶葫蘆的門坎上：他的餘生究竟可以優哉遊哉，還是永沉苦海，立即就有分曉。於是他猝然把門打開，走進馬棚。

在馬棚深處角落裏的一堆麻袋布上，停着一具穿粗布襯衫和藍褲子的男屍。一方血跡斑斑的手帕覆蓋着他的面孔。插在瓶子裏的一支劣質蠟燭發出劈劈啪啪的爆裂聲。

道林打了個寒顫。他感到自己沒有勇氣伸手揭去那方手帕，只得叫一個僱工進來。

"把臉上那東西拿掉。我要看一看，"他說時扶住門柱支撐自己的身子。

僱工照他的吩咐做了。道林跨前幾步，一聲驚喜的叫喊從他口中迸發出來。在樹叢中飲彈身亡的那個人正是詹姆士·韋恩。

道林站在那裏，對屍體看了好幾分鐘。在回家的路上，他兩眼噙滿了淚水。他知道自己的安全已不再受到威脅。

第十九章

"你何必向我宣佈要重新做人呢？"亨利勛爵大聲説，他白淨的手指正浸在一隻盛玫瑰香露的紅色銅碗裏。"你本來就十全十美。還是不要變吧。"

道林·格雷搖搖頭。"不，亨利，我一生作的孽太多了，以後我再也不會了。我昨天已開始做了些好事。"

"你昨天在甚麼地方？"

"在鄉下，亨利。我一個人借宿在小客棧裏。"

"我的老弟，"亨利勛爵面帶笑容説，"在鄉下任何人都可以做好人，那裏沒有誘惑。這就是遠離都市的人處於未開化狀態的原因。文明決不是唾手可得的。只有兩條途徑可以達到文明：一條是修身養性；另一條是腐化墮落。這兩種機會鄉下人一種都沒有，因此他們停滯不前。"

"修身和腐化，"道林像回聲般沉吟道，"我都體驗過。現在我實在難以想像這兩者怎能並行不悖。由於我有了新的理想，亨利，我決定重新做人。我覺得自己已經變成另一個人了。"

"你還沒有告訴我，你到底做了甚麼好事。你好像説做了不止一件？"亨利勛爵一面説，一面把有籽的草莓倒在自己盤子裏，堆成一座鮮紅的小金字塔，再用有孔的貝殼形匙子把白糖撒在草莓上。

"我可以告訴你，亨利。這不是一個我可以隨便講給別人聽的故事。我放過了一個叫海蒂的少女。這話聽來有些浮誇，不過你能明白我的意思。她長得極美，與西碧兒・韋恩像得出奇。這大概是我被她吸引的首要原因。你還記得西碧兒嗎？那是多麼遙遠的往事啊！當然，海蒂不是你我這個階級的人，她不過是個鄉下女人。但是我真心愛她，我確信這是愛情。在今年整個美妙的五月，我一星期要去看她兩三回。昨天她在一座小果園和我相會。蘋果花不斷落在她的頭髮上，她笑得挺歡。我們本來打算今天黎明時分一起私奔。但我突然決定讓這朵花保持我初次見到她時的原樣。"

"道林，我想這種新奇的感覺一定使你得到某種真正快意的刺激，"亨利勛爵把他的話打斷。"但是我可以代你敍述你們這首田園詩的結尾。你給了她忠告，也撕碎了她的心。這就是你脫胎換骨的起點。"

"亨利，你真可惡！你不應該説這樣刻薄的話。海蒂的心沒有碎。當然，她哭了，這是免不了的。但是她的名節保全了。她可以像珀迪塔一樣生活在薄荷飄香、金盞花開的樂園裏。"

"並為負心漢弗洛里扎爾哭泣，亨利勛爵靠向椅背，笑着説，"我親愛的道林，你的孩子氣真古怪。難道你認為這個女子現在會滿足於任何一個跟她同一階層的男人嗎？我估計她某天會嫁給一個粗魯的馬車夫，或是一個只會傻笑的農夫。是啊，跟你相識相愛教會她鄙視自己的丈夫，這件事足以毀了她。從道德層面來看，我不能説我有多欣賞你偉大的自我放棄，就算當作是一個起步，這也很糟糕。何況，你怎麼知道，此刻海蒂不是像奧菲莉亞一樣，飄浮在某個星光閃閃的磨坊水池裏，身旁有可愛的睡蓮陪伴着？"

"我受不了，亨利。你總是把任何事情變成嘲笑的材料，然後又憑空描繪最悲慘的情景。我後悔告訴你。不管你對我說甚麼，反正我知道自己做得對。可憐的海蒂！今天早晨我騎馬經過那個農家時，看見她雪白的臉蛋像一枝茉莉花緊貼在窗上。這件事再也別提了。你也不必説服我相信，多少年來我做的第一件好事，我有生以來作出的第一次自我犧牲，實際上又跡近罪惡。我要洗心革面。我正打算洗心革面。談談你自己的事情吧。近來倫敦有些甚麼新聞？我好多天沒上俱樂部了。"

"人們還在談可憐的貝澤爾失蹤這件事。"

"我還以為這一陣子人們已經談膩了呢，"道林説着，給自己倒了點葡萄酒，同時略微皺起眉頭。

"我親愛的孩子，他們只談論此事六星期而已。若英國羣眾三個月裏有超過一個話題，他們的神經就會崩緊到受不了。不過他們最近很幸運，他們能談論我的離婚案和艾倫·坎貝爾的自殺，而現在又有畫家神祕失蹤可談。倫敦警察仍然堅信那個在十一月九日穿着灰色大衣，午夜乘火車去巴黎的男人，就是可憐的貝澤爾。而法國警方則宣稱貝澤爾從未抵達巴黎。我猜兩星期內，我們會聽到他在三藩市的消息。這真奇怪，每個失蹤的人都被目擊身處在三藩市。那一定是個迷人的城市，擁有所有來世的魅力。"

"依你看，貝澤爾出了甚麼事？"道林問。他舉起一杯勃艮第紅酒放在燈光下細看，對於自己竟能如此從容自若地議論這件事，心裏也很納罕。

"我一點也想像不出。倘若貝澤爾願意躲起來，這不關我的事。倘若他死了，我不願想起他。唯一使我心驚肉跳的就是死亡。我恨死亡。"

"為甚麼？"道林有氣無力地問。

"因為，"亨利勛爵說時把一個打開了的鍍金嗅鹽盒放到鼻子底下聞了一下，"如今的人甚麼都熬得過，唯獨死亡例外。死亡和庸俗是十九世紀至今得不到圓滿解釋的現象。我們到音樂室去喝咖啡，道林。你得彈蕭邦的作品給我聽。跟我妻子一起私奔的那個人彈蕭邦的作品彈得非常出色。可憐的維多利亞！我倒是挺喜歡她。她走後家裏怪冷清。家庭生活固然僅僅是一種習慣，而且是壞習慣，但即使壞習慣也捨不得丟掉。也許恰恰是壞習慣最叫人難以割捨，因為它們已經成為我們不可或缺的組成部分。"

道林沒有說甚麼，只是從桌旁站起來，走到隔壁的音樂室裏，在鋼琴前坐下，手指按在黑白分明的象牙琴鍵上彈了起來。咖啡端上來後，他停止彈奏，望着亨利勛爵，問道："亨利，你有否想過貝澤爾可能被人謀殺？"

亨利勛爵打了個哈欠，"貝澤爾的人緣很好，而且經常戴着隨處可見的沃特伯里手錶。他為甚麼會被人謀殺呢？他沒聰明得足以樹敵。當然他是個厲害的繪畫天才。但一個人能像委拉斯凱茲般畫畫，亦同時擁有極其乏味的性格。貝澤爾確實非常無聊，他唯一一次令我感到興趣，就是當他幾年前告訴我，他對你有種狂熱的崇拜，你是他藝術創作的主要動機。

"我曾經很喜歡貝澤爾，"道林的語調帶着一點傷感。"這麼說，人們並不認為他可能被殺？"

"有幾家報紙提出過這種猜測。我認為這根本不可能。我知道巴黎有些可怕的去處，不過貝澤爾不是會到那裏去的人。他沒有好奇心。這是他主要的毛病。"

“假如我告訴你説我殺了貝澤爾，你將有何感想？”道林説這話時聚精會神地注視着對方。

“我會説，老弟，你在扮演一個不合適的角色。一切犯罪行為都是庸俗的，正如一切庸俗行為都如犯罪一樣。道林，你不配做殺人的勾當。很抱歉，我這話傷害了你的自尊心，但我確實如此認為。犯罪是下層百姓的行當，我絲毫沒有譴責他們的意思。我覺得，犯罪之於他們，猶如藝術之於我們一樣，無非是尋求刺激的手段。”

“尋求刺激的手段？那麼，照你這樣説，犯過一次謀殺罪的人還可能再犯同樣的罪嗎？別告訴我真是這樣。”

“哦！任何事情只要多做幾次就自有樂趣，”亨利勛爵笑道。“這是人生最重要的祕密之一。不過，我認為殺人永遠不足為訓。凡是不能在酒後茶餘談論的事情決不要做。我們別再議論可憐的貝澤爾了。我很願意相信他被你説中，得到一個真正浪漫的結局，但是我無法相信。他充其量只可能是從巴黎的公共馬車上摔下來掉進塞納河，而售票員把事情掩蓋起來了。對，我猜想他的結局八成是這樣。我好像看到他這時正躺在濁綠色的水下，滿載貨物的駁船在他頭上來來往往，他的頭髮和很長的水草纏在一起。老實對你説，我看他再也畫不出多少好作品來。最近十年他的畫大不如前。”

道林歎息一聲，亨利勛爵踱到房間另一頭去撫摸一隻珍異的爪哇鸚鵡的腦袋。那是一隻冠頂和尾巴呈粉紅色，其餘都是呈灰色的大鳥，它蹲在一根竹竿上保持平衡。亨利勛爵細長的手指碰到它身上，鸚鵡立刻垂下白色鱗片狀的皺眼皮，遮住玻璃球似的黑眼睛，身子開始前後搖擺。

"是啊，"亨利勛爵轉身繼續說，並且從口袋裏掏出一方手帕；"他的畫已大不如前，好像失去了甚麼似的。看來是失去了理想。自從你與他不再是知己朋友，他也不再是偉大的畫家。是甚麼把你們分開？我估計是因為你對他日久生厭。如果真是這樣，那他永遠不會原諒你。凡是討人厭的人往往如此。對了，我要問你一件事，他給你畫的那幅出色的肖像後來怎樣了？自從他畫好了之後，我好像一直沒有看見過。哦！我想起來了，幾年前你告訴過我，你把它送到塞爾比莊園去，可是在途中遺失了或是被偷走了。你始終沒把它找回來嗎？真可惜！這是一件真正的傑作。我記得我曾想把它買下來。現在我仍希望擁有它。這是貝澤爾創作巔峯時期的作品。從那以後，他的作品多半是很好的構思和糟糕的技法的奇怪混合物，憑這個條件就有資格被稱為有代表性的英國畫家。你有沒有登過啟事尋找那畫像？應當登報。"

"我忘了，"道林說。"大概登過。不過我從未真正喜歡它。我後悔為它做了模特兒。這幅像留下了令人討厭的回憶。你為甚麼提起它？它常常使我想起某一個劇本，大概是《哈姆雷特》裏邊挺古怪的兩行詩，不知我有沒有記錯——

"不過是做作出來的悲哀，

"只有一張臉而沒有心肝。

"是的，這正是它的寫照。"

亨利勛爵笑了起來。"一個人要是能用藝術的眼光看待人生，他的頭腦就是他的心，"說着，他在一張扶手椅上坐下。

道林·格雷搖搖頭，在鋼琴上彈出輕柔的和弦。"不過是做作出來的悲哀，"他還在那裏自言自語，"只有一張臉而沒有心肝。"

亨利勛爵向後躺，眼睛半閉半開地看着道林。"順帶問一下，道林，"他停了一下再說，"一個人如果得到了全世界，卻失去了——那句原文是甚麼？——自己的靈魂，這對他有甚麼好處？"

琴聲戛然而止，道林·格雷全身一震，向他的朋友瞪着眼睛。"你為甚麼向我提這樣的問題，亨利？"

"親愛的，"亨利勛爵驚異地揚起眉毛說，"我問你是因為我想你大概能給我答覆，如此而已。上星期日我正步行穿過海德公園，見一小羣衣衫襤褸的人圍在大理石牌樓近旁聽一個街頭傳教士講道，無非是老生常談。我從那兒經過的時候，聽到他正在向他的聽眾大聲提出這個問題。這個充滿戲劇性的場面給我留下深刻的印象。類似饒有興味的景象在倫敦還有不少。不妨想像一下：一個下雨的星期天，一位穿雨衣的粗野教友，滴水的雨傘拼湊成的臨時簷棚下幾張沒有血色的面孔，忽然用歇斯底里的尖嗓門喊出這句出人意料的話。這句話確實別具一格，發人深思。我本想對那位傳教士說：藝術有靈魂，人沒有靈魂。可是我擔心他不能理解我的意思。"

"不要這樣說，亨利。靈魂是一種可怕的現實存在。它可以買賣，可以用來作交易，可以被腐蝕，也可以改邪歸正。我們每個人身上都有靈魂。這一點我知道。"

"你有十分把握嗎，道林？"

"有把握。"

"啊！那它一定是幻象。凡是我們絕對肯定的東西就不可能是真的，那是信仰的致命傷和浪漫的教訓。你多麼嚴肅！別太認真，我們跟這個時代的迷信有甚麼關係呢？沒有，我們已從心底裏放棄了信仰。為我演奏一曲，一首夜曲。道林，在你彈奏的同時，輕聲告訴我你是如何保持青春。你一定有些祕密。我只是比你大十年，但我已經滿臉皺紋，憔悴不已，臉色發黃了。你實在不可思議，道林。你從未比今晚更有魅力，你令我憶起最初遇見你的時候，那時你是有點調皮、靦腆，但絕對超凡脫俗。你改變了，當然不是外表上的改變。我希望你把祕密告訴我，我會做任何事來取回我的青春，除了運動、早起和不失體面。青春！沒有東西像青春一樣，把它說成無知的人真荒謬。我現在只會聽比我年輕得多的人的意見，他們看上去比我走得更前，生活向他們揭示它最新的驚奇。至於比我大的人，我總是反駁他們，我是按原則而這樣做的。如果你問他們對昨天發生的某件事的意見，他們會一本正經地告訴你一八二零年的流行觀點。當時的人穿長筒襪，相信所有東西，又對一切一無所知。你彈的這些曲子真好聽！不知道蕭邦是不是在馬略卡島上創作的這首曲子呢？那邊的別墅周圍有大海在嗚咽，帶鹹味的浪花撞擊着窗戶。這首曲極為浪漫。我們多幸運，有這樣一件不是仿作的藝術品留給我們！別停，我今晚需要音樂。你就像是年輕的阿波羅，而我就是聽你演奏的瑪敘阿斯。我有一些悲傷，是我自己的悲傷，連道林你也不知道。老年的悲劇並不在於年老，而是年輕。我有時對自己的真誠感到訝異。啊，道林，你多麼快樂啊！你擁有多精緻的人生！你沉醉於一切，用舌尖抵在上顎碾碎葡萄。這一切對你來說都不過是音樂。時間沒有糟蹋你，你依然如初。

"我已經不是原本的我了，亨利。"

"不，你還是原本的你。但不知你今後的生活將是怎麼樣子。可不要放棄而糟蹋了它。現在你是完美的典型，小心不要給自己製造缺陷。目前對你一點毛病都挑不出來。你別搖頭，你自己也知道這是事實。還有，道林，不要欺騙自己。生活不是由意志或願望駕馭的。生活取決於神經、纖維，慢慢構成的細胞，思想就在那裏藏身，慾望就在那裏醞釀。你自以為高枕無憂，無所畏懼，但只要偶然看到一間屋子或早晨天空的色調，嗅到某種為你所喜愛和令人依稀想起往事的異香，無意間讀到早已忘懷的一首詩中的某一行，聽到你久已不演奏的一部作品的某一樂段——告訴你吧，道林，凡此種種，都會影響我們的生活。白朗寧在甚麼地方寫過上面這樣的話，我們的感官也有這樣的經驗。有時候，不知哪兒忽然飄來一陣白丁香的清芬，我就得把我一生中最不可思議的一個月重新回味一遍。我真想與你交換位置，道林。世人把我們兩人都罵得狗血淋頭，但他們只崇拜你一個人。過去如此，將來還是如此。你是我們這個時代所要尋覓的典型，而覓到後他們又害怕了。我感到高興的是，你從來沒有雕過一座像，畫過一張畫，或者造出任何一件身外之物。生活就是你的藝術創作。你把你自己譜成了音樂。你過的日子就是一首首十四行詩。"

道林從鋼琴旁邊站起來，用手掠了一下自己的頭髮。"是的，生活確是美妙的，"他喃喃地說，"但我再也不願過這樣的生活了，亨利。你也不要向我發表這些奇談怪論。並不是我的一切你都了解，否則恐怕連你也會轉臉不認我。你笑甚麼？不要笑。"

"你為甚麼不彈下去，道林？去坐下來再給我彈一遍那首夜曲。你瞧，那蜜黃色的大月亮掛在暗沉沉的空中，正等着你去誘惑她。只要你的琴聲一起，她就更加挨近地面。你不彈了嗎？那麼我們上俱樂部去。我們度過了一個愉快的晚上，應當有始有終。懷特俱樂部有個人一心一意想跟你結交，就是那位年輕的浦爾勛爵，邦茅斯的長子。他已經把你打領結的式樣學到了家，並一再央求我給你們介紹介紹。他很討人喜歡，我看他有許多地方像你。"

"但願不是這樣，"道林眼神帶着幾分憂鬱地説。"不過今天我已經很累，亨利。我不上俱樂部去了。現在將近十一點，我想早些回家睡覺。"

"再待一會。今天你彈得比任何時候都好。你的指法有一種出神入化的妙處，比我以前聽過的任何一次更富有表現力。"

"那是因為我想要重新做人，"他微笑着回答。"我已經起了一點小小的變化。"

"在我心目中你不會改變，"亨利勛爵説。"你我將永遠是朋友。"

"可是當初你通過一本書把我給毒害了。這件事我永遠不會原諒你。亨利，你得向我保證：再也不把它借給任何人。那是一本害人的書。"

"老弟，你真的做起道德家來了。看來不久你將成為一個改邪歸正的改宗者、一個信仰復興運動者，到處現身説法，告誡人們不要作那些你已經感到厭倦的罪孽。不過，你怎麼扮也不像這樣可惡的角色，你太可愛了。何況，這起不了任何作用。你我是怎樣的人，就是怎樣的人，將來仍然如此。至於説一本書可以把人毒害，根本沒有這回事。藝術不可能促進行動，只會打消行動的願望。藝術絕對不結果實。有些書被稱為傷風敗俗，無非因為向世人揭示了他們自己的醜態。好了，我們不必辯論文學問題。你明天再來。我打算上午十一點去騎馬。我們一起去吧，然後我帶你到布蘭克瑟姆夫人家吃午飯。這個可愛的女人打算買幾張掛毯，她要向你請教。可不要忘了。或者我們去同嬌小的公爵夫人一起吃午飯，好不好？她說近來你連人影也見不到。大概你對格蕾狄絲已經膩煩了吧？這是意料中事。她那副伶牙俐齒叫人受不了。好吧，反正你十一點到這兒來就是了。"

"你非要我來不可嗎，亨利？"

"當然，這個季節公園的風景很美。打我認識你那一年起，丁香還從來沒有開得像今年這樣盛。"

"好吧，我十一點到這兒來，"道林說。"晚安，亨利。"他走到門口，猶豫了一下，像有甚麼話要說。後來只是歎了口氣，就出去了。

第二十章

那是一個醉人的夜晚。因為天暖，他把大衣脫下來搭在胳膊上，脖子上連絲巾也沒有繫一條。他一路吸煙，一路漫步走回家去。有兩個穿晚禮服的年輕人從他身旁經過。他聽見其中一個向另一個悄悄地說："那就是道林·格雷。"他回憶過去被別人指指點點、注視或議論的時候曾是多麼得意，現在他對自己的名字已經聽厭了。近來他常常到一個小村子去，那個地方的可愛之處一半在於沒有人知道他是誰。他幾次告訴那個被他誘入情網的女孩，說他是個窮光蛋，她也信以為真。有一次，道林向她承認自己是個壞人，被她取笑了一通。她說壞人總是又老又醜。她笑得多甜啊，好像一隻畫眉鳥在唱歌。她頭戴大帽子、身穿布裙子的模樣十分招人喜歡。她天真無知，但是她有着道林失去了的一切。

到了家裏，他發現自己的侍從還在等他，便打發侍從去睡，自己靠在書齋裏的沙發上，開始思量亨利勛爵對他說的話。

人是不是真的永遠改變不了？他無限緬懷自己白璧無瑕的少年時代，亨利勛爵一度稱之為白玫瑰般的少年時代。道林知道自己玷污了自己，腐蝕了心靈，毒化了想像；知道自己對別人產生了壞影響，而且從中獲得一種殘忍的樂趣；知道在自己結交的人中裏性最純潔、前途最光明的人都被他引入歧途而身敗名裂。可是這一切難道都不能挽回了嗎？難道他已無藥可救了嗎？

唉！當初他在虛榮和慾望的一時衝動下，祈求上蒼讓畫像代他承受年齡的負擔，使他自己永葆光華照人的青春。想不到那一刹那竟成千古恨！如果他造的孽椿椿件件都毫釐不爽地馬上得到報應，倒也痛快。懲罰就是淨罪。人向無比公正的上帝祈禱時不應當説："寬恕我們的罪孽吧，"而應當説："懲罰我們的不義吧！"

亨利勛爵不知在多少年前送給他的一面雕鏤精細的鏡子，此刻正放在桌上，鏡框上白白胖胖的小丘比特依舊在笑。道林拿起鏡子，就像在初次發覺要命的畫像起變化的那個恐怖之夜一樣，睜大了一雙模糊的淚眼向光潔的鏡子望着。曾經有一個愛他愛得快要發狂的人寫過一封癡情洋溢的信給他，末尾是這樣兩句偶像崇拜者的話："有了你這樣一個牙雕金鑄的人，世界也變了樣。你嘴唇的曲線將重寫歷史。"現在他想起了這幾句話，一遍又一遍地默念着。隨後他對自己的美貌突然憎惡起來，就把鏡子扔在地板上，用鞋跟把它踩成無數銀色的碎片。正是他的美貌毀了他，正是他祈求得來的美貌和青春葬送了他。要不是這兩者，他的一生可以不沾上一個污點。事實上，他的美貌不過是一張面具，青春不過是一把笑柄。青春究竟是甚麼呢？往最好處説，也只是一段缺乏經驗、不成熟的時間，充滿了淺薄的見解和不健康的思想。他何苦老是穿着這身號衣？青春把他縱壞了。

過去的事還是不要去想。反正已經甚麼都不能改變了。他應該考慮的是自己和自己的未來。詹姆士·韋恩已埋入塞爾比墳地的一座無名塚。艾倫·坎貝爾某一天夜裏在自己的實驗室裏開槍自殺，但是沒有泄露他被逼知道的祕密。貝澤爾·霍爾渥德失蹤一事所引起的紛紜之說不久就會平息下去，眼前已經不是那麼沸沸揚揚了。總而言之，他完全可以高枕無憂。事實上，貝澤爾‧霍爾渥德之死還不是他最感到沉重的心病。不，是他自己半死不活的靈魂使他不得安寧。貝澤爾畫的肖像害得他好苦。這件事他不能原諒貝澤爾，禍根全在於畫像。貝澤爾向他說了許多極其難堪的話，但他還是忍氣吞聲地聽了。殺人完全是一剎那的瘋狂行為。至於艾倫‧坎貝爾的自殺，那是他自己的事。他要走這條路，誰攔得住？

重新做人！這才是他所需要的。這才是他所渴望的。事實上他已經開始了。至少他放過了一個無辜的少女。他再也不引誘無辜，他要做一個好人。

關於海蒂‧默頓的思緒使他聯想到被鎖在空室裏的畫像，不知它是否變好了些？也許不像以前那樣猙獰可怕了吧？如果他從此潔身自好，或許能把邪惡的慾念留在畫像面部的痕跡一個個清除乾淨，或許邪惡的痕跡已經消失了。他要去看一看。

道林從桌上拿起一盞燈，躡手躡足走到樓上。當他啟鎖開門的時候，一絲欣喜的微笑浮上他異常年輕的臉龐，並在嘴角上逗留了一會。是的，他要做一個好人，被他藏匿了這麼多年的醜東西將不再使他害怕，他覺得壓在心上的石頭已經搬開了。

他悄悄地走進房間，照例把門反鎖起來，然後把紫紅緞罩從畫像前拉開。一聲痛苦夾着憤怒的叫喊衝口而出。除了眼睛裏現出狡猾的目光，嘴角刻上一道偽君子的皺紋外，他看不出任何變化。畫像上那個傢伙還是那樣面目可憎，甚至比以前更加可憎。沾在一隻手上的殷紅濕斑似乎更鮮亮了，更像新鮮的血跡。他禁不住哆嗦起來，難道他做唯一好事的動機純粹是出於虛榮心？難道他只是想追求新的刺激，像亨利勛爵帶着嘲笑所暗示的那樣？難道正是那種裝腔作勢的癖好使我們偶爾做出比自身更高尚的行為？還是這一切都兼而有之？為甚麼那塊紅斑比先前更大了？它像是一種惡瘡在皮膚皺縮的手指上蔓延開去。畫像的腳上也有血跡，莫非是從手上滴下來的？甚至沒有握過刀子的那隻手上也有血。自首？這是否意味着他必須去投案自首？任憑發落，等待處死？他笑了起來。他覺得這個念頭荒唐之至。再說，即使他去投案，誰能相信他？無論何處都沒有留下被害人的任何痕跡。屬於死者的一切已全部銷毀，是道林親自把貝澤爾留在樓下的東西燒毀的。如果他和盤托出，人們一定會說他神經錯亂。倘若他堅稱確有此事，就會被關進瘋人院去……然而他應當自首，應當為人所不齒，應當受到社會的制裁，這是他罪有應得。上帝還在，上帝要人們對天對地同樣不隱諱自己的罪惡。除非他供認自己的罪行，否則無論用甚麼辦法都不能把他洗刷乾淨。然而，到底哪些是他的罪行？道林聳聳肩膀。貝澤爾·霍爾渥德之死在他心目中已算不了甚麼。他想的是海蒂·默頓。不，此時他正在照的這一面鏡子沒有如實反映他的靈魂。虛榮？好奇？偽善？難道他懸崖勒馬的行為就只因為這些原因？應該還有，至少他認為還有，可是有甚麼呢？……誰也說不出來。別的甚麼也沒有。他是在虛榮心的驅使下放過了海蒂。他是出於偽善的目的而套上德行的面具。他是為了好奇心的緣故才作這一番自我克制的嘗試。現在他意識到了。

但是，這樁殺人的罪行難道要跟着他一輩子嗎？難道他將永遠背着自己的往事這個包袱？他是不是真的該去自首？不。他還留着的罪證只有這麼一點，那就是這幅畫像，必須把它也消滅掉。他這麼長時間留着它做甚麼？觀察畫像逐步變化，漸漸老去，一度是他的樂趣。近來他已感覺不到甚麼樂趣。這東西常常使他夜裏不能成眠。他不在倫敦家裏的時候老是提心吊膽，生怕別人窺見他的祕密。這東西在他縱慾的過程中摻入了憂鬱的成分，有不少歡樂的時刻往往因為惦掛着它而大煞風景。這東西好像成了他的良心。對，的確成了他的良心。他得把這東西毀掉。

道林四下環顧，看見了曾經捅死貝澤爾·霍爾渥德的那把刀子。道林曾把它擦過好多次，直至上面找不到任何一點痕跡。這時它又在那裏閃着寒光。既然它殺死過畫家，那就讓它把畫家的作品及其象徵意義也一起毀了吧，讓這把刀子切斷與往事的一切聯繫。一旦往事逝去，他就自由了。讓這把刀子結束這種不可思議的靈魂活動。只要聽不見靈魂的駭人警告，他就可以得到安寧。於是他抓起刀子，對準畫像猛戳過去。

緊接着，只聽到一聲慘叫和甚麼東西訇然倒地的聲響。那臨死前痛苦的叫喊極度恐怖，驚醒過來的僕人嚇得紛紛衝出臥房。當時有兩位紳士正好從樓下的廣場上路過，聽到了叫喊聲，停下來朝這所大房子樓上張望。他們叫來了一名警察。警察響了好幾次鈴。但是沒有人應門。除了頂層一扇窗子有燈光外，整座樓宅一片黑暗。過了一會，警察從門口走開，去站在毗鄰的柱廊觀看動靜。

"警察，這是哪家的公館？"年紀較大的一位紳士問。

"道林·格雷先生的，先生，"警察回答説。

兩位紳士交換了一下眼色，冷笑一聲走開了。其中一位是亨利·艾森頓爵士的舅舅。

　　公館內部的下房裏，衣履不整的傭人們在緊張地竊竊私議。年事已高的管家婦黎甫太太一邊抽噎，一邊使勁交替地握着自己的手。弗蘭西斯面無人色。

　　大約十五分鐘後，他把馬車夫叫來，加上一名聽差，三個人一起放輕腳步登上頂層。他們敲了敲門，但是沒有人應。於是他們大聲叫喚。依舊毫無動靜。在嘗試破門無效之後，他們終於爬上屋頂，翻到陽台上。陽台的長窗沒費多少力氣就被打開，因為插銷已經很舊了。

　　他們走進房間，發現牆上掛着東家的一幅肖像，與他們最近一次見到他本人的時候一樣容光煥發，洋溢着奇妙的青春和罕見的美。地上躺着一個死人，身穿晚禮服，心窩裏插着一把刀子。他形容枯槁，皮膚皺縮，面目可憎。如不仔細察看他手上的戒指，他們怎麼也認不出這個人是誰。

完